SHADOWRUN:

DOWN THESE DARK STREETS

THE COLLECTED STORIES OF

RUSSELL ZIMMERMAN

SHADOWRUN: DOWN THESE DARK STREETS
By Russell Zimmerman
Cover art by Peter Tikos
Design by Matt Heerdt and David Kerber

Published by Catalyst Game Labs,
an imprint of InMediaRes Productions, LLC
5003 Main St. #110 • Tacoma, WA 98407

INTRODUCTION

I was supposed to be doing something else. I was supposed to be buying other people holiday gifts. I was supposed to be spending some time at the mall in Florence, Kentucky (beneath that famous "Florence Y'all" water tower), looking for stuff for my family and my friends. But I knew ahead of time what I'd GET, not GIVE, for the holidays; gift cards were coming my way! Gift cards, in particular, for B. Dalton and Waldenbooks, the twin pillars of my local bookselling community.

So I wasn't just on a job to buy stuff, oh no. I was pulling a RECON MISSION. Thirteen-year-old Rusty, he was on a deep scouting patrol, digging up the good stuff he'd come scurrying back to buy a week or two later with his pockets bulging with gift cards and his grubby paws out to snatch up cool, geeky prizes.

When I saw Larry Elmore's SR1 cover, it smacked me upside the head and demanded attention. When I OPENED that cover and read my first-ever piece of RPG intro fic, it got the hooks into me. Deeply. I saw those same characters from that intro fic show up again and again, the more *Shadowrun* I read. So I kept reading, and I never looked back.

Shadowrun was the first RPG I ever actually played. I loved it for undergrad semester atop semester, as late-90's games came and went and we slung dice for all of them, *Shadowrun* was always there. Years later, playing on the Shadowland BBS with familiar faces like the real-life Pistons and Demonseed Elite, I wrote my first fiction (describing the down-time of my characters between runs), then I wrote more fiction pieces for fun, then I wrote some fiction pieces for Dumpshock forum contests. Those fiction pieces would eventually get me my first freelancing jobs. Lots of stuff spiraled from there.

Y'all, I met my WIFE playing *Shadowrun*.

So when I say that the trajectory of my life changed thanks to that Larry Elmore cover and that chrome-flashing intro fic, that's not just street bluster, chummers. That's the chip-truth. I wouldn't be the person I am today, I wouldn't have the family and friends that I do, much less the job, if it wasn't for that cover art...and that intro fic.

Ghost-Who-Walks-Inside, Sally Tsung, and The Artful Dodger changed my life when they hauled me into the shadows.

And now, thirty years later, I'm writing those intro fictions. I'm writing those novels. Heck, I'm writing those characters! I'm seeing my name on the spines of books, I'm seeing my characters in card games, board games, and as miniatures. I'm tagging territory on Seattle corners.

I'm telling stories that are drawing people into the shadows. Some of them are getting pulled back into the Sixth World thanks to my stuff, but some have reached out and let me know that it was my stuff that introduced them to it all, my stuff that first got the hooks in them, my stuff that first got them to keep reading.

Imagine that!

Because high-school-freshman Rusty? He sure as hell COULDN'T imagine that.

He just thought he was finding the only game where he could have a robot arm and still cast Fireball. He thought he found the only RPG that let him be an elf on a motorcycle. He thought he found a way to play "Hardwired" but also be an ork. He thought he found the only world that had Tron and Tolkien all tangled up together. He thought he found his first RPG where combat wasn't a binary hit/miss affair, and where greater skill meant greater damage.

Young Rusty had found all of that, but so much more. And with the "so much more" came opportunities he never dreamed of, couldn't possibly imagine, wouldn't believe if you told him. First off, of course, *Shadowrun* is how Rusty met his wife! But then came podcasts and paychecks that funded his geeky hobbies, signing stuff and giving seminars at conventions, fan art of his characters, COSPLAYERS of his characters (hi Sandy!), and dozens—a hundred, or more?—of his best friends. Young Rusty couldn't imagine the emails from *Shadowrun* line developers asking him lore questions, the boxes of books with his name in them, or the fun he would have telling these stories.

Young Rusty couldn't imagine walking into his local comic book shop and seeing his work on the wall.

This book is...all of that.

This book is how I started to run the shadows with my first hesitant steps ("Untethered Life", in *Attitude*), how I started to stretch my legs a little ("A Warrior's Edge", *Way of the Adept*), how I really found my niche and picked up steam ("Layers", *Land of Promise*), how I first started trying to tie my little fictions together (Saber and his crew), and how I really found my stride (literally anything with Ms. Myth and her rag-tag band of would-be Prime Runners).

This book gathers together all of my side gigs over the years. All the asides. All of the little stories I tried to finish under editorial word count. All the little street legends that didn't quite make it into a novella or a novel, all the little plot hooks I left hanging, picked up, and threaded together over the years. Some of these stories feature the children of the heroes and villains I grew up reading. Some of these stories will come up again, later, as you keep reading my novellas and novels and you see familiar faces. Some of these stories won't—not every shadowrun has a happy ending—but that's life in the Sixth World, chummers.

This book has Kincaid in it, too, of course. Because if *Shadowrun* changed my life, Nigel Findley changed my *Shadowrun*, and Kincaid is my hat-tip to Nigel. No single voice colored my perception of the Sixth World the way Nigel Findley's did, no other set of eyes have seen *Shadowrun* in the same way I do since his. If *Shadowrun* made me, Nigel made my *Shadowrun*.

And Jimmy Kincaid—an elf, a down-on-his-luck PI, a hero from and for the streets rather than the high-rises or even shadows—is a little of all of that. Nigel taught me how to tell stories about *Shadowrun* without quite being stories about shadowrunners, Nigel (literally) wrote the book on Seattle's elven neighbors, Nigel taught us all that being a half-step removed from the shadows was a heck of a way to build a world and find a voice, and without that idea I wouldn't be the writer I am today.

So here. Have at it. This introduction told you how I got here. It told you how I found *Shadowrun*, and what *Shadowrun* found for me. But this book shows you instead of tells you. This book shows my story by showing the stories of Saber, Ms. Myth, Frostbyte, Gentry, Agent Thorn, Jimmy Kincaid, and more.

Welcome to MY shadows.

Enjoy your stay.

–RRZ

PART ONE:
MS. MYTH'S CREW

MISCHIEF IS MY BUSINESS

(Shadowrun: Beginner Box)

Going from the core rulebook to the Beginner Box was a fun little step backward, in that I wanted to take Coydog and The Boys from being a comfortably experienced team BACK into, well, being Beginner Box characters. They all got extensive write-ups in the Beginner Box (from me, natch, lots of words flying willy-nilly), but we also wanted some straight-up fiction, to show the team–as a group of brand-new shadowunners, just like a group of brand-new players–coming together.

So I wanted to characterize everyone enough to get Coydog and Gentry's playfulness, Sledge's gruff demeanor, and Hardpoint's not-much-nonsense attitude to shine through, but ALSO to tell a neat little self-contained story, and ALSO to highlight some of these key roles in Shadowrun, and ALSO to highlight the gear disparities between starting characters and more experienced ones, and ALSO to just have some fun with it. It turned out to be a pretty neat little story, I think, and hit all the marks I needed it to.

—RRZ

Coydog tucked her hair behind one pointed ear as she carefully backed her beaten-up old Gopher truck into a parking spot. The engine growled and idled for a second before she killed it, then gave herself a long look in the mirror. It was time. She'd slung spells to help out her brother and his friends, and been feathered for her courage. She had shown her teacher each of the five spirits, summoned and tasked, and controlled them all. Four-Paws-Laughing had told her she was ready. Coyote hadn't disagreed. She had everything she needed, even her *méstəm̓'s* old duty Browning and her *tum̓'s* favorite set of armor-lined clothes; she could do this. It was time for her first real shadowrun. Why not? She had the skills, the power, and her totem's faith; she might as well get paid for having a good time, right?

She clambered out of her truck and thumbed her scuffed-up commlink to life. She was five minutes early, which Four-Paws-Laughing had always said was on time. She made sure her fake SIN was being broadcast instead of her real one, checked that her pistol was hidden beneath the folds of her shirt, and headed into the Café Sport. Downtown wasn't her usual neighborhood here in the Seattle Sprawl, but the smells inside this particular restaurant reminded her of growing up; real fires fed by real wood, real fish being grilled. No soy, just actual food.

The prices, of course, were astronomical. What Coydog and her family took for granted back home, and even here on Seattle's Council Island, these poor saps had to pay out the nose for. She waved off the server and nodded at a table in the back. Coydog smirked as she slipped past tables full of suit-clad salarymen and their families, knowing they were spending a week's wages on food she'd been cooking since she was a little girl.

The crew assembled at the table her commlink had told her about—the Juggler was a lot of things, but as fixers went he was pretty honest—could only be the rest of her team. The most eye-catching was the big ork with the bold tattoos and armored-up arms. He loomed over the dwarf who sat next to him, who had some external headware and gray streaking his beard. A human shared the booth with them, a datajack on his left temple and friendly smile on his face. Apparently she was interrupting an argument between the ork and the dwarf.

"—I'm just sayin' I ain't a fan of Prop 23," the bigger one scowled. "It ain't up to outsiders to give the Underground laws. It's up to us orks."

"My father helped build that place, Sledge, before he got evicted out by you orks. It's got all manner of changelings and other metahumans in there, even today. It didn't start the 'Ork' Underground, and it's never been ork-exclusive. If those people want law and order, their voices count just as much as yours."

"More, I guess," the ork—Sledge?—sulked and crossed his arms across his wide chest. "Since it ain't like I'm crashin' down there no more."

The human rapped on the table to quiet the two, then gave Coydog a bright smile as she approached.

"I'm betting that's not our Mr. Johnson," he said to the other two with a grin. He got up from his edge of the booth and gave her a polite bow.

"*Se'thinerol. Telegit thelemsa.*" He sure did say it like he expected Coydog to understand him.

"Sorry chummer." She bit down a laugh as she breezed past him to snatch up his seat. "No habla elfy-elf."

The pair at the table laughed loud enough to catch a few glares from nearby patrons. The dwarf shot back by making a face, the ork by glowering and looking like he was about to stand. That table emptied, scurrying away in a flurry of polite excuses.

"I, ah. Sorry." It had been ages since Coydog had made someone blush that red. "I thought you would..."

"Speak that Sperethiel stuff, just 'cause I'm an elf? Nope. Salish and English, pal. My momma was Sinsearach, not Cénesté. My folks stuck with the Council, didn't run off when the Tír started recruiting."

"So what's your story, breeder?" Sledge cut in with a big orkish snort. "Some kind of dandelion-eater wannabe?"

Coydog rolled her eyes at how casually he used the meta-racial insult, as though an elf weren't sitting right across from him.

"The name's Gentry," the human said, features a little colder towards the ork than they'd been to Coydog. "And no. I'm just from down there, is all."

"Yeah? What do you do, Gentry? Why should I wanna work with a breeder like you?" With cyberlimbs as obviously dangerous as his, no one had to ask the ork what he brought to the team. Every crew needed muscle.

"You watch Urban Brawl, Sledge?"

"I got eyes, don't I?"

"Gentry the Jinx ring any bells? Played fifteen games as a Scout for the Bend Borderers."

"Yeah?" Sledge sized Gentry up openly, eyes flashing just a hint of chrome as he looked the human over. "I remember seein' a few trid-clips, sure. You're some kind of fancy-pants hacker or something, too, right?"

"Decker," the dwarf next to him corrected. He reached out across the table—Gentry's longer arm making the handshake possible—and as they shook he nodded down at the bulky wrist-module strapped to the human's forearm.

"Nice hardware. Renraku core, looks like? You should upgrade to the new Shuriken when you can. I know a guy. The name's Hardpoint, I rig. Zero-zone experience, and plenty of it. If it's broken, I can fix it. If it ain't broken, I can fly it."

"Good to meet you," Gentry quirked an eyebrow and nodded toward Coydog. "What do you think, Hardpoint? I crash and burn hard enough I shouldn't try again?"

Coydog snickered and shook her head. "No need, pal. Name's Coydog. I'll be your mojo for the evening, boys." She waggled her fingers and put on her best faux-menacing face. "Spells, spirits, and inscrutable tribal wisdom, at your service."

"Nice ink," Sledge grunted and nodded to her bare arms. Coydog had a neo-circuitry design, top-end nanotattoo work.

"Thanks. Got it from Lou's after my first fight. Yours, too." She glanced down at the ork's blocky ink. It was sloppier than hers, hardly the high art Lou, right here in Downtown, put into his pieces. Maybe it was prison work, maybe just Underground standard. Skraacha ink, maybe? The gang had a lot of sway in the subterranean city.

Gentry and Hardpoint had already turned away from the tattoo conversation and were exchanging electronic pleasantries through their commlinks—Coydog pouted a bit when she saw just how outclassed her cheap Meta Link was, but she'd kind of expected it—when a newcomer arrived to their booth. Several nearby tables had been quietly cleared out, and the lights in this corner dimmed a bit.

Right on time.

Coydog glanced up and saw almond eyes, salt-and-pepper hair, a crisp, dark suit, and a small corporate pin glinting on one lapel. She opened her mouth to drawl out something halfway polite when Hardpoint surprised her by clambering out of the booth with deceptive speed. The dwarf bowed deeply at the waist, and straightened up very formally.

"*Konbanwa*, Johnson-*sama*."

She quirked an eyebrow at Sledge and Gentry while their temporary employer returned the greeting without the honorific, and Hardpoint scrambled to grab a chair for their Mr. Johnson.

<Old habits dying hard?> Coydog looked down as her Meta Link vibrated and alerted her to an incoming text message. Instead of quipping back, she glared over at Gentry, wondering how he'd gotten access to her system so quickly.

"And good evening to each of you, as well." Mr. Johnson cut off her silent accusation, switching to English to address the rest of the group. Hardpoint settled back into his seat as though nothing unusual had happened, but even Sledge didn't press the matter.

"Juggler-*san* and I appreciate your willingness to accept this task on such short notice. He has entrusted me with some basic contact information. Check your inboxes now, please, and feel free to ask me any questions that come up as you read."

With her Link already in-hand, Coydog opened the attachment he'd just sent them. As the images slowed her loading time, she felt sure that Gentry and Hardpoint—spirits, maybe even Sledge!—were probably hip deep in confidential information by now. She started to scroll down slowly, and paused when she saw a violently severed cyberlimb.

"My previous team has been...inconvenienced." Mr. Johnson spoke up right on cue, his subtly chromed eyes flicking from face to face. "They were scheduled for this employee transfer some time ago. They handled the legwork, relayed information to the potential new-hire for me, and did a reasonable job of all of it. However, due to an unrelated incident, they find themselves now incapable of performing this final task, the extraction itself."

His voice was clinical, calculating, and showed only disappointment—no concern—for whoever that savaged, glossy-black cyberarm had once belonged to.

"I am in need of a driver, an electronic security specialist, a mundane combatant." He nodded to Hardpoint, Gentry, and Sledge in turn. "And you, miss, will be the icing on the proverbial cake. My former employers lacked an overt magical operations agent. It is my hope that you will be something of an insurance policy. Magical security is not expected."

An unfair fight, then? Coydog's favorite time! She tried not to smile as she slowly scrolled through the document. Blah blah blah, Kirsten Haines was an executive assistant to slick NeoNET big-shot Andrew Rolf, Mr. Johnson's mysterious company—who Coydog was sure she'd figure out by asking Hardpoint later—couldn't get Rolf and his plans, so they were going after Haines and her headware. Haines was onboard with the exchange, thanks to Johnson's terribly unlucky but otherwise competent old crew, and the pick-up was slated for...

"Tonight?" Hardpoint somehow made the word both deferential and incredulous.

"Timeliness is critical here. Ms. Haines has been a covert employee of ours for some time now, and has made it clear she requires immediate extraction. Our mutual acquaintance, Juggler-*san*, should be offering you a substantial bonus for this being such a short notice task."

"And it's just her?" Gentry glanced up from his sleek Transys commlink, and Coydog stifled a grumble about how fast these drekheads were reading.

"Ms. Haines is unmarried, has no children, and has no family she wishes extracted with her, that is correct."

"Lots o' security for some secretary," Sledge grunted. Coydog wanted to punch someone. Even *he* was out-pacing her?!

"Ms. Haines is the administrative assistant to an important man. The security detail is for him, not her. I had hoped that four of them wouldn't be too much for four of you. Is my hope unfounded?"

"Ain't sayin' we can't do it," the ork's voice rose a bit, bristling. "I'm jus' sayin'—"

"I don't think we have any more questions, Johnson-*sama*," Hardpoint cut Sledge off before he could get them all fired or assassinated.

Mr. Johnson waited a heartbeat for someone in the team to disagree, then nodded politely at them. "I'll see you in two hours, then."

Coydog opened her mouth to ask where, when an incoming text—<The hand-off point's at the end of the message>—buzzed onto her commlink. Gentry looked smug, but Coydog closed her mouth. She'd get him for that, later.

Later.

Mr. Johnson nodded to the kitchen before he strode off, and a handful of eager wait-staff scurried to the table. Sledge dug in with orkish gusto, Hardpoint waited until Johnson was out of sight before going for some salmon, Gentry stuck to a fresh salad, and Coydog picked at her meal while they planned. She figured a beer wouldn't kill anyone, but their waiter fell all over himself apologizing and insisting that Mr. Johnson had left them explicit instructions. *Bah*!

They ate, they planned, and—in well under an hour—they left. Sledge had been sitting with a big Ares handcannon in his lap the whole time, she saw as they stood up. A tiny spy-drone zipped down to rest on Hardpoint's shoulder as they walked off. Coydog saw a holstered Colt on Gentry's hip as he reached for some scrip to leave for a tip.

They all went out the back door, and she strode along with them like she'd been planning on a surreptitious exit all along, herself. She was a shadowrunner now, after all.

They had agreed to simplify their travel logistics over dinner, and everyone left their vehicles at the Café Sport except Hardpoint.

"It's no drone," he said as he climbed into the driver's seat of his big Bulldog step-can. "But I can make it fly."

On the drive over, Sledge meticulously loaded and unloaded a few magazines for his autopistol.

Hardpoint hummed to himself as he drove. Gentry seemed to be playing a videogame, unless Coydog missed her guess. Just like the plan called for, though, she worked during the trip.

"Little brother," she whispered so that only the air could hear it. "I need your help."

Hardpoint had all the doors and windows closed, but a breeze filled the back of the van.

"Little brother..." She breathed in her power while Coyote smiled. "Aid us in mischief."

Her magic worked, as Coyote had willed it to. The minor spirit was enough to conceal them. No one noticed as the van pulled into an employee-only curbside parking spot. No one noticed as a surly ork with a gun and military-spec cyberarms climbed out. No one noticed as a swimmer-lean human in a courier jumpsuit—blinking commlinks all wired together to mimic the processing power of a proper cyberdeck—hopped onto the curb, adjusting his sling-bag. No one noticed as the big loading doors at the van's rear swung open, and Coydog sat on the edge of the van and swung her boots in the wind. It didn't matter how little they fit in on this curb full of corporate-approved delivery vans and shining limousines. No one saw them, really saw them, enough to care.

Gentry and Sledge loitered at the back of the van with her, half a car-length from a Mitsubishi Nightsky whose driver had just straightened up and tried to look attentive. The tinted doors of this NeoNET branch office slid open, and their target walked into sight; right on time. With her was a terribly important-looking human in a suit that probably cost as much as Coydog's truck, and a foursome of serious-faced men who looked like cookie-cutter copies of each other. The four bodyguards had implanted optic shields, permanent sunglasses, that made their faces unreadable and likely hid a half-dozen cybernetic modifications.

None of them helped against Coydog's spirit, though. No one glanced twice.

"You sure you can do this to his wheels, breeder?" Sledge elbowed Gentry to hurry him up.

"I've been boosting cars since I was twelve, Sledge." Gentry didn't look up, he kept his attention on the sleek keypad strapped to his arm, now linked directly to him by a thin cable. His left hand hovered just above it, hitting imaginary keys, adjusting files, tweaking processors, or maybe—hell if Coydog knew—still just playing *Star Lords* or something. He knew his way around augmented reality, though, she could tell that much. "So yeah. I'm pretty sure."

The suit-clad targets approached the limo, and the bodyguard in front reached out to pull open the door. He started and they all looked frustrated when it didn't open. Coydog fought a snicker.

In the front compartment, the driver looked terrified. The engine purred itself to death, and the driver's eyes whitened. He started frantically adjusting controls on the dash, but was locked in a powered-down car. The security foursome milled around and looked concerned and alert. Gentry flashed a very pleased with himself smile.

Sledge drew his big Ares and stalked across the sidewalk.

"Think I should remind him this ain't a full-on invisibility spell?" Coydog glanced Gentry's way, then back to watching the ork.

"Ah, he'll figure it out." The decker grinned at her, then cheerfully flipped off the limo driver as he strolled off after Sledge.

They drew attention pretty quickly once Sledge started shooting. Point blank, muzzle a hairs-breadth from the security guard's temple, the gel round dropped him like a poleaxe. Suddenly—and unsurprisingly—the ork wasn't so easy to overlook any more.

Mr. Rolf grabbed Ms. Haines and shielded himself with her. Hardpoint howled with laughter. The three remaining guards went for their guns, so quick Coydog could barely see them move. The ork looked surprised, cursed, and dove, scratching paint the whole way, across the parked Nightsky. Rounds ricocheted off the limo's subtle armor plating, and Sledge growled his frustration, but stayed low and out of sight.

Gentry hauled a stun baton from his little messenger-bag hack-pack and waded in. One guard's wrist was broken and gun was sent flying from two quick chops, then the third big overhand swing connected with his head and sent him, herky-jerky, to the pavement. Pistols barked in Sledge's direction and Ms. Haines and Mr. Rolf cried and begged. One guard turned to line up a shot on Gentry and Coydog reached out and threw a bolt of pure mana. Blood poured from his nose as he tumbled to the ground next to their extraction target and her boss, who still huddled beneath her for cover.

Sledge popped up from the rear of the limo—not the front, where he'd vanished—and dropped the last exec-protect company man with a pair of gel rounds. He slid across the trunk, Coydog was sure it was thanks to a steady diet of action trid-flicks, or maybe just to muss up more of the paint job, and silenced Rolf with a swift kick. His ork-sized combat boot won out over Rolf's flawlessly styled hair, and the suit crumpled and let go of Haines.

"Let's go, lady!" Sledge hauled the bawling woman up by one arm and dragged her toward the van.

"It's okay, Kirsten," Coydog tried to sound a little nicer than the ork, which wasn't hard. "We're here to help you, not hurt you. A...secondary team."

"You're from...?" Haines' eyes were wide, but a lifetime of corporate obedience had her climbing into the back of the van.

"*Hai*, Haines-*san*," Hardpoint turned in his driver's chair to nod to her. "Just have a seat, we'll get you there in no time."

"Hustle it up, breeder!" Sledge hollered as he buckled himself in, shouting back to Gentry.

The human stooped over Rolf's unconscious form, then straightened up. He still had his buzzing shock baton in one hand, but his other held a chrome-shining commlink. "Bossman might toss us a bonus for some goodies if I can de-encrypt this puppy." He idly tapped the side of the parked limo with his baton, arcing blue-white sparks as he trotted toward the back of the van.

"This wasn't so bad," he smiled, tossing the stolen commlink up into the van for Sledge to smoothly snatch out of the air, chip-quick. "In the movies, something always goes wrong on a shadowrun."

Coydog smiled at him sweetly, then pulled the van door shut in his face.

There were chuckles from the driver's seat and the Bulldog started rolling. Coydog peeked over Hardpoint's shoulder and saw a dashboard monitor display showing that, sure enough, Gentry had clambered onto the back of the van and clung desperately to the ladder there, kicking the back of the van and cussing at her in Sperethiel.

She filled the back of the van with peals of laughter, Sledge chuckled and flashed his tusks in a laugh, and Ms. Haines looked like she was going to go back to crying any minute now.

"Give him about half a block before we let him in," Coydog laughed out over the sounds of Gentry's pounding and hollering.

That's what he got for being a show-off.

ANOTHER NIGHT, ANOTHER RUN

(Shadowrun, Fifth Edition)

You wanna know what's a really nice ego boost AND pretty terrifying? Writing the intro fiction to a brand new edition of Shadowrun, *the first RPG you ever saw with intro fiction, the first RPG you ever played, and the RPG that introduced you to your wife.*

When I got offered the intro fic to SR5, I knew two things: I was gonna have to knock this outta the park, and I was gonna HAVE to have the cover art. I was always so impressed by the one-two punch of the first Shadowrun *cover and the first* Shadowrun *intro fic, and I wanted to hit the same sweet spot. I wanted my piece to tell the story of the cover.*

To recapture that, I needed the art, then. I needed to see who I was creating, who I was naming, what story I was telling. Sledge, Gentry, Coydog, and Hardpoint were born thanks to that amazing, dynamic piece of artwork. Ms. Myth got added later, to finish the team off...but this story (which was itself a nod to "Night On The Town"), started it all for this crew. I had a blast naming them, filling them in based on their looks, and working on future art notes for them after they all became fleshed-out characters.

—RRZ

Smoke filled the air, cut through by the dancing, impossibly-straight, crimson lines of laser beams. Lights strobed all around him, showing Gentry still-frame images of bodies clashing violently, muscles heaving, chrome flashing razor-sharp contrast against scuffed black leather. Belly-deep, he felt as much as heard the staccato thrums of too-loud percussions, shaking him to his core. He ignored it all and concentrated on the AR feed piped straight to his brain by top-end hardware and his customized implants.

This was Gentry's first trip to the Skeleton, and the last thing he wanted was to get turned around in the press of thrashing bodies on the dance floor, dazzled by the lights and fog, smothered by the hordes of metahumanity all around him. Hardpoint had sent them all directions for the half-secret—and, Gentry dearly hoped, well-soundproofed—back rooms, and ignoring reality for his AR overlay had gotten him this far in life, hadn't it? Meatside light shows had never done him any favors. The Matrix was where the action was. Augmented reality or full-on virtual, that's where Gentry did his best work.

The heaving crowd jumped and roared in time to the Archfiends on stage, an all-elf rock band with more guitars and good looks than talent. Truth was, their sound made Gentry feel at home. He hadn't been back into Tír Tairngire since his sentence had been commuted, but seeing a rock band of nothing but elves and electric guitars reminded him of home. The crowd had enough humans in it Gentry wasn't as self-conscious as he'd been back in the Tír , though. Here, his rounded ears didn't stick out.

Here, he was just one of many, wedging his way through a brawling pit disguised as a dance floor, overcrowded with everything metahumanity had to offer, humans included: weekend warrior wannabes slumming from Downtown and Renton, soaking in the dirt and danger of a trip to the edge of the Barrens. Then there was the everyday Redmond populace, as tough and stained as the denim and leather they all wore. Redmond being Redmond, though, a sizable chunk of the crowd was gangers. Gentry saw a tight knot of orks from the Crimson Crush, louder and more violent than the slam-dancers near them, a lone woman in the green and black that marked her as a Desolation Angel, looking for trouble, and pretty enough that some idiot would offer her some before the night was out, and a troll looming head and shoulders over everyone else, not wearing any gang's colors in particular, but big enough he didn't have to. Metahumanity, sweating and panting, moving in time to the wailing strings and shouting voices from the stage, flash-lit by a retro light show and the lasers and commlinks some of them waved around in white-knuckled fists.

Gentry wrestled his way clear and sucked in a deep breath. Chip-truth, he didn't really care for that metahumanity, or at least not packed that tight around him. Coydog was waiting for him just outside the press of bodies, though, elf-thin and elf-pretty, with hair as dark as raven's. The leather fringe of her outfit swayed just a bit as she let the Archfiends' latest guitar riff make her move, and a light sheen of sweat covered her bare arms, showing she hadn't been afraid to partake on the dance floor while the night had still been young.

By way of greeting, the Salish elf just laughed and shook her head, then tapped her wrist where someone else might wear a watch.

Gentry made a face and said terrible things about her mother in Sperethiel, knowing that despite her pointed ears and high cheekbones, *he* knew more of the elven language than *she* did. She got the gist of it, though, and—still laughing, teeth flashing elf-perfect and white—her little fist thumped into the armor over his shoulder.

"This way!" Coydog hollered, turning to show him which hallway to take. Or, upon reflection, Gentry supposed she might have just called him an asshole. So that he'd know next time, he set his snugged-in earbud's sound filter to pick up her voice. "Myth set everything up!"

Their final teammate wasn't present for tonight's action, but she rarely was. Ms. Myth was a troll, and a heck of an organizer, but she tried not to be on-scene whenever she could help it. She managed. She manipulated. She mothered. She didn't murder. If she said everything was set up, everything was set up.

Coydog sauntered through the shadows of the back halls easy as you please—Gentry was used to that, with elves—but it took him a few seconds to adjust. He thumbed the dimmer-display for his cyberdeck and sent all the secondary lighting to full power. The last thing Gentry wanted to do was stumble into Coydog from behind. She'd never let him live it down.

Hardpoint and Sledge were waiting in the back room with a half-open window letting moonlight and soft traffic sounds in, and probably a couple of Hardpoint's drones out. The dwarf killed time in the middle of the room, juggling a trio of small KnowSpheres. MCT had designed the drones about three weeks after the Horizon Flying Eye had hit the market, but if you tried to tell him Mitsuhama had copied the design, Hardpoint was liable to kick you in the shin or punch you somewhere uncomfortably higher. He'd been in the business long enough to have gray streaks through his beard, but the dwarf was stubbornly loyal, despite what life had thrown at him.

Sledge, meanwhile, did what he normally did; glowered. Gentry knew the ork was vain enough, in his street-tough way, to keep a synthflesh covering over most of his cyberarms, not wanting his augmentations to ruin his tattoos and the biceps that were so central to his self-esteem. His forearms, though, were no-frill monstrosities, Evo-specced combat chrome that didn't pretend to be anything but armor plating and hidden weapons. Right this second, those arms were crossed across his broad chest, and he took turns glaring at Hardpoint for his goofing off, Coydog for the perpetually amused smirk she always wore, and Gentry for being late.

That glare settled on Gentry, natch. Just the decker's luck.

"You're late," the razorboy grunted, showing tusks in a snarl. "We're supposed to be professionals, breeder. Johnson'll be here any minute."

Gentry shrugged, armored jacket rustling and soft lights from his hack-pack sending beams throughout the room. "Traffic, Sledge. Hardpoint's directions had me rolling through contested turf. S/A skirmish started up an' traffic went for crap. Spikes and Ancients going at it again, you know how it is."

Hardpoint didn't seem to notice he'd been blamed, just kept juggling his KnowSpheres. Coydog looked for something clean to sit on.

Sledge didn't let it lie, though. "So next time that happens, you just geek the elves, end the firefight, an' get here on time. You ain't back in your precious Portland. You gotta earn your nuyen in Seattle, kid."

"Right. *Here* I've gotta earn my nuyen." Gentry sighed and rolled his eyes, ignoring the "kid" and knowing that, if anything, he was a year or two older than the ork. "What, you think being a human criminal in the Tír was just a walk in the park, huh?"

"You musta treated it like it was, breeder." Sledge pushed off from the wall he'd been leaning against, arms uncrossing as he took a few steps toward the human, "Since you got your ass locked up and put to work, didn't you?"

Gentry's eyes narrowed. It wasn't about timeliness or professionalism, it was about machismo and pride. Both of them had too much of it. Sledge took a perverse pleasure in rubbing Gentry's nose in the fact he'd been arrested back in the Tír and had to work off a long sentence playing the hyperviolent sport Urban Brawl, whereas Sledge had so far avoided Knight Errant. The violent ork also resented that he wasn't the team's leader any more, and—knowing that—Gentry had long since been ready for a confrontation. He bet Sledge wouldn't talk so tough with a backdoor to his personal area network taken advantage of, and those fancy arms shutting down for diagnostics.

"Before you two cripple each other, I thought you might want to know our boss is outside." Hardpoint's voice interrupted the brewing stare-down, all business. A fresh bevy of lights blinked on the external display panels of his MCT-issued headware, a sure sign he was actively monitoring one of his recon drones. "Maybe we should take the job and burn off some steam, boys? Having both of you along for the gig helps our odds, I'm sure."

"I dunno, HP," Coydog teased and flashed a wicked grin, "If one of 'em geeks the other, it does mean bigger shares all around!"

Sledge kept up the glare, but Gentry lost interest and turned away.

"You guys are right. We need to focus, Sledge." The decker sent mental commands to his hack-pack, shoving icons around and canceling the viruses he'd been about to upload into the ork's PAN.

"Let's go meet the boss and get the details."

The Meet was over. It had gone as well as a Meet ever did, without the team's fixer, Ms. Myth, around to help out.

Sledge wasn't thrilled with leaving his Harley back at the Skeleton, but a short conversation with the righteous tusker running the door, and he was satisfied his bike would be looked after. That punk Gentry's sleek Mirage looked fast but fragile next to Sledge's chopper, but Coydog's muddy Gopher pickup dwarfed both of them. Satisfied they'd all be there when they got back, the big ork clambered into Hardpoint's big van, a GMC Bulldog.

But right away, Gentry started whining and wrecked what should've been a quiet ride. "I'm telling you, facial recognition pegged the guy. Mr. Johnson's *from* Ares. You can see him in this fundraiser picture, he's part of a security detail, if you'd just take a look at—"

"Well, I ain't takin' a look at it," Sledge cut Gentry off with an angry chop at the air. His new sword was sheathed, but he still liked waving the thing around to interrupt the wannabe daisy-eater. "It ain't our job to care, chummer. We took the job and the up-front payment, so now we do it. Period. We go in, download the specs, record the infiltration. That's it. That's all. It's simple."

"No, it isn't. It's never that simple! This guy's hiring us to do a run against *his own company*, and you don't think that's a little weird?"

Sledge rolled his eyes. "I'm saying it don't matter if it's weird. It's just another night. Just another paycheck." He reached across the van and jabbed Gentry in the shoulder with his sheathed blade again. "Maybe he's Ares internal affairs or somethin'. Maybe he's from another department. Maybe he's angling for his boss's job an' wants us to make 'em look bad. Lots of maybes, but none of 'em matter. It's just another run."

"Listen, if you'll give me five minutes to—"

"No time, shadowkiddies." Hardpoint's voice cut off their argument, and the dwarf unplugged himself from the Bulldog's dash. "This is our stop. Sledge, you're on point."

Sledge hopped out of the van smoothly, leaving Gentry to fumble with this seatbelt and strap his goggles and headset on. The ork's movements came herky-jerk quick now, his enhanced reflexes turned on and running hot. He had a blocky AK-98 in his hands, an Ares handcannon holstered at his hip, and his new pigsticker, long and thin, slung over his back. It was an official *Neal The Ork Barbarian* repro, all thin, curved, and fantasy-stylized right out of a high budget tridflick, but it had a wicked sharp mono-edge, and that's all Sledge cared about.

The team had a block and a half of broken-down Seattle to cover, and Sledge knew the streets better than the rest of them. He led the way from cover to cover, alley to alley, hurrying them through the rain-slick shadows. The Seattle shadows were his home, and urban gunfights his way of life. They knew he'd get them there.

Sledge shot a glance backward as he waited at a corner, and flashed his tusks in a smirk at Gentry, who was second. The decker had a Colt 2066—which wasn't the worst gun in the world, the ork grudgingly admitted—in his hand, but the real skill he brought to the team was strapped all over his body. It was some sort of drek-hot Renraku hack-pack rig Gentry'd sometimes babble on and on about like anyone but him or maybe Hardpoint gave a damn. His eyes weren't chipped up like Sledge's, and the breeder had to wear those goggles of his, half-shooting glasses and half-supercomputer, to use a smartlink or see in the dark.

Sledge snorted.

Hardpoint was next, following in his scuffed-up security armor, MCT logos long since scratched away, but still the dwarf's favorite outfit. Sledge understood loyalty. He got where the dwarf was coming from, trying to stick with the folks who'd brought him up; the only reason it didn't make sense, in Sledge's eyes, was that the halfer was so doggedly protective of a megacorp, especially one that had cut him loose. Still, the ork didn't mind all the firepower Hardpoint's drones brought to the team. He'd been arguing for them to park closer, of course, but eventually they'd compromised; this way Hardpoint's previous van was close enough to lend indirect support, but far enough away to avoid notice.

Coydog and her cowboy boots came last, and Sledge couldn't help but let his gaze linger a little. The elf was different. Salish tribal born and raised, but here on Seattle's Council Island and Everett neighborhoods, she had a foot in both worlds. Native and Anglo, backwoods and city streets; Sledge liked her. Everyone liked her. She had a big Browning pistol holstered at her waist in a sleek, modern gunbelt which didn't quite fit in with the feathers in her hair, the strings of colored beads, the leather fringes on her clothes. She was an interesting gal, Coydog. Sledge saw her lips move, saw hints of color flash and ripple from her hands, and then felt a cool breeze swirl around them all. He knew what that meant, and would've smiled if smiling was his style. The shaman had gone to work and called them up a friendly spirit. They'd be hidden from prying eyes, at least partially, but Sledge sure wasn't going to let that trick him into relaxing.

The ork stopped at the building's loading entrance, back to the wall, watching the team as they approached. It was time for Gentry to do his job. His smartgoggles brightened and his Colt was holstered as he began to work with his own brand of magic. No, not magic, really, just skill. Soft blue lights flared and danced while the decker's fingers wiggled and tapped, pecking at an imaginary keyboard his Renraku hardware spun into existence. Sledge covered them while the decker worked, smartlink reticule and the muzzle of his AK sweeping the streets.

Sledge growled impatience low in his throat like a junkyard dog. Coydog laid a gentle hand on the human's shoulder and whispered something encouraging to him, but Sledge didn't have a chance to say something snarky about it. Maybe a half-second later, the doors slid open. *Fraggin' finally.*

The ork nodded to Hardpoint, and the rigger lifted his hand and several drones leaped to answer his call. A sleek little glossy-black beetle drone, an MCT FlySpy, lifted off from his palm and led the way into the building, with Sledge and his AK just behind. Then Hardpoint rummaged in his pockets and tugged out his KnowSpheres, too, and soon enough the trio of little black globes were buzzing through the air near him, recording the job per Mr. Johnson's request. The FlySpy, nimble and silent, sped down the hallway as the team hurried inside, getting out of the Seattle drizzle and the putting walls and doors between them and the external security teams.

The FlySpy led the way. Hardpoint's tiny drone buzzed along ahead of them, making sure that security cameras were where they were supposed to be, that a corpsec kill-team wasn't lurking around every corner. The dwarf worked his left hand to pilot the little machine, fingers splayed, twisting and planing his hand this way and that, angling his palm to orient and maneuver the spy-drone, headware and extensive control rig electronics making it unnaturally responsive to such simple commands. He had one eye looking through the drone's optical sensors, the other squinted half-shut, and Coydog led him through the halls and kept him from bumping into anything.

Gentry was the slowest of them here; every camera the FlySpy tagged on their team's heads-up display—visible to all of them but Coydog, she said she kept losing her AR glasses, but HardPoint kept insisting she was breaking them on purpose—was his responsibility. Sledge gave Gentry a little nudge and a grunt each time he spotted one, just to make sure the geek was on top of things, and to hurry him up.

Gentry reached out through the Matrix, his AR-goggles bright with streaming data and security override commands, cracking into their nodes one at a time and convincing each camera to run a loop of the last minute over and over again before they stepped into the frame. Coydog's magic might convince security there was nothing to see here, face to face, and buy them half a second if some corpsec jerk caught a quick glimpse. Gentry's skills, instead, convinced corporate cameras to shut their eyes tight while the team snuck past. If the decker kept it up, Sledge knew their job would be a whole lot easier.

It was slow going, and tense. The FlySpy took point, Sledge cleared each hallway with the muzzle of his sturdy Kalashnikov, then came Hardpoint and Gentry, only half there, most of their attention sapped away by the dazzling electronic reality of the Matrix. The dwarf's three KnowSpheres swirled around the team, tiny dog-brains programming them to record their movements. Coydog rode herd, listening for doors opening and closing behind them, the stomp of security boots, the wail of alarms. Slow and tense, and careful, too, but Sledge got them there. They didn't see another living soul. Together they threaded a careful path through winding Ares corporate hallways and stairwells, slicing their way deeper and deeper into the belly of the beast.

And then, suddenly, there they were; data terminal 501. Sledge took a knee and braced his rifle against a cubicle wall, nodding for Gentry to move in. It was showtime.

Sledge watched as he settled into this corporate spider's chair—he had to admit that hacking into a Matrix security agent's terminal as a way into the whole system was a decent plan, assuming Gentry could pull it off—and adjusted a few of the sub-systems that made up his Renraku deck. Then Gentry pulled a long, slender cable from a spool on his right bracer and reached towards a port on the Ares counter-hacker's workstation.

Sledge thought about wishing the decker good luck, but decided against it.

Maybe he should have.

Hardpoint knew better than Sledge or Coydog what the decker was up to. The dwarf was no expert console cowboy like Gentry, but he had a handle on the basics of illicit Matrix interfacing. He knew how fast things happened in full virtual reality, how every nanosecond counted and how everything—from your own icon to the intrusion countermeasures that threatened it—moved at the speed of thought. Gentry flew in VR when he could, but Hardpoint preferred to keep one foot in the real world. That was the difference between them, really. The human liked to escape reality fully in the Matrix, where the dwarf preferred to influence the meatworld, just through drones instead of his own two hands when he could help it.

But the speeds were the same. The electronic rush. The stakes. Hardpoint knew, even if the rough-edged samurai and the city shaman didn't, how quickly things could go wrong in an electronic contest.

He heard and saw it through his own eyes and ears, as well as the audio and optical sensor suites in four different drones, when the Klaxons started to howl and the security lights began to flash. It hadn't taken long, but Hardpoint hadn't expected it to. Things moved fast in VR. Sometimes too fast.

The dwarf watched through his FlySpy's optics as Gentry shifted in his chair, lurching side to side. He called his littlest drone—no point in stealth, now—back to him and stowed it in the armored pouch on his belt. He kept his KnowSpheres running and recording, one swooping all around the team on autopilot, the other two racing away to scout. The decker jerked again in the big chair, body going tense and rigid, somewhere between a seizure and taking a punch. Then again. And again.

"He gonna die?" Sledge didn't look up from the sights of his AK, unperturbed by the security alert.

"Spirits, I hope not." Coydog bit her lip.

"I doubt it," Hardpoint said, half his attention elsewhere. He piped commands through his headware to the waiting Bulldog, disabling security measures, firing up the engine, and getting it rolling in their direction for a quick escape.

"No," Gentry himself said, reaching out with one hand twitch-quick to unplug himself. The human stood and brushed the back of one hand under his nose to wipe away some blood.

"Got the file by the tips of my ears." He shook his head, still unsteady on his feet, and Hardpoint watched through a drone as he blinked heavy eyelids that suddenly had deep bruises beneath them. Gentry patted the main drive of his Renraku deck, a sleek black box that rested on his hip not far from his Colt. "Almost got iced, but me and my baby got the job done."

Intrusion countermeasures—IC—could tear a Matrix icon to shreds in nanoseconds. Some IC, the blackest of the black, could do the same to a decker's brain through custom-programed biofeedback. Judging from Gentry's condition, the files were more heavily protected than Mr. Johnson had known.

Hardpoint started to get fresh information from his recon KnowSpheres, his reliable MCT headware giving him several datastream overlays at once.

"Left, down three stories," he said, monotone, matter-of fact. He recorded and reported all at once, telling the others about the incoming security teams even while his headware showed him black-clad security troopers, armored head to toe, faceless beneath their glossy helmets. In their midst loomed a taller, broader, figure, a massive troll, too big to even fit in the full-body security armor the rest of them wore.

"And right, one floor down." A second group were jogging up the opposite stairwell, looking to trap them. A pale woman in a dark suit led a handful of heavily armored guards. Behind them, Hardpoint recognized combat drones when he saw them; Duelists, the experimental bipedal drones Ares was manufacturing in this very facility.

"Trouble," was all he said. Gentry and Sledge could see just what the problem was over the teams shared cam-feed. Before that KnowSphere could get a better look, the woman raised a hand and whispered a word; a flashing bolt enveloped Hardpoint's little spy drone and that display window turned to static.

Sledge didn't speak, just led the team down the left hallway where they'd have a better chance of making it into stairs unimpeded. He shouldered the door open and threw a pair of metallic spheres down the stairwell in one smooth motion, then took a knee. Gentry hurriedly led the rest of them up the stairs. Sledge's broad, orkish frame blocked Hardpoint's curious KnowSphere from being able to track the grenades as they bounced down the stairwell, but there was no denying that the ensuing explosion was impressive. Hardpoint's own ears rang from the twin blasts, but he was able to hear the wailing of injured guards through the audial suites in his drones. Sledge hadn't moved, just waited there with his AK shouldered.

One of Hardpoint's drones watched as Gentry kicked twice at the roof door, the other floated above and behind Sledge. Hardpoint and Coydog burst onto the roof behind the decker just as Sledge's AK started to bark and fill the stairwell behind them with muzzle flashes and fast-moving bullets. The first heavily armored guard to recover from the grenades and stumble into view caught a burst for his trouble and tumbled back down the stairs. Then came a second and third, and Sledge burned the rest of his magazine knocking them back out of view.

Slivers of Hardpoint's attention flitted from drone to drone, watching as the Ares security troll lumbered into view. He swung up a huge gun and the dwarf's KnowSphere and Sledge both scrambled out of the way. Hardpoint felt the gun go off, even two stories away, on the roof, as the Panther Assault Cannon roared like thunder and sent a round smashing a fist-sized hole through the wall where Sledge had been just a second earlier. His drone whirred loudly as it tried to keep up with the impossibly quick ork, flying up the stairs after him as he ran to catch up to the rest of the team. Just as the security door opened up with the second Ares team burst into the stairwell near them, the drone's audio equipment picked up the sound of a pair of metallic spheres bouncing down behind the ork.

The dwarf fought a little smile as he heard the second pair of grenades go off, but that hulking troll and his assault cannon worried him. Ares was so concerned with securing the facility that they were willing to blast giant holes in it to try and stop a few shadowunners. Security, not practicality, mattered to them here, and that made them unpredictable. Unpredictable people were dangerous to get into firefights with.

Hardpoint tssked under his breath and shook his head, sending out a fresh series of mental commands. *The only way to fight fire...*

Coydog still wasn't exactly sure how everything had gone so wrong so quickly. One second Gentry had been doing whatever he did in the Matrix, and the next their whole night had gone to pot. Klaxons everywhere, emergency lights painting the whole building red, and Hardpoint and Sledge rushing them up stairs, a half-a-breath ahead of a bunch of security goons.

The crew darted across the roof, heading toward the nearest building and starting to cross over. The Ares security team burst up the stairwell behind them, missing maybe half of their number, several of the survivors with armor scratched and scarred from Sledge's explosives. The troll stood head and shoulders over the rest, the slender, pale, woman in her dark suit pointed, and they lifted their guns.

Gentry lurched across the gap between buildings, firing blind behind him with his big Colt autopistol. Sledge sprinted across a ventilation pipe, chip-quick, and spun to unload a second magazine from his AK. Coydog carefully holstered her Browning and leaped across the gap, nimble as a deer. Hardpoint stood where he was, letting his stubby little Ingram hang by his side, and just lifted his arms and grinned.

A flurry of grenades fell onto the roof, fired, one after another, from a trio of miniature helicopters that swooped low overhead. Coydog recognized Hardpoint's beloved MCT-Nissan Roto-drones a second before their retreat was covered by thick smoke and a fresh wave of explosions among the security team. The dwarf cackled as he scampered to join them on the new rooftop. Sledge's AK fired and fired, and was soon joined by a trio of autoguns mounted in each of Hardpoint's fire support drones. Coydog ducked as one of the little KnowSpheres flew by, turning to take in the firefight while the larger drones traded fire with the Ares security squad. Between the drifting clouds of thermal smoke and the protection of her own friendly spirit, the security forces had trouble getting clear shots at Coydog and her friends, but the drones' mobility and armor plating were their only real defenses.

She heard Sledge's AK stutter out a long burst, and saw the Ares troll stagger but not fall. In the corner of her eye she saw Gentry kicking again and again at the rooftop door that would get them clear of the fight, and everywhere else she looked she saw smoke and muzzle flashes, swooping drones and black-clad security. She reached out with a simple spell and sent an Ares goon stumbling and staggering, exhausted, but didn't quite drop him. She heard Coyote bark laughter at her failure and frowned, drawing up a fresh wave of mana to throw at him. The black-armored thug turned to fire at her, no doubt shouting into his helmet, but then he wavered and fell unceremoniously on his face.

Coydog smiled and started to say something smug to no one in particular when the security woman across the way lifted her arms. A sickly blue glow filled the rooftop as she chanted with a voice that scratched at Coydog's soul. She transitioned to Astral sight to get a look at what the other magician was up to, and her blood turned cold. The spirit in mid-summoning was terrible, but just as disconcerting was the black, lifeless, no-aura mass of drones that emerged from the stairwell.

"Oh, Ghost," the elf cursed under her breath as the wave of Duelist anthro-drones led a fresh charge across the rooftop. Her mana spells wouldn't do any good against such soulless automatons. She blinked and dragged her vision back to the material plane and started to drag at her holstered Browning as though it would do her any good.

Sledge appeared out of nowhere, blocky AK nowhere to be found, with a blue-glowing sword in one hand and the bucking, death-spitting, mass of a big Ares handgun in the other. He barreled into the lead drone with a simple shoulder-check, then she lost a clear view of him as he blurred into motion. A fresh wave of smoke grenades dropped onto the roof, and all she could see of him was the faintly-glowing blade and the occasional muzzle flash of a point-black shot. Coydog wasn't sure she could have made him out clearly even without the smoke, though, she was moving so quickly.

There was a flash of too-bright light and a faint droning in her ears. Coyote yipped in horror and anger in the back of her head, and the elf looked up at a twisted insect spirit, all mandibles and outstretched, wriggling legs, and felt bile fill her throat.

And the worst part was, they couldn't even run.

Smoke filled the air, cut through by the dancing, impossibly-straight crimson lines of laser beams. Lights strobed all around him, showing Gentry still-frame images of bodies clashing violently, muscles heaving, chrome flashing razor-sharp contrast against scuffed black leather. Belly-deep, he felt as much as heard the staccato thrums of too-loud percussions, shaking him to his core. He ignored it all and concentrated on the AR feed piped straight to his brain by top-end hardware and his customized implants.

They needed him to open the door. They needed him to dive back into the Matrix, or at least dip in his toes, and get just this one door open to save all their lives.

Gentry ignored the stutter-flashes of muzzles spitting out round after round, whether from Hardpoint's swooping drones or the Ares Alphas shouldered by corporate muscle. He pushed aside the curses and grunts of exertion where Sledge was, single-handedly, dismantling a half-dozen purpose-built close combat drones. He didn't flinch when the Ares troll's cannon sent a round close enough to tug at the edge of his armored jacket, or turn to stare in abject horror at the clawing, chittering, nightmare that loomed over Coydog.

He decked. He could more than hold his own in a fight, and had some subtle combat augs to back it up, but more than that—more than anything—this was who he was, what he did. His mind ran through program after program, subroutine after subroutine, thought about security protocols and lockdown practices faster than the computer could. He knew electronics backward and forward, literally inside and out, and all he had to do—all he had to do in the world *right now*—was beat this maglock and the hardwired security system supporting it.

His Renraku hack-pack screamed wirelessly in the back of his mind and ran hot, back-up systems getting shut down and processing power shunting from secondary processors. Bullets flew by and chipped paint from the wall next to him, and Gentry just reached out, irritated, to snap a return shot without looking.

One pop-up window out of many, all juggled at once by Gentry's headware coprocessors and his top-end smartgoggles, started to show him what he was missing through his gun's smartlink camera. Hardpoint alternated between twitch-quick piloting and wild cheers as his Roto-drones strafed the looming Ares troll and dodged assault cannon rounds. Sledge hacked the last drone apart and blasted the wreckage point-blank to disentangle it from his trid-flashy sword, then staggered as an enemy burst tore into his armored vest. Coydog raised her hands and chanted something in a language Gentry didn't know.

"I'm sorry," Gentry's earbud picked up Coydog's voice, wedging past all the background cacophony to hear her whispered apology to empty air.

There was a thunderclap and a flash of sorcery-bright lightning. The enemy spirit, assaulted by Coydog on one plane and by her spirit on another, shrieked in pain and tumbled to pieces. There was a cyclone hanging in midair for a half-second, impaled on the ephemeral insect's claw, before it, too, vanished.

Gentry gave the door locks open and disengage commands thirty-seven different times and one finally got through. Coydog swayed and fell, elf-thin and elf-fragile, having given almost everything within her to blast the spirit to nothingness. Sledge, covered in equal parts blood and oil, dove to snatch her up and—firing with his free hand—haul her toward safety.

Hardpoint's FlySpy led the way past Gentry's just-opened door, and directions and building schematics began to scroll across the team's network.

"Straight down, Bulldog's out front," the dwarf whooped and flashed a thumbs up. His sole remaining KnowSphere, the other one the victim of a stray bullet, hovered just over his shoulder as he started down the stairs. Sledge was next, half-carrying Coydog, shouldering roughly past Gentry but—just for a half-second there, in the doorframe—nodding to him.

Gentry covered their escape with his Colt in one hand and Coydog's Browning in another, while the trio of Roto-drones flew off to one side to split the corp-sec attention. A fresh wave of smoke grenades made the cross-building jump risky, and Gentry knew they'd make it clear before the Ares troops caught up to them.

He had the data. Hardpoint hard the footage. Mr. Johnson would profit from it, somehow.

It didn't matter how sideways it had gone, didn't matter what eldritch horrors had been thrown at the team, didn't matter what curveballs the night had pitched their way. It was just part of the job.

Just another night. Just another paycheck. Just another run.

CAUGHT IN THE CROSSFIRE

(Shadowrun: Crossfire)

Immediately after (a) making Coydog, Sledge, Gentry, and Hardpoint for the core intro fiction, then (b) rolling them back to being starting characters for the Beginner Box, during peak Year of Shadowrun time, I suddenly had to (c) pair them up with the box art for the Crossfire *card game, where THEY WERE FIGHTING MOTHERFRAGGING RED SAMURAI.*

You wanna talk about some whiplash? Going from a "starting character" story to a "fighting Red Samurai" story was a heck of a leap, but I had a good time doing it, and I think I made it work. I got to highlight how tech-hungry deckers are, I got to show a clear gear upgrade, and I got to show the oh-drek moment whenever a team of runners bumps into top-tier opposition. There was a last minute cover art change that made a FEW story details not quite line up, but I'm proud of the work I did, and glad that I got to contribute to a card game as fun as Crossfire.

Not gonna lie, I still grin like a fanboy every time I see Hardpoint or Gentry (or Jimmy Kincaid) flip up in a Crossfire *game.*

—RRZ

Shadowrunning is an art, not a science. There are times in this biz when you do everything right and a plan *still* falls apart. You can do your research, call in all the right favors, have a good team backing you up, get all the right gear, and still have things go utterly sideways for no good reason at all. Doing everything right isn't what makes a shadowrunner a shadowrunner. *Improvising* does that, staying cool under fire, working as a team, and recovering from the unexpected.

My name is Ms. Myth, and my morning was *not* going as planned. Internal walls and floors in this Renraku facility were pockmarked with bullet holes, scorched here and there from magical bolts of power, and stained with rather a lot of blood. Hordes of black-clad security guards ran through the hallways, a wagemage was locked in a sorcerous duel with my teammate scant meters from me even as a beetle-black security chopper, a sleek Nissan Hound bristling with weapons pods and covered in Renraku logos, rose in the air at my unprotected back. To our front, my team was confronted by several of Renraku's elite, the Red Samurai, the razor's edge of corporate security, perhaps the best in the world.

That last part, in particular, had *not* been part of my plan.

In my defense, I had done my homework. I'm a troll known for her attention to detail, and I take great pride in my work and in the web of connections I've harvested because of my competence. I'd spent six weeks on the job, literally, having been hired on as a consultant at this particular facility thanks to an old acquaintance who answered to Satou or Johnson, depending on who was asking. I'd gotten building security used to seeing "Ms. Smith" walking their hallways, gotten personal psych profiles on each of them, gotten them accustomed to the moderate authority that my security clearance, no matter how temporary, granted me. I'd spent more than a month getting the young one in particular, Yu, to watch how I grinned at him every morning, half a friendly smile and half a troll-nasty flashing of silver-capped tusks, just to get him accustomed to seeing me, obeying me, and being a tiny bit scared of me. I'd cased the hell out of this joint, plotted out a great little extraction, shared the details only piecemeal to maintain operational security and compartmentalization, and then someone upstairs—literally, not metaphorically—had tossed a monkeywrench into things.

Oh, my day had started fine. Everything had been perfect.

I'd stood in the AR cattle chutes with the rest of the salarymen, waiting to file through the security checkpoint. I'd used all my little social tricks (and believe me, I've got plenty) to get the crowd feeling impatient, to make my own displeasure at the security wait clear, to give off near-palpable waves of frustration. I'd tapped my feet, shifted my weight around to make the workers around me uncomfortable, pointedly looked at my tastefully expensive watch, clicked my nails loudly on my commlink as I impatiently checked my messages. I had just generally made a pest of myself to make the security guards feel pressured, worried, hurried. A troll-sized pest about three times bigger than anyone else in the room, mind you.

Well, *almost* anyone. The big, orkish maintenance worker, one of a set of three blue-jumpsuit-clad contractors, had skewed the average mass a bit. They were the reason I'd made such a bother of myself, of course. Sledge, Gentry, and Coydog didn't fit in at Renraku, whether their cute little human had hacked themselves onto the maintenance schedule or not. Yu, the fresh-faced, nervous, young security guard had stammered his apologies, but insisted on a more thorough search, and that was the last thing I'd wanted. No, that wouldn't do. So I put the pressure on, gave him a silver-capped smile coupled with an angrily furrowed brow, made him feel the pressure of an entire lobby of eager, loyal employees being slowed down and frustrated by a few day-laborers. He'd eventually waved them through, just like I knew he would.

The four of us regrouped in the elevator on the way up, and I felt rather pleased with myself. My extraction team had gotten on-site, my meticulous planning had paid off, my site preparation had been flawless, the weak link in the security team had broken for me. The target of our extraction was nervous, but prepped and ready. Everything had been going fine.

And then, falling from on high? monkeywrenches. monkeywrenches *everywhere*.

Some bigwig advisor to Orito Sasaki, Director of Renraku America, had decided on a surprise inspection of this humble Seattle facility *today*, for some reason or another; the why didn't matter, only the whom. To our team, the visiting Vice President wasn't the issue. No, the problem was who he'd brought with him. Red Samurai. Renraku's bloodiest. Hyper-lethal, cybered to the gills, trained, armed, and armored arguably better than any other fighting force on the planet. The personal security detail of Sasaki-*san* and his entourage of data gatherers were prowling the hallways of this little research building for reasons totally unrelated to my simple extraction.

Of course, Sledge's luck being Sledge's luck, our ork had literally stumbled across one of them as he'd rounded a corner. Sledge, still in his blue workman's jumpsuit, had been walking on the right-hand side of the hallway; to the Japanocentric employees milling around us, he was driving the wrong way. He'd taken the corner Westerner-tight and plowed right into the red-armored officer in charge of the Red Samurai detachment.

There'd been an audible *clank* as the ork's armor-plated cyberarms had thumped squarely into the guard's glossy red *dou* breastplate, then came a split-second's pause as one warrior sized up another and recognized death somewhere around the eyes, and then my morning had been shot all to hell.

First had been that initial fight itself, of course. The confused swirl of herky-jerk wired reflexes kicking in, the bracer of the officer's armor lighting up as a cutting-edge cyberdeck screamed Matrix warnings after a mental command, the stylized red armor tangling up with blue worker's jumpsuits in a twitch-quick melee, the flash of a shining katana against Sledge's street-lethal spurs, Gentry's stun baton twirling amidst it all, Coydog's startled little "oh!" and then a sizzling blue-white bolt of energy that missed the Red Samurai despite her best effort.

I'll be honest, I'm not really sure just how it all went down, because my own few augmentations just don't make me quick enough to follow that sort of thing. It ended a heartbeat after Gentry twisted and wrenched the Red Samurai's katana away from him, giving Sledge a reach advantage. The ork's spurs skittered across armor but finally found a gap, and the injury slowed the samurai down enough that a dazzlingly bright spell from Coydog created another, lethal, opening. In the blink of an eye, Sledge had won, but found himself cut in a handful of places and nursing a broken nose; Red Samurai were not to be trifled with, even their deckers.

It wasn't until a few seconds later, mind you, that any of us had realized the Red Samurai's katana had been stuck right through Gentry. It was wedged tight by the high-impact plastics that laced his bones, and had been wrestled from the samurai's grasp by the momentum of the slender decker falling to the ground, soundly impaled.

Then there'd been all kinds of running around, let me tell you. Lots of screaming employees, an alarm wailing, Coydog's frantic chanting as she tried to heal Gentry, Sledge's cursing as he tore off his stupid jumpsuit, Gentry's insistent refusal to sit still and get healed as he, instead, dragged himself across the floor to grab the Red Samurai's cyberdeck. Then it seemed like the only sound in the place was the terrible slithering *scratch* as Sledge had impassively withdrawn the meter-long blade from the decker's belly, leaving the human to clutch the looted Cyber-5 'deck to his chest with white knuckles, almost cracking the casing as Coydog had poured on the mana. Everyone hurried out of their jumpsuits—no point in trying to hide any more—and we settled on grim faces as the mission went sideways.

Oh, what a bother it had all been. All that planning for nothing!

Gentry and Sledge both had a few keepsakes, at least. They'd traded blood for them, so I didn't mind the decker keeping the deck, or Sledge *swish-swooshing* through the air with the well-balanced Renraku katana and syncing his smartlink wetware with his new Yamaha assault rifle. Boys and their toys.

Then had come the running gun-battle to get to Ishida's cubicle, of course. I had called him while Gentry writhed and Coydog healed, ordering Ishida—*ordering*, not asking, using a tone I'd never used on him in all our preparations—to stay under his desk, out of the line of fire and where we could reach him. Sledge had led the way with his new Raiden autorifle, Coydog and a hastily-summoned spirit next, then Gentry leaning and bleeding on me and my brand new Vashon Island outfit, the little scamp.

Sledge had gunned down a half dozen or so black-clad building security, I imagine. Adrenaline up and using my commlink to pipe directions to the rest of them, I didn't really keep count; the gunplay wasn't especially my job, was it? Coydog and her spells did for a few more of the everyday guards, I'm sure, and a tiny sliver of my mind wondered if Yu was among them.

Then we'd gotten Ishida, my nervous nelly of an extraction target. Oh, but he was a wreck. Weeks of negotiations and preparations, all out the window. I'd given him a high probability of a quick and quiet extraction, and he was rather upset that the numbers just hadn't fallen into place. An engineer with a head built for math instead of danger, I suppose I couldn't blame him. He also kept trying to talk to Gentry instead of any of us metahumans, though, which didn't exactly endear him to any of us. Coydog's feathers were ruffled because the sweet girl's just not used to being ignored. Sledge, dear boy, is irritated whenever anyone ever talks to Gentry instead of him (though in fairness Sledge tends to be irritated whenever anyone but Coydog talks to *him*, too). Gentry himself was flustered because his belly hurt and he was trying to crack into his new cyberdeck. I, of course, did what I could to get Ishida back under control, tugging the proverbial leash by handing Gentry off to him (since he wanted to talk to his fellow human so much); it made Ishida feel important, but also meant one of my shadowrunners would be within arm's reach if the engineer panicked and tried to run off.

For a few moments, I thought maybe we'd still be able to pull this whole mess off. We just had to get back downstairs, I told myself, and find some way out in all this confusion. Sledge could handle light doors, Gentry could open armored ones. Coydog's magic gave us an edge, and if she'd spread her spirit out to help hide us all, perhaps we could slip away and leave them all none the wiser. Improvisation, right? Staying cool under fire, working as a team, and getting the job done? Another Ms. Myth shadowrun, complete and added to the record books.

And then, in a voice still a bit thin from blood loss, Gentry piped up and ruined everything. Renraku data streamed across his smartgoggles, a slender cord linking his brain to his pilfered commlink.

"They work in teams of five," he'd said from just ahead of me, half-leaning on Ishida. "There are four more in the building, using a tac-net to coordinate and close on us while they get building security to—"

And then, like he'd summoned them, there they were.

More shooting, more noise. Sledge's Raiden chattered out a long stream of autofire at black-clad work-a-day security, savaging cubicle walls and leaving streaks of red on walls and floors. Coydog's spirit manifested in a swirl of claws and fur square in the middle of a security fireteam, howling and savaging, and for a moment her shamanic mask—a snarling coyote's toothy grin—was terrifying despite my trollish bulk and our friendship. Ishida balked when Gentry started shooting his big Colt handgun right next to him, skittish like a horse at gunfire, but as the firefight wore on I knew that the building security was just slowing us down; they were a tarpit, not a wall, meant to keep us busy until their red-clad murderers arrived.

They arrived. The other four Samurai flowed from one firing position to the next in their glossy red armor, moving faster than Sledge and smoother than Gentry, like spirits made of blood. Each one shouldered a Raiden autogun, and began to pin us down while they advanced.

We were stranded twelve stories up, running low on ammunition, injured, and with Coydog increasingly fatigued by the stress of spellcasting. Her feral spirit was torn to shreds by incoming bolts of magical fire and the will of a Renraku spell-slinger that rivaled the elven shaman's power, and searing lights flashed up and down the hallway as they matched wills and wits. My girl was tired, though. The black-clad human who clashed with her was fresh to the fight, newly dispatched from the security office I'd cased so meticulously.

Gentry manipulated augmented reality in one hand while he laid down pistol fire with the other, even belly-stabbed and distracted he was winning out against the few remaining building security. He cast me a questioning look as he intercepted an outbound call from my commlink. I gave him my sternest glare and he shrugged and went back to whatever else he was doing with his commlink, occasionally snapping off a shot sighted-in solely through his smartlinked goggles.

Sledge, poor boy, had to be everywhere at once. Sliced in a few places by that first Red Samurai officer, healed up as an afterthought when Coydog had finished with Gentry, he had still led the charge all morning. He used his new Yamaha like he'd been born with it, shrugged off incoming fire that peppered his armored vest or ricocheted off the bulky armored plating of his cyberarms, and killed perhaps half of the building's mundane security crew all by his lonesome. I'd *thought* the promise of a reflex upgrade would motivate him, mind, but I hadn't expected him to go above and beyond the call like this; I made a mental note to speak to Khayyim, my street doc, if we weren't all killed. Sledge had more than earned his move-by-wire.

The ork put in his last magazine, roaring defiance and frustration at the four red-clad Samurai as their guns tore into his cover. I was certain he'd be the first of us to die. He shouted, frustrated, for anyone on the team to do *anything* at all and help him out. Perhaps my improvisation was a little lacking. In fairness, I imagine most improvisation is found lacking against Red Samurai. Far-off, muffled, I heard the rhythmic whirl of a helicopter approaching.

Gentry crowed and fist-pumped in triumph, and in the same instant the oncoming Red Samurai stiffened. The magazines of each of their Raidens ejected simultaneously, bolts of their blocky autoguns locked back. The decker hauled himself to his feet with newfound enthusiasm as the four fumbled—for maybe a whole quarter-second—with their hacked guns.

Then, moving as one, each of the Red Samurai flowed into drawing their katanas instead, and rushed Sledge.

"That ain't much better!" Sledge shouted, but as they broke from cover he emptied his Raiden at them.

His firepower didn't drive them back, but he did split them; two dove to cover and the other two slowed down as their armor took impact after impact from incoming fire. None of them fell, but the ork was rewarded by some blood spattering the carpet near them. They could hurt, they could die.

It wasn't going to be enough, though. They were just too fast, too tough, too strong, too well-armored. Too unflappable. They were, each and every one of them, the sort of street-lethal killing machine men like Sledge worked to be; and, monkeywrenches being monkeywrenches, there were *four* of them.

No, it was time for me to take a more direct hand. You always miss the shot you don't take, right?

I slid my slender Fichetti from the concealed and magnetically-shielded holster in my blood-ruined Vashon Island suit. It barked once, and suddenly the wagemage matching spells with Coydog had more on his mind—several millimeters more—than his duel with the elf. He fell in an awful spray of blood and gray matter. Coydog immediately whirled and shouted words of power at the oncoming Red Samurai. They were too quick, her flurry of lightning spells hadn't hit or hurt them, but her firepower, combined with Sledge's, had bought us a few more seconds as they took cover.

Then the Nissan Hound, the Renraku attack helicopter, lifted to our floor. Red-on-black corporate logos gleaming, angular, predatory, it hovered and flanked us. Ishida wailed in terror. Coydog's shoulders slumped from resignation as much as fatigue. Sledge snarled around yellowed tusks, ready to go down fighting. The Red Samurai, emboldened by this latest arrival, renewed their charge. Gentry, blue augmented reality interfaces hovering all around him, data scrolling across his smartgoggles, laughed like a madman.

Hardpoint, the dwarf that handled the driving and flying for our little team, gave the decker a stubby thumbs-up from the cockpit of the attack helicopter. I'd kept him up all night painting the thing, and he'd spent most of the morning installing the electronics my Renraku contact had finally supplied me, the daily security codes that made the Hound look like a loyal Renraku flier on the virtual, not only the physical, world.

The twin machine guns mounted on weapon pods opened up, and the hallway between us and corporate security veritably disintegrated. Suit-clad and black-armored Renraku security were torn to shreds, glass flew everywhere, walls were sheared away, the roar of the chopper's winds blew debris everywhere. Red Samurai scattered, chip-quick, impossibly dodging, ducking, pinwheeling, spinning everywhere but where the bullets were. Sledge added pinpoint-accurate bursts to the volley of fire, though, and blue-white spears of pure mana were hurled by Coydog. The Samurai weren't dying—somehow—but they weren't advancing, either.

Hardpoint swiveled the chopper sidelong, still firing, and Gentry—before anyone could move to stop him—vaulted across the gap like the fall wasn't there, like we weren't twelve stories up. The former freerunner cleared the gap between building and helicopter and rolled to a landing inside the Hound, then stood back up holding up the Nissan's harness and sling.

I allowed myself a satisfied smile as the hacker hurled the coiled rope to me, and I turned to strap Ishida in. *Improvisation.*

Coydog and Sledge augmented Hardpoint's incessant fire on the Red Samurai, building security savaged and openly falling back while the four lethal elite were hapless and pinned, unable to stop us. *Teamwork.*

Ishida got strapped tight and Gentry slammed the controls to haul the engineer clear of the whole mess, dragging him into the Hound and relative safety; the rest of us would follow. *Recovering from the unexpected.*

WHIRLWIND TOUR

(Seattle Sprawl Box Set)

"Whirlwind Tour" came about for two reasons; first, I wanted to just plain write more about Myth and her crew handling the fallout from their introductory story ("Another Night, Another Run.) There was an arc I had in mind, consequences from that cover art that had to be examined, and, duh, just more fun to be had with Sledge, Coydog, and all the rest.

Second? I wanted to showcase Seattle. This was the intro fiction for a boxed set that covered the whole city, and I needed some zany fraggin' scheme that would get them driving all over, talking about at least a few different neighborhoods.

There's a high-speed chase, there's a chance for each character to shine a little bit, there's a Panther Assault Cannon...what more do you need?

—RRZ

"This—" Sledge growled between his tusks, hanging onto the back of Hardpoint's tire-squealing Bulldog with one hand, boots slipping on the rear bumper, rain running down his shaved head, bullets whizzing by, "—is a bad plan."

"Sure is!" Gentry heaved and strained, pulling at the big ork by the back-strap of his combat vest, hauling him back inside the cargo compartment, the pair of them falling on their asses while Hardpoint seemed to be dutifully finding every pothole in Redmond's shitty streets. "But it's working!"

Sort of.

Yes, they'd raided an Ares facility for the second time in their team's young career. Yes, they'd filled Gentry's headware with the files their Mr. Johnson had needed. Yes—and this is where Sledge's complaints had started earlier—they'd succeeded in getting an Ares security squad chasing them. And, yes—more complaints—they'd been able to confirm that the sec-team had a certain very special combat mage leading it.

All, technically, gold stars.

"Well, *I* think it's a great plan," Coydog defended their leader, stepping over the boys to glare out the back of the Bulldog, all equal parts elven grace, balance, and disdain. A sickly green bolt of acid was hurled at her as soon as the Amerindian's profile presented itself—oh yes, they had that enemy mage, all right!—but the shaman flashed a Coyote-cunning grin and pushed, hard, to counterspell it.

The incoming spell dwindled, then fizzled entirely. Coydog half-turned to flash them both her best I-told-you-so grin, but then the Bulldog bucked as Hardpoint rammed something, and it was her turn to almost tumble out.

The ork and human fell all over themselves scrambling to help her. Gentry's prowess had recently been increased by the addition of a suprathyroid gland, as he was always so eager to yammer on about. Sledge blew the human out of the water, though, where raw speed was concerned, with his cyberarms chipped in directly to his new black-market move-by-wire system. He had mass on the hacker, too, straight-arming him to one side effortlessly as his other arm reached out to grab Coydog's waist and haul her inside.

Instead, an impossibly, inhumanly long arm reached past the pair of them, and a gloved hand gently wrapped around Coydog's bicep, steadying her and easily pulling her inside.

"Thank you, Coydog." Ms. Myth flashed her white-toothed, white-tusked smile. She was decked out head-to-toe in her urban combat gear, as armed and armored as any of the rest of them, with even her normally-gleaming horns subdued with a quick swipe-on matte varnish, but there wasn't a stealth suit on the market that could keep her teeth from gleaming. "I'm sure it will work out just fine."

Myth's armored bulk filled the doorway—shoulders broad enough there was precious little chance of her falling out—and she lifted first one Ingram Smartgun, then another. Whole magazines were sprayed out, the troll's fire inexpert but enthusiastic rounds chattering out a long burst that left a Knight Errant pursuit special smoking and sputtering to a stop, tires shredded, the pair of officers inside cursing and shouting into headware or helmet-mounted radios.

"Hey, 'Point," Myth spoke into her own comms system, ducking back into the van while Gentry scrambled to pull the armored door shut against a fresh wave of fire from their pursuers. "How're we looking?"

"*On track,*" the dwarf's clipped tone came back, all business when he was jacked in. "*Johnson's called in. They're sweeping the place now. Oh, hang on.*"

The on-ramp caught them and left the cramped foursome in the back lurching as the Bulldog accelerated, turned, and swept upward, all at once. The back end skidded wide, sparks flying as the rear corner skidded along against the steel barrier topping the ramp's concrete wall, but Hardpoint never slowed. None of them commented on the light show, half-visible out the bulletproof windows of the step-van; they knew what the rigger could make a vehicle do, and trusted him and his abilities completely.

They'd *had* to, with a plan this bad.

TWELVE HOURS EARLIER

"—and that's the plan."

Ms. Myth nodded matter-of-factly, trying to end the discussion. She had a fantastic personality, forceful and firm, a voice that could turn soft as satin or hard and rough as a cinder block, and a gaze that could turn as steely as Sledge's cyberarms when she needed it to. She wielded all of it, now, trying to sound confident, certain, mind-made-up.

Instead, a dam broke for Hardpoint, Gentry, and Sledge to start complaining, waving their arms, cursing, kicking chairs across the room, or, in the decker's case, saying "I told you so" about their Johnson having been an Ares insider in the first place. Only Coydog was on board. The shaman had to be; she'd been with Myth during the follow-up Ares meet after their last job for this Johnson, and she'd conferred with the Johnson's mage about what they'd run up against.

More importantly, it was Coydog who best understood the severity, the cosmic importance of what they'd found. She'd spent weeks conferring with her shamanic teacher on Council Island, confirming the worst.

"*Enough*." Coydog stood her full elven height, tilted her chin just so, didn't let any of her usual easy charm and lazy smiles shine through. "That. Is. The. Plan." A sudden wind stirred her long, dark, hair. They were indoors. Mundane as they were, the rest of the team knew that wasn't good. Coydog had a special love for air spirits, and they for her. Getting her too angry was like playing chicken with a thunderstorm that brought friends.

"Running around the whole town?" Gentry sulked.

"That's the best way to draw them out, yes. This is important, you guys." There was enough genuine emotion in her voice to get the job done. "She's not an insect shaman. She's not been...turned...all the way. But she *is* compromised. She is insane. And she is very, very dangerous."

"Then let Ares clean up their own fraggin' mess," Sledge crossed his chromed arms, voice ork-low and ork-nasty. "You ain't gotta risk your neck over it."

"Ares *is* cleaning it up. Mostly." Myth met his baritone with her own trollish grumble. "We kicked this wasp's nest, we've got to take care of it to clean our slate with Mr. Johnson."

Coydog winced at the analogy, which gave Hardpoint time to chime in.

"This is gonna be—" The former corp-rigger hated to use the word "impossible," especially when referring to his own skills. He pulled at his beard in frustration. "—tricky. I can shake a pursuit team, no problem. But stringing 'em along like this? That's harder."

"An' what about K-E?" Sledge interjected. Knight Errant, Seattle's contracted law enforcement company, was also the militant wing of Ares itself. "They'll have half the city up our butts in no time."

"Knight Errant's taken care of. Or will be, after the fact," Myth said with a hint of a smile. "Johnson's got that taken care of. As long as his secondary team finds evidence of hive activity—"

"—and they totally will—" Coydog nodded.

"—we're in the clear, after all this. Johnson'll pull security footage, handle all the reports, flag all of this as one big incident, one big internal affair. If we're right about that crazy mage—"

"—and we are—" the elf cut in again.

"—then we're fine. We just have to keep them chasing us, give Johnson's other team the time they need to take and lockdown that joint. Retroactive immunity. As long as we complete the objective, and keep casualties to the... *compromised...*security personnel, we're good. No geeking regular Knight Errant guys, and no geeking the mage."

"I hate to say I toldja so." Sledge reloaded as they heard more shots clatter off the van's armored hide. On top of the pursuing vehicles, they had a half-dozen Ares gun-drones chasing them down, too, with Hardpoint's little autonomous air wing dogfighting them overhead.

"The hell you do." Myth gave him a thump on the back that sent him toward the rear exit again. It was his turn on provocation duty. Gentry had dived into the Matrix head-first, Coydog was taking a breather, and Hardpoint's drones were busy. It fell to him to dissuade their pursuers.

The ork braced himself near the rear door and took a deep breath before nodding for Myth to fling it open. He was toting a new toy, and the muzzle led the way.

A Panther Assault Cannon is a ridiculous thing for a street samurai—for any shadowrunner, really—to own. Sledge had said so when Myth had given it to him.

"Why th'frag you even have this thing?" he'd asked.

But now, using it? Feeling the skillsoft slotted in his new chipjack port, *GUNNER.0* guiding his fire, with the gel-padded buttstock of the cannon braced against his armored shoulder, the heavy barrel stabilized by—ironically, perhaps?—an Ares brand *SmartHarness* gyro-mount system, the boneshaking *THOOM* of the gun rattling his tusks, and with a single shot simply *obliterating* the entire engine block of the Knight Errant pursuit/interceptor vehicle he aimed it at, Sledge understood.

"This *norgoz* is *hez*!" he grunted, and Myth—understanding Or'zet, the orkish tongue—laughed loudly in agreement.

Oh, dumb as a box of devil rats, sure. As subtle as a fraggin' bazooka, as quiet as a tank, as concealable as a small car under a trenchcoat. It would never be something to pack for an actual gig, never something safe enough to use—never, *ever*—without getting the National Guard called out on you. It was a once in a lifetime bang-bang, something Myth had given him to use, just this once, because of the arrangement, the get-out-of-drek-free card they were all carrying.

It left a grin on his face and craters in the 405 as they raced down the arterial line of Bellevue. As he ducked back inside against a half-hearted spray of return fire, Sledge played back slow-motion clips from his Trijicon cyberoptics and the smartgun mounted on the big Panther. Wiz. It was just like an action movie. Neil the Ork Barbarian never had nothin' so sweet.

Ares pursuit cars swerved and skidded to avoid the wrecked vehicles he left behind, to dodge the war-zone potholes he made, to slip past lethal collisions with the harnessed-in, crash-foam stabilized cops in their mauled cars.

"That helped." Hardpoint's voice, calm and level, crackled across the team comms system, piped directly into Sledge's inner cyberear. Backing off the hostiles bought him time to redline the engine in a straightaway, gave him time to coordinate with Mr. Johnson.

"We're on schedule," he said, and Ms. Myth nodded. Coydog craned her neck to peer down the 90 as they whipped past it, and let out a little sigh as the saw the subdued lights of Council Island in the distance.

The rigger kept them on course, though, and stayed far, far, from that NAN territory. The job was already a clusterfrag by design. The last thing they needed was to get Salish soldiers on their tail, too. But she wished Four-Paws-Laughing was with her. He knew so much. But he *had* taught her a new trick over the last few weeks...

"We get in. We get the data. We pick a fight. We get out... *then* the job actually begins. The chase starts here." Hardpoint flicked his wrist, a casual mental command sending the team's commlinks playing. Coydog's flickered unsteadily, but she got the gist.

A map of Seattle, softly glowing green, was displayed, the Emerald City in fact as well as nickname. A boxy little icon stood in for their GMC Bulldog, and sped away from their target facility. It was in Downtown, and Downtown hadn't gotten any easier since last time.

"We have to leave Seattle proper as quick as we can," Hardpoint said to nothing but agreement.

"We don't want no beef." Gentry bobbed his head. Downtown was Seattle's beating heart, and corporate security ran those streets.

"So we floor it. North—"

"Hold up." Sledge tapped his screen to pause it, right off the bat. "Why not take the 520 across to Bellevue? Cut east right off the bat, through the 'Belle, straight into Redmond?"

"The bridge," Hardpoint said, face grim behind his beard. "Traffic's too unpredictable there, and it's way, way too easy for them to choke us off. If we move from district to district fast enough, that's K-E precinct to precinct. With Mr. Johnson behind the scenes, that exacerbates their response problem. And remember, we're doing this to eat up time. Mostly we want surface streets. Options at every intersection. Fluidity."

The ork grunted his assent, so the rigger kept going. "We start here, then head north. Snohomish is easy mode. The cops don't take it seriously, they're too spread out. Rural geography, rural population per kilometer, rural fees. Knight Errant doesn't care. It's our warm-up phase, when we'll just have Buggy-*san* and her personal retinue on us."

"She's not actually 'buggy,' she just wants to be, and—"

"We know, 'Dog." Myth smiled. "Hardpoint, keep going."

"So, Snohomish. Rural country, we spin our wheels a little, make sure they're hooked. Then Redmond, 'cause we know Knight Errant won't do much there—they'll need time to get a real tac-team put together, CityMasters can't catch us and they won't roll anything else into Redmond without heavy armor support—and it gets us moving in the right direction. Redmond's our playground. They follow us there, we know we've got 'em. Bellevue's where things will get tricky—"

"More than tricky," Gentry cut in. "Bellevue's got just about the toughest 'trix in the city, bro. I know you've got basic GridGuide handled, 'Point, but their Matrix protocols are gonna fry us if I'm not on the spot. Drones like crazy, top-end traffic flow control, and they're white-collar enough Knight Errant takes it very, *very* seriously."

"Yeah. Tricky." The dwarf's understatement was met with sighs and multiple eyerolls around the room.

"Then south. Fast as we can. Knight Errant standard pursuit protocols will mean trying to keep us out of high-profile, high-income zones. Every surface street they're worried about keeping us off? That's one less car on our ass. We keep Buggy-*san* engaged, shoo away any straight cops we find, and make time. Renton will be more of the same, but a little easier. If we make it to Renton—"

"—'if,' he says—" Gentry groaned.

"*If* we make it to Renton, we're on the downhill slope. We get to the southwest corner of Renton, and we keep 'em guessing. Knight Errant doesn't know whether to call for support from Tacoma or Auburn details next. If we head towards 167 at speed, then they've got to worry about us going to Puyallup, too."

"But we don't," Myth said.

"Nope," Hardpoint adjusted the little AR display, and the boxy little Bulldog spun crazily. "We double back. The finish line is here, right in Ares industrial turf, vacant factories. No civvies to worry about, and their team will think they've boxed us in. Johnson's got our back, though."

"Sure he does," Sledge grumbled.

"Tell me we're fraggin' close," the ork snarled, bleeding. It had been a long night.

"I've almost got it," Coydog said soothingly, slender hands against his bloody chest. She called on Coyote to trick his injuries into healing, and the ragged punctures were closing up.

"Not that!" He almost swatted her away before he caught himself—cheeks flushing, feeling guilty—and turned it into an angry gesture behind them. Sirens wailed at them and flashing lights winked through dozens of tight little holes punched neatly through the back of the van. Knight Errant had started leaning on anti-vehicular munitions in response to the Panther. "I mean are *we* close? On the fraggin' map!"

"ETA in one minute." Hardpoint's monotone came through over the snic-snak of Ms. Myth reloading Sledge's borrowed assault cannon. She handled it and the massive ammunition magazines as easily as Gentry did his sleek Colt handgun and its own, comparatively puny reload.

"So gear up," the dwarf finished unnecessarily.

They were ready. As ready as they'd get. Coydog finished her healing spell and Sledge gave her a smile—a real smile, rough face softening immeasurably, getting a beaming response from the slender elf and a sulk when Gentry noticed it—before hauling himself to his feet. Gentry had his pistol in one hand, the glowing screen of his Shiawase Cyber-5 strapped to his other forearm. Hardpoint's second wave of gundrones hummed to life in their concealed launch pods atop the van, loading into a ready state. Ms. Myth had her game face on, goggles down, a locked and loaded SMG in each massive hand. Sledge strapped on the bulky harness for the Panther again, face turning ugly and mean again.

Coydog crooned to someone—something—only she could see. A wind swirled inside the van as Hardpoint's tires squealed, as the looming warehouse consumed them, as they received ready-set-kill messages from the Ares ambush team arrayed throughout the building. An armed and armored fireteam materialized from behind hard cover, guns pointed to cover the van's entrance, ready to loose hell when the rogue, corrupted Ares agents raced into the kill zone.

Mr. Johnson had come through. Gentry's tactical network lit up with cool blue symbols for each of them against the ugly red of the Insect-cult-tainted hostiles, the white of the semi-neutral Knight Errant cops who'd fallen into the hunting pack. Suppressing the mage was Coydog's job. Subduing her with less-lethal munitions was the Johnson's. Protecting Coydog was theirs.

Hearing the elf's friendly call, heeding her mental command, responding to the Initiate shaman's powerful summons, a whirlwind engulfed the battered van, helping it skew to a flawless halt.

The air spirit, the most powerful one she'd ever asked for help, burst to life as a roiling black cloud, lit from within by flickers of lightning, growling low with a nonstop rumble of thunder. It wasn't a Great Form, but it wasn't far from it. The potent storm-spirit understood the need, understood the danger, and stood ready to help its elven friend. Coydog's rematch against this insect-twisted mage, and any corrupted spirits she called up, would be a lopsided affair.

"This—" Coydog said with a manic grin, hair lifting as she called up a crackling bolt of lightning and prepared to fling it, "—was the best plan ever!"

EXTRACTION ACTION/REACTION

(Game Trade Magazine)

Ready for a mission impossible scenario? The Powers That Be had several pages coming up in Game Trade Magazine, *but just one page per issue, and they wanted to drop some* Shadowrun *short fiction in there. They wanted to tell a story as a cohesive whole, filled with cool action, iconic archetypes, and plenty of exposition to introduce completely new readers to the world and the game.*

Cool action, iconic archetypes, and plenty of exposition...in one page shots? Telling a good story? Released across five months?! Were The Powers That Be high?!

So naturally, I dove right in. I couldn't even write up an outline or a pitch, not really. Not with something this short, but also this detailed and punchy. How could I describe for my editor what the finished product would be, and sell it to him...without just writing the finished product? How could I write a one page synopsis of a one page-at-a-time story?!

So I sat down and threw together the shortest short fictions I've ever written, trying to give each one a coherent beginning, middle, and end. Trying to explain the high points of the setting and the game to absolute newbies. Trying to show off each character in a way that would make readers go "wow, I want to role-play THIS one!" Trying to be true to the existing characters as written. And, of course, trying to do all of it in just 800 teeny tiny words per shot.

Myth and her crew (holy drek, should I call them the Mythfits?!) fit perfectly to show off each archetype, and in the end, I had a BLAST with this one. It was so weird to try and do so much in so little space, but in some ways I think this is the purest, leanest, sharpest slice of "tie-in franchise fiction" project I've ever done. I've never tried to do more in less space.

And, even though I like how it turned out, I hope I never try to again.

—RRZ

THE MEET

Ms. Myth was a troll, nearly three meters tall, weighing in at a dainty 280 kilograms, with patches of skin toughened and roughened by thick, dermal deposits, and her face featuring prominent tusks and framed by horns that curled from her forehead. But none of that meant she wasn't still a lady, pleased with her curves, style, and grace, who stood proudly, minimized her skin conditions with a thorough self-care regime, whose tusks were as white as the dentistry of 2080 could manage, and who polished her horns every day.

And she *knew* she rocked this year's Vashon Island Little Black Dress™.

So, as she ignored the maître d' of *Trente et Un* and headed to her table in the dining area of Seattle's premier spot for Michelin-starred elven fine dining, she didn't stomp. She sauntered. Strutted. Swept.

"Miss Smith," she introduced herself to her appointment with a pleasant smile, enjoying, as always, the pun.

"Mr. Johnson," he replied, returning her smile with one just as flawless. He was human, but she could tell he'd had work done, too. He was corporation-perfect, lantern-jawed, symmetrical, aesthetically pleasing...but insincere. His smile hid a shark's hunger, and his cyberoptics were all business.

She had already known his name, though, or at least the name he would give. Corporate clients hiring extralegal professionals—called *shadowrunners*—always went by Johnson; it was a tradition of anonymity.

A trustworthy Mr. Johnson was a rarity to shadowrunners, so they turned to fixers like Ms. Myth to vet their employers and ensure honest, if not fair, deals. The Seattle shadows were a tangled web of fixers, crime bosses, arms dealers, and swindlers. Ms. Myth, as the face and brains of her team, *lived* in that web; she'd recognized several peers, rivals, and former employers while walking through the restaurant this evening (and she kept the maître d' on her payroll).

So Myth and Johnson sat and talked like colleagues, despite never having met prior. Appearances mattered at a clandestine meeting like this, and their fig leaf of privacy came not from whispers or electronic countermeasures, but civility, decorum, and a projected air of propriety. Ms. Myth, given her druthers—and she did love her druthers—preferred the civilized approach, and had the rep and street cred for places like this. If a good Mr. Johnson was rare, Ms. Myth was downright unique. A female, shadowrunning troll with her network of contacts, ledger of favors owed, cognition-boosting headware augmentations, and her skills and demeanor? One-of-a-kind. She'd taken the street name "Myth" for a reason. She might as well be a fraggin' *unicorn*.

So she held court here rather than in the damp back room of some dingy bar in one of the city's lawless z-zones. She listened to Mr. Johnson's request, coaxed information from him, discussed terms, and enjoyed herself immensely while doing so. Myth represented one of Seattle's hottest teams, and they both knew it. Shadowrunners might be disposable in the long run, but right now, she could demand respect—and receive it.

This Mr. Johnson represented Ares Macrotechnology, one of the world's premier extra-national entities. They were one of the "Big Ten," the AAA Prime megacorporations that literally ruled society through their wealth, industry, and Corporate Court influence. Ares was respected around the globe for its defense and aerospace tech, and boasted that more people were gunned down by hardware sporting their signature than any other brand on the planet. The megacorp more than lived up to its bloody war-god's legacy.

Ares, by way of Mr. Johnson, had a simple request: an extraction. They wanted another company's researcher, and her data, stolen. Interrupting a rival's project and co-opting their work was a common corporate move, the extraction itself—either a kidnapping or a prison-break, depending on the target—was a common shadowrunner mission.

Mr. Johnson's target, though, was another megacorporation with an even darker reputation. Saeder-Krupp Heavy Industries dominated global markets in energy and oil, and they cast a wide enough shadow over aerospace tech that clashes with Ares weren't uncommon. Saeder-Krupp had an edge Ares didn't; its CEO, President, and Chairman of the Board was a dragon—*the* dragon, the ancient beast Lofwyr, perhaps the single most powerful living creature on Earth. Lofwyr had awakened decades earlier when the ages had turned and the Sixth World had dawned. As magic had returned and brought with it elves, dwarves, orks, and trolls, so too had dragons and their hunger for dominion returned, Lofwyr most of all.

Ares might have been named after a mythological war god, but Saeder-Krupp was run by a *living* legend, who lent it terrible power and fearsome repute.

Mr. Johnson's assignment would be straightforward, but dangerous, then.

Still, Myth smiled around a dainty mouthful of elven haute cuisine.

"Dangerous" let you charge extra.

OVERWATCH

Gentry liked Seattle best at arm's length; running courier gigs on the rooftops, or, even better, seeing the Emerald Grid, Seattle's virtual reality Matrix, instead of meatspace.

A human, born ostracized in the nigh-fascist elven nation of Tír Tairngire, he had whitewashed memories of where he grew up. *Literally* washed. During his time in especially unsavory prisons, he'd been subjected to a full spectrum of sorcerous and mundane brainwashing that had left him, among other quirks, feeling like his old home was pretty perfect, and that human/barbarian nations were pretty gross. Even knowing the feelings were implanted, he still felt what he felt.

And, brother, what he felt right now was disgust at these Seattleites and their drekky-ass mall. Why risk your sanity and dignity amidst a cacophony of gaudy augmented-reality spam, real-life salespeople squirting you with noxious perfume as you walked by, squalling children, and on and on and on? Why be around all these *people*, when you could just buy anything you wanted online?! Everything here stank.

Ugh. Maybe the food court hadn't been the best place to hole up for his attack run.

"Hey," he grumbled into his team-band comms as he thumbed on his cyberdeck, "I'm going in."

Edging out even roof-running, virtual reality felt *right*. Gentry saw it more clearly than most, with his novahot cyberjack linked to a top-of-the-line Fairlight cyberdeck, and he loved to push his hardware to the limits; virtual reality just looked *better* to him. Servers, hosts, and nodes were crisper than crisp, cleaner than cleaner, sharper than sharp. There was no smog, no dirt, no stink, no litter.

Plus, in the Matrix, you could be anything.

Gentry's avatar—a fantasy elven ranger, painstakingly customized—crept through the mall's virtual overlay. The archer wore a hooded cloak that shadowed his features while animated storm clouds roiled within its folds; Sleaze protocols making him a virtual ghost. Beneath the voluminous cloak he wore a mixture of dyed leathers and enchanted chainmail; Firewalls. A rune-etched bow and quiver of arrows were ready for any intrusion countermeasures he might encounter; Attack programs. His faintly oversized eyes took in everything, node-by-node; Data Processing subroutines.

His lithe, slim hunter stalked through the mall's electronic tiers, following the digital signatures of their extraction target, Dr. Ichika McDougal, and her plainclothes mandatory security detail.

Gentry's legwork had shown that the research-driven doctor had split custody of her teen daughter, was allowed to visit only in public, and that she was scheduled to be here, now—in this upscale mall with a limited security detail and a single Matrix agent on overwatch—all of which gave the team their window.

With the awkward visitation done, Gentry watched the daughter's icons vanish safely into the distance. He stalked his real prey from node to node, smugly invisible to the crude icons of their target and her boneheaded security guards.

But not so invisible as to make up for bad luck.

Even as he blocked their outgoing calls, Gentry's virtual elf had wandered right into view of Dr. McDougal's Matrix overwatch agent, the Saeder-Krupp electronics specialist remotely tasked with her security. They'd styled their avatar after the company's draconic logo, all red and black scales, claws and fangs, fire and death.

Dragon saw elf. Elf saw dragon. Gentry could tell from his "keen elven eyes" that he was facing a Living Persona, the virtual projection of a Technomancer; hackers naturally weaned on the Matrix, who manipulated virtual reality without Gentry's need for headware and cyberdecks. They were, literally, naturals at this.

Cybercombat happened very quickly. The violence was nova-sharp, Matrix-fast, at the speed of thought and processors.

Gentry's Sleaze-cloak was shredded by her chrome talons. His Firewall-armor barely held against her digital flame. His Attack-bow, Data Spike after Data Spike, struggled against her dragonscales. He got tagged, and more than once. The Techno was good, she was fast, she was dangerous.

But Gentry was better. Only just.

The digital elven ranger crouched over his foe's avatar the millisecond it fell. He didn't crouch-spam—a century-old tradition when it came to taunting—no, he just knelt, a warrior respecting a fallen foe.

"Gentry," he introduced himself, tagging the pixelating icon with a harmless signature-bomb.

"Nym," the dragon responded, her voice a threatening growl. "I'll see you around, punk."

Fair enough.

Gentry logged off and came to. He took in the returned greasy mundanity of the food court half-nervously. Nobody'd noticed his biofeedback nosebleed, though. Good. He scanned Hardpoint's ongoing spy-drone info, and spoke up.

"I, uh, *effortlessly* took out McDougal's Matrix overwatch totally on purpose. They're isolated on the third floor, and her sec-detail's comms are blocked." He slung his deck into his messenger bag and started toward the rendezvous point. "Gotta take her now."

"*You heard him*," Myth sounded off. "*Elevator fight. Hit it.*"

CQCHESS

Sledge and Coydog, orkish boyfriend and elven girlfriend, walked hand-in-hand through the upscale mall. Their shadowrunner-couture outfits—all leather, denim, and barely-hidden armor—and Sledge's mean-mug face kept anyone from slinging any overt metaracism their way.

The pair had tailed their targets in peace. They were headhunting, snagging a researcher to take from one megacorp to another.

With every step, Sledge's mind worked. Street samurai were a special breed. Everywhere his cyberoptics scanned today, he saw weakness, slowness, and softness. Not one citizen was carrying firepower, only three lame corp-kid "rebels" had even had knives on them, and every uniformed guard carried just a mid-caliber automatic.

Every person Sledge saw, he played out a fight, a chess match, in his head. He felt pretty sure he could kill every motherfragger in this mall if he had to.

Except *maybe* them; their extraction's security detail. Saeder-Krupp, a global titan led by a global dragon, did *not* half-hoop it when it came to security.

Sledge had reconnoitered, though, and prepared to chess-match against each of the five. He knew how they'd all move. The biggest man had cyberspur ports, but a slight limp. The woman moved with the herky-jerkiness that came with a recent speed upgrade. Their elven man had a few fine, distinctive facial scars; common signs of fingertip razors. Another man looked faintly out of place in the team, a half-step off-piste from the rest of the squad. New transfer? Mage? Both? Finally, their sellout ork moved with a fluidity that worried Sledge. All day, he hadn't made out any chrome at all on the last two, nor spotted any telltale surgical scars.

The group and their researcher stepped into an elevator, all brushed steel and glass. Sledge and Coydog stopped holding hands to double-time it and stay on-target, then the team comms rippled with the go-order.

Breathe.

The elevator doors opened. Everyone's eyes met. Coydog smiled and waved. Sledge triggered his reflexes.

Geek the mage first, that's the queen. Sledge's palmed Streetline Special led the way, and a shot to the forehead—a gel round from his lucky all-polymer holdout—dropped the Maybe Mage security man like he'd been poleaxed.

Sledge drove the little handgun into Twitchy The Too-Quick Knight's belly before she could trigger her speed and pinned her against the elevator wall as he emptied the magazine till she fell, writhing.

His initial stance blocked the others so Coydog could get the target out of the elevator and start hustling the "king" to safety, but then the melee began in earnest. He had to keep his cyberarms close to protect his most fragile, least augmented body part—his head. He ate a few fists, blocked a blade, then launched a low roundhouse kick that wrecked Cyberspur Knight's bad knee, followed by a brutal twelve-to-six elbow, cyberarm-lethal, that brained him.

Sledge swung on the other ork, but the bodyguard slipped it, sidestepped, and closed on him in a tangle of arms, a too-tight, too-clean, too-sudden embrace.

Drek. Grappling wasn't Sledge's forte, but he knew good jiu-jitsu when he saw it.

Too-Quick tried to get to her feet, so Sledge kicked off her to keep her down and throw himself against the wall, smashing the grappler on his back and spiderwebbing the security glass. Scarface The Elf Bishop slashed in a flurry, despite Sledge's roaring push-kick to buy space. A red death of a dozen cuts was promised in the elf's nimble fingertips as he swiped again and again. Sledge dropped his choke defense to return the favor with a proper cyberspur, and thirty centimeters of mono-edged murder swiped forth from his cyberarm. The elf fell, holding in his guts.

The Grappler-Rook—*had* to be an adept, he was too strong to be unaugmented, too smooth to be chipped, too calm to be mundane—almost locked Sledge in a rear-naked choke, and the only thing that saved the samurai was pure orkishness. The adept had the big arms and meaty hands common to *homo sapien robustus*, and Sledge had the distinctive jawline and powerfully muscled neck, plus his armor-plated shoulders to help out his just-enough training; the bodyguard couldn't get a proper blood-choke going, so Sledge had the chance to gasp and fight back.

He rammed them back against the cracked glass again, trying to dislodge his assailant. No luck. The adept had him in check and kept fighting for position. Eventually he'd twist Sledge to pieces—checkmate—unless the samurai did something truly unexpected.

Sledge grabbed the bodyguard's choking arm with both cyberhands, then sent them a *lock lock lock* mental command.

He hurled himself with both legs, and body-slammed both of them through the weakened glass—and out the side of the elevator. It was only a two-story fall, right?

Flipping the game board.

THE STORM

Coydog preferred shopping and hand-holding to broad-daylight murder, running down stairwells, and getting shot at by confused-but-angry mall security. Sometimes, though, life puts shadowrunners in uncomfortable positions.

"Nice to meet you," Coydog kept up a friendly facade for the clearly frazzled Dr. Ichika MacDougal as the pair of them trotted away from intermittent gunfire, "I hope someone told you to expect us."

"To expect...*something*, perhaps, but not..." The currently-Saeder-Krupp, Ares-shortly researcher gestured broadly to... everything.

"That's fair." Coydog nodded matter-of-factly. "We're kind of an experience."

As Ichika stopped to catch her breath, Coydog cast the most powerful defensive spell she could. A rippling barrier poured into existence, cutting them off from the pursuing security guards and their sporadic fire.

Coydog almost opened her mouth to say, "see, you're safe now," but then, on cue, two orks fell out of the sky to almost land on them.

"Oof!" Sledge oofed.

"Aah!" MacDougal yelped.

"Hon?" Coydog gawked.

"*Did Sledge just–*" Myth's voice crackled over comms.

"Gottacallyoubacksorrybye," Coydog had disconnected for worse reasons before. Sledge was *hurt*.

He wasn't dead, but neither was the other ork; one of MacDougal's close protection watchdogs. As the last one standing against her Sledgeypoo, he was probably their best. He'd been twisting as they fell, and landed feet-first where Sledge had impacted bodily. No. Not feet-first. *On his feet*, rolling with the impact, at least partially.

"Nuts."

Coydog waved Dr. MacDougal away behind her and summoned a cupped palm of pure energy. Clearly this ork had skills, but she had more. She had Coyote laughing over her, powerful totemic focus items to help her channel and harness mana, and years of shadowrunning experience. Not just elves and orks had returned with the Awakening those many decades ago, but true magic.

Magic she now tapped into with skill and grace in equal measure.

She chanted in her native Salish, black hair whipping around her in a storm nobody else could feel, and turned raw power into refined energy. She threw an eye-searing bolt of lightning at the orkish killer.

Which promptly fizzled out a good meter away from him.

"Nuts!"

Coydog knew a countered spell when she cast one, and with the ork looking as surprised as she was, it meant *he* hadn't done it. Who, then? Where? It was only when she cycled over astral vision—the true reality, with rippling auras and skeins of energy all tangled up with living things, including those most short-lived of things, spells—that she was able to untie the roiling masses of colors and figure it out.

Oh, it was *that* guy.

Two stories up, leaning against a pane of unbroken elevator glass, was the other untainted guard from MacDougal's lockdown detail. Sledge had been worrying about him all day, the human who didn't move like a chipped-up razorboy company man.

They'd *all* appeared mundane when 'Dog had scanned their auras earlier, but now, disdaining subtlety and suffering from a concussion at the *very* least from Sledge's headshot, the sorcerer's Masking defenses were down. He was *yes, no duh, very clearly* a combat mage.

And he was one clearly capable of protecting his less-magically-inclined teammates, like the ork. The ork that was really close. The ork with his own aura rippling with unmasked power now, power honed with lethal intent.

Coydog figured his Plan A was to kill her, then secure MacDougal and get a promotion.

If he was hurt badly, though, Plan B would be "secure MacDougal's secrets" with an execution, then possibly die fighting; but die having done his duty to Saeder-Krupp rather than being eaten by Lofwyr, or whatever the punishment was for losing your researcher.

The ork methodically lifted his lethal-weapon hands into a combat stance. He leveled his gaze, meanness of his eyes highlighted by the hemorrhaging in one of them, straight at Ichika MacDougal.

That was clear intent enough for Coydog. The good news was it meant he was probably hurt real bad. The better news was that Coydog never fought alone. You can't counterspell a spirit.

A cyclone encapsulated the lethal ork, plucking at his suit, first, then whirling stronger, then stronger still. Coydog focused *herself* on counterspelling as her storm-friend manifested fully, shielding it from the elevator-mage's harmful spells; between his concussion and her abilities, she blocked two direct attacks before he just glared.

Abandoned to his fate, the ork was handily, if messily, suffocated. Coydog didn't quite have her hastily-summoned Air Spirit turn him inside out, but came close. Hurt as he was, adept or not, he went down, hard.

Coydog flipped off the elevator-mage as she hurried to Sledge's side for some hasty healing magic, then, after helping the big ork unsteadily to his feet, she turned her earbud back on.

"Hardpoint," she summoned the team rigger's attention grimly. "Elevator fight."

CONTROL

Hardpoint was a simple dwarf who enjoyed simple pleasures. One such pleasure, any self-respecting combat rigger will tell you, is bringing superior firepower to bear.

"Don't bring a knife to a gunfight" was an old adage that saw surprisingly little use in the Sixth World, with all the nimble elves and powerful trolls running around, the street samurai and razorboys made flicker-quick with chipped reflexes and racer-tuned cyberlimbs, the implanted blades and the blunt trauma caused by armor plating or reinforced bones. Monoswords and combat axes sold for a reason, and plenty of people brought knives to gunfights. Stupid phrase.

In certain circles, it had been replaced by, "Just don't even show up to a drone fight."

At Coydog's request, Hardpoint showed the Saeder-Krupp combat magician why that was.

His primary combat drone for the day was a Mitsuhama Computer Technologies/Nissan Roto-Drone (Tactical Assault variant, customized). It brought to bear an MCT drone-customized assault rifle, a carbine built specifically to be mounted on unmanned vehicles instead of worrying about metahuman ergonomics.

He was able to swoop it in on an attack vector triangulated with tactical input provided by his MCT "Fly-Spy" mini-drones. He flew directly via mental commands piped through his MCT-specced Level III-Platinum control rig headware, and did so ably thanks to MCT's training and the precise controls sent by a top-end MCT rigger command console.

The attack run was, in short, a coordinated effort between a great many moving parts of cutting edge technology, but every piece of that technology came from the same corporate source.

And so, when one long, chattering, autofire burst roared forth, and a full magazine of armor-penetrating rounds turned the Saeder-Krupp combat-trained hermetic into a wet, red mess?

Very decisively, the day's score became Mitsuhama Computer Technologies: ONE, Saeder-Krupp: ZERO. Hardpoint was brand-loyal for life.

MCT's zero-tolerance, Z-Zone mentality paid dividends after one target earned a whole mag. He didn't even need to shoot at any of the mall security after that show of force! His Roto-Drone just swept near them melodramatically, flew back and forth in an aggressive pattern, and covered the team's hasty retreat without firing another shot.

Simple pleasures for a simple man. Overwhelming firepower topped the list, but getting your friends to safety afterward? That was important, too.

So the former MCT security rigger took a great deal of pleasure in watching his teammates pile into his long-since-customized getaway van.

Myth had never left, overseeing affairs—still armed and armored up, ready to provide direct support as needed—from relative safety, as they all preferred she do. Gentry was the first to get back, due to the young courier's athleticism as much as their planned order of operations. Then, package in tow, Sledge and Coydog arrived. The ork was beat all to hell, the elf was clearly fatigued from casting and summoning too heavily, but they were there, there were alive, and they had Dr. Ichika MacDougal and her head full of data.

Hardpoint battened the hatches and peeled out once all were aboard and his drone nested. The squad's home away from home sported armor plating, pop-up machine guns, and a very, very powerful engine.

For this daring daylight getaway, Hardpoint knew he'd need it all.

Every single upgrade got a workout during the Downtown chases that ensued with mall security (off-site licensed), then Knight Errant (until their Mr. Johnson got the Ares-owned city security force to back off), and finally the much more sincere efforts of Saeder-Krupp's nearest fast response/urban pursuit team.

Through it all, Hardpoint's meatbody—dwarven, wild-bearded—barely twitched. He drove purely in virtual reality, piped commands wholly through his MCT hardware, piloting by feeling, living in the moment, being a part of rather than apart from, the van. His eyes were shut, he saw through the rigged vehicle's sensors. His feet didn't touch pedals, they were the tires squealing and smoking like a street-racing drifter's. His hands didn't touch the wheel, they were the van, reaching out and touching oncoming S-K pursuers with fingers of automatic fire spat from angry Hardpoint-mounted weaponry. Pursuers never stood a chance, Hardpoint smoked 'em.

Throughout the escape, Ms. Myth and Coydog patched up Sledge as best they could while Gentry ran comms-interference and kept one eye on their prize. Finally, though, all seemed clear, and Mr. Johnson—Ares—awaited. Sledge's soreness ratcheted up his surliness, and Myth leveraged it expertly as evidence of their extra effort, scoring them a bonus for going in with non-lethal options and only piling up a body count when Saeder-Krupp had responded bloodily first.

Before long, Dr. MacDougal was chatting with Mr. Johnson about research budgets and benefit options; already settling into her new home, ignoring the trail of corpses that had brought her there.

All's well that ends in payment.

SYNCHRONICITY

(Shadowrun: Anarchy)

Shadowrun: Anarchy *was a book that a LOT of time, trouble, and thought was put into. It wasn't just another supplement (which we already put a lot of time, trouble, and thought into), it was a whole new mechanical way of seeing the Sixth World, a whole new set of rules that needed to be playable (and awesome) on their own, while still FEELING like* Shadowrun.

The first characters I made–the first characters WE made, on the whole project!–were Ms. Myth and her crew, who were also the faces of the GenCon Anarchy preview. Between that and the original cover art (Sledge plummeting from the sky), it only felt right for them to score the intro fiction, too.

As the cover art changed, though, we had a handful of new characters we wanted to introduce; so I added them, tweaked the 'run, folded in a second team to spice things up and give new faces some time to shine.

And then the cover art changed AGAIN, and you know what?

By then, I didn't care. I liked the story too much. It stayed.

—RRZ

"I don't like it," Sledge said into their huddle, casting a wary glance clean over Hardpoint's head.

"You don't like anything," Gentry said, then stuck his tongue out. "It's barely even worth saying any more."

"Boys." Coydog shot a glance between the two of them, quirking an eyebrow.

"Listen here, you little squi—" Sledge started in, but got cut off.

"*Boys.*" Ms. Myth's troll-deep voice ended the argument before it really got started. "We need in the building to get the focus. They need in the building, too. There's no need for two teams to be at odds with each other, is there? They're short on technical support, so we've got an advantage if things go sideways, and Sledge's worst fears come true."

"'M'not scared," the big ork mumbled to nobody in particular.

"It just makes sense," Hardpoint cut in with dwarven certainty. He didn't speak up as often as the others, and when he did, they listened. "I say aye."

"Aye." Gentry nodded, shooting a glance at a particularly leggy member of the other team.

"Aye." Coydog nodded with a bright smile.

"Nay." Sledge crossed his blocky cyberarms over his broad chest.

Myth spoke last, like she so often did. "Ayes have it, not even countin' mine, sweetie. If they're in, we're in."

"I don't like 'em." Lefty shot the larger group a concerned look, glaring a bit at the decker who kept staring at her. Her chromed-up left hand flexed and straightened with tension. Her right hand—her shooting hand—didn't move.

"You rarely do," Alyosha teased, the good-natured dwarf shooting her a smile that took the edge off.

"I know Myth," Tiny's bass rumbled. The troll easily doubled Alyosha's height and even loomed over the elf-lanky Lefty. "She's a righteous tusker. An' I've heard good things about her crew. They'll do fine."

"Yeah, but what will they be fine at *doing*? I heard 'em say they're after some magical doohickey—"

"A focus," Alyosha said, since he was the one who was supposed to know magic for the rest of them.

"*Doohickey*," Lefty doubled down. "And this isn't a retrieval job for us, as you two well know. We can't let 'em slow us down. In and out, maximum speed, minimum time, that was our plan."

Alyosha sighed. Precision was great, right until the moment that it interfered with actually getting the job done.

"Well without 'em, I'm our only way through the front fraggin' door, Left-o, and same with every other stinkin' door we come across. That's gonna slow us plenty, right? Highball's still down, and can't run offsite info-tech for us. Without a decker, we're hosed, and they got a decker."

Lefty peered over at Gentry, who smiled at her. "Some decker," she grumbled.

"I and great Bear—" Alyosha Duska gestured everywhere and nowhere in particular, as he often did when talking about the spirits he could call, "—vote aye."

"Aye." Tiny's massive head shifted in a nod.

"Nay," Lefty pouted. "Fat lot of good it'll do me. Fine. If they're in, we're in." She glared again at Gentry, who lifted a hand to wave back at her. "But I'll be using an 'I told you so' later."

"Hey." Sledge introduced himself to the massive troll—massive even compared to Ms. Myth, who was particularly proud of her girlish figure—with open hostility and only grudging civility. The ork carried a sleek assault rifle and had a *Neil the Ork Barbarian* reproduction mono-sword over his shoulder.

"Yo." Tiny looked down at the chromed-up ork, showing wry amusement. His weapons, his arms, his style was visibly and overtly lower-tech. Sledge knew the type, runners who thought older, simple stuff was more reliable. Tiny rippled with trollish mass, and his most obvious weapon was an absurdly heavy chopping blade, a machete writ large and in bold.

The two sized each other up, then fell into a tense silence, just waiting at the front of their pile-up for the rest of their teams to get in line. Everybody on both crews knew who'd take point. The two of them filled the alley, regardless, it would've been tough for anyone else to get past them to be in front of they'd tried.

"*In position.*" Hardpoint's voice came through both teams' commlinks, lacking inflection, as was always the case when the dwarf rigged. He'd stay in the van, but sure enough, shortly after his announcement, a pair of low-flying hoverdrones zipped into view, stubby autorifles held aloft on whirring gyroblades.

"Neat!" Coydog clapped her elf-thin hands as Duska finished his quiet, guttural chanting and a ripple of power flowed from him. Nobody else on either team was Awakened, nobody else had their eyes open to the astral and the tricks of power the two shamans could pull, but the elf seemed impressed with his summoning work.

"Your turn," the dwarf said with a wry smile, only to tilt an approving eyebrow a moment later. There was, again, no obvious display of power as Coydog finished her crooning call, but a light breeze teased at her long, dark, hair, and apparently her own incantation was complete.

"Nice. Multi-spirit support," Lefty grudgingly admitted.

"Hey! Uh, you want me to take a look at your firewall?" Gentry sidled up, trying his friendliest smile. "I heard your usual Matrix dude wasn't—"

"Nope." She started screwing her oversized silencer into place on her long rifle, not even looking at him. "I'm good."

"Oh. Yeah. Okay, *raé*, I feel ya." Gentry looked halfway cool for about a second. "But what about the latest patches on your smartlink software, though? I bet my download speed is pretty wiz. I've got this sweet Sony Cybe—"

"I'm good." Her tone was chillier this time, a box magazine slapped home with a metallic *snick-snack* of finality.

"Yeah, okay, cool, I'm just gonna, uhh..." And then he was in a hurry to be somewhere else.

Sledge grunted in amusement. Tiny shook his shaggy head. Alyosha chuckled openly. Coydog giggled and offered Lefty a long-distance fist bump. Hardpoint's metallic, far-off "*heh heh heh*" rang into earbuds and cyberaudio suites across both teams. Gentry's cheeks flushed red, and he was abruptly very busy with something in augmented reality.

Myth split the night with a big-palmed clap and a bright smile. Lefty took off up a fire escape, long gun barely slowing her down. Gentry slunk past the motherly troll, who reached out to tousle his hair, easing the sting of yet another elven rejection.

"Okay runners," Myth said, nodding at the door. Lefty clambered into her sniper's nest, Hardpoint's drones whirred and climbed. Tiny and Sledge readied their weapons. "Let's get running."

Lefty leaned and twisted to swing her scope around and watch their progress. Hardpoint's gun-drones spread to cover each flank, the two shamans huddled next to Myth in the middle of the group, the street muscle—ork and troll—waited at the door, ready to commit terrible violence as needed.

Gentry handled the camera just below the glowing Wuxing logo, then the door just below the camera, then the camera just inside the door. The human might not be all that socially adept—especially around elves—but even Lefty had to admit he was damned good at his job.

No security assault team came boiling out to welcome them.

Lefty didn't have to kill any welcoming party, didn't have to line up her old-fashioned sights and cutting-edge smartscope, didn't have to adjust the rifle's front-end with her inhumanly precise cyberlimb. Lefty didn't have to squeeze with her flesh-and-blood trigger-finger for the exactly two pounds, five ounces, that would smear some idiot guard's grey matter all over the nice, clean, *feng shui*-fancy facility walls.

Good.

She watched the last of them go in—did that Coydog girl shoot her a thumbs up?—and then Lefty swung her scope to scan upward, toggling through light-amplification mods and looking through what windows she had access to.

"There's been some gang activity, though, Chipped Razors," Duska worried, voice carrying more than Sledge liked, "So I'm a little worried about leaving Lefty alone out there. Perhaps I should have left my spirit out there to protect her?"

"She seems nice." Coydog smiled, then straightened her features, "I mean, for a professional killer and all. Very competent and confident! I'm sure she'll be fine."

"You two are gonna get us killed," Sledge turned his head over his shoulder to grumble. Omni-directional grumbling wasn't something he'd had implanted—it was just a natural knack.

"Shh." Coydog glowered, "We're communicating and coordinating between teams. Transparency is important in a *healthy* relationship."

Duska lifted an intrigued eyebrow. Tiny winced on Sledge's behalf. Myth snorted in a supremely unladylike fashion. Gentry snickered, but kept hacking the elevator controls.

"And besides, I have a spirit concealing us." Coydog timed it just right so her explanation coincided with Sledge opening his dumb mouth to say another dumb thing. "Nobody'll hear anyways."

"*Heh heh heh*," Hardpoint weighed in via audiolink.

Sledge wisely stayed quiet.

"Ninth floor's us." Sledge stepped out as the elevator doors slid open, sweeping one side of the hallway with his Raiden assault rifle. At his back, Tiny swung the other way, huge blade up.

"You sure you're okay, boss?"

Myth gave them both a warm smile. "We'll be fine without you. Tenth floor's where Coy does her magic."

Sledge's cyberoptics had already slid off of the troll leader, though, and he cast a worried look at Coydog.

Gentry pointedly looked away.

"Go cover Tiny while he does his job. I've got Myth and Gentry and Alyosha and—oh yeah!—fraggin' Bear *and* Coyote coverin' me while I do mine. I'm good."

She didn't blow him a kiss or shoot him a wink or call him sugar-wooger-noogums. Sledge's cheeks still flushed, though, Myth still stifled a smile, Gentry still looked away.

The elevator doors closed, and the car kept lifting.

"*Still clear. Hostiles on floors four and way up on twenty*," Lefty said through the microphone built into her cyber-wrist, near enough her face in her prone shooting position. "*Proceed as planned*."

She emphasized the *planned* enough to make Tiny roll his eyes and Alyosha to feel a little guilty, but nobody else seemed to pick up on it.

Just like she, alone on her rooftop, didn't seem to pick up on the pair of gangers whispering at one another, blades out, as they climbed up the fire escape behind her.

Inside the facility, Coydog moved fast, squeezing out of the elevator ahead of Myth and even Gentry, Duska in her wake. The facility—the whole megacorporation—was well-known for meticulously arraying every little thing just so, aligning their offices with the flow of *chi* energy that surrounded and enveloped metahumanity, whether they were aware of it or not. Some attributed it to ley lines, others to emotional claptrap, others to simply nature's will; what mattered was that Coydog could see it, could *feel* it, and she followed this tenth-floor's flow of power to her target.

Duska was just a step behind her, the spirit whisperer as attuned to the supernatural as Coydog, in his own way. Gentry chewed at his lip and hurriedly wiped cameras as he trailed them, and Myth took up the rear of the group, her shadowy bulk a reassuring presence at their six.

"Ooh." Coydog finally smiled, casting a glance at Gentry and knowing the decker would already be working on that last security door. Through the thick safety glass, inside the central experimentation chamber of this floor of the building, an ornate metal bracer veritably blazed with power.

"What's it do?" Duska whispered.

Coydog shrugged. "Somethin' neat." The mundane security was Gentry's job. The wards, inlaid into the floor, were hers. "Johnson's paying a pretty penny, that's all we really know."

"Orichalcum?" The dwarf peered over on his tip-toes.

The magical metal was phenomenally powerful, and equally expensive.

"The inlays for sure." Coydog nodded, "And maybe some of that big stuff, too."

Her wrinkled nose and gesture took in not only the gorgeous bracer they were here to steal, but also larger, heavier pieces. Broken lengths of pillar, an ancient-looking section of wall covered in runic carvings, a lovely marble statue that looked to be wearing metallic jewelry.

"I think so, too," Duska sighed. None of the heavier items would leave the room, he was sure. "They're beautiful. That's too bad."

Sledge stalked the cubicle walls with paramilitary precision, his move-by-wire upgrades making every footfall sure and certain, his street-earned experience keeping his gun steady.

"So what's with 'Tiny,' anyway?" he grunted.

"Hmm?" Tiny didn't look up from his satchel.

"It's ironic, right? Call the big guy 'Tiny,' I mean?"

"Prob'ly." The troll shrugged, busy.

Sledge grunted back, then the pair moved most of the way across the room. They were near the central area, ducking from cubicle to cubicle.

"So, uh," Sledge tried to remember Coydog and Myth's lessons on the importance of small talk. "How'd you meet Myth?"

"Hmm?" Tiny was halfway under a desk again, shoulders too broad to fit, stretching out one long arm to reach something.

"Ms. Myth." Sledge tried not to sound grouchy. He really, really tried. "How d'you know her?"

"School," Tiny said as they moved to their fourth such pit-stop. His big machete was never quite in the way, he seemed as practiced at moving with it as Sledge was with his rifle and sword.

"Like a...a tech school or something?"

Tiny looked up, clambering to his feet after wedging himself beneath this last desk. "Why?"

Sledge shrugged.

"Figure smoothies won't let a troll into most schools. Thought, like, a vocational school or whatever might've been it. Myth there as some long con, you lookin' for work before The Man kicked you out—"

"*Movement*!" Lefty interrupted them, a heartbeat before Hardpoint's static-crackling voice did the same, a split-second before his gun-drones started firing a floor above them. Lefty sounded out of breath. Sledge didn't notice it. Tiny did.

The pair of them began to move—straight at the stairwell, running toward the trouble—but then flashlights split the darkness of the work-stations behind them. Underbarrel-mounted flashlights, carried on guns, carried by guards.

"Go help the others." Sledge dropped to one knee, bracing his Raiden against a flimsy wall, half-concealing himself and ready to open fire on the first guard that stepped fully into view. "I'll hold 'em here, you finish the gig."

"I will."

Tiny ran for the stairwell, and Sledge—firing a tight burst into an armored guard—didn't notice the troll went *down*, not *up*, the stairs to complete the rest of his job.

The guards had a security mage. *Had*.

Gentry's Colt snapped off quick shots whenever he wasn't ducked behind something and hacking furiously. Myth's Ingram Smartguns let out long roars of autofire as she sprayed and drew fire, hollering orders to the rest of the team over the chattering guns. Hardpoint's drones swooped and roared, laying down suppressive fire or flying up to flank a hunkered-down guard. Occasionally a window got a neat little hole blasted in it, and somewhere across the room, as if by magic, a security thug went down, as—across the street—Lefty shifted her aim for another shot.

Coydog and Duska? They had to handle the mage. The young combat magician, fresh-faced enough he looked like a fuzzy-cheeked recent graduate of Something-Or-Another Tactical Sorcery Academy, had started strong. Very strong. Too strong. Coydog had barely countered the fireball he'd decided to open with, and the elf 's features turned grim when she thought about what would've happened had she not snuffed out the spell.

Going straight to a loud combat-casting like that was a rookie move. It showed impatience with the ebb and flow of combat, a lack of willingness to wait for the right moment, an inability to pause and survey the opposition. It showed an eagerness to prove oneself to peers or superiors. Pulling out a big gun so early showed immaturity, maybe even fear.

Most of all? It showed you were the mage.

The young Wuxing caster got hit with a tornado, essentially, sucked into a raging whirlwind of Coydog's current air spirit, dashed against the ceiling, then the floor, then cast aside.

Then, getting shakily to his feet, glowing with power—again—as he mustered up a healing spell to try to repair his bruises and cracked bones, he got entirely, messily mauled by a rather unexpected bear.

Duska shook his head sadly as the team's fighting withdrawal continued amidst the roars of ursine fury and Wuxing pain.

"So young." The dwarf 's glowing blue bear spirit roared and clawed and charged off toward some heavily armored troopers that had Gentry pinned down. Duska sighed. "You should've stayed down, my boy."

Lefty saw Tiny first, the massive wall of troll-meat smashing the front security doors open—the wrong way—with a battering ram—more precisely, a dwarf in now-cracked Wuxing combat armor. The troll's big machete was wet with blood, and Lefty suppressed a shudder as she lined up a shot and squeezed her trigger again.

Hardpoint's van rushed onto the scene next, a GMC Bulldog, as customized as you could hope for. Security came spilling out of a side door, but the van slewed to a sideways halt just in time for its armored hide to deflect incoming fire. The doorway was covered as Alyosha, Myth, and all the rest came stumbling out, fighting a rear-action as they did.

No. Lefty lined up a headshot, applied another kilo of pressure, and ended a life. *Not all of them.* She checked the chronometer in her heads-up display.

"Tick, tock," was all she said, and all she had to.

"*Sledge*!" Tiny went rushing back down the hallway for just a few seconds, and when he came back out, there weren't any more guards firing from inside the building. "*Sledge, you gotta get outta there, big guy*!"

Lefty shifted, squinted, saw figures still moving on the ork's ninth floor, muzzle flashes still barking. She wondered—another squeeze, another fallen guard—if Tiny or Alyosha had ever told Myth's crew why they were here.

"*Frag off*," Sledge's fire didn't cease, but Lefty watched his bulkier silhouette move sidelong down a hallway. Moving and shooting, never standing still. A real pro. It'd be a shame if he didn't leave soon. "*I'm holdin' my own. You bein' tech-school buddies with Myth don't mean you get to tell me*–"

"*It wasn't technical school, sweetie. Not that there's anything wrong with that*," Myth cut in as she reloaded her Ingram, then she leaned back around the van to lay down another whole magazine of fire. "*Sledge, Tiny's got his Master's. He's a structural engineer*."

The twin-team's commlinks buzzed with a hurried image message, a photo showing a detonator and a dwindling countdown, a tiny-looking electronic device held in Tiny's massive off-hand.

"*You really should jump soon, Sledge-a-roonie*," Tiny growled.

"*Or don't*." That earned Gentry a punch from Coydog.

Oh. Sledge squinted at the heads-up AR display that showed Tiny's detonator, and highlighted the building with hotspots pinpointing just where demolition charges had been planted. *Well, drek. Guess I* ***do*** *gotta get out of here.*

The ork eyed the building schematics, swallowed, and gritted his teeth in determination. *Everything's easier with a running start.*

He chewed at the nearby wall with a long burst of expensive, explosive ammo, emptying his Yamaha Raiden in the process. The mirror-shined windows gave way, splitting the night air with jagged edges. He ran, built up speed, and leaped.

His cyberarms cleared the way for him, battering aside the last brittle edges, and the few small cuts that got through to his meat were nothing compared to the fact he was, well, leaping from a ninth-floor window.

Got a job to do, gravity or not.

The ork twisted, kicking his feet to bring his body around, flailing to orient himself as his move-by-wire kicked in and time slowed down. He got his Ingram in his hand as the ground—and the knot of Wuxing security troopers that had his team pinned down—loomed up at him.

Falling straight at them, Sledge lined up his smartlink targeting pip and let fly. His Smartgun barked and bucked, a long, nonstop burst, and Wuxing guards fell dead, shot at from an unlikely angle, no cover to be found.

No reason not to try.

His free hand groped over his shoulder for his sword—a wiz blue-glowing replica from *Neil*'s latest tridflick, but also a monofilament-sharp blade in its own right—and Sledge tried to angle his fall to land on one last drekhead. Might as well take one more with him.

Sorry Coyd–

Suddenly a tornado hit him, and Sledge was falling sideways instead of down. The world turned into a bouncing, shuddering, shower of sparks and bruises as the street rose up to meet him and he skipped along the pavement.

The rear of Hardpoint's van loomed at him, the inside crammed full of too many shadowrunners. Myth and Tiny took up half the space back there, and Alyosha ducked, and there was Coydog by one door, and at the other was Gentry, and then this weird shaggy-looking blue glowing thing—and then the world turned black, because Sledge was out cold.

Lefty watched the ork skip like a stone once, twice, and then slam right into the back of Hardpoint's van. Or, rather, into a shaggy bear-spirit who'd tried to soften his landing, and then into Gentry, and then into the van.

Neither of the two meatheads got back up before the doors were slammed shut by gale-force winds and the van started to peel out.

Lefty scrambled up from her shooting position—again—and hurried to the edge of the building. She stepped over a pair of Chipped Razors, a local gang that had, according to recent reports, about a seventy percent chance of trying to pull some drek tonight.

They'd tried. The two corpses were mauled terribly, almost looking like one of Alyosha's ursine spirits had done a number on them.

One hadn't.

Lefty's chromed-up arm was sticky with blood as she used it to help her vault off the roof, even though all her blades had been tucked back into their concealed positions. She fell right down onto a three-point landing—rifle slung over one shoulder, safe from the impact—atop Hardpoint's van.

She gave the Bulldog a *thump-thump* with her metal fist and they sped away. Just before they rounded the next corner, she looked back and saw the Wuxing facility split in half by a fireball.

It then crumpled, folding at the mid-point like a pocketknife. Tiny'd been right; the judicious application of controlled explosives *would* disrupt the flow of chi in a pretty long-term way.

Two teams, one facility...*almost* one job.

PART TWO:
AGENT THORN

LOOSE ENDS

(Street Legends)

Agent Thorn was a (semi)-retired covert operative I cooked up to be the voice for my sections of Spy Games, *the SR4-era espionage book. Expanding upon him for* Street Legends, *I knew I'd need to pin down as much fiction as I could, to show/explain/build his backstory. It's hard to introduce someone as an experienced veteran, so I needed to really lay out some details where I could; and that was in "Loose Ends," here, every bit as much as it was in Agent Thorn's actual write-up.*

The word count I was given was generous, and gave me the chance to do just that. I could lay out what he'd done, lay out that he'd done it for quite some time, drop hints about just how deadly he was, and just generally play up the badassitude of one barely-equipped guy ninja'ing a whole tactical kill-team in full gear; but even more importantly, what this story let me do was show how tired of it all he was, and, most of all, how listless. He was a guy with a very peculiar set of skills, but no idea what to do with them now that he'd turned his back on the company that gave him those skills.

—RRZ

Lieutenant Rudi Vollstedt shouted the *"gehen-gehen-gehen"* command over his integrated comm system. His eight-man team burst into action as his order crackled in their ears; half of them, including their mage, gained entry through the windows of the target's living room, where he'd last been spotted. Two rushed through bedroom windows to seal off that avenue of escape. Vollstedt himself and his last team member blasted the lock from the townhome's front door with a Mossberg combatgun and rushed in.

At first, things were precisely as Vollstedt expected. It was music to his ears, all the shattering glass and splintering doors, the muffled *thump* of flash-bangs going off, the pounding of booted commando feet on faux hardwood floors.

Then, however, he heard the muted cough of a firearm and the sound of one heavily armored body crashing down, then another. He heard the chattering return burst of unsuppressed fire and a shotgunner's blast, the rush of booted feet, another muted cough. He and his breacher bolted down the extravagant entryway through disorienting smoke—who on his team had used a *verdammt* smoke grenade?—toward the ringing echoes of more gunfire, sweeping left to clear the kitchen, then bursting back out into the sprawling living room.

Through the haze of smoke, dizzying and half-blinding him even as his cyberoptics cycled through vision modes, Vollstedt managed to see an armored corpse lying on the floor. One of his.

Then there came another silenced gunshot from somewhere up ahead, another gurgle of a dying soldier over the lieutenant's headware. Vollstedt's breacher, just a step ahead of him, rushed toward the action until he stumbled over the corpse of Greta, their aspected spellcaster, and Vollstedt slowed to let him catch his balance.

The shotgunner kept falling though, tumbling toward the floor, until he lay sprawled out on his face, bleeding, and only then did the mercenary officer see the tattered hole in the back of his teammate's balaclava, just between his helmet and armored backplate.

A second later he registered the sound of a silenced weapon from somewhere behind him, hidden by their hurried, heavy, boot steps. The lieutenant started to spin and raise his submachine gun.

"*Anhalten*."

The warning froze him. So did the feel of a weapon's muzzle pressing against the back of his neck.

"In the spirit of my new mailing address, I'd like to speak with you in English. Fair enough?" The muzzle was warm, and it wedged itself up under his helmet just a bit. He'd be dead before he hit the ground if the trigger was squeezed. "I know you speak English, laddie, or they wouldn't have sent you on an op here in Denver. Give me a nod."

He nodded, tried to swallow past the sudden fear gripping his throat. Vollstedt's mind raced.

"Swap your Praetor to your left hand, and with your right, drop the magazine and work the bolt for me, aye?"

Vollstedt did as he was told. Obedience came instinctively, not only because of the feel of the muzzle at his neck, but also due to a certain something in the lilting voice at his ear. He awkwardly held the empty submachine gun out with his off hand.

"Good boy. Now just drop it. Take off your helmet, toss it down the hall."

Vollstedt hesitated, and his assailant gave him a little nudge with the muzzle. "I know all about the flash-pak built into the helmet's front, by the by. I helped field-test the things, after all. Now do it."

He obeyed again, then slowly turned when he felt the gun drift away from him. The smoke was starting to dissipate, swept out of the spacious hallway through ruined windows. He saw an elf dressed in sweatpants and a sweatshirt standing just a meter or so away from him. Vollstedt's headware computers buzzed through a half-dozen recognition protocols, and told him he'd successfully found his team's target; Rory Caolain, Agent Thorn. There was no trace of blood on the elf, nor any other sign he'd been in a firefight. The elf held an Ares Viper Slivergun trained on Vollstedt. Both the gun and his flashing green eyes stayed steady even as the elf reached, without looking, inside the nearby kitchen. His hand returned holding a steaming cup of tea.

"I'm afraid my kettle finished just before you lads decided to come bursting in. I wasn't where you planned me to be from pure, dumb luck," the elf said with his Irish lilt, amused more than anything else by the fact that the smallest of things can make the biggest of differences.

Vollstedt had been warned their target would likely have weapons secreted throughout his flat, but they hadn't been expecting a grenade custom tailored to foul both standard vision and thermographic imaging. Upon their chaotic entry, he imagined the elf plucking the grenade and the pistol from a shelf in the refrigeration unit, just alongside the creamer, next to the butter. There was something surreal about that. There was something strange about his voice, too. Vollstedt couldn't help but listen as the elf continued.

"It was all downhill for you lads after that, wasn't it? Only eight men to attack me in my own home, and with no spirit support? Only one spellcaster, and that just wee Greta Schmidt, the junkie?" he said with an empathetic little sigh. Smoke drifted behind him, revealing more corpses. The elf tsked. "Overconfident work, that. Sloppy. And here I thought a man your age would've known better."

"You killed..." Vollstedt licked his lips as the elf calmly sipped his tea, trying to find words. "You killed them. All of them are dead, *ja*?"

"Oh, yes. More's the pity, but you lot knew the rules when you came in like you did. Not a silencer in sight, no real effort made at discretion, and not a one of you with zip ties handy? Not to mention two of your lads with those Mossberg CMDTs. They only fire buckshot, boyo; the chamber doesn't handle non-lethal munitions quite right. There's no chance the rest of you lot are here for a capture instead of a kill, not with your breachers carrying those. Oh, and let's not forget little miss Schmidt, comma, Greta, hmm? A trained combat hermetic, being the second through my window? She may be past her prime, but I know full well what damage she could have done. I know the spells she likes."

Vollstedt got drawn in the longer the elf talked, that voice holding his attention in ways the muzzle of the Slivergun couldn't. Then came another sip of tea and the slightest droop of elven shoulders showing something like resignation, maybe even regret.

"So yes, they're dead. You lot decided to play by big boys' rules. I know a bloody kill team when I see one."

"And me?"

"You and I both know who sent you in the broad sense, aye? Taking off your unit flash doesn't hide the fact you're MET 2000. I want to know who sent you, specifically, though. How high up the chain of command. And why."

"You know why."

"Fine. I want to know who."

"*Nein*."

The elf 's wrist flicked down and the Slivergun answered, sending shards of steel into Vollstedt's shin. They hit just below the reinforced kneecap of his armor and just a hair above where the Kevlar-woven fabric of his combat boots stopped. The old soldier's leg buckled, and he stumbled against the wall to keep from falling.

"Listen to me," the elf said, turning emerald-green eyes on Rudi. Something in those eyes made it impossible for the mercenary to look away. Something in that voice cut through the pain of his ruined leg and made him pay attention. "I know a hundred places that armor doesn't cover, and I'm pretty sure my dossier told you what kind of shot I am, aye? So please. Let's save time. Who was it that...that..." The elf let out another sigh.

"Ah, damn. Why even bother?" The elf let the Slivergun's muzzle drift downward. He leaned against the same wall and looked almost his age, for a moment, there in the half-light. "I'm so bloody tired of going through these motions. I'm tired of playing this game."

His sullen, exasperated tone made Vollstedt feel like he'd awoken from some spell. Green eyes swept the bloodstained hallway, spotting where frantic merc fire had sent rounds blasting through the decorated interior walls. For an instant the elven gunman looked like any other homeowner just frustrated with a mess made in the sanctity of his condo.

"I suppose this Baird cover of mine's well and truly fucked, and it only now just hit me. Damn it. I was really starting to like Denver. A place this big, it's not cheap, ye know." The elf took in a long breath, then let it out in a deeper, heartfelt sigh. "Listen. I'm sorry about your shin. But, believe you me, they'll love to buy you a new one."

Vollstedt spat something in German, knowing full well from the elf 's dossier that there was an appropriate level of fluency there for the insult to hit home.

"Stop being rude. I'm doing you the biggest favor of your life right now." The elf 's eyes turned a little sharper, and the Slivergun's muzzle drifted back up and into play. "So you listen to me. I'm just tired of all this. That's why I quit, and that's the only reason. I've got plenty of money squirreled away. I didn't stop working for them in order to sell a single damned one of their silly fucking secrets. I don't need the money, you hear me? I'm not going to sell anyone anything. You tell them that."

The elf threw the teacup down and let it add to the chaos and destruction on his floor, looking disgusted. Frustrated. Angry.

"You tell them I've always *had* money to vanish, and enough covers. I've been at this game a long damned time, and everyone who plays it knows the rules and has back doors open as a matter of bloody principle. I've got enough SINs set up to keep trading them for your eight-man kill teams, every time you find me. *Tell them that.*"

His eyes turned hard as emeralds, and his tone made Vollstedt lock eyes with him, made him listen, made him want to relay the message.

"You tell them I can play the attrition game and that they're losing money on trying to kill me. I've got plenty of boltholes and covers ready to go."

Vollstedt blinked before the elf did, shaking off the melodic power of his soft lilt. He cleared his throat a second later.

He'd always known this job would kill him.

"What if..." The merc coughed, then looked back up at the elf with a defiant smirk on his face. "What if it's more than an eight man kill team?"

Emerald eyes narrowed in understanding. The Slivergun coughed, and Vollstedt's other shin splintered. He grunted in pain as his knees hit the fake hardwood floor, then he glared up in anger as the elf stooped to pick up Vollstedt's Praetor and slapped the magazine home. The elf 's head tilted a bit to one side, as if he was listening for something. A heartbeat later he heard it, judging by the way he started to turn and walk down the hallway.

"Don't be smug. No one likes that." He half-turned back, regarding Vollstedt over one shoulder. The elf racked the slide on the Praetor, chambering a round and shouldering it smoothly. "All you and your headware have done is get more of your own lads killed."

He vanished around the corner, leaving Rudi Vollstedt to bleed in the hallway and think about armored corpses.

"Oh. I just remembered..." said the elf as he leaned back around the corner, the muzzle of Rudi's own carbine leading the way. His eyes, past the weapon's iron sights, were hard and cold. "Right shortly, I'll have eight more lads to choose from, finding me a more likeable messenger."

The Praetor fired. Vollstedt joined his team.

Rory Caolain—Agent Thorn—was going to miss his Michael Baird cover identity. He'd had a week and a half of cross-continent travel to get used to the idea Baird was gone, but that didn't mean he was happy about it. As he wove his café racer through Washington, FDC, traffic, he held a funeral in his head. Whenever a cover identity was well and truly blown, whenever it was time to say goodbye forever, Thorn gave them a proper imaginary send-off, celebrating the work he'd done as them, cutting all ties with them, and reminding himself they were gone and untouchable in the future. He'd spent eighteen months as Baird the first time, dropped the identity when he was sent off on other assignments, and then picked it back up and had now spent almost four years as the man.

They'd been heady times, the Baird jobs. He'd been running guns and explosives through the Denver smuggler pipelines into Portland, then giving tips to the anti-Tír insurgent groups on how best to use them. "Military Advisor" was an innocuous term for very bloody work. Argus had sent him there because they knew about his INLA days, about his clashes with the other Tír back across the Atlantic, and because they knew he was an expert on surviving in the face of an oppressive magical regime. What's more, he could help the locals get in a good swing every now and then, and blacken the eye of even Tír Ghosts. The work was hard and dangerous, but seldom dull. So when he'd formally quit Argus all these years later and decided on Denver as a place to settle down, the Baird identity—SIN matched up to a Denver mailing address, never pinned down for criminal activity in the UCAS, and with fond memories and plenty of local contacts attached—had seemed a reasonable choice to dust off and wear again.

Sadly, what had provided eighteen months of cover in both UCAS and Tír systems, then forty-six more months of wild Rinelle ke'Tesrae work years later, had been peeled open and savaged by the heavy-handed idiots of MET 2000 in barely a month.

Damn their databases. Damn him for forgetting how many Argus files existed about his successes as Baird.

And damn that red light! Whoops!

His Triumph motorcycle was flashing a red warning at him, his AR visor filling up with notices of an impending collision. He scowled as he braked, working handlebar lever and foot pedal in tandem, barely stopping the thing in time. Eye-flicks sent warning popups out of his field of vision as his SmartHelmet registered and responded to his commands, and before long, he had a clearer view of the street ahead, overlaid only with his basic GPS navigational map. He forced himself to focus—this lovely machine had spent far too long under a dust cover in storage, and Agent Thorn was a little rusty on it—by telling himself getting crushed by some politico's limousine would be a horribly anticlimactic death.

He leaned low over the handlebars, trying to worry only about the road and the ride, banishing Baird, both Tírs, Argus, MET 2000, and all the other clutter from his head. After all this, he still had a lunch date to keep, and it wouldn't do to keep a lady waiting. Traffic here in Kansai Village wasn't the worst in the city, but he wasn't the only one on his way to lunch at the Waterfront, either. What's more, he knew he'd need his head cleared to handle a conversation with her.

She was stunning. Thorn had to admit it as he parked and swung a leg over his Triumph. He'd known what she looked like ahead of time, of course. He had done his fair share of homework prior to their meeting and knew more than most people did about how to change his appearance. All the same, the resemblance was remarkable. Daviar look-alikes were a dime a dozen, even if the fad had peaked nearly a decade ago, but this one was remarkable.

Something about her, or about the streetside café she'd chosen, reminded him of Paris.

Her, he thought as he wove through tables, *not the café*. The tables and chairs might look like something from a Paris café, but the background noise was all wrong. DC worked too hard, especially in this Shiawase-controlled part of town. Paris had different priorities.

"Miss Corinna, I presume?" Agent Thorn smiled as he slid into the seat opposite hers, helmet settled quietly onto the ground near his feet. His comfortable Irish lilt was gone, his accent of the moment pure public schooled English. "Dreadfully sorry to be late. I'd underestimated traffic."

"Not at all. You're just in time, Mister..." There was a hint of a questioning tone as she trailed off, politely letting him know she wasn't certain what identity he was operating under at the moment.

"Carter, ma'am." He smiled wider, all blond hair and blue eyes that day, a fair-skinned British icon since he'd chosen this SIN. Wire-rimmed glasses rested lightly on the bridge of his nose, giving his elven look a faintly academic spin. A glowing Union Jack on his t-shirt peeked out through the front of his unzipped Ace of Clubs Vashon Island jacket. "But please, call me Michael."

"Michael, then." She graced him with a smile as she reached across the table to politely shake hands. She was darker than him, somehow earthier. He knew she was a fake, knew she wasn't really the Estonian who'd worked as the face of a dragon, but from everything he'd read and seen about the original, this one was a flawless copy. The accent was off, but that was to be expected from someone living in DC as long as she had.

They shared small talk as a waitress arrived, and Corinna, as the café regular, got Thorn's blessing to order for them both. When their drinks arrived, and they knew they had time before their waitress's return, the foreplay was finished, and talk turned to business.

"Everything I arranged is ready?" He sipped his ice water, blond eyebrow quirked.

"And awaiting your pick-up at this address." She smiled again, leaning forward slightly as she slid something across the table.

She knew the old plays, Agent Thorn realized; the smile, and the way her reach made the Zoé suit-dress fall open just enough for cleavage to catch the eye. They were tricks used to conceal the act of passing a note, tricks an elf-gorgeous operative like Corinna could use to draw the eye away from some slip of paper. It made sense for her, working as she did and where she did, to know the rules to this particular game. The actual hard paper note was a refreshing change of pace, though. He thought of his own bike, and suppressed a smile. He reminded himself that retro was fashionable—and besides, no one could hack a slip of paper.

"And the new commlink will be there?"

"With the rest of the information you requested, yes."

She smiled again, all sugar and spice, broadcasting for anyone nearby—and the pair of them caught a few curious eyes—that they were just a pair of friends eating lunch. That was the trick to talking shop in public, both of them knew. Chat like you always would. Whispering made people listen. Talking casually made people ignore you.

"Our Japanese associate is in the contacts list of your new Hermes Ikon."

They'd both gotten what they were after, and the meal continued. They were just friends eating lunch, elves sharing overpriced ciabatta sandwiches at a trendy organic café. Neither of them used words like murder, or target, or assignment, or even favor. Neither discussed ammunition, firearms, detonators, or explosives. He'd transferred the credits already; they'd worked out the details through intermediaries—one last favor from Baird's old contacts as Thorn had been driving east—long before he'd arrived in DC. The face-to-face meeting was just a courtesy; one professional vacationing in the territory of another, with the both of them wanting the chance to politely appraise the other.

Agent Thorn finished his sandwich, shook hands again over polite small talk concerning the media interest in recent mystical disturbances, and they parted ways.

As he saddled his Triumph again, and she strode away toward a sleek BMW, he knew they wouldn't meet again until someone died.

THE PRESTIGE

(Street Legends)

Street Legends *gave me the opportunity to share Agent Thorn's backstory, to show why he was burned out and looking to change...and in "The Prestige," I was able to show what he was doing now, and to tie him in with the rest of the Sixth World in the moment. And nobody ties you into the Sixth World quite like Nadja Daviar.*

I wrote this piece with James Meiers, alternating our perspectives and points of view, and essentially–in a way–role-playing it as though Thorn was my PC, and Nadja was his. It's something I've only really done this one time, but we had fun with it, and told a pretty cool yarn.

—RRZ

Rory knew she wasn't actually staying at the suite, but for politeness' sake they played as if she did. Thorn waited in the hallway for a tick before Corinna smiled and invited him in. He complimented her on how comfortable and spacious the room looked and that sort of thing. Politeness was a game, and it was right and proper that he should go through the motions.

"Sure and that's a marvelous picture, too." He'd dressed and colored himself like Michael Carter again, but once he saw the white noise generator humming away on a Brazilian cherry coffee table, he dropped the public school Brit accent and slid back into his comfortable Irish lilt.

Thorn nodded to one wall of her suite's living room, enveloped as it was in a massive tridscreen display of evening programming.

"It's just the news," she said idly, swiping a negligent hand across the sensors built into the wall, muting it but leaving it on. Talking heads kept talking and neither of them listened, so she turned away from it to regard him again. "A ridiculous number of channels available, and not a thing worth watching."

"Oh, there's plenty worth watching in this room," he said through a little smile, winking playfully. She was in a the same suit as before, but the Zoé tailoring seemed to be a slightly different cut—something more restrained, but still tailored for her curves. As Nadja Daviar clones went, she was one worth looking at.

"Plenty to watch, and plenty to talk about, as well." Corinna's arms crossed, and she arched a brow at him. And there went the pleasantries. Business time. "All nineteen, Mr. Carter?"

"Oh, Rory's fine. Mr. Caolain if you want to sound formal," he said with a shrug and a nod at the anti-surveillance device he'd already noted. He was sure the room held more of them, and the knowledge made him relax enough that his hair began to change color. In a span of heartbeats, his cool blue eyes had turned the green of fresh-cut grass, and his pale blond hair had gone black-Irish. "So long as you keep your little doo-dads on, I'll thank you not to call me an Englishman's name."

Her pointedly arched brow didn't lower, and her question still hung heavy in the air.

"Oh, and yes, all nineteen." He threw his hands up, fighting a grin even as he explained himself. "You read over the files before sending 'em to me, I'm sure. It's not my fault Kanagawa sent his security detail out in six little three-man teams, for Christ's sake. You have your patrols working in bite-sized crews like that, an' it's no one's fault but yours when I come by an' kill 'em all."

"We were under the impression that your interest in Mr. Kanagawa was professional, not personal, Mr. Caolain." Her arms stayed crossed, her tone dissatisfied. Behind her, the news program's talking heads just kept moving their lips with nothing worth hearing coming out.

"Aye. Well, that was the impression I wanted to give." Rory shrugged, unapologetic. Behind his glasses, his green eyes turned hard and sharp as emeralds as he remembered a Russian winter spent in misery and anger, and why he'd had to endure it. "I owed him, and I took it out on his men as my way to take it out on him. I'd do it again if I could."

She scowled through his answer, but her fine features softened at his final proclamation. "Would you? Do it again, if you could?"

"Shedim notwithstanding," he said with a quirked eyebrow, "as a general rule, you only get to kill someone once."

"Not him," she said ignoring his joke. "Not him precisely. But others like him. Ones you might not have the same personal motivation for approaching, but for whom financial motivation might be offered..."

"Haven't you heard, lass? It's all over Puzzle Palace and the other trendy shadowrunner boards. I'm retired."

She smirked. "Mr. Kanagawa and eighteen of his employees would disagree."

"Ah. You're asking just how retired I am, in other words?"

"And if I was?"

He answered with a sigh.

"Mr. Caolain, I represent certain parties who understand your worth and who are willing to provide you with the information and support you would need in order to keep..."

"Killing folks?" He scowled.

"Solving problems."

"By killing folks," he said with a nod. "Miss, I understand you came into this confused about my motivation, but I want to make it perfectly clear. I hated Kanagawa. He and I hated each other from the moment he picked me up from the Kobe airport twelve years ago, because his employer wanted me for a job she didn't trust to him alone."

"Miss Kanematsu?"

"Don't be coy. You know full well who he handled security for, or you wouldn't have given me a green light and a dossier." His face was serious, his earlier laughter gone. Corinna, too, was businesslike. Politician smooth. Along with something that wasn't quite the same about her...

"So are you saying, Mr. Caolain, that it was personal motivation alone that sent you after Kanagawa? That you aren't willing to engage in this sort of activity again?"

He stared past her at bland-featured newscasters and old B-roll being intercut on the trid as he mulled over her question.

"I'm saying," he eventually answered, "that I don't particularly want to 'solve problems,' but I don't know what else I'm good at. I don't know how else to make up for the things I've done. Kanagawa was a bloody arsehole, and he betrayed me a long time ago. When MET 2000 fucked up me laying low, and I heard Kanagawa was in DeeCee, I figured I might as well take a drive and go for him."

"Just like that?" She wasn't scowling or glaring any more, but appeared genuinely curious. "Travel through two countries to kill a man?"

"Three, actually. I took a rather indirect route, rode a good bit more than the crow flies. But, aye. Just like that." He snapped his fingers. "Because I didn't have anything better to do, he had it coming, and what's one more kill, really?"

"Nineteen more, actually, given his security detail."

"Nineteen drops." He shrugged. "Just nineteen more drops in a very big bucket."

"Speaking of MET 2000, Mr. Caolain, and that unpleasantness in Denver with your previous employer..." Her sentence ended with an inquisitive lift in her tone. It was half a question, half a demand for information.

"Not worth worrying about, truly, miss. There were only sixteen of them." He shrugged, leaning into the new turn of conversation as smoothly as he would a twisting road on his bike. "It was just a mid-level bastard who's always hated me calling in favors and scrambling a few kill teams. A few washed-up old officers, a junkie for a mage. They were trimming the roster as much as anything else. It wasn't a proper Argus op."

"You're certain there won't be further entanglements?"

"Certain? No. But then, who's certain of anything, really?" He shrugged philosophically. "Like I said, though, it wasn't *really* Argus, and they didn't *really* want me. If they did, they would've used proper explosives or sent another agent after me, not some infantry knuckleheads and a single half-mage. You know those MET 2K boys, aye? Bloody worthless outside their tanks. No big deal."

"Sixteen assault troopers, one of them an aspected spellcaster, might be considered a big deal."

"To some. To me, it was just an irritated major back in Hanover who thought he had a chance to get me back, who used some dull tools for the job. If Argus wanted me dead, well and truly dead, they'd send someone like me. It won't ever be a squad of lads with heavy footsteps that does me in, I promise you that."

"Argus has more men like you?"

"Oh, sure. Thousands of us, haven't you seen the commercials? And I trained every last one. There's Agent Thorn, of course, and then I went and taught everything I know to Splinter, Needle, Nail, Staple, Thumbtack, Safety Pin..."

She sighed and interrupted his list by standing and walking away. It was a relaxed stroll, and Thorn assumed he was supposed to follow her.

She walked into the suite dining room where a champagne flute sat, untouched. Keyed to her, the tridscreen images danced along the wall in her wake, following her faithfully from room to room. He wasn't sure if this was a psychological ploy on her part, or if she just felt better about the anti-eavesdropping measures in the windowless room. If this was a game, though, he was more than capable of playing along.

She sat at the head of the table while Rory remained standing at the opposite end, his body positioned toward the wall of trideo newsfeeds. Her expression did not change as he stood away from her.

"Agent Thorn, Mr. Caolain, let me be clear. I'm trying to approach you with a serious offer of long-term intelligence and financial support. I'm not here for jokes."

He gave a jaunty little shrug, either as an apologetic gesture to show he was listening or a flippant one to show he didn't care what she was there for.

She took it as the former and continued, "You know the business I'm in and the people I deal with. I can read men very, very well. What you lack, Mr. Caolain, is very simple, and I'm here to give it to you."

She tilted her head up just a shade, matching his gaze without fear despite knowing just how many lives he'd ended.

"It isn't ability you're missing, Rory. It's purpose. Direction."

His eyes did not break contact with hers. "Sure and aren't we all?"

"Not in the slightest. I know exactly why I'm here, and exactly what I'm here to do."

"And do you know..." he spoke slowly, carefully, eyes squarely on her to read her reaction. He pulled his wire-rimmed glasses off, tucked them into a jacket pocket as he got more serious. "Exactly who you are?"

That made her pause.

"Enlighten me." Her voice was flat, but she raised a curious eyebrow.

"You aren't Corinna. Your attitude is all wrong, body language is colder. Your heels are shorter and your dress is longer, despite this being a more private meeting. But it's more than an outfit change. Your posture is different, you don't arch your back quite like she did to exaggerate your chest. You've certainly got the build to use your sexuality, lass, don't take it as an insult, but you're not as quick to do so as she did. She'd be trying to seduce me right now, all alone up here in the bedroom. Lad or lass, you lot have read my files. You know what I fancy."

As he talked, Rory began to tick differences off on his fingers.

"The eyes match perfectly, but not the lines around them. It's not age, no, so you're a natural elf, but yours are more like mine. A couple crow's feet. A few wee tiny lines to show that you squint and glare a bit, that you pay attention, and that you've done so much more than Corinna has. You've been in the game longer than her."

Another finger, another count.

"Now, your accents are close, but both of them are faked. You've each cultivated the DC twang, and done a fine job of it. Start with a CAS drawl for all-American appeal, accentuate the clipped New England bits to imply political power, round it out with a hint of those long Canadian o's; all perfect, politician-bred, to make sure it appeals to a broad spectrum of UCAS voters. The difference is hers is native, yours is forced. There's something like Finnish hiding under yours, unless I miss my guess. Comes out in your v's when you're not careful."

He raised his eyebrows, curious how close he was to hitting marks. He knew he was closer than most.

"And Corinna is a bit harder in the eyes, too, and meaner around the mouth. She hides it well, don't get me wrong, but God's own truth? I think she might just hate every man she deals with. She manipulates us to show herself she can, and because she doesn't remember how not to. You, though? No. You, I think, manipulate everyone. Man, woman, and whatever else crosses your path. And you don't do it because you hate who you're talking to. You do it because you need something from them."

Rory watched her shoulders as he spoke, the lines of her neck. Faces lied. It was the rest of the body that gave things away. He hadn't missed his guess.

"So you're not her. You're friendly enough for all that, your organization came through with the information and the tech support I needed to do my job, and everything went smoothly. I'm here, because part of the arrangement—on your end—was an insistence on a follow-up meeting. I'm not terribly *concerned* that you're not Corinna, but my curiosity's piqued."

When she still didn't deny it, still didn't speak at all, he continued.

"So then, having established who you *weren't*, I then wondered who you *were*." Those minuscule lines he'd mentioned, the only hint of his true age, appeared around his eyes as he smiled. "It struck me as unlikely, women being territorial creatures every bit as much as men, that you'd be just another knock-off. No, no. Not just another clone, taking over on her debriefing, on her turf. Corinna's too much like a cat to let just another vat-job come along and take over a deal for her. But mostly? It was the trid that did it."

He nodded to the wall, where the trid still flickered away and lit both of them in its glow. She stonily eyed him instead of following his gesture.

"Lovely things, newscasts. Whenever they're not letting you read lips, they're writing out exactly what's going on all along the bottom of the screen. Continuing chaos and upheavals in Dunkelzahn's pet organization, they say. Rumors and whispers about Foundation security in the wake of Chief Consultant Kanagawa's disappearance, they say. Assumptions that he fled back to Japan and left Midori high and dry, they say. Midori dangling in the boardroom, ripe for a power play, they say. Draco Foundation board shuffling all over in the wake of a certain someone's triumphant return and restructuring, they say."

Rory gave her a sunny smile.

"You know the trick to figuring out who hired an assassin, ma'am? It's easy. Know who's going to profit from the trigger being pulled. Kanagawa was the rug under Midori's dainty wee little feet, and snatching him away knocked her on her arse."

Her lips pursed. When they opened, in that split-second between her taking in a breath to start talking and her actually speaking, he cut her off behind a wide smile. "It's nice to meet you, Madame Vice President. Or do you prefer just 'Miss Daviar' these days?" He winked at her playfully. He knew when he landed a bullseye. Nadja Daviar herself, in the flesh. The original.

She smiled. "All right, let's talk. Please, have a seat."

Rory walked to an armchair at her right hand and sat, while she leaned toward him. "My offer is genuine, Rory. I have a specific plan for what I need to do, but I cannot pursue my goals with people like Kanagawa or some of the board members in my way."

"I do not have the capacity for violence that others have. Not hard men like yourself, of course, but also not those people like Kanematsu and Dupree who are comfortable with issuing the orders that send men and women to die like they were chess pieces."

Rory watched her eyes and her measured inflection, and he could tell she had something in mind. "Aye, but at the same time, you were the head of the foundation and the vice president for...what? Seven years? Eight? Sure and you've had to make those same calls a time or two."

"Indeed. That is my point. As much as I do not have a taste for it, I am not going to pretend that your particular brand of violence is going to disappear. It is a necessary evil to make this world function. In this particular case, Corinna let me know that you were headed this way and carrying out the same sort of acts that had upset me concerning his position within my foundation."

"You mean Dunkelzahn's foundation, of course." Rory fought a smile.

"Dunkelzahn is dead," Nadja said with a voice hardened in a way Rory understood perfectly. He stopped smiling. "I seem to be the only person to truly understand that our actions are his legacy. It is not what we think he wanted that matters, but what we do with what he left us."

"I hope you now understand my concern about some of your violence. I approve of your action against Kanagawa, but I am not entirely comfortable with the collateral effect. We can discuss just-war theory and the writings of St. Thomas Aquinas all day, but suffice it to say that I am intent on minimizing collateral damage in the future. That is something Dunkelzahn insisted upon, *and* it's a goal I continue to seek."

Rory leaned forward, elbows on his knees, hands steepled, listening. Intent. Focused.

"Leaving aside for a moment that I know just the sort of men Kanagawa had working his personal security detail, why me? What about your drake lad, Mercury, or any of his protégés? All named after metals, his elite drakes, aren't they? Those aren't bad sorts to keep up those tailored sleeves of yours."

"Ryan has his own path to follow, and that path is tied intrinsically into another effect of Dunkelzahn's legacy. The Watchers that are amenable to a new way are also still known for being tied to that network. Even these clones of mine have only a limited value. They're mercenaries, and they don't necessarily have much regard for me—for obvious reasons."

"Fair enough, then. What's your actual pitch?"

"Come work for me, and we can change the world. In the last twenty years the world has been allowed a certain amount of new opportunities, but the fact is that increases in efficiency and comfort are not synonymous with freedom and advancing humanity. It's time for that to change. What is worse—and what I hope to impress upon you through your long history of siding with the underdog—is that things are coming back around.

"Horizon is a perfect example. It does good work, but like the Draco Foundation it is a large institution that has people in it acting in hostile ways, doing things I would rather not see. Moreover, people have become so suspicious of the concept of corporate social responsibility that many of them are just waiting to see some 'true face' appear from behind this façade. The fact that it's a media producer is an inherent liability, since an entity based on shaping and manipulating reality for its own ends, and the ends of its clients, is suspicious, at least to those who know how the world works.

"It's time for a page to turn, Mr. Caolain. You can step up and help it happen, you can roll up your sleeves and do work, *and* you can train Mercury's recruits for me, make them as subtle and dangerous as you are...or you can sit on the sidelines and watch others do the heavy lifting."

Her smile was stunning, brilliant, radiant. She held a hand out to him, not just for the symbolic handshake, but to make him lean even more toward her, to change his position both physically and mentally.

"From reading your files, Rory, I know you'd rather have a more active role than passive."

She knew she had him. His psych profiles and work history had him in her clutches before she'd even started talking. He was hers, now, in part because he had nothing better to do and no one better to do it for, and also because hers was an attractive offer to a man of action.

He would do what she wanted him to do, right up to the moment that he—simply, suddenly—wouldn't. He'd wander off, declare himself under one of a dozen new identities, and live a new life. Her job, then, was to get the most out of him while she held his attention.

They shook on it, and a page turned in the killer's history.

PART THREE: MISCELLANEOUS

OVERBOOKED

(ANARCHY 2050)

Remember how I talked about Dodger, Ghost, and Sally Tsung? Remember how I loved them in the very first Shadowrun *rulebook ever? Remember how I marveled at a sense of continuity that came from them launching from a rulebook's opening text to (Sally) showing up in the sample adventure, and from there into novels, and from those into (later) adventures?*

I love them. Ghost-Who-Walks-Inside, Sally Tsung, and especially my beloved Artful Dodger, were icons to me. And I got to write a little something with them in it. I hope you enjoy.

—RRZ

And there...we...go!

Dodger snapped open one more button on his black leather jacket, and flashed himself a crooked, confident smile in the bathroom mirror. It was a dirty mirror in a dirty club filled with dirty people, but it got the job done and let the elf admire himself. A dashing mish-mash of lucky charms, souvenirs, and trophies—an ancient arcade token, colored beads, polished shells, slender silver chains, plastic gems, and other street-merchant nicknacks—hung around his neck, but he knew that, to all the right admirers, the real visual treat was his utter lack of a shirt beneath. The sleeves of his jacket got shoved up to show off both forearms, smooth and unblemished skin except for his augmentations, and the bundled-up material made his biceps look bigger. One last look in the mirror did the trick.

I am a treat.

The elf ran one hand through his silver-white hair, flopping his fauxhawk to one side to make sure all the world saw the gleaming datajacks at his temple, and sauntered out of the bathroom that *clearly* did not deserve him. No, no. He had a wider audience to impress. Everyone. Underworld 93 awaited! All the world was a stage to the Artful Dodger, and every metahuman upon it was his to charm or spurn as he desired. He was at his novahottest at home, in the Matrix, of course, but there was no reason he couldn't draw more than his fair share of admirers here in the dingy meat-space of this warehouse-turned-nightclub, too, right? He let the bone-deep throbbing bass of the evening's performers put a roll into his hips as he jandered back to his no-doubt-impatiently-waiting compatriots.

"Behold, noble companions! Lady, gentleman, and Kham."

He bowed low, his grandiose wave—chrome ports at his knuckles flashing—taking in the golden-haired, leather-fringed Sally Tsung, the face-painted and rippling-muscled Ghost-Who-Walks-Inside, and, last and least, the scowling, broad-featured, broad-shouldered, orkish gang leader.

"I. Have. Returned!" Dodger straightened with a flourish, and gave Sally his winningest smile as he did so.

"Took your fraggin' time, elf," Kham grunted, oh-so predictably. "Think you were in there powdering your nose for long enough, we coulda gone and done this job without you!"

Ah, the shortest-lived among us are only naturally the most impatient. The poor dear.

"That, my dearly betusked friend, I quite sincerely doubt. For, indeed, which of you would have seen to the Matrix wizardry for which I am rightfully held in such high esteem? The beauteous Lady Sally? Ho-ho, would that 'twere so, and she might accompany me on my dances in the Matrix, but, alas, her aptitudes lie thoroughly elsewhere, and so I am denied the pleasure of her company on my electronic jaunts! Or perhaps the noble Sir Ghost, master of blades, barrages, and brooding? I think not! His lethal skills are of an altogether different bend. You, Sir Tusk? Oh, what a sight that would be to see. Indeed, I know only of *one* orkish decker, and I'd wager you've never met him. Electronics elude you, Sir Kham! When last I saw you try to answer it, alas, even your humble pocket secretary seemed to leave you thoroughly flummoxe—"

"Jesus, Buddha, and Zeus, Dodger," Sally grabbed Kham's drink and finished it for him, slamming the glass onto the table as an exclamation point. "You never shut up, do you? And Kham, you know you only encourage him!"

Then she stood, fetish beads clattering, feathers dangling, long legs stretching, Roomsweeper on one denim-clad hip, magesword comfortably low on the other. "We've got a job to do, boys. Zip back up, put 'em away, save it for Saeder-Krupp, and let's go get paid, *so ka*?"

Ghost allowed himself a small smile and stood at her side. Even here, he was bristling with firearms, most notably his twin Ingram smartguns. Even here, Dodger knew Ghost didn't need them much.

"S-K won't know what hit 'em. Let's roll," the street samurai said with a nod to the door. The pair of humans took off, Ghost's shoulders and street rep carving them a path, Sally smoothly jandering along in his wake.

Kham was left trapped in the booth with his blocky assault rifle. If he stayed put and got back to work complaining about Dodger making them late, he'd be the one making them even later.

The unfortunate fellow's only winning move is not to play.

Dodger spun on his heel and started toward the door, casting a smug look over his shoulder at the flustered ork. Kham's lips were moving the whole time he stomped along behind them, and Dodger smirked as the ork grouched the whole way to the nightclub's exist.

Just as the throbbing synth-rock of Underworld 93 faded behind them and Kham's grousing threatened to reach his ears again, Dodger was saved. Sally's red and silver Yamaha Rapier screamed to life to drown out the ork's complaints again, and Dodger was certain he saw another small smile on Ghost's war-painted face as he twisted his wrist and set his Harley Scorpion to growling and chugging next to her slender, graceful, street bike. Dodger slung a leg over his own Rapier just in time to see Kham throw his big, scarred, hands up in frustration, and felt no small surge of smug satisfaction as the ork stopped his complaining entirely to clamber onto his own scratched, weathered, combat hog.

The foursome—two howling, slender Rapiers and two roaring, broad Scorpions—carved a path 'cross town. The Yamahas nimbly wove between the numerous potholes and the rarer other drivers on Puyallup's battered, bloody, nighttime streets. The Harleys and their riders were less graceful, but no less effective, riding aggressively and with the engine to back it up, bypassing the same obstacles in an entirely different way.

Sally led her team perilously close to the elven ghetto of Tarislar, but good fortune smiled on them, and Dodger's silver-tongued Sperethiel wasn't necessary; the Ancients weren't out to hound anyone tonight, and none of the other local toughs had a toll booth set up, no gunners had overwatch as leather-clad Silent P's demanded tribute. Kham's leaden tongue, fierce snarl, and heavy street cred weren't put to the test, either, as the foursome of bikes skirted the edges of Black Rains turf in Carbanado, nor even as they screamed past a knot of Forever Tacoma orks (and one looming troll), all in blaze orange ponchos over obvious combat armor. Their luck held, and the lot of 'runners even avoided the Asphalt Devils, which was for the best; neither Dodger's quips nor Kham's rep would have saved them from that thrill-killer go-gang's love of violence. It would have fallen to gunplay and sorcery, two of Dodger's least favorite things.

Ah, Puyallup. Such a charming neighborhood.

That luck broke, however, as they reached their destination. Ghost—ever tactical—had helped Sally plot their course, but Kham had decided on the ideal location to leave their bikes as they went about their night's business; the street-savvy ork had found them a rare dead spot in Puyallup's gang-riddled landscape, a block of territory left temporarily vacant due to the internecine violence of a turf war that had required the Yakuza to step in and declare an end to.

For the moment, they were on neutral, empty turf. There would be no need to bribe a gang to watch over their things, to pay protection money to keep their bikes unmolested, to leave a trail of certified credsticks in order to ensure they could ride safely home at the end of the night. No gang to double-cross them, rat them out to nearby corporates, and get paid for feeding shadowrunners to the beast.

They could skulk the few blocks they needed to reach their target—a juicy Saeder-Krupp facility dripping with newtech schematics and prototypes ripe for the stealing—get back, and leave, all before any local warlord could throw a monkeywrench into their plans for professional corporate subterfuge. S-K was always a hard target, the dragon-run megacorp was feared for a reason. So why make life harder by tempting fate with local gang-troubles, too?

Except that the turf might well be nominally neutral, but it surely wasn't *empty*.

First, a a half-dozen or so of the Barrens' hungriest denizens, bristling with weaponry, milled about, scowling, fingering their autoguns and fire axes, and doing their very best—which was, Dodger had to admit, pretty good—to look intimidating. An assortment of humans, orks, and dwarves, and an impressively broad troll, they were, surprisingly, motley. Unaffiliated. Not in uniform. Independent of any gang.

Second, the lot of them were in a rough, aggressive, circle around a van. A van that sported precious little Puyallup graffiti, a van that rather suspiciously wasn't stripped of tires and up on long-suffering cinder blocks, a van without bullet-riddled body panels, without shattered windows, without a cheerful fire blazing away. A van that was entirely right-side-up and unmolested.

"Well," Kham grunted in surprise as the lot of them idled their bikes across the street and began to park and stand. "That ain't been there long."

Puyallup wasn't kind to abandoned vehicles.

"Buzz, drekheads!" the Barrens-troll's voice was a belly-rumbling bass, like rolling thunder when he raised it. "This ain't no parkin' lot!"

"*Hoi*! Ain't out to hose your gig, brother." Kham held his hands up in a non-threatening gesture, but one that showed his size. "We're just in your 'hood looking to do a little work. You watch our rides same as you watchin' that one, everyone wins, *so ka*? Elf'll slot you a credstick, hundred nu per ride."

Wait, what? "I will do no such thi—" Dodger sputtered, only for Sally to cut him off with a hiss. Ghost, the elf noticed, seemed to have entirely vanished.

"One-twenty-five. The elf plus me, yeah? Solid wage. He'll pay you seventy-five per ride, I'll pay you fifty. Solid biz, chummers. You're already here, right? Easy payday."

The gall of these so-called professionals!

"Why am *I* paying the seventy-fiv—" Dodger began again.

"I said buzz! Frag off outta here!" the troll rumbled at Kham, ignoring Sally entirely, stepping to mid-street, away from the GMC Bulldog step-van he'd clearly been heavily bribed to watch over.

So much for neutral territory being cheaper. For a band of civvies, even Barrens-civvies, to try and glare down obvious shadowrunners *and* to turn down a secondary payday meant they'd been paid nifty nuyen, indeed, to see the van left unmolested and the street kept otherwise empty.

"We got good 'stick to keep eyes off this van, so we's doin' it. Jander on, trog!" The troll's mind was *entirely* made up.

"Trog?!" Kham bristled, his upraised hands turning to fists. "Who are you callin' trog, trog?!"

"M'callin' you trog, *trog*, an' we'll straight-up frag over your whole night, if you and your joyboy don't slot and run." The troll waved his hand—the one with his huge revolver in it, *of course*, at Dodger as he finished his threat.

"Joyboy? *Joyboy*?! I'll have you kno—" Dodger's indignant squawk got cut short. Again. He reached for his machine pistol in a huff, deciding he might as well point something at somebody, too.

"Chill, chummer. We got biz, we ain't gonna buzz. Now you can take the money to watch over our rides, or not, but trust me, *mundane*, you ain't doin' anything to frag over our night." Sally's voice never turned shrill, just calmer. More certain. Dodger knew that was when the street mage was at her most dangerous. She sent a little crackle of raw mana dancing across her knuckles to help make her threat clearer.

"Shut it, slitch. Men are talkin'." The troll looked her way only long enough to sneer.

Dodger snorted. Before Tsung could kill the lot of them with a fireball and trash their van on principle, besides, the troll's life got saved by a sharp whistle. A whistle from the alley *behind* the hotly contested Bulldog van.

The toughs behind him all went wide-eyed and jumped half out of their britches at the whistle, and gawked open at their looming leader's broad back. A bit of smog got blown just right by the stinking Seattle breeze, and Dodger could only just barely make out twin reddish beams in the haze, for an instant.

Laser beams.

Ghost-Who-Walks-Inside took a few steps out of the shadows of the alley he'd used to flank them, his twin Ingrams held shoulder-high and rock-solid-still, painting the troll's spine with their underbarrel-mounted lasers.

"Uh, Bones?" As the assortment of metahumans scattered and half-turned, trying to keep an eye on the street samurai *and* on Kham, Sally, and Dodger, one of them piped up.

The troll—Bones, apparently?—grunted and spun, then sighed in defeat.

Ghost flashed his teeth like a dog, lips bared, a threat instead of a smile, and the Amerind nodded a "yeah, you get it," nod. The samurai kept one Ingram trained right on the troll's center of mass and pointed the other at the crew fanning out nervously.

Ghost's steps were measured, careful, perfectly balanced, and his voice was perfectly certain and calm. "No need for anyone to get geeked tonight, 'least none of you. You do your biz. You watch your van. You watch our bikes for *fifty* nuyen each from the elf."

"Hey!" Dodger was beginning to feel *entirely* too insulted and—worst of all—overlooked to have made all that business with undoing his jacket *at all* worth it.

"And nobody gets hurt. You get fair payment, our rides are safe, and this crew's job don't go sideways 'cause nobody's minding the van." Ghost tossed his head at the Bulldog, his shaggy black hair glossy in the moonlight. "*So ka*?"

"Oh, don't worry, handsome. The van's *definitely* minded." The flirtatious threat, or threatening flirtation, came by way of subtle external speakers, the sort that might have let out a banshee wail if an alarm were triggered, but the voice was, while tinny, thoroughly understandable.

Augmenting the warning came the whir of a rotordrone, a cylindrical hunter-drone with a pair of blocky Enfield combat shotguns attached, each of them sporting an altogether alarmingly large drum of ammunition. *It* emerged from the same alley Ghost had.

It was the samurai's turn to sigh; arms flung akimbo, now, so that one of his sleek Ingrams stayed trained on the troublesome troll, the other laser sight hovered over the drone's primary sensor array.

"*Aww, frag*," All three of them, the rest of the team, whispered under their breath as one.

Kham gave up his simple posturing and went for his gun. Sally rested a hand on the hilt of her magesword, drawing power from it for a devastating spell. Dodger shouldered his Heckler and Koch machine pistol, scowling.

The good news was that the combat drone bristling with streetsweeping firepower wasn't a Saeder-Krupp model, a hunter/killer patrolling nearby territory at random, or fed paydata about Sally Tsung and her crew and sent here to wipe them out. No logos emblazoned it, it wasn't marked as corporate property the same way city blocks were marked as a gang's turf.

The bad news was that the hover-shooter wasn't *alone.*

Well, this is entirely vexing.

A shadowrunner team emerged from the same dark alley, panting and moving at a quick trot that both explained why Ghost's lurking hadn't spotted them—they and their air support were moving fast, and simply hadn't *been there* to be spotted—and *also* made it clear they weren't out for a casual stroll.

There was no mistaking the look of Seattle street-professionals. One was a leather-skinned human with severe slash-cut hair that was the latest in Barrens high fashion. He had a blocky polymer case in one hand and a handcannon—already pointed Ghost's way—in the other. Just behind him came a troll and a half, nearly three meters of toughened hide, scars, and the nodules, commonly miscalled warts, common to his race. More troubling than his complexion, the troll was toting a massive Ares machine gun. Third and finally, they were joined by another human, dressed not terribly unlike how Dodger figured a U-Dub professor might dress, and with a faintly rippling aura of magical power crackling around him; shields hastily erected should Sally finish her spellcasting any time soon.

There was, frankly, no telling which of them was the most dangerous.

Dodger and the rest of the team hedged their bets, then—Dodger last of all, elf-quickness put to shame by the combat-honed reflexes of his nominal peers—as *their* side of the street bristled with weapons. Ghost kept one Ingram on the murderdrone, the other pointed at the human whose huge wheelgun had him covered. Kham's blocky Kalashnikov centered on the massive troll's massive chest. Sally's beautiful eyes narrowed and she locked gazes with the other mage.

Dodger's HK turned to survey the problematic civilians—troll and all—who the rest of the team seemed content to ignore. They knew when they were winning (and their generous patrons had surely turned the tide in their favor), but none of them had reached anew for the weapons they'd lowered after Ghost had outplayed them.

"Drop it!"

"Put it down!"

"I don't put things down!"

"I'll put *you* down, trog!"

"Who you callin'—"

"Easy, everybody."

"Null persp, chummers!"

"Nameless, my friend, remain calm."

"No need to get geeked, let's just—"

"Can't we talk about this?"

"Frag off, let's zap these fools, Neddy!"

"Already did our job, we gotta wax 'em!"

"Ease up, Kham, let's not get carried away."

"Smedley, don't drop that thing, you hear me?"

"—all Dodger's damn fault, Sally, I swear, he spent half an hour in the fraggin' lady's room and—"

"Wait...Smedley?"

"Neddy?"

"Sally?"

"Nameless?"

"Dodger?"

"Hello, pleasant eve, and how fare thee, friends?" Dodger lowered his gun to point it at the street instead of anyone's face, and gave the threesome of shadowrunners his second-best smile. Then he carelessly swept the whole damned street with the muzzle of his HK as he bowed politely to the whirring combat drone.

"Lady Iris, yes?" Dodger gave the drone his *very* best smile. "*Telegit thelemsa!*"

"*Siselle,*" the tinny speakers of the van answered him, "*Thelemsa-ha.*"

Ah, Sperethiel. Bringing elves together since best-not-to-listen-to-rumors-about-exactly-when.

The driver's side door of the Bulldog van opened, and a silver-haired elf—filling out a set of grease-stained mechanic's coveralls, and with the front unzipped almost as far as Dodger's leather jacket—turned in the seat to settle her combat-booted feet on the running board of her van and regard the stand-off with the amusement that can only come from someone who's meat-body was never in the line of fire.

Dodger pressed on, one hand reaching up to unsnap one *more* button on his jacket. "Unless I am thoroughly mistaken—and, in truth, I *never* am—I believe I may have accidentally spied 'pon some Matrix chatter that your noble band of ragamuffin ne'er-do-wells was planning a job ahead of time, yes?"

Iris rolled her eyes at him and his jacket, then tossed her head to the suit-clad professor-looking-fellow. Dodger had heard of him, a thoroughly over-educated combat mage who called himself Dr. Fortesque, but who the streets called Neddy.

"Quite right, good sir." The hermetic magician gave Dodger a polite nod, and let his shields lower after just the barest of wary glances at Sally. "Targeting a local Renraku subsidiary, you must have heard, and securing a prototype of a new spy drone."

Nameless, their cold-eyed samurai, kept a good grip on his locked-tight polymer case.

Dodger arched an eyebrow.

"Indeed. And 'twould be possible then, Sir Mage, that when traveling the same digital social circles, you may have heard we, too, had a quest before us this very same evening? An appointment to keep at a nearby Saeder-Krupp facility."

"So they ain't?"

"So *you* ain't?"

"You lot ain't after this dumb thing?"

"They didn't go and get security riled up, then?"

"No need to scrap, huh?"

"Aww, we ain't doin' this?"

"What a *hilarious* misunderstanding." Dodger let his stupid HK hang by its sling, an idle hand swiping to the *other* slung weapon, his *real* weapon, the Fairlight cyberdeck that hung at his side.

"Boys, can we just go?" Iris tore her gaze from Dodger's bare chest and swung her long legs back into the driver's side of her Bulldog.

They went, in a flurry of apologies, chagrin, and one last staredown, troll-to-ork, where Kham flashed tusks in a smile as Smedley had to look away first (in order to climb into the back of his team's van).

"Now then." Dodger gave Iris a cheery wave as the van rolled away, then spun to beam at the grouchy neighborhood troll and his band of miscreants. "Might my friend Ghost here see to your payment, and you lot of angels look over our noble steeds for us, while we are away to free the princess from the castle?"

"And," Sally added with a wry smile, "I won't give you the ol' magical mind-whammy, like Neddy did, to keep you loyal. Just good, clean nuyen. *So ka*?"

PLAN B

(Chicago Chaos)

Chicago Chaos *was the second book in the* Anarchy *game line, and presented another chance to tell a neat story without any particular theme; it wasn't narrowed to any particular aspect of the fantastic* Shadowrun *setting, I could do basically whatever sort of storytelling I wanted.*

"Plan B" was another story I threw together to match up with some cover art...and another time where the cover art got yoinked and rethought at the last minute. I was able to tie it in with several of the characters/archetypes I built for the book itself (which is always cool), and the cover art game me a heck of a plot hook and story idea...so much so that I kept it instead of whipping together something new, even after the artwork changed.

There are times I've changed a story (or tried to) at the last minute to match an artwork change, but this one represents another time I just didn't WANT to, 'cause I dug it too much. Luckily, my editors agreed.

—RRZ

"And that—" Grimm's Reaper smiled as he swung his sword down, two-handed, and the blade cleaved neatly through skin, bone, flesh, and magic to part emaciated head from emaciated shoulders. "—is that."

The vampire was dead. Head removed by weapon focus; there was no coming back from that. Reaper knew a done deal when he saw it, and this deal was very, very done.

The elf turned his head to glance at the sleek gun-drone hovering nearby. One buzzed and whirred near the entrance to this sewer's reeking chamber, covering the exit. The other hovered just about an arm's reach away, a blinking green light showing it broadcasting. He looked it square in the smartlink camera lens.

"You get that footage?" he said loudly enough to be sure the aerodynamic Transys combat-bot could pick up his question on its external mics. The tunnels were a too-deep maze lined with too many old metallics, the short-range radios they'd scrounged up for communications weren't working any better than his commlink had. Reaper'd had to leave his back at the tunnel entrance with his getaway man, the two 'links spliced together to boost Sharky's signal so *he*, at least, could maintain clear communications with their electronic support duo, clear and away, topside.

And so, without proper communications, Reaper had learned to settle for yelling at a gun-drone and hoping either microphones or facial recognition subroutines linked up to lip-reading protocols did the job.

Looked like it was still working, at least. His question got through.

Elsewhere, a rigger sent a mental command and twitched her wrist just so. The drone hovered in place, but its mounted assault rifle's muzzle bobbed down and up several times in a virtual nod. Footage received. Rigger confirmed.

"All righty! Kill documented and verified, then." Reaper nodded matter-of-factly, sheathing his mageblade at his hip. "No need to collect the corpse. I'm in the clear to get the frag out of he—"

He heard them coming just as the second drone reacted, suppressed Typhoon autorifle coughing and spitting death. Reaper's mageblade leaped back into his hand, and the scythe-sharp tattoos on his forearms blazed as he tapped into his internal reservoirs of power to fuel himself with supernatural speed. Grimm's Reaper was hard to catch unawares, and even harder to pin down.

The first wave of howling, blood-mad, feral ghouls fell to combined waves of high-velocity death spat forth by the Transys combat-drones, several well-placed swings of Reaper's preternaturally sharp sword, and a single, focused, blast of pure magical power. Nothing dropped threats like manabolt, that's what Reaper always said.

There were more claws in the darkness, more sets of glowing eyes peering at him from all around.

"Where the frag is my exit?!"

Reaper said that a lot, too.

"I've got no word from Sharky. How's Grimmy doing?" Dot-Execute *almost* sounded like she cared. Caring wasn't like her. She might've been faking it—she did that sometimes—but maybe she liked Reaper 'cause he was easy on the eyes. Or maybe it was an elf thing. Or maybe it was the potential payday he represented. Or, yeah, given how she was leaning carelessly against the van, maybe she was just faking it.

"You know he hates it when you call him that. And he's doing fine." Loop took a few seconds to answer, shrugging her ork-broad shoulders. Half or more of her attention was invested in manipulating her gun-drones, guiding them via her top-of-the-line control rig, flying them based on the visuals she saw projected through her augmented-reality goggles; they were flying and shooting a few klicks away and underground, so the signal noise had her lagging a bit and kept her from piloting them at full speed. She pretended it was a video game, like she'd played as a kid. Making the vampire hunt and ensuing chase feel unreal made it easier to swallow. "But he'd be doing better if he followed my fraggin' drones more closely."

Like all right-thinking gamers, Loop hated escort missions.

"No, left!" she growled, agitation making her raise her voice. There was no way for the elven mage to hear her—not any more than her AR gaming rigs could've heard her, ten years ago, playing just for fun—but she didn't let that stop her from voicing her frustration. "Left! Turn le—ah, damn it Reaper! My drone!"

Dot-Exe rolled her eyes and busied herself with her own cyberdeck, but half-heartedly. The elf didn't seem to care very much, after all. She shrugged, elf-graceful even in her disdain for others.

"I guess I'ma call Sharky and see what's what," she said, a sharp nod sliding her AR goggles down from her forehead and over her eyes. It was only fair, Dot had been the one to talk Sharky *into* this gig, she was the one that knew him from around the way, and she *wasn't* the one that was overseeing the drone fire team. It was only fair the elf do *some* work on this gig, right?

Reaper ran. He didn't trot, jog, jander, saunter, or stroll, no. He ran. He ran like he hadn't in a long time. He wasn't in bad shape, far from it, he was just rusty at running away. He didn't like the taste it left in his mouth, the coppery taste of pure fear and the primal, animalistic acknowledgement of another creature as a superior threat.

Pride like that was dangerous for a monster hunter, naturally, but Reaper seldom claimed he was perfect.

So it stung, but he ran.

He ran away from the spark-spewing gun-drone he'd last seen emptying its magazine while feral ghouls tore it apart and raged about a lack of meat within. He ran away from the muzzle flashes and whirring engine of Loop's *other* gun-drone, letting the machine draw fire and attention as he—and his precious meat—hoofed it down a side passage. He ran as he heard claws skittering and bare feet splashing in the darkness behind him. He ran.

Reaper's feet slid but the elf kept his balance as he rounded the last corner to the surface entrance where he'd left his bike and his sidekick. Sharky was local muscle, Chicago-born and bred, that'd been picked up by another local Reaper'd just started to work with. She vouched for him. Sharky'd been seduced into coming along on his own set of wheels, to standing shotgun over his and Reaper's bikes, and to getting paid half in advance and half after they both made it clear, post-vampire encounter.

"Aww, drek. Damn it, Sharky!"

Reaper's skittering stop drew the glowing-eyed gaze of a knot of ghouls, feasting, bloody up to their elbows.

The good news was that Reaper hadn't ever grown very close to the local muscle. The better news was that Sharky wasn't going to need the second half of that payment. The bad news was that a whole pack of bloody-chinned ferals with bits of implanted musculature stuck in their teeth stood between Reaper and his way out.

Halfway between him and the snarling, staring monsters, the elf saw a clear, glowing screen. One of their commlinks had survived Sharky's getting snuck up on and torn open, and a tinny voice rang out from it, high-pitched. Disinterested. A terrible lifeline, as lifelines went.

"–en I guess try Plan B, or whatever. Anyway, I don't know if you can even hear me, Grimmy. Sharky's Meta went offline, which could just mean the drekky battery died, could just mean that dummy dropped it, or could mean he, I dunno, got eaten or something. So if you can hear me, then I guess try Plan B, or whatever. Anyway, I don't know if you can even hear me, Gri–"

A ghoul crushed the commlink under one bare, sewer-filthy foot as the mob of them howled and rushed at Reaper.

What the frag was Plan B again? He just had time to think before his mageblade and sparking bolts of pure sorcerous power busied themselves trying to carve out a little space for him. And, for just a second, *Maybe it's time to get a regular crew instead of trying this drek solo.*

"What do you mean, it went dead?" Loop gawked over at the elf, managing to glare even as her attention remained split, one eye—literally, thanks to her AR monocle—on her remaining gun-drone, the other leveled incredulously at Dot-Execute's casual posture.

"Uh, I thought I was pretty clear." The elf rolled her eyes. "It went dead. No return when I ping it. No response when I call, no answer when I text, no icon remaining when I full-dive in to check on it."

She shrugged. "I set a loop—" A very un-elven snort escaped her lips as she grinned at the ork, Loop. "—to give them a heads up and remind them of our back-up plan, and wide-cast it to both 'links, but, drek, girl, I don't know. They might both be dead, I guess."

"You guess?" The ork growled.

Dot splayed her hands in front of her in a what-you-gonna-do flail.

"Girl, get your skinny ass in there." Loop nodded to Dot's cyberdeck, and by extension the Matrix. "And check again. Scan for nearby sec-cams, check on their bikes' location signals, hit up the bikes' diagnostics checks I installed, *do something.* If they're both dead, we don't get paid!"

That widened the elf's disinterested eyes and got her to work.

Loop wasn't *technically* telling her the whole truth, of course. The footage of the vampire's execution *was* recorded, and Loop *had* saved it already, three different places. So they could probably still get paid, even if Grimm's Reaper and Sharky were both ghoul-chow. It would be a hassle—forging up a proper license and all, since Reaper was the only one with the paperwork to do this sort of gig—but Loop knew she'd be up to the task, if push came to shove.

She just *also* knew threatening the nuyen was the surest way to get Dot-Execute's hoop in gear. Dot had promise. Dot had potential. Dot had a conscience problem. She was pure merc, and Loop tried not to hold it against her, but she *did* also know just how to motivate the younger console cowgirl.

"Plan B—" Reaper panted as he ran, "—is stupid."

Swimming wasn't his strong suit, any more than running was. But if he had to run, then swim, then pedal a damned bike like in some old Ironman competition, by Jesus, Buddha, and Zeus, that's what he'd do; he wasn't going to get eaten by ghouls, he had a reputation to keep up!

So he continued to trek toward Plan B, which was a nautical exit. It would mean leaping right into the oh-so-polluted Chicago River, and just hoping these ghouls weren't natural swimmers. There was a tendency—Reaper read a lot—there was a tendency for ghouls and assorted other Infected to shy away from aquatic encounters, and they seldom ventured into areas rich with running water. Some speculated it was a side effect of the Human/Metahuman Vampiric Virus (Krieger Strain) that made ghouls so ghoulish, others that it was a purely psychological holdover, with evidence that non-feral ghouls could swim just fine, while only ferals seemed to avoid the water. Others suggested that it had to do with a ghoul's blindness, their utter reliance only on astral vision to see, and that they found water disconcerting or disorienting in some way.

Long story short, Plan B hinged on Reaper out-swimming ghouls who, for whatever reason, often weren't strong swimmers.

But damn, was that a weak assumption to be betting his life on.

Limping as well as panting now, Grimm's Reaper tried to ignore the steady trickle of warmth running down his side, past one hip, and along his leg. It was the bite of a ghoul that was likely to spread their disease, not just a rake of their claws, but hell if it wasn't still an open wound and he wasn't running around an actual sewer with it. And double-hell if he wasn't about to jump right into the Chicago River with a few extra holes in his body.

"If," he said to nobody in particular, wincing in pain. "I can even find it."

They hadn't mapped Plan B out very meticulously, no. He'd uploaded a basic mapsoft to his goggles for emergency reference, but the local hacker girl—the elven one, Dot-Execute—had been honest about it being years out of date. Wary, even, when she'd announced it. Worried, no doubt, that providing years-old tunnel plans might endanger her payment.

"Maybe it should have," Reaper grunted as he ran unevenly along the route his goggles displayed for him. He had to run. They were still behind him. He could still hear them breathing, snarling, growling, splashing, and skittering after him.

Frag the map. It was time to just navigate by instinct. A monster hunter's got to trust his gut sometimes, and that means, when in doubt, running *away* from the ravenous horde of ghouls. Not north, not south, not measuring in meters...just orienting in terms of *away* and *fast* and *far*.

Until, the huffing, puffing, limping elf realized he heard snarling and the skitter of long-grown claws *in front* of him, too.

Grimm's Reaper sighed and resigned himself to another fight—his last?—and figured a proper fireball would be a better way to die, if it came down to it, than yellow teeth and splitting claws. He leveled his mageblade, found the confident, balanced center of himself, and called up his power.

Just as the shadows swarmed in from all around, every nearby mouth of every nearby tunnel, *just* as he felt swollen and pregnant with the terrible, raw fire he was about to loose in the too-tight confines of the sewers, *just that second* as he felt certain it was too many claws, from too many different directions...there was a bright light and a muted roar.

A Transys Typhoon autogun, mounted in the sleek, polymer body of a custom-rigged security drone, firing on full auto.

Grimm's Reaper pivoted on one foot and slung his fireball far down a side passage, a streaking blur of fire that cast crazed shadows on the walls as it burned its way past a half-dozen ghouls, exploded behind them, and sent charred, blackened, bodies and parts of bodies back in his general direction.

"*Hey*!" he shouted over the muted, suppressor-stuttering, sound of the drone's continued autofire. "*Where the frag is my exit*?!"

Loop sighed, shook her head to re-orient her far-off, lag-heavy drone, and got herself back into the game. She fired and fired, swung and pivoted, swooped, climbed, and raced through the too-tight tunnels, her barking muzzle leading the way. She was acutely aware of her drone's dwindling ammunition count, but also acutely aware it wasn't like she could reload the thing with fresh mags from here.

All she could do was keep shooting, keep flying, and keep guiding Reaper's shapely, spell-slinging, elven ass toward the river.

"What're you doing?" Dot piped up from her spot safely out of arm's reach.

Loop ignored her and focused on the shooting.

"What're you do—"

"—I'm getting Reaper out of there," Loop growled. "Or trying to. I'm running low." Low on bullets. Low on patience. Low on hope. And soon, low on tunnels; they'd be hitting the exit pipe before too long, and then it would be up to Grimm to show how well he swam. Or, more specifically, how well he swam with a bunch of holes in his belly.

"Okay." Dot shrugged, chewing on some gum. "Plan B still, right?"

"Slitch, it ain't like we *got* a Plan C, is it?"

"That's fair." Dot shrugged again. Her fingers danced across her cyberdeck's battered, button-worn control panel, even as she half-assed her conversation with Loop.

The ork really hated that.

"I really hate this." Reaper stood at the edge of the tunnel, which protruded a few meters out over the river.

The drone didn't—couldn't—answer, it just kept hovering behind him, firing. It was shooting double-taps, now. Earlier it had been full-auto. Then short bursts. Now just pairs of shots, into the darkness, carefully dropping a ghoul at a time or, at least, hurting them enough to send them scurrying back around the nearest corner, gathering their numbers.

The Infected were content to wait and collect a few more members, it seemed. Maybe they could smell his uncertainty—Reaper couldn't call it "fear"—about what remained of the plan. Maybe they knew the layout of their tunnels and were aware he was about to leave. Maybe these ones just weren't hungry, and were waiting on some alpha-type feral pack leader to come along and choose the choicest cuts of his meat.

"You hear me?" Reaper hollered at the drone, the tip of his mageblade scraping against the tunnel's floor as he leaned on it, exhausted and hurting. "I really hate this! I hate that I'm either about to die alone except for some mostly-stranger's murder-drone while I get torn to shreds and eaten, or that I'm about to die alone *without* that drone even nearby, because I'm gonna be in the bottom of a river, and that drone's just going to fly away!"

He was still yelling, but he wasn't sure why.

"And I hate that I don't even know that idiot Sharky's real name, and that he died 'cause of a job I was totally gonna stiff him on. And I hate that you're just some gun-drone working for Loop, who I barely know, and that despite that you're, like, my best fraggin' friend right now."

A little part of Reaper was worried he had a fever.

"And I hate that Dot-Exe-whatever got her friend into this, and I don't even know *her* real name, either. Like, I hate that, if by some miracle, I don't drown in this filthy river or just die outright from chemical shock or whatever, I hate that I'm gonna have to say, 'Hey, Dot, sorry about Sharky,' like some kind of total asshole. I hate street names! I'm not a shadowrunner, what do I ha—"

"*Hey.*"

Reaper blinked as he heard a voice, clear as day, ring out. He looked around and saw nothing but the muzzle flashes of the gun-drone and the glowing eyes of the amassing pack.

Then looked down and saw an idling Suzuki Watersport, a jet ski, idling in the water, almost within reach.

"*Stop moaning and get on the thing,*" Dot said, voice harsh as it was broadcast through the hacked Watersport's sound system. The engine revved and the Suzuki lurched right up to the tunnel's mouth, water churning below it as jets and propellers worked to turn the sleek watercraft in place, presenting it to him. "*Let's get you out of there, float your hoop upriver, and discuss Sharky's cut of the bounty on the way to a street doc I know, huh*?"

Grimm's Reaper cast a look behind him, to the sets of eyes blinking at him, and to the dwindling fire from Loop's last combat drone. He looked away as the claws began to skitter again, as the growling and snarling grew louder behind him, and he leaped out onto the bobbing, idling Suzuki.

Reaper let out a triumphant whoop as the Watersport lurched away from the tunnel's open mouth, and the dozen ghouls and *their* open mouths, and he flipped them off as it splashed away from the riverbank. The filthy creatures roared and charged out after him, splashing in the narrows and clambering for the banks of the river, and Reaper threw them a going-away present, a blast of pure mana, as his scythe-tattoos burned with power.

He was gonna make it! Loop's drone and Dot's swiped Watersport—his half-assed local support—had made all the difference in the world.

Maybe Plan B wasn't so bad after all...and maybe it was time for a Plan C.

A proper team. Regular support staff. Shadowrunning.

BACK ALLEY BRAWL

(Shadowrun: Hong Kong)

"Back Alley Brawl" is one of my favorite pieces of short fiction I've ever written. The only real direction I had for it was "Hong Kong, set in the 2050s," and I ran with it pretty hard. There are plenty of role-playing games, video games, and (especially) movies that are full of epic kung-fu action and legendary-sounding names, and I just rolled in with that bouncing around in my head and let loose.

An open-air market in Hong Kong sounded like a great stage on which to tell a story, an adept was a natural fit for some over-the-top martial arts action, and the rest of the pieces just fell right into place (including the chance to name-drop a minor character who's shown up in a few other places of mine, a young Bing-Lei "Billy" Shen). It was a fun read with a neat mixture of comedy and action, and I'm really proud of how it turned out.

—RRZ

The Four Thunders were on a roll. Seven Resplendent Tigers had gotten them together just six months ago—he'd already worked with Storm of the Road prior to that, but getting Dog Emperor and Smiling Cat on board had really rounded out the crew—and they'd already started to build a reputation in the Hong Kong shadows as a reliable shadowrunner team. They specialized in mobile ops, Storm and Dragons in the van, Cat and Dog running interference on their combat-specced racing bikes, and right off the bat they'd started to get regular work with the Red Dragons Triad.

Their current gig, Seven Resplendent Tigers assured them, was going to seal the deal. The Red Dragons had been having trouble chasing down the Chungking Chargers, a go-gang who'd been undercutting the Triads' reputation, horning in on the fringes of their turf, making them look slow and clumsy. The Red Dragons were a behemoth, a monster, a titan. They were built for slick, glossy-black SUVs full of shooters, they were designed for running whole neighborhoods, they were prepped to fight off the White Lotus Triad and other criminal giants; squashing scuttling cockroaches was hard when you were that big.

So they'd outsourced. The Red Dragons had put up a standing offer, and so far no one had been able to claim the prize; whoever put the Chungking Chargers in their place, the Triads would hook up with positions—legit positions, totally legal, high-paying, high-profile—on Hong Kong's superstar Combat Biker squad, the Cavaliers.

The Four Thunders, with their tricked-out wheels and their combat wires, their gleaming chrome and their chattering autoguns, were out to move up the ladder.

Smiling Cat and Seven Resplendent Tigers were winding their way through the bustling back-alley marketplace, a maze of warbling sellers, neon lights, and the rich, clashing smells of a dozen or a hundred food stalls all competing for your attention. Open-air body mod artists and crude street docs spilled blood next to cleaver-swinging butchers, fried noodle stands glared through the crowd at one another all day and night, pocket secretaries and other portable electronics were hawked or disassembled for parts, and portable stalls selling cheap clothes and cheaper knock-offs vied for every traveler's business.

And then, of course, there was the protection rackets, the business within the business, the shadows within the shadows.

The Red Dragons' boys had come through earlier in the week. Every Tuesday, like clockwork, slick men with slick hair and slick suits rolled through, eyes hidden behind implanted cyberoptic shades, hands held out for their weekly take. Everyone paid. Everyone had to.

But it wasn't a Tuesday. Days later, while the Triad crews were off working a different alley, a different sprawl of buyers and sellers, pickpockets and hustlers, joyboys and joygirls, while the Red Dragons' mighty eyes were elsewhere, the

Chungking Chargers rolled in. Their nimble little bikes, souped up for sound as much as for speed, howled their arrival, and they took turns unmounting, jandering from stall to stall, flashing some spurs, some implanted muscles, or a cheap street gun, to get money and fear because they couldn't quite manage respect.

"*In position,*" Dog Emperor said, straddling his own armored-up Yamaha Rapier combat bike down at one end of North Point Alley. He spoke into a mic built into his motorcycle helmet, the only member of the team without *any* cyberware, even just implanted comms.

"*Still all set,*" Storm of the Road's electronic voice chimed to the team, the rigger sprawled in her van, implanted hardware translating her thoughts to the team as vocals. Her meat-body was snug in the van at the other end of the alley, but her attention was in her combat rotordrone, high overhead.

"Eyes on," Seven Resplendent Tigers said, a subvocal microphone implanted somewhere in the razorboy's jawline, the least of his chrome.

"*I'm workin' on it, fraggers, be patient,*" Smiling Cat snapped, scowling despite her street name. She had her head shaved high on one side, freshly smooth, not a hint of glossy black stubble near the cluster of datajacks that rode high over her left ear. Cat, the Four Thunders' electronics wizard, was on point tonight, being watched over by the protective Seven Resplendent Tigers, charged with bugging a Chungking Charger's bike.

"*It's not like these boys ever get far from their toys,*" she grouched, frowning toward the nearest knot of go-gangers from her spot in line at a pork bun stall.

Two Chargers were on foot, shaking down an old man with a table covered in knock-off watches. Their arguing was louder than the wizened old merchant's blaring radio, a Mercurial tune ringing out and fighting against the perpetual background noise of the night market. Four more Chargers hovered nearby, straddling their bikes or leaning against them, all with a hawkish eye on the crowd.

The Four Thunders had a simple plan. Bug a Charger's street machine, follow them to wherever their base was, and wade in, combat drones leading the way. If any Chargers made it to their bikes to blast out of there, the Thunders would chase them down and beat them at their own game. At the end of the night? Sell the bikes to Red Dragon chop-shops, show off the bodies to Red Dragon bosses, and grab the glory, the street cred, and the chance to go Combat Biking.

Only bugging a go-ganger's bike was easier said than done.

"I can cause a distraction," Tigers offered in a growl, his augmented muscles rippling. "A little brawl, get their attention, bug out before things get too seri—"

"*No need*," Storm's robotic voice cut him off, but the eye in the sky didn't apologize. "*They're moving. Look*."

Visible now to the ones on the ground, the Chargers were distracted by something; no, some*one*. They'd started hooting, laughing, pointing. They sounded like hyenas. They sounded like punks. They sounded like trouble.

"*Isn't that Shen's old lady*?" Cat squinted.

"So what if it is?" Tigers' voice was flat. They'd never gotten along.

"*So Shen did right by us*." Dog Emperor tried to see from behind his helmet's faceplate, idling bike rolling him a little closer. "*He vouched for us, and got us a good gig*."

"Sure, but now he's dead," Tigers didn't care.

"*She's with his kid*," Cat didn't have to fake disinterest, everyone else in line was craning to watch.

The Chargers had swooped down at a fish stand and had started pitching carcasses at the woman, one of them flashing a switchblade to silence the frantic fish-seller. Mrs. Shen, a Triad killer's widow, didn't turn away from the reeking onslaught, just twisted to protect the skinny boy next to her from it.

"Just a dead traitor's wife and a pixie brat," Tigers grunted. "Not our problem. Cat, tag the bikes."

"*But we can't–*" Dog started.

"We can. We are. Tag. The. Bikes."

Smiling Cat slipped out of her line, hands in her jacket pockets, and Tigers slid sideways to block line of sight—not that any of the Chargers were paying any attention to their forgotten bikes—with his sheer bulk. Cat dropped to a low squat and got to work, snaking her small hands to find out-of-the-way places to hide her sensors.

"*Aww, frag*," the curse lacked all inflection, Storm's tinny voice sapped the urgency from it.

One of the Chargers was howling and cursing even more sincerely, a little folding knife jutting out of his denim-clad thigh, the fish-seller's bucket of blood and slime held over his head, about to toss it onto Shen's widow.

The dead man's son, a coltish boy, elven-tall but elven-skinny, didn't let up after the quick stabbing; he started punching, angry, eyes narrow with rage, fists flailing.

"*They're gonna kill him,*" Dog said, engine revving.

"Maybe. Not our problem. Bikes are tagged. We fade." Tigers shook his head, staring right down the alley and frowning. Cat slipped back into the crowd.

The beating started. Two Chargers grabbed the boy and held him from behind, while the leg-stabbed leader limped over and started punching. Two more had Mrs. Shen in a handsy tangle, making her watch while her son took a few shots to the belly. The last was laughing and watching, not sure which dogpile to join in on.

Chao Shen had been a strong man, a feared man, a man protected by the Red Dragons Triad. Chao Shen had kept his family safe. He'd died trying to redeem his name after being charged with disloyalty; the Red Dragons hadn't gone after his wife and son for his crimes, weeks earlier, but they also hadn't extended their protection. Seven Resplendent Tigers was just glad his team's reputation hadn't been sullied by the whole thing. He'd vouched for them early, after all, and the Incense Master could have easily questioned their loyalty by extension.

Chao Shen was gone now. His family was fair game, and the Chargers were having their fun.

Young Bing Lei Shen spat blood and curses—not at the glowering Charger beating him, but at the ones grabbing his mother. Another few punches took the air out of him, but not the anger. His eyes went wide with worry as his mother was thrown to the ground. A more immediate threat loomed before the boy, though, as the gang leader grimaced and ripped the little knife from his leg, spitting and preparing to turn it against the elven youth.

"We *fade,*" Tigers said again, trying to keep his team on a leash. The bugs were planted. They just had to be patient. "We just wait. We follow them. We do the job an—"

"*–can't do it, boss.*" An engine growled along with the response.

Dog Emperor's sleek Rapier knifed through the crowd, headlight and horn clearing the way, red-lining his engine to build up speed despite his short lead-up room. Dog slipped the brake just so, slid the back tire out wide to one side, laid the bike down as it swept down the alley—a sideways wedge—low, and he leaped airborne at the last instant.

The three Chargers standing over Mrs. Shen had time to look over stupidly before his bike slammed into them. One of them went down with his knees and shins and thighs all wrong, bones jutting and denim ruined. The second scrambled for the relative safety of a side street, eyes wide. The third felt very clever as he hopped over the bike, until the airborne adept, Dog Emperor, flew into him with all a racing bike's momentum behind his jump kick.

The Charger didn't get back up. Dog Emperor did, barely scuffed. He tugged his helmet off and held it in front of him, eyes bright, teeth flashing, hair wild.

"Let the kid go," he said, giving the three that were left just that one chance to pick up their friends and go about their brutish business elsewhere.

They threw young Bing Lei into the filth next to his mother—she already checking on him, him already checking on her—and charged instead.

Dog Emperor dropped his helmet and kicked it like a soccer ball, the sphere of impact-resistant polymers smashing the lead go-ganger's nose in a spray of blood. The second Charger thrust with a chrome-flashing switchblade, but Dog sidestepped it, backpedaled away, slapped at the ganger's wrist and forearm and hand, making him miss—only just barely, but miss—again and again and again. A quick front kick shoved the Charger away and bought him a second.

Another Charger scrambled for a weapon and came at him with a fishmonger's cleaver, swinging it in big back-and-forth arcs, and it was all Dog Emperor could do to sidestep, duck, and weave away from the fresh onslaught. Dog jostled the watch-seller's table and rolled backward onto it, just as a wild cleaver-swing split the flimsy table.

"Crap," he said, lying in a heap, tangled with a dingy tablecloth, as the cleaver went up again.

"Damn you, Dog." Smiling Cat still wasn't smiling as her extendable baton swept out—*crack, crack, crack*—and lashed out at the cleaver-wielding Charger in a flurry of strikes. She was quicker than he was, and probably just as strong, but he had size and reach on her; while any one good hit from her club might break bone, any solid swing from his cleaver could split her open. Her rush bought Dog Emperor time to kip-up and brush himself off, though, shooting her an incorrigible grin.

"Couldn't let the kid get shanked, Cat." Dog Emperor faced off with the switchblade wielder again. His left hand flipped a knock-off watch at the Charger's head to distract him, then a second, then a third. Hup, hup, hup, flick, flick, flick, and then just as the knifeman fell into the pattern of swatting the irritating little distractions away, Dog stepped into it and swung with the watch-seller's blocky radio. With all his adept power behind it, the makeshift club smashed into the Charger's head, breaking into a dozen pieces but not doing the ganger's skull any favors, either. The Charger dropped, out cold.

The Charger with a bloody nose—helmet-face!—came at Dog Emperor, a length of chain clattering and whooshing through the air. Dog got battered with it once, twice, and then lashed out with his left forearm the third time, metal rings clanking as they looped around his biker-jacket-armored limb. The Ganger's eyes went wide for a second, realizing his mistake, and then Dog gave a hearty pull. Off-balance and over-extended, the Charger got tugged right into Dog Emperor's follow-up head kick. Falling like he'd been poleaxed, the ganger fell into a puddle right next to his switchblade-wielding friend.

Dog saw Smiling Cat had her Charger down—cleaver nowhere to be seen, one hand holding his bloody mouth, the other hand a purplish mess with bent-wrong fingers—before another foursome of go-gangers burst into sight, drawn by all the commotion. Cat ran to intercept them, her whirling baton leading the way, just as Dog felt a burning pain low in his back, and spun around.

The leader of their first little pack, the one who'd taken a knife to the leg and had wanted to return it to little Bing Lei Shen, had finally limped into the fray...and stabbed Dog right in the back.

Ignoring the lance of pain and the spreading warmth, Dog Emperor brought up his chain-wrapped left arm, using it as a shield against the flurry of knife-strikes. Sparks flew and chains rattled as the men shouted and advanced at one another, sideways like fencers, knife and chain weaving before them, one stiff-legged from a stab, the other tense from the wound near a kidney.

Dog snuck in a few quick snap-kicks and a good high punch, but the Charger wasn't dropping easily. Just when he felt like he had the measure of the man, two more go-gangers arrived—a quick glance showed Smiling Cat had her hands full with the other two—and Dog had to get back to scrambling, ducking, dodging, backpedaling, and making due with whatever he could find.

A fish stall blurred past, and Dog Emperor kicked a bucket to make one Charger's arms pinwheel as he scrambled on the extra-slick alley. Knock-off blue jeans were wadded and thrown, cracked like a whip, used to tangle one Charger's eyes as Dog drove a rising knee at his face just afterward. A noodle stall turned into a battleground, Dog Emperor staving off a flurry of knife strikes and fresh cleaver swings with a hot wok, a split second after emptying the pan in one attacker's face. A vendor's stool was used as a shield until cleaver strikes pared off two of the three legs, then Dog spun it, twirled it, struck with it, and eventually waded back into the fight with the hacked-off legs spinning like escrima sticks, ratta-tat-tatting out a pattern of pain as furiously as he could.

Dog Emperor found himself back to back with Smiling Cat, the woman's cyberdeck still snug against her back, her trusty little baton a little bent to one side but the striking tip slick with blood, as yet more Chargers rushed into the long-emptied market alley.

The pair of them spun warily, eyes all around, as snarling thugs swept in closer, feinted to see what the shadowrunners would do, hurled insults and threats, and worked up the courage to rush.

One came in, and swiftly regretted it. Cat dropped him with three quick strikes to the head, Dog snatched up his baseball bat and gave it a balance-checking spin, and the two of them gave each another satisfied nods.

Three came next, all roaring. Fists and feet flew, Dog swaying against Smiling Cat's back at first, then spinning away from her. He checked a front-kick, followed it up with a jab of the bat that left a Charger spitting blood and teeth, tossed his shaggy-long hair out of his eyes just in time to catch a punch to the mouth, and retaliated with an angry *qi* strike of his own that left his attacker a heap on the wet pavement. Cat hissed and danced, long legs leading with deceptively quick kicks, then finished off her opponent with the butt-end of her baton to the temple.

The stood back to back again, the calm in the eye of the storm, ready.

A Charger shouldered his way through the pack of them, a head taller than his peers, ork-broad in the shoulders, ork-ugly in the face. He pulled a big wheelgun from his belt with a nasty sneer, thumbed the chromed revolver's hammer back, and very pointedly sighted down the long barrel right at Dog Emperor.

The adept lifted the bat like it was a sword and gave the big Charger a minuscule nod past it; *go ahead*, the nod said, *If you need the gun to beat me, show the whole world that.*

"Do it," Tigers grunted into his headware microphone.

Dual assault rifles chattered from up high, Storm of the Road's gun-drone raining death on the line of Chargers, starting with the Ork and his gun.

The roto-drone swept low, chattering away the whole time, dakka-dakka-dakka, parting the crowd and carving an escape route for Dog and Cat to scramble away; Cat kicking a cowering Charger in the vitals as he didn't move quickly enough, Dog breaking the bat over one's head as he passed.

They dove into Storm's waiting van, and the rigger's gun-drone swept high and away on autopilot as she threw her attention into driving. A whole wave of bike engines roared to life behind them, headlights blinking to life, glaring at them like the eyes of a hungry wolf pack, ready, now, to chase down and maul this creature that had bloodied them.

Seven Resplendent Tigers cursed at Dog Emperor as the young adept could only shrug to defend himself. Storm of the Roads lay immobile in her driver's seat, strapped in securely, her up-engined van already adding distance between the Four Thunders and their pursuers. Smiling Cat settled into the passenger side, swung her cyberdeck around into her lap, and gave them a Cheshire's grin.

"A beacon's on the move." She twisted to look smug at Tigers in the back, saving Dog from their boss's wrath. "So all we gotta do now is ditch these guys, and the plan's back on! Storm does her job, I do mine, and your boys' plot is saved after all."

"*Ha. Ha. Ha,*" the rigger's tinny voice rang out in the team comms. "*Cavaliers, here we come.*"

"See, boss?" Dog Emperor tried his best smile. "It'll all work out. Plus I got you this watch!"

Seven Resplendent Tigers didn't quite throw him out the back of the van for the scratched, bloodstained knock-off the adept offered—but he was tempted.

PAYING GIG, PART ONE

The last couple of years sure have been something, haven't they, chummers? "Paying Gig" is a story I started to put together not-too-far into lockdown, and like a lot of my stories do, it started to get away from me and turn into something more. Luckily, I ended up liking the something more, and leaned into it, and turned it into a pair of short stories that go together pretty well in my humble opinion, while also standing on their own as individual stories.

Part One here is a paying gig we don't usually see in Shadowrun*—a musician, doing what he does best. It's not a distraction for a heist, it's not the front for a wandering gang of burglar-assassins, it's not a guitar case full of six-shooters instead of a six-string, no. It's just a rocker rocking, all by his lonesome self, entertaining a room with charisma and finesse, by opening up and letting some music come out.*

Oh. Plus he's an ork.

—RRZ

Sojourner's had been a Los Angeles staple since 2040, when the eponymous rockergirl had retired her stage persona, shifted gears, and become something softer around the edges, more authentic, and more lived-in. For all that the brewery/coffee shop avoided the concrete-and-chrome flash of the original Sojourner, the place still seemed to have adopted her good luck.

It was still here four decades later, markets be damned, riots be damned, earthquakes be damned, fads be damned, and now, damn the Pueblo Corporate Council who collected their tax money. Run by her granddaughter now, still serving drinks day or night, Sojourner's was a quiet cornerstone for the up-and-comers, the wannabes, and the perpetual faintly underground sorts who loved to know a musician before they went mainstream.

Sojourner's was where talented young artists went to almost make it. Some caught the wave and rode it to bigger venues. Most faltered, fell, failed.

Tonight's would-be star had all the regulars murmuring to one another before he started, attentively silent while he played and sang. He was utterly alone on stage, just an ork, his guitar, a mic to sing into, the house's borrowed amp, and a place to sit. He was pinned to a humble wooden stool by the spotlight, settled in place by the eyes and ears of the crowd, and held there by his hunger for more. Letting out a long sigh, preparing himself, the ork grabbed a lazy handful of his shoulder-length steely-white hair and tugged most of it into a sloppy ponytail, suddenly a warrior-poet's topknot, strands out of his face as he prepared to begin.

Sojourner's had been a Los Angeles staple since 2040, and they'd never quite had an ork like Tommy Portland.

He was ork-tall, ork-fit, ork-tusked, but not quite ork-rough or ork-ugly. Some whispered snidely about metatype reduction surgeries, some put it off to good genes, others simply enjoyed the view. His backstory was pitch-perfect for orkish talent; a hardscrabble story of coming up the hard way in the elf-dominated Tír Tairngire. Safe-havened as a child (and thus named after his hometown), doing time as a youth, becoming a grizzled rocker's protégé while behind bars, and then turning his life around to try and turn his talent into an honest living. Rags to roots rocker riches, every young publicist's dream.

He wasn't bedecked in the classic orxploitation trappings, though, wasn't leaning hard on all the concrete-criminal stereotypes. Alone, that would've been fine, but he *also* wasn't giving them up for just the right look from any other archetype that audiences expected. No tight jeans and button-up Americana for the Orkountry look like Rattlesnake Smile favored, no subtle Western wear with a few token feathers for Native-chic like Wyldkat, no corporate casual business shirt with just-so rolled shirtsleeves and one button too many undone to get the swooning teen corpo-girls like VeePee. He wasn't head-to-toe denim and leather like the notoriously

Ancients'-affiliated Archfiends or countless other feathered-haired, made-up, glam rock acts.

No, he just *was*. Half-atop, half-leaning on Sojourner's worn stool, he wore a simple urban brawl team shirt with the Mountain Dragons logo softly glowing in augmented reality, worn-in blue jeans, canvas shoes, and off-the-shelf smartglasses. The stuff he walked down the street in, not out of some dressing room. He looked more like a grown-up skater than any sort of rock star, shadowrunner, or anything in between.

"How's it going, everybody? My name's Tommy. Thanks for coming out tonight."

As Tommy Portland's self-introduction continued, he showed only a faint Tír accent, and he didn't sneak in any Or'zet or Sperethiel; the way he talked was West Coast through and through, rather than leaning hard on just the Tír. He wasn't the Chrome Bard, the city of Portland's latest street poet. He wasn't a brooding, resentful, orkish stereotype either, he wasn't angry. Just like his look, his persona didn't quite fit what anyone expected of him. Portland was affable, flashing a boyish-bright smile as he also introduced Laina, his electric-acoustic smartguitar, to the audience and demanded she get half the credit and none of the blame for what they were about to hear.

The guitar might've been his first love, but there was no doubt she wasn't his favorite any more. As the crowd cracked grins and shared quiet chuckles, Tommy's eyes fell on the chestnut-haired elven woman he'd arrived with. Even as the spotlight, darkness, and music took his attention elsewhere, she barely tore her eyes off him. The elven beauty used his sticker-covered guitar case to save his seat, she wore a jacket clearly sized for him, and she mouthed every word to every song with all the perfection of someone who'd soaked up the lyrics and melodies by listening to endless hours of practice.

Her name was Loriel, and not a single soul in Sojourner's—except the young adept on stage—knew she was, honest-to-Buddha, an actual princess. She had magic, she had privilege, she had Peace Force training and experience, hermetic training from her momma and a daddy on the Council of Princes. But sitting there, that night, all she had was a boyfriend under the spotlight, a table full of pub grub she devoured and washed down with ice water, and a heart filled with pride.

There was a reason she was proud of him; his talent, once he got started, was undeniable. His nimble fingers danced on the strings of his smartguitar, his voice, as smoky and deep as one of Sojourner's dark malts, rang against walls that had heard four decades of hope and talent come and go.

He'd started the night lazily, casually, comfortably noodling about with his strings, seemingly just tuning. Idle strums turned into a nameless, shapeless, little hopscotch from note to note, an aimless meandering through sound, and then suddenly, opening his mouth, all the pieces fell into place and he breathed life into a *song*.

His opening piece was "Hallelujah," the century-old cover-artist's dream, the guitarist's rite of passage. It, and only it, Tommy hardly tinkered with. He just left it alone, loyal to the twencen version he'd decided felt right. Nothing else on his playlist was safe, though, because at Sojourner's you either *stuck* out or you *struck* out. For the rest of his playlist, he took songs and made them his own, ignored convention, ignored expectation, ignored cover-artist tradition. Laina's carbon fiber and mahogany frame adjusted for him, shifted, worked with her internal electronics, his wireless synth, and his dancing fingertips to create magic out of other people's classics.

He slowed down and twisted one of Maria Mercurial's classic rock-love hits, "Breathless," into a minor instead of major key, leaving half of the audience shifting uncomfortably in their seats as his guitar wailed eerily. He turned Johnny Banger's "I Do What I Want" punk classic into a song that spoke less of frenetic defiance and made it more of a call for help, the cry of someone fighting manic episodes and their own loss of control. The augmented-reality dracoform on his Mountain Dragons urban brawl shirt crawled and glowed as he leaped headfirst into the *Isabelle* Mercurial tune, "Dragonfire," her heaviest tune, about watching the devastation of Italy's GeMiTo sprawl during the draconic civil war. Next up was Sojourner's own hit, "Yet Untitled." He wasn't the first guitarist to come into her house and take a stab at honoring one of her tunes in front of her granddaughter, but he *was* the first to settle it in the middle of his playlist instead of putting it up on a pedestal as his opener or closer, which got him a smirk. Portland took CrimeTime's *Djoto* chart-topper, "Haven," and tweaked the lyrics just enough to make it a love song about CT's famous girlfriend, Tiffany Brackhaven, not a hate-song about her bigoted grandfather. His slapping hands and the ratta-tat-tat of his slide turned his guitar into a beat box, creating a backdrop for him to spit out Glock .50's poetic, street-brutal, hit "Curbstomp" with all the fire of the original piece.

Despite rumors of his prison mentor having been Rustbucket, infamous guitarist from the Fragging Unicorns—or *because* of those rumors?—Tommy didn't go for a single Unicorn rock tune. Maybe for the same reason—it would be too easy—he and his acousto-electric stayed away from traditional Tír Tairngire favorites like Darkvine adored. His whole set avoided the obvious picks, he veered nimbly away from what would've been the low-hanging fruit.

Instead, his final song of the night was an Orxanne smash hit, arguably *the* Orxanne smash hit, "Oakland Rage." During an infamously butch phase, she had released her hardest, roughest song ever, a novahot bass-thumping trog-rap war chant, a call to arms against General Saito's Imperial Marine invaders.

And this damn fool ork went entirely acoustic—no guitar trickery, no reverb or loop pedal, or anything, just using his synth and his amp for nothing but clean, pure, volume—and turned it into a motherfragging ballad.

We're from where the sun goes down
And everyone knew tusks run this town
We marched around with booted feet
We tagged everyone corner, we marked our streets.
When we had to, some Imp got domed,
And in the end, Orkland stayed home.

He'd taken "Oakland Rage" from the present tense to the past, adjusted almost every line, and shifted it into something mournful. He'd made it something resigned, something sweet and heavy and sad about the bloody gutters, split knuckles, and cracked skulls. He'd turned a bass-driven howl for war into a dirge for the fallen.

And, as the final haunting notes were dragged from the belly of his guitar, rang out, and faded, nobody knew just what the frag to make of it.

Nobody but his one-elf-audience, his only fan, the knockout with the green eyes, wearing his ork-sized synthleather jacket. Loriel Taylor whooped loud enough for everybody, lit the room with a smile that rivaled the spotlight, and cheered for her boyfriend with the gusto and zeal of the most fervent football hooligan or screaming, concert-going woo-girl.

The lights lifted. As Tommy drank in the sight of her and let out a spent sigh, everyone present understood he'd been playing for her, not for them, not for scouts, not even for Sojourner's at all.

"Thank you, everybody. G'night." He leaned into the mic one last time, then stood up.

His tired smile and the way she beamed up at him made it look like the whole thing had been a dare, a challenge, a calculated risk to just play what he wanted, how he wanted, while she had the best seat in the house.

The applause was confused at first, uncertain, sporadic. Sojourner's was something like a spurned lover. But as Tommy Portland lifted Laina and left the small stage, the response grew. Swelled. Rolled in like the waves from the Pacific. They couldn't deny that he'd done his job, and done it well.

His exhausted smile recharged and turned into a beacon for the whole room, tusks flashing as more and more of them gave him the glory he'd refused to leave on the table.

Sojourner's. There was nowhere else in the world *quite* like it—and that night, Tommy Portland called it home.

PAYING GIG, PART TWO

The second part of "Paying Gig" was actually the first mental image I had of it. I've had a certain bounty hunter I first wrote up almost as a joke, and who got more and more real-feeling the longer I thought about and wrote him, and my initial short-story idea was just to let this gunslinger loose. Everything that came before was just what he was interruptin'!

Chase is fun to write when I'm trying to capture an almost-satire (the way reality tv is) of that Western swagger Shadowrun *first edition leaned into a bit. Seattle was the "Wild West" in 2050, everyone wore a duster, and if your gaming group was like mine, lots of us tried to see who could get the highest, craziest initiative score.*

So this second half of the tale is about our boy Chase, everyone's favorite "Errant Knight" bounty hunter tridshow star, doing what he does, and doing it in Ares-approved style. His quarry in this piece, Loriel and Tommy Portland, stand on their own two feet just fine, I think, and there's a good bit more of them to come in a couple other places. The prey makes a hunt interesting, just like the hunter does, and these two make for a fun odd-couple.

—RRZ

Audience approval rolled and thundered within the confines of Sojourner's, a Los Angeles watering hole with a reputation for up-and-coming musicians. More than one scout was in the crowd, more than one media department kept a keen eye through drones flitting about or sponsored hard-wirings straight into Sojourner's systems. More than one person had stepped off the stage at Sojourner's and right into something better and brighter.

Chase didn't give a cowpoke's damn about any of it. He *had* his gig, and it wasn't music. He *had* his own whirring spy drones, and didn't need anyone else's. He *had* his fame and was, truth be told, a little too used to it.

He enjoyed, briefly, the novelty of not being the center of attention, but the rest of the night's performance was lost on him. He wasn't the world's biggest music fan, and both country and rock had begun to grate on his nerves, in particular, after a decade of Ares force-feeding him both as part of their standard fare.

Besides, he was a performer himself. Working on his tenth season as *Chase: Errant Knight*, the gunslinger was accustomed to eyes aplenty, and he was carefully maintained and manicured, like a lawn, to be just exactly what fans of the show expected.

He was an Americana-Western blend custom-tailored to appeal to CAS, UCAS, and several NANner states alike. He was every bit as whip-thin and sharp as an elf, a cowboy, or an elven cowboy ought to be; a tall drink of water, straight up and down. He wore tight jeans, a button-up denim shirt with the sleeves rolled just so, a leather vest begging for some sort of badge, and a leather hat *literally* made for trid-appeal and to accentuate his handsome features. He was decked out, head to toe, in subtle, brand-name armor, and was topped off with tactical accessories Ares wanted him to sell.

Chase was a walking stereotype. He was iconic. He was so recognizably himself he had people dress up as him for Halloween and at corp-sponsored fan conventions. There was a whole *show* Lone Star had made to copy him and his style. He wasn't a poseur, he was an *archetype*, in all the ways Tommy Portland—the yahoo on stage—wasn't.

Tommy Portland was some nobody, with nobody's style. An ork from up north, come down to sunny L.A. to turn his life around and make a living with his guitar and blah-blibbity-blah-blah-blah, Chase didn't get paid to care. The guitarist just wore an urban brawl t-shirt, no-frill jeans, plain canvas shoes, and assortment of lucky bracelets and a few bits of similar claptrap woven into his long, silver-white hair. He wasn't ugly for his metatype, but the best-looking thing about him (and probably the most expensive thing he owned) was the carbon-fiber and wood hybrid in his lap, a smartguitar. The ork had just wrapped up an electro-acoustic set, and Chase had sat through the audience murmuring, *ooh*ing and *aah*ing, and now applauding. He was getting impatient.

Unfortunately for Tommy and his little elven girlfriend, Chase was on the clock. The registry was clear on Tommy needing to be taken down, but it didn't say anything about a bounty on the elf woman, there wasn't money on the barrel for other known accomplices. "Loriel," the file said her name was, the gal in the front row, wearing Tommy Portland's ork-big armored jacket, with the shining smile and the warm chestnut hair. She didn't have a bounty or a list of crimes against her. It was just her bad luck to be with a guy that *did*.

Chase had work to do. A simple pick-up. Down the ork, take the ork, deliver the ork to some sour-faced elf that wanted him. The girl would, Chase hoped, mostly stay out of the way.

A bounty hunter's work is never *really* done, even a celebrity one. He was between regular seasons, but there were always holiday specials that needed action sequences, small-game hunts for petty criminals that could give good footage, and contractual obligations for product placement.

Tonight, Chase stood at the far end of Sojourner's bar, with one eye on the ork, and the other—thanks to his augmented-reality contacts—on the ork's own AR overlay.

> <CHASE: ERRANT KNIGHT IS BROUGHT TO YOU BY ARES LITELENS!
>
> LITELENS SOFTWARE IS A REVOLUTIONARY STEP FORWARD IN SMARTGOGGLE, SMARTGLASS, AND SMARTCONTACT TECHNOLOGY, SYNCING UP YOUR AUGMENTED EYEWARE, YOUR FIREARM, AND YOUR LIFESTYLE MORE EFFICIENTLY THAN EVER BEFORE!
>
> LITELENS: WHY COMPROMISE WHEN CLARITY IS ON THE LINE?>

Chase saw the animated Mountain Dragons logo, a Western Drake crawling across the ork's torso. He saw the icon for the young musician's own AR-glasses, saw the ork's projected cone-of-vision was squarely on his gal-pal, then slid over to his guitar as he packed it away. Chase saw a string of alerts as pop-ups announced new comments tagging and following Tommy Portland on MeFeed.

And Chase saw, most of all, Tommy's P2.1 score, that aggregate metric of his popularity, the eyes on him, his number of followers, his footprint. It was that score that mattered to Chase. It was that score that would tell him just when to strike.

Tommy's bounty wasn't worth writing home about. It was some secondhand gig, a Northwest heavy hitter who had street channels gunning for the kid, too, but also an official government-sanctioned arrest request. A couple grand wasn't enough to get Chase's attention, or his producers'.

But the drift-in media buzz *Chase: Errant Knight* might get from going after an up-and-coming minor social media star, instead of just some *other* random orkish street tough? *That* made it worth the quick hunt. Chase's job wasn't about bounties and bullets, not really; it was about product placement—and product placement needed ratings.

Chase wasn't here to grab Tommy Portland. He was here to hijack the guy's social media spike.

So as the ork's 2.1 numbers plateaued, Chase tore his gaze away to down the last of his bitter Southern Gentleman dark stout, a Sojourner classic. For a half-assed bar/coffee-house combo named after some old rockergirl, they made a decent beer, he had to give 'em that.

He flicked his fingers a few times and handled his AR tab, shucking off the order and a 1,000% tip to his Ares expense account. He let out a sigh, rolled his shoulders and neck to work out a kink, and looked back at Tommy P while steadying his breathing.

He saw the ork's P-score start to dip for a second on the ticker, another, a third. That was it. They'd peaked.

Time to draw 'em back in.

Chase slid through the crowd as Portland and his tusk-bunny girlfriend in that oversized coat shared a kiss, then the ork thirstily gulped down the Wanderlust pale ale—an irritated flick of his eyes sent a pop-up advertisement and a comfortably high review rating sliding *out* of Chase's field of vision—that she had saved for him.

Chase came up in front of Tommy Portland, and half to-the-side, half-behind, his elf. The cowboy stopped when his Ares *TacSmart* rangefinder subroutines told him he was a comfortably-close 3.25 meters away.

"Tommy Portland!"

Chase was an elf, but a loud one. His lungs might not stack up compared to a broad-chested, trained singer, but he could hold his own in the volume department. He'd been trained in what Ares called the command voice, and he used it well. He had ten seasons of practice.

There was no mistaking it for an excited audience member, or as anything *but* a challenge and a threat. Heads turned. Chairs scraped. People started to move, a nervous herd.

Chase's booted feet slid a little apart and he squared off. He blinked twice to zoom in his smartlenses for a nice close-up shot as the ork gave him a confused look, then it slowly dawned into awful realization.

"I'm callin' you out!"

The drifting herd of citizenry turned into a stampede as the situation became tridshow-clear to them.

Chase's voice rang with Thunderbird's own fury as his hand hovered just off the grip of his Ares Carnivore revolver. The elf was an adept, and he leaned heavily on that power in times like this. His mentor spirit, Thunderbird, spread wings as big as the Texas sky and spoke with a voice like all nature's fury. His patron liked challenges. His patron liked stare-downs. His patron liked pride. There was a ritual to it, the glare, the call-out, the posturing. Chase filled his belly with supernatural talent and Thunderbird's favor, and he gave Portland a half-second to let the fear sink in.

But only a half-second.

Chase's elven quick-draw was, of course, flawless. He'd practiced it for ten seasons, after all, he had *literally* written a book on it, and he had an adept's flair for perfection. His hip cocked just so, he leaned back to shift the angle of his body and clear the muzzle a hair faster, his right hand barely twisted, his left hand slapped the hammer back, his gun barely lifted, and in the *exact* moment the muzzle cleared the leather, he fired, held the trigger down, let the muzzle flip help his off-hand cock the hammer again, and got off a second shot. A double-tap with a hand-cannon revolver, all in the blink of an eye. Better than any normal human. The Fastest Gun In The UCAS, according to his season three ad campaign.

<CHASE: ERRANT KNIGHT IS BROUGHT TO YOU BY THE ARES CARNIVORE LINE OF TACTICAL AND HUNTING REVOLVERS!

NOW WITH A CRISPER TRIGGER ACTION, SHORTER HAMMER STROKE, AND INTEGRAL RECOIL REDUCTION PORTS! YOU NEED FOLLOW-UP SHOTS LESS THAN EVER WITH THIS BIG-BORE BAD BOY...

BUT WOULDN'T YOU RATHER HAVE THE CAPABILITY AND NOT NEED IT, THAN NEED THE CAPABILITY AND NOT HAVE IT? THERE ISN'T A TROLL OR A BEAR THE CARNIVORE CAN'T BEAT!

THE ARES CARNIVORE: BECAUSE BIGGER REALLY IS BETTER!>

Tommy Portland took both shots square in the dracoform AR-crawling across his t-shirt, a pair to the ten-ring, dead center of his chest. If he'd been a paper target, the holes would've been touching. He fell backward like he'd been mule-kicked, all the air blasted from him, and with, Chase assumed, a rib or two being worse for the wear.

Ork or not, the Ares Carnivore was the not-fragging-around gun. When you shot someone, they dropped.

The ork wasn't a paper target, though, and there was no ragged hole. No bloody ones, either. For tonight's half-assed episode Chase was just packing gel rounds, inasmuch as there was "just" anything when it was loaded into a Carnivore.

That should've been it. Problem solved. Ork pole-axed, right? Time to flash the smile and credentials, maybe toss out an AR autograph or two, haul him outside, and go get paid. The elven gal, Loriel, should've been shooed away, should've been cowed by some AR spam, should've been sent packing when she recognized that the star of *Chase: Errant Knight* had gunned down her betusked boytoy.

But no. The problem wasn't Tommy Portland, as it turned out. The problem was the girlfriend. Chase knew the sound of an Ares Light Fire by heart, but was surprised—genuinely surprised, that hadn't happened since *maybe* season two!—by the immediate return fire, since he hadn't *seen* the gun at all!

A pair of smoking holes and muzzle flashes blasted through the lining of her ork-sized synthleather coat as she fired at him *through* it, gun snug against her side, hidden by the armorjack. The gal must've seen him coming, kept her head, and tucked the muzzle right in a gap between armor plates. Her aim was high—way high—but that could've been to keep from hitting someone in the panicking crowd more than sloppiness. Credit where it's due, she was clever.

A little integrally-suppressed small caliber fire wasn't going to stop *Chase: Errant Knight* easily, but the elven woman seemed to know that, so "easily" didn't seem to be part of her plan. Even as Chase was reflexively ducking from the first sloppy-quick pair of shots, the girl twisted—reluctantly tearing her gaze away from her still-falling beau—and raised her Light Fire fully and properly. Loriel slid into a textbook-accurate, modern tactical shooter's stance and squared off against Chase's classically, cinematically, old-school gunslinger pose.

Chase's arm straightened and he lifted the gun to eye level, lining up his LiteLens-emblazoned smartlink pip, the big front sight blade of his Carnivore, and his target. He thumbed back the hammer for a lighter trigger pull—and for effect—instead of relying on the wheelgun's double-action innards.

Nice and slow. Nice and smooth. Nice and dramatic. Thunderbird spread his wings.

The pair of elves eyed each other, her over her black, polymer, light tactical piece, him down the long barrel of his brushed chrome and wooden-handled moose-killer monstrosity.

"Now, miss, I surely do appreciate your fine taste in Ares firearms." Chase let his drawl shine through just like the producers loved. Thunderbird backed his play, and he stared her down as hard as he could. "But even if you are outgunned, there ain't no Ares in the world that's a *toy*, so your Light Fire, well, I'd really rather you point it somewhere else, ma'a—"

Chase's voice caught in his throat as his smartlenses took her in and projected tactical threat displays—tagging the firearm and helpfully pointing out it was pointed in an unsafe direction, spotting the collapsible baton she had on her hip, finding the armor weave in the bulky jacket she wore—but it wasn't his contacts that saw it.

It was Chase himself, and Thunderbird's keen eyes, better than any falcon or *every* falcon in the world, that made out two things; both of them problems.

First off, Loriel-the-elf, who Chase had no meaningful record on, was clearly *rippling* with arcane power. She was sustaining some sort of mojo, some slight blur lingered around her hands and her hazel eyes, some augmentation that helped explain her uncanny accuracy. That wasn't great, but it wasn't insurmountable, it just shifted the balance of power a little closer to fair.

More of a problem, though? She wasn't just wearing the ork-sized jacket to keep off the cold, wasn't just wearing it for luck, for tradition, no, nor for cuteness' sake. As she stood, now, body bladed and gun held on him, Chase saw the bump in her belly.

She was wearing Tommy Portland's jacket because the mass of it helped hide, and helped *protect*, her pregnancy-swollen stomach.

Chase blinked, uncertain for the first time in *several* seasons. Gel rounds or not, his momma hadn't raised him to shoot some *pregnant* lady. He clicked his wheelgun's huge hammer back down, carefully.

"Ma'am? Whoa. Okay. All right, listen," he began again. His Carnivore twirled once around his trigger finger and he reversed it. He kept his long, nimble finger tucked into the reversed trigger guard, though. He was ready for a road-agent's spin if he was gonna need it, but for now, he had his left hand splayed and open and harmless-looking, and his right holding the wheelgun pointed entirely the wrong way.

Time to defuse. Quickly. His drawl was a little less thick, his tone a hair more earnest. Chase was being himself, not his stage persona. "Ma'am, now, let's think about this before the situation gets ou—"

She shot him. *Repeatedly.*

The Light Fire coughed and spat, uncannily muted gunshots muffled terrifically by Ares Arms' innovative system of integrated baffles and spacers. She advanced as she shot, another page right out of the textbook, her upper body a stable weapons platform—arm, arm, shoulders, a flawless triangle held steady and on-target—as her lower body moved her at him and to his left at a smooth 45-degree angle.

Chase's denim was armored, of course, and he was blessed with Thunderbird's own speed, but she was *good*, and Ares *did* make a fine firearm.

He got tagged twice before he made it to the bar, then two more times as he was vaulting up and over. His earbuds helped him count the shots, projected the data onto his LiteLens smartcontacts, and he cussed under his breath. Four shots, for four hits. *Damn*. Those initial pair of misses, the warning shots through her own coat, were the odd men out.

Even worse, two of the flurry—nope, three—had gotten through his armor and drawn blood. Chase gritted his teeth and a flick of his gaze shoved aside his suddenly-urgent DocWagon alerts. Two early misses with the through-the-jacket trick, four shots now. That meant she was down six rounds in a sixteen-round mag. Okay. Chase could work with that.

"Tommy? Baby?" the elven woman called out in between gunshots. "We gotta move, hon!"

Shots seven and eight sent pieces of the bar and shards of glass flying around Chase's head, pinning him in place. It was all he could do to angle his Carnivore and, looking through its smartgun as the data was piped to his LiteLenses, watch his prey. There was no way Chase could manage a shot at this awkward angle, though. Not without either having a cyberarm or needing one very quickly; the Carnivore *was* the not-fragging-around gun, but that meant it was hell on your wrist if you got sloppy.

Loriel fired again, and shot nine busted a bottle, too close. She wasn't interested in letting him up. For a standard autopistol, she was managing pretty serious suppressive fire.

"Mmnghn..." Chase's smartgun showed him Tommy struggling to his feet, shaking his head and wincing, then balling his hands into fists as he straightened. He had on an ugly, angry face. "Ugh! M'gonna frag that daisy-eater up so bad—"

"Tommy!" Shot ten, and her voice went harsh as glass showered over Chase. Loriel kept angling, kept sidestepping, had been sliding toward the door the whole time.

"Sorry! Sorry!" The orkish singer half-croaked it out, grabbing his beloved guitar case. "I mean 'elf,' not 'daisy-eater,' baby. Didn't mean to be racis—"

"Thomas *motherfragging* Portland, will you *please* just get your ass outside?!"

The ork made a face but staggered toward the door.

Shot eleven and shot twelve spat out. Chase grimaced as wood and glass and booze fell all around him, and his smartgun followed them toward the door. Loriel's movements were textbook-precise, as smooth and certain as if she had skillwires installed. Portland's were stiff, angry, like an alley cat as offended as it was hurt.

Shot thirteen. Fourteen. She was close to running dry. Chase tensed up and got his boots under him, ready in a low crouch.

Problem was, she never emptied the gun and gave him the chance. She had two shots left in the magazine as she shoved her ork out the door, followed, and they turned to run.

Chase snarled in equal parts pain and anger as Thunderbird lifted him up and over the bar, leaving a trail of blood on Sojourner's polished wood. He lurched after them gamely, but by the time he shoulder-checked the door open and raised his Carnivore to sweep the lot, he saw her, yes, but saw her leaning out the passenger window of a pick-up, her Light Fire still trained on him.

Neither of them fired, so Chase blinked and zoomed his contacts as he limped to his own waiting truck. This week's set of wheels were an Epoch, a panzer pretending to be a pick-up.

<CHASE: ERRANT KNIGHT IS BROUGHT TO YOU BY THE ARES EPOCH.

DOESN'T YOUR BUSINESS, YOUR CARGO, OR YOUR FAMILY DESERVE THE SPEED OF A TOP BRAND TRUCK, BUT THE SECURITY AND RELIABILITY OF A ROADMASTER? THEY DESERVE THE BEST. SHOW THEM YOU'VE GOT IT.

IT'S TIME FOR SOMETHING NEW. IT'S TIME…FOR THE ARES EPOCH!>

Chase climbed into the up-armored cab of his streetfighting pick-up (that held the soul of a tactical urban assault vehicle) and flashed a feral grin. His was a broad-faced machine with a hybrid-diesel V8 that packed hundreds of horses under the hood and torque for days. It was a juggernaut. There wasn't a civilian vehicle on the streets of L.A. that could stop his Epoch, Ares had made sure of it. Its crash bars and sheer mass would let him barrel *through* anything he couldn't go *over* or *around*.

But the news wasn't all good.

Chase's commlink searched up make and model information he stole from that lens-enhanced glimpse of the couple's truck. Tommy Portland's two-bit criminal record scrolled by again, reminding Chase of his history as a wheelman.

Both were problems, especially since the orkish roots-rocker and his elven protector were in an Andalusian Manticore. The Manticore Sport was the company's top-end model, their most popular and their most customizable. It was a bootlegger or a street racer's dream, popularized by rally car racers and the Tír action-tridshow *Dare*, where the brave border guard patrol of D-squad routinely used their Manticores to run down smugglers, poachers, and go-gangers.

If someone knew how to drive it, it was a hell of a thing to drive, and every record made it look like Tommy P was as comfortable with a steering wheel as he'd been with a guitar.

Still, hell if Chase wasn't gonna try.

As the Manticore squealed out of the parking lot, his Epoch rumbled after it. Chase clipped the corner of a parked Americar and didn't notice until external sensors alerted him to it. He hopped the curb, taking a tighter exit corner than Tommy had, and even the truck's sensors didn't register it. There was no point in *having* all this horsepower if you weren't going to *use* it, right?

Production hadn't up-gunned his Epoch, though, so there was nothing Chase could do to stop the Andalusian getaway except ram it, and that was gonna be a tough sell. The good news was that the Manticore's truck bed didn't seem to be filled with a machine gun or—considering the Epoch he drove—rocket launcher or anything, so Chase wasn't too worried about his safety. His *speed*, yes, his *physical well-being*, not in the slightest.

The Manticore increased its lead on every straightaway, a lighter truck rocketing through late-night traffic with reckless abandon. Chase made up for it by traveling in *entirely* a straight line every time he could, clipping and brushing aside lighter cars and only thinking about the ratings he was racking up, not the damages. Damages were a producer's problem. Excitement was Chase's gig.

In the end, it wasn't the Epoch *or* the Manticore that made the difference. It was Loriel. Chase saw her twist in the seat, slide the old Manticore's back window open, and glare his way as he barely kept line-of-sight and the Manticore rounded a corner. It wasn't an Ares Light Fire she pointed, though, it was a slender wand, mahogany flashing the same color as her hair for an instant, then a ripple of light came Chase's way just as he began to turn.

His Epoch didn't turn, though, wheel be damned. He was on a ramp, suddenly, a glowing, red-white, platform of shimmering light and pure mana, a child's toy-car playset writ large. Large enough to send the Epoch skittering against it, sparks flying, in a straight line; not around the corner and after the Manticore, just straight ahead, past the intersection, until finally the mass of his huge Ares truck broke the mana-construct.

"Well, frag." Chase kicked the burly vehicle into reverse and cast a longing stare as Tommy P's bounty—and his gunslinging, spellslinging girlfriend—vanished into the distance. With that momentum lost, there was no catching up to them. He was a powerlifter chasing a track-and-field star.

"Next episode," he sighed as his engine loosed a disappointed snarl, then transitioned back from diesel to electric mode. Chase tapped at the console, pulling up another case. Tommy Portland and his badass girl were someone else's problem now. Frag 'em, anyways. He could blame the chase on his producers, too, they'd given him too much truck for the SoCal streets.

"There's always another gig."

VECTOR

Chummer, Sprawl Gangers *was gonna be great. One of the things I did for the unfortunately-aborted skirmish-scale wargame was flesh out some gangs by statting up some unique characters to go into one gang or another.*

One I really loved was Bushido Blitz. He was my "iconic Ancients member" that spun out of my control and turned into a dude I started to sneak into other fiction, long after Sprawl Gangers *was consigned to the dustbin. Blitz's first appearance was actually a reveal that his momma was pregnant, back in the* Shadowrun Returns *anthology (which is also where readers first "met" Belial, the same way)!*

Canny readers will, as always, notice a few OTHER characters they know, too, all spun together in my Rustyweb. Lots of my characters know one another, or know someone's sibling, or had a job with (or against!) each other, or get a plan ruined by someone else's frag-up halfway across town...you name it. In my world, the shadows are big enough to have room for everybody, but the shadows are small enough that everyone knows everyone, too!

—RRZ

The good news was Blitz was on his rugged Harley Scorpion brawl-bike, wind in his hair, rolling down the street at a good fifty-five, sixty kilometers per hour.

The bad news was Blitz wasn't really *on* his bike, or rather, his bike wasn't really on the street. He was roaring down the street sideways, at a psycho-ganger's pleasure.

His trusty Harley was pierced through—front wheel and back, speared cleanly—by the sharpened front forks of a dumpster truck. The beast was an armored-up war-wagon customized by the Seven-7 Boys and now being used, right this very second, to defend their claim on turf, long-held, here at the corner of Seventh Street SE and Seventh Avenue SE.

The Seven-7s didn't hold a lot of turf, but what they had, they were apparently pretty determined to hold onto.

So Blitz and his Ancients—all gleaming chrome and black leather, green hair and faded denim, elven superiority and street-tough certainty—had what you could call a motherfraggin' *fight* on their hands. They'd expected a scrap. A turf war always meant a scrap, sure. Blitz wasn't stupid, he'd brought his boys and girls in hard, fast, brutal. The usual.

He'd dueled a few Seven-7s, knocked a couple off their bikes, all that fun stuff. But then he'd gotten t-boned by a fraggin' *garbage truck* that had only kept from rolling right over him and his Scorpion by the grace of laughing, dark gods and the unfeasible accuracy of sharpened front forks. So this was surely a fight, not just a scrap. If things kept up, it might even turn into a battle.

Battles were bad news.

"Welp," he managed to grunt, several heartbeats *after* the impact of the side-on crash had taken the wind out of him, after his hair had been ruined by his skull spiderwebbing the windshield, after he'd realized his predicament and looked up to see Lucky, the manic, face-painted leader of the Seven-7s crowing obscenities at him from the driver's seat.

"Frag you, too." Blitz rolled the throttle with one hand—fat tires long since lifted clear of the street, nothing happening but the chunky engine's low-throated growl—and flipped the bird with his other hand. Then he reached down to the mag-clamps on his bike, checked that his sword was snug on his belt, and started climbing.

The good news was Blitz was a natural at climbing stuff. Well, an augmented natural, at any rate. He'd always been fairly fit and athletic, sure, and his elven build—long arms, narrow hips—helped, but what also helped was the work of every Ancients-sanctioned street doc in Puyallup, and a few in Portland during an eye-opening, eye-rolling trip to "the motherland." Blitz had been tuned up. He had a balance augmenter, the raw physicality of a suprathryoid upgrade, all sorts of toned and augmented muscles. "Blitz" was half of his street name, and it came in part from his strength, his speed, his aggression in a fight. Climbing was a snap, even given the, to put it mildly, stressful circumstances (what with climbing free of his twice-impaled, dying Harley while pinned to the front of an up-armored dump truck driven by a combat-drug-high maniac bent on killing you).

So, good news, he climbed just fine.

The bad news was Blitz made it all nimbly-pimbly up and over the driver's area and into the back; and landed in the rear of the dumpster truck, which had four Seven-7's in it, *also* hyped up on combat meth, and taking turns shooting at his brother and sister Ancients out the back of the war-wagon.

"Oh." Blitz slide his feet apart a little, checking his balance after his not-quite-parkour tumble and landing. "*Hoi*, chummers."

He let one hand slip down to the matte black hilt of his matte black sword—a Tír-issue combat katana, mono-edged, lethal as all get-out—but lifted the other hand as a conversation started.

"Hang one just a second here," he said, holding out his pointer finger. "Let's not be hasty."

From that finger dangled the pin of a grenade.

Blitz's big Harley engine blew up, with a Tír-issued grenade mag-clamped snug up against the "gas" section of the hybrid engine. The front end of the dumpster-truck vanished in a fireball. The rear end, though, plated in steel and protected by the huge truck's sturdy engine block and formerly-safety-rated passenger compartment, just *heaved* and lurched and then skidded, sparks flying, to a stop up against an unlucky building.

Blitz kept his footing during all of that, through the grace of street augs and elven finesse. The rest of them didn't, the Seven-7s back there with him, orks and humans all. They tumbled down together, a tangled mass of angry limbs, bristling with street-ready weapons and aggression.

He reached down with just his left hand and thumbed the *tsuba* of his combat katana, sliding it a few centimeters out of the polymer tactical *saya*, but otherwise taking no aggressive actions toward them. His right hand was well clear of the weapon, still waiting. Still gentle.

"Be certain," Blitz said softly.

He gave the Seven-7s a second to rethink things as they groaned, shook their heads, and clambered to their feet. He gave them a chance to realize their prized defensive machine, their mighty war-truck, was down and out. A chance to remember that Lucky Sevens, their boss, had died with it. A chance to surrender.

The four of them didn't take that chance. They roared upright and began to charge him, one with a baseball bat, one a fire axe, one a long chain with a cinder block tangled in the end, and the last with a pair of claw hammers. In close. Dirty work. Brutal tools.

Blitz finally brought his right hand down to the hilt of his sword and exhaled, eyes going half-closed.

He centered himself.

He *flowed*.

An instant later, he was in the back of the truck's "cargo" bed instead of the front of it, and every one of the Seven-7s was behind him. In pieces. Limbs off, a head severed, a torso sliced diagonally from shoulder to hip, a bloody, meaty, mess, stewing together in the bottom of the truck.

Their choice. Their loss.

Blitz flicked his blade clean and sheathed it, lifting the *saya* to meet it and click it home. The "Blitz" largely came from his strength and quickness, but it was only half of his street name. Most of the Ancients called him "Bushido Blitz" properly. Because of the sword. Because of how he used it. Because he was an adept, too, not just a Puyallup-gutter razorboy. He was Barrens, but he was more than Barrens. He was an Ancient, but he was more than an Ancient. He was an elf, but he was more than an elf.

He was a true street samurai.

He leaped up the side of the truck and balanced there smoothly, then stuck his fist in the air with a bellow.

"Ancients Forever!" he roared, taking in the street's bloody views.

"*Ancients Forever*!" It came back to him, echoed through a dozen smoke-raw throats, a war-cry, a rally, a rock-star chorus.

He watched the rest of the fight—and it wasn't much of one—from that elevated perch, standing up atop the rear walls of the dumpster-truck-turned-war-wagon. Rather, he *posed*, really, back-lit by the full moon and neon of nearby signs, and well aware of it; long, dark hair free from his topknot and blowing in the wind, feet together, one hand resting on the hilt of his sword, watching his brothers and sisters clean up the Seven-7s that remained.

Belial, the Seattle Ancients leader, had taught him the importance of a good pose, just like the importance of letting the gang clean up fights instead of the officer-champion always wading in.

Bushido Blitz raised his voice as the squealing tires died down, the staccato bursts of gunfire tapered off, the war-screams dwindled. In the near-silence of a finishing fight, it's important for a leader to grab the reins.

"Standard rules, boys and ghouls." He gave his street-rat followers a smile alongside the shout, Seattle-born and Seattle-bred, all of them. The Tír-born Ancients mostly ran with Rook. "You keep what you kill. Take or break weapons, for personal use or cash-in at the clubhouse! You know our street docs are open for organs and augs! Drugs are fun, but save 'em for later. Prizes are ears and tusks taken as appropriate."

His smile vanished. It wasn't all fun and games.

"But remember, no elves. If they're down, help 'em back up. They get to quit, or they get to try and join us. They're our kin. Treat 'em right."

He hopped down from the top of the ruined truck, lightly, nimbly, effortlessly. Standing at eye level with his bloodthirsty mob, he dared any of them to challenge that rule.

They knew better. Most scattered, off to deal with prisoners, check on brothers and sisters, loot and scoot.

One did approach, though. Squire. She'd been one of their leader Belial's favorites when she was just a kid, something like his mascot, good luck charm, and assistant all rolled into one. She'd followed the burly, brawny, charismatic rockerboy around Seattle for years, carrying his huge sword, toting his guitar, taking care of his bike. She wasn't just a hanger-on any more, though, wasn't just "some kid" who rolled with the Ancients and fawned over their boss, no; she'd earned her stripes, spilled her fair share of blood, and come up through the ranks the messy way. The hard way. The right way. Blitz loved her, as more than just a sister Ancient.

She had a pair of neon stripes on her face tonight, warpaint, with a splash of Seven-7 blood turning the perfect picture of her all asymmetrical and postmodern.

"Good night." Squire flashed a white-toothed smile.

"Good fight." BB nodded back, and they fist-bumped.

"Bummer about your wheels, though." She nodded past him to the smoking wreckage of the dumptruck's front-end. "She did you good. You had her for a while, yeah?"

"Yeah." Years of hard road, through all kinds of fights. Blitz sighed. "But I'll find something."

"You better, and you know I've got your back if you need a hand. But you know the rules." Squire lifted an eyebrow, concerned.

Every Ancient knew the rules. Not just tonight's rules, not just Bushido Blitz's rules for his personal retinue, his pack, his band of street-warriors, no. *The Rules.*

Chief among them was "you ride." Everybody. No matter your rank, no matter your years of service, no matter your role, where you were from, or how good you were at what you did. If you're an Ancient, you ride. The Ancients were the best go-gang in the world, and every single member had to be ready, willing, and able to prove it. To show it. To ride fast, hard, straight, and true. To *ride.*

"I'll find something." Blitz met her gaze and tried to make his nod reassuring.

She wasn't a rat. She wasn't a snitch. She loved him, as more than just a brother Ancient. But she *was* an Ancient, through and through. She'd been raised in the gang, every bit as much as Blitz had. Gasoline was in her blood, headlights instead of stars were in her eyes, and she wasn't happy unless her ears were filled with roaring engines, gunfire, or the wail of an electric guitar; preferably two out of three. She lived by the rules, and someday she'd die—happily—by the rules. She needed him to do the same.

Squire held the eye contact long enough to show she was worried, but gave Blitz a sliver of a smile and a half-mumbled, "I'm sure you will," before turning to go.

She helped out, keeping Ancients on-track when it came to their squabbles over who'd gotten what kill, disputes over what loot they got to keep, and keeping the gang's combat mages focused on healing hurt enemy elves, not just their brothers and sisters, now that the fight was over. Squire was a good egg. She was also one of the Ancients' best at talking up potential new members, getting folks to ditch their old colors and join the winning side.

She already had one fresh new convert shaking up an acid-green paint can and spraying *ANCIENTS FOREVER* on a wall, right over their old Seven-7 tag.

Blitz left her to it. He *did* know the rules. He had one day to get some wheels back under him.

More than that, though, Bushido Blitz was *Bushido Blitz*. He wasn't going to just go to some dealership and lay down some nuyen. He wasn't going to saunter into a showroom and leave on some gleaming corporate-approved ride, no. He'd had his Harley for years, had it customized, tweaked, rigged up just right. He'd ridden it hard, treated it well, made it his own. Every Ancient did. You didn't stay the world's premier go-gang by not worrying about the *go*. Nobody showed up with a store-bought bike, any more than they'd stroll into Ancients turf in clean new denims and leathers, sporting some Ancients-brand streetwear fresh off the rack in their local mall.

No, no. Street-legal was for noobs. Bushido Blitz was second-generation, Ancient-born and bred, child of Ancient heroes, and Belial's right-hand elf on the mean Puyallup streets. With great reputation came great expectation. He had a day to get a new bike, but that new bike had to be impressive.

The good news was he had options.

The bad news was he had to think big.

He could have just found another gang and swiped something. He might have rolled up to a clubhouse tomorrow atop a troll-sized chopper, still wearing the blood of a Spike or two, or with a massive troll-skull mounted on the handlebars.

He might have called in favors from the intricate webs he'd spent literally his whole life spinning across Seattle, networking, keeping track of blood feuds, honor debts, and street reps. He knew people. He knew people who knew people. Some up-and-comer gang the Ancients had sponsored would *love* to brag about hooking him up with new wheels, some Princes of the Blood would be eager to get back in the Ancients' good graces by handing over a customized racer, some young Ancient would fall all over themselves to try and boost him a ride.

He even thought about calling Scout. An ex. Scout-Who-Kills-Six-Times, the swaggering First Nations lieutenant, the ganger who'd turned urban brawl superstar for a night and scored a half-dozen kills in a league-sanctioned match. They'd had some good times, and Blitz had rigged together a nice ride for Scout, back in the day. He could call him. He could cash in chips, ask for the bike back, and be back on the streets in no time.

But no, BB wanted something *special.*

So he called his mom.

The streets had called her Comet for decades now. The 2040s had been a heady time, the gang had been in its infancy, and she'd been there; everything had been grimy and new, from people growing into their metatypes to the broader dispersal of street magic, from changes to augmentations to the steadying of megacorporations and rise of brutal, magnificent, new gangs.

And Comet had been there for it all, along with her partner, Blitzen. Slinging combat magic from the back of her man's bike, one arm around him and the other flinging a fireball or worse. They'd left scars on their foes, skid marks on the city's streets, and an indelible mark on the young Ancients gang.

Then he'd died. Bushido Blitz's father, Blitzen—his namesake—had given his life to protect Green Lucifer, the Tír-born lieutenant, from a Tír-backed assassination attempt. Thirty years ago, the elven assassin Blackwing had tried to murder Lucifer and ended up killing Blitzen instead. The gang had been tangled up in Tír bulldrek every since, for better or worse.

Green Lucifer was Belial's father.

Blackwing was Rook's.

Blitzen was Blitz's.

And now here they were, the three of them, leading the gang.

Rook kept one foot in the Tír, where his father was now a Prince. He was the Ancients' pipeline to the lucrative West Coast run, their hook-up to the Peace Force and their "lost" weaponry, their connection to all things Tír Tairngire and beyond.

Bushido Blitz kept the Seattle Ancients grounded in *Seattle,* he and the other old guard, like the venerable Sting, kept them tied to Puyallup especially, and the elven ghettoes of Tarislar in particular. He kept them legit. Kept them real. Kept them living and free, not slaves to the elven fascists.

And Belial, their Seattle leader, swayed from side to side; wanting to stay street-lethal, but also wanting the edge the Tír connection gave them. He reported to his father, Green Lucifer, the gang's West Coast captain, but before he did so, Belial always listened to his angels and devils, he kept Rook on one shoulder and Blitz on his other.

The more the gang drifted away from the local streets, the more Blitz's mom had drifted away from the day-to-day gang life. It had been years since she'd cast a spell in anger. She didn't have to fight any more, so she didn't. There were always new kids for that, always new generations, always bright-eyed young elves with headlights in their eyes and electric guitars in their ears. She coached them, now, taught them, mentored them. She'd lost a little of her fire when BB's dad had been taken from her. She was, maybe, the Seattle chapter's strongest living combat mage. She wasn't much for the "combat" any more, that's all. She was wiser. She was softer. She was sadder.

But still, she was an Ancient. Through and through. She might not go out of her way to get bloody any more, but by hell, she wasn't afraid to get a little grease under her nails. She still rode. She'd still help.

BB went home. They pulled aside the tarp. They waved away the dust. They spent the night drinking, talking, and working.

They had the pull they needed to clear out one of a dozen Ancients-friendly shops, the street cred to go take the parts they needed from Black's junkyard, the know-how to do the work. It took them all night. Old machines were stubborn.

"Gods, that old pic!" Comet laughed. "I'll never forget those chaps, that *outfit*! I don't know how I squeezed into it!"

Blitz shook his head and didn't fall for the fishing trip; she was an elf, after all. She knew full well she looked as good today as she had that night, decades earlier. She'd shed his baby-weight in no time. She wasn't getting older, or weaker, or slowing down. She wouldn't for a long time. Being an Ancient? Probably not ever. Ancients didn't retire. Ancients didn't die of old age.

Ancients Forever wasn't just a slogan.

Blitz smiled softly down at the picture. It was something of a gang relic. It had made headlines a-plenty back in the day, and lazy journos still used it, here and now, all up through the

’50’s, ’60’s, and ’70’s, whenever the Ancients were accused of some street violence.

In the middle of an early gang war, the Ancients had slaughtered their rivals with combat-mage cavalry, a bold maneuver that paired the firepower of hermetic spellslingers and the speed of their best riders. In the middle of the fight, someone’s wayward pocket secretary had snapped a photo. *The* photo. Mid-fight, beneath the night sky, the gleaming neon, and against the fires and chaos of the gang war, there they were.

Blitzen, BB’s dad, slung low over the bike. Muscles rippling beneath Ancients ink, wrists studded with spikes, fingerless gloves, combat vest, face paint on his half-Japanese, half-NANner bronzed skin. Comet just behind him, machine pistol spraying, fist crackling with power, golden hair flying wild in the wind; and wearing the gaudiest, day-glo orange chaps and halter top you could imagine. Blitz was in the pic, too, if you thought about it; she hadn’t quite started to show yet, but he’d been in there, tucked away in her belly, early in her first trimester.

Blitzen had died later that very night, snatched away from the streets he loved by a Tír-born killer that was all cyberarms, katanas, and death; but his boy had used that very same sword since he’d grown large enough to wield it.

Blitzen and Comet. They were legends, thanks to that pic.

Legends.

Heroes.

Ancients.

“You’re the best parts of both of us.” Comet leaned past the photo and kissed her boy on the forehead.

BB had his father’s size and dark good looks, hair as long and thick as his mother’s, and eyes as bright and wise. His street code, her smarts. Modern versions of his street augmentations, an adept’s internalized version of her magic. That iconic picture, that iconic duo, two of the Ancients’ founders, and he kept both of them alive in the gang.

Blitz rolled up to the clubhouse the next morning, sleep-deprived, but high on life. His presence was announced well before he was within sight, as he was carried down the street by the banshee wail of a hybrid pressurized-hydrogen engine. *The* pressurized-hydrogen engine. His dad's.

The roaring heart of their old bike, the iconic wheels that had stormed Seattle's streets thirty years earlier. Restored, retuned, gleaming as brightly as it had that night, when it had been photographed during the Ancients' most famous, media-hyped fight.

All carbon fiber armor plating and neon green highlights, low-slung, spiked chrome and angular headlights.

A Honda Vector. *The* Honda Vector. The hottest model there was, the most exclusive, the most powerful; a Vector Sport, officially only ever sold to top-end combat biker and urban brawl teams, the pinnacle of combat cycle design, second to none when it came to being fast, tough, and nimble, all at once.

Blitz let it idle, planted a foot, and gave Squire an unrepentant smirk.

She smiled and stole a kiss. He tossed his head for her to get on, and she swung a leg over. She whispered. He shook his head.

The Vector roared like a dragon and launched like a rocket. The streets were theirs, all theirs. For a little while.

PREGAME

(ANCIENT PAWNS/ELVEN BLOOD)

"Pregame" was one of my earliest pieces of published Shadowrun *work. In retrospect, I think that shows, and there are certainly things I'd've done differently if I wrote the same story today; but in the limited word count I had to work with (it was just very short fiction in the front of an adventure), I think it still gets the job done.*

It was meant to set the stage for the GM to get a handle on certain characters and their attitudes, to see what the stakes (and the powers behind the challenge) were, and to just generally introduce the basics of the scenario, even if they happened off-stage. I'm a sucker for the Ancients and Tír Tairngire (always have been), and that will become increasingly clear over the next few stories.

—RRZ

Sting moved well for a woman closer to fifty than forty, lithe and balanced, silk-smooth and razor-sharp; but then she would, she was an elf. It wasn't age that would slow her down, not living the life she was living. It would be a bullet someday, or a gillette's spurs, a troll's axe, maybe a bike crash.

"Ancients Forever" wasn't a rallying cry on accident. Ancients didn't die of old age, and if there was anything Sting was, she was an Ancient. She was a Seattle-born ganger girl who'd clawed her way up in the old days, gone to war beside Wasp, then led the sprawl's most powerful gang for two decades next to the exile Green Lucifer. Sting wasn't just an Ancient, in many ways she was *the* Ancient.

And right now, she was very, very angry.

She twisted and grunted, sidestepped imaginary counter-attacks, lunged in at her target and lashed out. Her chrome-tipped fingers ended in lethal cybernetic razors, and even a feather-soft swipe of her claws could draw blood. She wasn't doing anything feather-soft, right now. A thin sheen of sweat covered her as she danced with shadows, slashing and kicking at the old mattresses duct-taped to steel girders in this practice hall.

Normally other Ancients would be here, practicing *Carromeleg* or Ghost-brutal strikes, prodding at the bundled mattresses with switchblades, combat knives, and slender swords. Normally their weapons hall would be ringing with the sound of fencers at practice, gloved-up brawlers sparring with one another, and Tír Peace Force retirees critiquing everyone's work. Normally the lights would be on.

Tonight wasn't normal.

Sting danced alone, venting her frustration and tension on mattresses in the dark. Her implants compensated for the gloom in the air, but nothing could overcome the gloom in her head. She relished the opportunity to lash out with her hands and her razors and her chipped-up reflexes, knowing that for most of the rest of the night—*Jesus, Buddha, and Zeus, maybe for the rest of another twenty fucking years*!—she'd have to do her fighting with her wits and her words again.

She missed the simpler days. Days she thought she could take on Seattle with just a fast bike, a gun in her hand, and a few favors from a street doc. The whole world had been simpler then, somehow.

Now she was a politician, of all fucking things. A mattress opened up, "guts" spilling out between layers of duct tape, and she sidestepped to another girder, worked at disemboweling another one, started with kicks that would cave in a normal man's ribs.

If only, she thought, hands gliding through another dazzling routine, blades leading the way. *If only everything could be attacked so directly.*

Not for another twenty years, she swore to herself, as her razors danced across the sloppy smiley face someone had scrawled onto this mattress at head height.

I'm not dealing with it for another twenty years. Gods damn him for doing this to me! *And Gods damn his father for knowing he would*!

Her thoughts didn't show up on the astral, of course. Life would be a lot simpler for some—and a lot more complicated for others—if it were so very, very easy; if cartoon thought bubbles blinked into existence to cleanly, neatly share someone's innermost secrets.

Instead, the mage spying on her made due with the roiling, raging tempest of her aura. The darkness of the building bothered him even less than it did her, the only shadows he saw were the ones where cybernetics had muted her aura here and there. Invisible to her on the astral plane, slipping through Ancients wards because he'd been the one who had raised them, he watched as Sting lunged from target to target, slashing each to ribbons and dancing off to the next.

The mage smiled, watching the colors of her soul flash and storm. He knew how to conceal his own aura, and how to peer through the layers of secrecy that existed when others tried to do the same. Sting didn't have any such training, and was as mundane as a brick. The mage read her like a tridsheet.

He whisked away in an eyeblink and slowly opened his eyes—real eyes, physical eyes—on a rooftop several blocks away. "She's upset," said the dark-haired, dark-hearted, young mage.

Rook flicked raven-black hair out of his eyes, reaching up to take a proffered hand that effortlessly hauled him to his feet. "And alone. Not calling a war council yet, not listening to anyone. Her lieutenants aren't even inside the building. She's angry. Off-balance, but angry. She's not calling anything off."

Even once he was on his feet, the elf that had pulled him up still loomed over him. Both were young, and both had the Talent, Rook's abilities with magic were quite different than his companion's.

"Good," the larger elf said, as broad in the shoulders as an ork, with a smile and a confidence as dazzling as a Tír Prince. He wore Ancients green and Ancients ink, had been born into the gang, and wanted nothing in life so much as to lead it. "If she's pissed, they won't be able to talk her down. This is really happening."

A dozen other elves, all Ancients, all young and lean and hungry, shared glances. A few looked nervous. Most looked cocky. One, smaller than the rest, and the only one without an Ancients logo on her jacket, stood in the shadows and teetered under the weight of a massive, two-handed sword. She didn't glance around. She just fawned on the big one, eyes bright.

"We're being taken seriously, boys and girls. Rook, make the call," the strong one said, unable to wipe his grin off his face. Tonight was the night. Finally. *Finally.*

"We all know the rules to this game. Let's recruit ourselves some players for the night."

LAYERS

(LAND OF PROMISE)

"Layers" came to be just after "Pregame," and as part of a very similar (and elf-centric) product. Everybody's favorite ork decker, Bull, gave me the chance to write a whole bunch of Missions adventures, together, as a campaign, and I went for it. Elven Blood *was the end result of those efforts, and a bunch of Magical ElfyLand adventures came to be.*

I wanted to update the Tír as part of it (as the setting of the adventures), but the longer I worked on it, the longer my update got, and the more it became a product of its own. The e-book Land of Promise *was the final result, which spun off into a whole book all by itself, separate from, but sister to, the* Elven Blood *adventure books.*

"Layers" here was the intro to that, a fun piece about a parkour-doin', badge-wearing, gun-totin', hacker-adept (AND the chance to characterize several new Princes). How fun is that?

–RRZ

To people with the eyes to see it, Portland is not a place, it's a thing. A living, breathing, eating, shitting creature. An animal.

Most tourists only see the outside, the shining fur, the bright eyes. They appreciate Portland—or Cara'Sir, if they want to sound like the new natives—for being beautiful, they keep a safe distance, and they think it's gorgeous and graceful. They're like people watching a tiger at a zoo.

They don't know it—really know it—like folks with a closer view. Patrolman Craig Young knew better. He saw the lower layers, not just the shiny veneer. He didn't spend much time amid the shining spires of Downtown, the lights of the Telestrian Habitat, or his brother Constabulary officers with their hokey horses and their paychecks triple the size of his. The tourists, the academics, the high society mavens, the good citizens—those were not his people, not the ones he dealt with day in and day out. He didn't simply admire the predatory grace of Cara'Sir from a distance; he was immersed in it.

He spent his nights tucked soundly in the belly of the beast.

As an elven officer with the wrong kind of reputation, he got the worst beats to walk, the worst neighborhoods to patrol, the worst parasites to deal with. Young saw the claws and fangs firsthand, with no intervening iron bars or glass.

He liked to classify the neighborhoods by how much augmented reality they indulged in; given his particular skill set and outlook, he spent more time in AR than most, and it colored his perceptions. The gaudy Downtown sights, the hotels of Elk Town, the conference centers and eateries of Westmoreland? What wasn't a magical illusion was an AR overlay, as often as not. It was all painted up, either with wonderful wizards or console cowboys, to dazzle and distract and impress. Their dark reflection, the other side of the coin, was Cara'Sir's ugliest neighborhoods. Guilds Lake, the half-renewed industrial park on Swan Island, the Meat Racks down by the port?

There the AR was more desperate, where it existed. Triple-X rated, thick with syndicate-sponsored subliminals, illegal tracking cookies, and occasional malware. The electronic overlay of Portland's underbelly was like top-notch tridscreens propped up in rotting, roach-infested BTL dens. It was there to hold your attention while someone took your nuyen, your blood, your soul. Or all three. Only the places in between showed their true colors. Tigard and Progress, Faloma and St John's, places where what you saw was what you got. The honest places. The middle places.

Part of Young liked avoiding those places in the middle. Even riding solo in his patrol car—Pritchett had, surprise surprise, gotten yet another last-minute assignment that kept him from having to ride with a "round-ear lover" like Young—he preferred the thrill of Portland's worst corners. Here in the dark, a cop could get away with things that were impossible in the city's nicer districts. Especially a cop with the right skills, magical aptitude, and headware.

Young idled in his sedan, chewing betel gum and doing what no one else in the Constabulary would or could. He'd spotted another one; an AR underlay, a crafty way some seemingly legit businesses advertised their less-than-clean secondary operations. This one was a basic list of options and prices for a massage parlor, but with the right password—or a powerful spoof program, which was what Young had—you could turn the special offers page into a list of less-than-savory actions with less-than-legal partners. At least the Shooters down at the Meat Racks ran clean parlors with willing participants.

Outfits like this, though? Here, the Peace Force couldn't just take a small cut and turn a blind eye. Or at least, Young couldn't. His headware commlink spun to life, and he danced with it.

Dipping into full VR—seat laid back, windows tinted, sedan armored—he and his Fairlight slipped through menu option after menu option, leaped and spun from node to node, sliced through their secure code neatly and smoothly. In an eyeblink, he skipped past their clumsy IC, and in a heartbeat he was a full administrator. He downloaded their lists of working girls, their clients, their employees, and sent instant data relays to friends in the Constabulary. He found their money, and the seventeen separate numbered accounts where it was kept.

He smiled and edited the base code of their sign.

As Young straightened his seat and pulled his green-and-white cruiser away, easing into light traffic to continue his patrol, bank accounts and passwords scrolled serenely on the animated sign. He knew how the animal of Cara'Sir worked. The bank accounts would be drained by the greedy and selfish faster than the parlor itself would be raided by law enforcement, and he didn't mind a bit. It was a win. Some of the city's poor would have a little extra spending money, one less thing to worry about with the Rite and the elections coming up. The pimps who rented out little girls would still lose their cash. The cops who cared more about glory than order would still get their busts, eventually. Young wouldn't get official credit for any of it, but he didn't care. The work was getting done, the girls would be freed, and this layer of the city would be a little better off. He'd done it before, and things had fallen into place just fine.

He was feeling pretty pleased with himself, then, when he came across the sloppiest burglary in Portland's history a few blocks later.

Three ork youths—gangers from the Spans, judging by their black-on-gray colors—were clambering into the shattered front window of a ¥-4-NERPS pawn shop. For a split-second he wondered how they'd gotten the bars off, even as a mental command got his patrol car's lights flashing while the siren warbled twice. His question was answered by one look at the shoulders of the burly teens, and the way the light dully gleamed off the crowbars two of them carried.

<Car 34 to Dispatch. 459 in progress at my GPS. Backup requested>, he piped silently and invisibly as he clambered out of his car, drawing in a lungful of air to bellow in his best command voice, "Peace Force! Put your hands up!"

His answer was a cinder block, hurled by the third ork ganger, that almost took his head off.

Young was too quick, though, lunging sideways to dodge it. Lying sidelong on the pavement, his Falcon pistol barked twice and a pair of gel rounds slammed into the ork's chest. The targeting reticule of his smartlink broadcast to his department-issue Oakleys centered on the ork's head a split-second later. The Span wasn't bright enough to take the hint from the first two shots, and raised his crowbar to attack. His head snapped back as Young squeezed the trigger, and the ork spun to the ground. The opening exchange was brutally one-sided, but it kept Young from realizing he hadn't received confirmation from dispatch.

He didn't have time to think about it a heartbeat later, either, when the two that were still awake came rushing at him. They were all high on jazz or kamikaze or—*I hope it's not K-10*—something, coming at him even as he emptied his magazine into the pair of them.

As a half-dozen gel rounds raised welts and bruises or bounced off armored street leathers, they bellowed about broken promises, ripping the ears off keeblers like him, and following orders. He let his sidearm clatter to the pavement after the slide locked back, empty, and his right hand darted to his duty belt for his baton while his left tried a stiff arm to buy him the space he'd need to draw it. What was coming was going to be ugly, and it was going to be up close.

A crowbar swipe almost broke his collarbone, a gut punch blasted the wind from him, and a ham-sized fist snapped his head sideways. Young gave as good as he got, though, keeping a cool head and lashing out with the shock baton, battering with hilt strikes when they got too close to properly engage the electrically charged end. A downward smash of the crowbar cracked the densiplast forearm guards hidden beneath his jacket, a hot gust of foul breath made his eyes water as gleaming fang implants shone centimeters from his smartglasses, and a full-shouldered shove sent him tumbling almost back to his squad car.

He came back with baton strikes to the head, a brutal elbow, a dirty kick from a densiplast-enforced boot. Young's world exploded in static and bright light, then, and as he clawed his shattered Oakleys off his face and let his eyes adjust, trying to ignore the ringing in his head, he saw one of his assailants was down and groaning. The other had gotten in a cheap shot and used the opening to run. An ork-sized blur of black and gray rounded a corner into nearby alley. Young stooped to recover his sidearm as he went, leaning down to trigger his stun baton one last time and jab hard at the Span ganger lying on the pavement.

Then he ran, and the chase was on.

<34 to Dispatch, 34 to Dispatch. Code Purple, 245 on an officer!>

<11-99! 10-73?>

By reflex, he and his Fairlight shot the data equivalent of emergency flares, calling for Constabulary back-up as he sprinted down winding alleys, dodging dumpsters and squatters. The ganger he was chasing was probably fifteen years younger than him, with ork-strong legs and ork-powerful lungs, high on some combat drug and riding a wave of adrenaline. The punk went out of his way to bull through anything in his path, knocking over garbage cans, sending piles of crates tumbling, throwing everything he could in Young's way.

Young was better, though. More experienced. He moved through the real world as smoothly as he did the Matrix, avoiding what he couldn't overcome. There was a grace to his actions—vaulting over a rusty trash can, taking three steps up a wall to grab a fire escape, swinging from it to the top of a dumpster, sliding across the rain-slick lid and down, feet under him, sprinting again—that the ork lacked, and where the young ganger went through everything in his path, Young slipped past it, over it, around it. He found a hole, every time.

He was gaining. Steadily gaining. Almost on him. All he needed was a good straightaway to pop in a fresh magazine and draw a bead, or one more little slip-up to let him get within arm's reach. Almost there.

Another alley mouth opened up to a street that needed crossing, and Young had the time he needed. He slid a cold polymer magazine into his Telestrian Falcon, the slide slapped forward to chamber a round, and instead of continuing the chase he raised the pistol.

"Peace Force!" The gun barked twice, Young's aim purposefully low.

"Halt!"

The Span ganger tumbled to the rain-slick pavement yowling in pain and clutching a bleeding leg. He tumbled and rolled, trying to scramble backward on all fours and pitifully raise his hands at the same time. Officer Young advanced with his pistol held on the ork, left hand dipping to his duty belt to grab some restraints.

He spared a skyward glance as he piped another command to his headware.

<Dispatch, this is 34. Come in, come in. 11-41 at my location, I repeat, ambulance needed at my loca—>

Suddenly, a limousine barreled into the ork fast enough to send him flying, the custom Westwind stretch-job low enough to the ground that it kicked him up for some real hang time. The low-slung machine stopped on a dime a split-second afterward, and Young was sure the brake lights hadn't engaged until after the impact.

The Span was a sprawled-out mess, limp as a rag doll, head pulped. Young registered it all in an instant, knowing he was dealing with a driver chromed enough to hit the ork or not, and that they had chosen—consciously chosen—to run him down.

Young leveled his sidearm as a rear passenger window slid down. Then, a second later, his vision was dazzled by flashing, stabbing lights.

A pair of squad cars and a trio of rotodrones had this block cordoned off, and every one of them lit him up with their spotlights at once. With his smartglasses broken, the light was a physically painful thing, knocking him a half-step back, but leaving the face he'd seen—the passenger in the limo—etched all the more sharply into his mind.

"I would holster that, Officer, before it gets you killed."

It was only after Young's kydex holster clapped onto his sidearm and he lamely lifted his hands in the air that the spotlights slid away. They didn't turn off, though. They all just swiveled, finding other targets, dazzling and spearing at an apartment window here, a storefront there, a couple on the street, a late-night food vendor at his cart. Each of the civilians was pinned in place as surely as Young had been; they all knew that a Peace Force spotlight came mounted on a gun. They all knew what that attention meant.

"Do climb in, please, and stop waving your arms around. You're embarrassing the Constabulary."

Still off-balance, Young stooped to enter the luxurious back seat of the Eurocar. He blinked away the darkness of the interior, then did his best not to gawk. Sitting across from him were Princes Conall Taylor and Jonathon Gant, two of the most powerful men in the Tír.

Taylor drawled at him again, with that famous amused edge to his voice, while holding up a slender flute. "Champagne?"

"I'm, um, on duty." It was the first thing Young thought to say, even as the limo pulled away and left his squad car behind.

"Your shift expired at 21:15, actually. You were, as it turns out, called back to the station and formally reprimanded for an unwarranted search of a privately owned node." Gant's deeper voice was almost robotic, clinical, detached, matter-of-fact. Wholly uncaring. "No one is turning a blind eye to your little game this time. You're facing official legal sanction for your tampering, and will likely face compensation charges from the businessmen you wronged."

Taylor lit up the back of the limo with a smile. "Or, rather, you will if we decide to have Johnny here hit send on a few messages he's got queued up. Perhaps you'd rather sit and talk for a few minutes, Officer Young?"

Young sat.

"As wise as you are athletic, Officer. A fine performance, by the way. We already knew you were mentally sharp, but it was nice to see you in action tonight. You didn't do a bad job at all with those Spans. No hesitation, solid shooting, and good stick-work." He paused for a cheery little toast and a sip of bubbly. "We already knew you were good at chases, though. Jon?"

"Young, Craig Joshua. Born October 2, 2040, Tír Tairngire Medical Center, to Michael and Cindy—"

"Oh, hold on just a moment, Jon." Taylor held up his flute of champagne to interrupt, nodding toward one door as the Westwind glided to a halt. "And scoot over just a bit, Officer. Who knows what she's wearing tonight?"

As it turned out, she—Prince Amy Joubert—was dressed rather conservatively, not wearing one of her splendidly formal, often magically decorated gowns. She slipped into the back of the limousine gracefully, as she did almost everything else.

Taylor handed her the champagne he'd offered to Young by way of greeting. "Prince Joubert, always a pleasure. We were just getting to the dirty secrets part. Jon started a bit early in the timeline, though. Do skip to the interesting parts, you're being dreadfully dull."

Jon Gant—head of the Information Secretariat, the shadowy espionage center of the entire nation—shot Taylor a glare that would have made an ordinary citizen fear for his life and that of his family. Nonetheless, he cleared his throat and continued. Young could only just barely make out the telltale glimmer on Gant's eyes, tiny slices of data shining over his cyberoptics, giving away that he was reading off a list from deep within his headware.

"Very well. Young, Craig Joshua. Formally joined the Rinelle ke'Tesrae in 2059, serving primarily as Matrix enforcement. Made a sysop of the Shay ke'Sallah, or 'forest of silence,' after less than a year's service as a data courier. Responsible for Matrix assaults on nine Netwatch officers in that time, directly involved in four operations that caused twenty-seven deaths and sixty-four injuries, handled data, coordination, and planning for at least eight more."

Taylor *tsk-tsk*ed loudly, and even Joubert frowned prettily. Gant didn't show that much emotion; he just kept ratting off sentence fragments like he was cribbing notes instead of describing a string of violent terrorist activities.

"Left the Rinelle during the amnesty period offered following the passage of the Zincan Act. Enlisted in the Peace Force, requesting a position in NetWatch and citing 'other' as qualifications. Served well from 2066 to 2072, with background records safely classified from all but higher-ups. In 2072, formally requested reassignment to the military branch, specifying the Ghosts as a desired position. Was transferred to Constabulary instead and put on Patrol, formally reprimanded for unnecessary paperwork and repeated requests. Transfer requests continued."

Taylor made a grand show of producing a commlink from within his jacket pocket, waving a finger to put it in speaker mode, and settling it onto the seat between Gant and himself.

"And, with Prince Parris joining us—" As Taylor spoke, the commlink broadcast an AR display of the perpetually scowling, dark-haired Prince, "—storytime is over, and I believe it's time for a little Q&A."

"Were you a Paladin of the Rinelle ke'Tesrae?" Prince Joubert's voice was softer than the rest. She lacked the perpetually amused edge of Taylor's and the clinical disconnect of Gant's. She was a Paladin herself, Young remembered.

"I swore Oaths to bring about change, yes."

"As part of an Initiation?"

Taylor's question caught him off guard. They had to know he was an adept, of course, but he wasn't sure they'd known how advanced he was. "Yes."

"And why turn your back on it, then? Why join the Peace Force?" It was Prince Joubert again, managing to sound almost concerned. Taylor was having fun with him, Gant was interrogating him. Joubert seemed almost worried about him, empathetic to what he went through, understanding.

"I didn't turn my back on anything. I became the change I thought the country needed, even after the Coup accomplished most of what we were after. The people got their elections. They got their Rites *and* their rights back. I wanted things to keep getting better, but thought I could do that from inside, not outside, the system."

"*And since then*?" The voice was tinny, a little cold. Sharper than Gant's, though. Parris. "*Why continue badgering your commanding officers with these demands to be transferred? They've made you a pariah in your own precinct.*"

"Because this isn't where I want to be."

"*Why*?" It was from Prince Parris again, piping from the commlink. It was a demand, not a question.

"Because I feel like I can do more good—"

"Stop." It was Gant, interrupting with those cold, dead eyes of his. "You should know I'm monitoring you in a dozen different ways to test the honesty of your answers and I'm reporting my findings to my peers real-time. Prince Joubert and her unique talents are also in play. Tell us only the truth."

"Lying to a Prince is a capital crime." Parris's voice carried more than the hint of a threat. "You were one of NetWatch's best, now you're just a beat cop, hated by your peers. You want to be a Ghost instead. Why?"

"I think I'd fit in better with the Ghosts than—"

"We can have you shot, you know. Why?"

"I feel the Constabulary isn't fully utilizing my potential to bring about greater—"

"If he lies to us again, Prince Taylor, kindly snatch the life from him with your bare hands."

"Will do," Taylor sing-songed, with absolute confident and another champagne toast.

Young sighed. Telling them what he *thought* they wanted to hear wasn't going to work.

"Because they killed him." He almost spat the words at them, feeling the anger rise up in him like bile. "You already know it, but you bastards want to make me say it? Fine. Because when the Rinelle got their leg caught in a trap, they acted like an animal and gnawed it off. With Horizon and the Peace Force coming in at them under the Zincan Act, some of the Brat'mael decided to go out 'purging' Rinelle cells they thought were weakening the movement."

"And so your mate was killed," Amy Joubert spoke softly, as though she'd lost a friend herself.

"Daniel was too moderate for them, *and* he was a human. That was enough for them to want him dead. I want them dead for it." The dam broke, and Young let the words pour from him angrily. "Fuck NetWatch! Fuck the Constabulary! I want to be chasing *them*. I want to be hunting down what's left of the Black Sun and killing them. I want to pay them back for what they did to me, and to him, and to my life. And you all know the Ghosts is the only place to do that."

"Not the only place," Taylor cut in again, this time without any sarcasm. His upper-crust, foppish veneer vanished, and there was a formality and seriousness to his tone that had been lacking before. "But we recruit from the Ghosts, too, so at least you have been trying to step in the right direction. We're short on Matrix overwatch since the Boise job, and Young fits what we need. I say aye. Those in favor?"

"Aye." Gant sounded bored, even as he agreed.

"Aye," Joubert said, sadness still touching her voice. "Though I fear the hunt will bring you no peace, Craig, I think you are the right hunter.

"Aye," Parris said, as though he'd been on Young's side all along.

"Very well. That gives us four direct votes. Joubert carries Foster's proxy, Telestrian and Demarco are formally listed as agreeing with the rest of the Council in these matters, which gives us seven. Rex couldn't care less, Zincan and Van den Berg don't know, and fuck Jaeger. We've got our vote, the matter is settled."

"The...matter?" Young rather wished he'd accepted the champagne now. Or any other drink, preferably harder.

"You're in. We'll have your things moved to the training facility shortly. Your brothers and sisters will take over for the formal initiatory rites, but in the meantime, the least we could do was give you a ride."

As the Westwind slowed, Young saw they were cruising to a stop on Royal Hill, outside one of the luxurious manors that had been so hastily vacated when the old Council was abolished. A fit-looking black human with a clean-shaven head and a salt-and-pepper goatee stood on the curb, hands on his hips. Prince Taylor nodded to him as their driver unlocked the rear door for Young to climb out.

"Marcus will take you from here. Welcome to the Moonlight Thorns, our nation's *real* elite paramilitary squad. And congratulations on your progression, *Sir* Young."

And just like that, Craig's life changed again.

WARRIOR'S EDGE

(Way of the Adept)

Way of the Adept *was my very first solo project for* Shadowrun*; the first thing I pitched, the first thing I thought up on my own, the first thing I wrote, start to finish, all by my lonesome. "Warrior's Edge" was, as such, one of my first fiction pieces, and, again, I feel like it shows (here, a decade later).*

I still think the story does what it set out to do, though. It showed the outlook of someone warped by elven supremacist propaganda, it showed the fanaticism that comes from a lifetime of rhetoric reinforced by magical certainty, and it shows the lethality that perhaps no one in the Sixth World is as capable of as a dedicated specialist adept.

—RRZ

The elf had taken the name Talondel after his Rite of Passage. He had shivered in the cold rain of the wilderness and survived his Bridging. Talondel then stood proudly in front of his parents, the Paladin he would serve alongside, and Count McCoy—a representative from Prince Ni'Fairra, who sadly could not attend that day—as the elf renamed himself for all to witness. Alongside that name came a purpose; with that purpose came service to his nation and ultimately his Prince.

The Warrior served Ni'Fairra still, these decades later. His Oaths demanded it.

His orders had been broad, and they left quite a bit of leeway as to how to carry them out. To sow discord, advance elvenkind, and disrupt Hestaby's plans, whatever they might be. He'd been given the initial assignment years ago, and hadn't heard from Prince Ni'Fairra since the great coup and upheavals. Talondel took pride in the Prince's trust and was quietly reassured by her confidence in his abilities. She was his Prince still, politics and orkish upstarts be damned; by Oath he served her, and one day she would be a Prince in name again.

As he had years ago, he lurked in the cold rain and waited for midnight. He'd chosen his target two days earlier when a police-band scanner reported, ahem, a "weedeater gypsy punk" being taken in. Their slurs made them easier to hate, and Talondel already had a terrific knack for hating.

He was on a roof in a small town between Redding and Shasta. Talondel had spent the previous night performing reconnaissance work, reminding himself that skulking around in shadows wasn't cowardice when it was part of his duty. It was merely preparation for the fight to come, and he had shaped the battlefield to his liking. The filthy round-ears of Wolverine Security hadn't seen or heard him, meaning they didn't know about the planted charges, the placed electronics, the ranges he'd measured, the head counts he'd taken, or the plans he'd made.

They didn't know they stood against a trueborn Warrior in service to his Prince. They didn't know they would all die.

At midnight, he heard muffled explosions and smiled grimly. One charge cut off the building's external power supply, while the other destroyed the emergency generators in the basement.

Darkness smothered the small security station, and Talondel's delicately pointed ears heard the first confused cries: the heckling to hide fear from the prisoner cell, the shouts from one Wolverine officer to another within the building. Even his magically enhanced hearing couldn't pick up the sound of the directional jammer, but he had set the timers, and knew it had begun at the same instant as the detonations.

Talondel married his cheek to the stock of his HK PSG Enforcer. The scope's magnification was set low, because the range was ridiculously short. More important than the Zeiss optics was the time he had invested into this rifle. The Warrior had used it for years, taken it apart and reassembled it more times than he could count. He knew the balance, trigger weight, and recoil like it was an extension of his body. He had used this Enforcer to end more lives than he had bothered to count, and it had never let him down. He knew it would not tonight.

Talondel leaned, shoulder snug against the stock and swung the muzzle around on a compact bipod that held the rifle. When he saw a security officer, he quickly caressed the trigger, twice, and then checked for movement at another window. The silencer and flash hider performed as they should have; no one outside the three-story police station would know what was going on. The signal jammer, not just his silencer, ensured that. He continued to shoot as targets presented themselves.

Magic fueled him, and he fired the rifle quicker than anyone wholly human. He would drop a target with two shots, find a target, adjust aim, and repeat; several heartbeats later he thumbed a small lever on the precision rifle and engaged the second magazine to continue sniping. Silencer or not, dozens of rounds in the Wolverine thugs revealed where he was firing from, but Talondel didn't let that stop him. Another pair of shots, and another; the targets were more careful now, giving him only wary heads and half-covered shoulders to fire at, peeking at him through shattered windows. They were still easy targets to him and his Enforcer though, he was as calm and confident as when he spent an afternoon at the range, until finally the second magazine was empty.

Talondel ducked below the lip of his building and quickly locked his rifle into its armored, padded case. It was tethered to a grappling hook by a slender line of stealth rope, and the elf hurled the locked case over the rear of the building. He had pre-measured the line and spooled out just enough that the rifle would be dangling a meter off the ground, two meters away from his waiting coupe when the night's work was done. His movements were calm, seemingly lax, but every action had been meticulously planned in advance. Warriors were not sloppy in service to their Prince.

He took a single, calming breath and then whispered in Sperethiel as he leaped over the rooftop's low wall. He recited his Oaths as the pavement rose up to meet him, twisting cat-like and effortlessly absorbing the landing's impact with his legs, magic, and faith.

Talondel glanced up as he darted across the street, spotting a round-ear who'd mustered the courage to stand in a window and level a shotgun. The elf snorted at the inelegance of the man's weapon, the ugly sound of the slide, and the slowness with which the muzzle tracked him. His left arm swung up, and a sliver of steel leaped from his hand. Talondel's eyes weren't even on the target as the corpse fell with a knife in his eye; he was already scanning the other windows. There were none.

Wolverine Security agents were only fearsome when attacking. Their brutality and bluster left them when they were on the defensive. They were bullies. Dead bullies.

A ripple of energy rolled off his shoulder as he slammed it into the front door of the station, buckling the metal as it gave way from the force of his magically enhanced impact. The door crashed off the hinges, but even before it clattered to the ground he was tumbling, rolling to one side, avoiding the fire he knew to expect. Talondel then sprang to his feet meters away from where they expected. His wrist flicked again, and a handful of sharp steel whistled through the air. Two more bodies slumped to the floor.

Another ugly policeman died to his throwing blades before he ran dry. Talondel relished the opportunity to rely on his Warrior's training and steel. A sword leaped into his hand, too quick for the next officer's eyes to register. It was a short blade, something like a gladius, but leaf-bladed like an old xiphos. It was similar to a secondary weapon an Old World archer might carry, but graceful runes etched in orichalcum ran the length of its blade ensured lethality despite its size. The edges were lined with monofilament wire; combined with the enchantments and Talondel's ability, it was enough to separate the surprised guard's head from his shoulders easily. As a boy, he'd been a master with a well-balanced hurley. After his Naming, Talondel had an altogether more lethal weapon.

The sword wasn't just a thing of metal, monofilament, rubber grips, and orichalcum. It was his Prince's will made manifest, a gift from her hand, a symbol of his fealty and of his place. He wielded it as she wielded him; and they were unstoppable.

The blade sang in the darkness of the security station, led unerringly from room to room by his flawless vision, making examples of every night-blind, ugly human that dared to stand in the way of a thrice-Oathbound Warrior.

It was more than a sword, just as he was more than a swordsman; they were symbols, and symbols do not die easily. The slaughter finished as quickly as it started. Talondel had barely broken a sweat.

He dipped gloved fingers in the pool of blood left by his last victim and swiped it across a bare spot of wall. He was not an artist, but within moments the sketch was complete. He tilted his head and narrowed his eyes in mute critique, but there could be no mistaking the graffiti's sinuous neck, slashing tail, or broad-spread wings. A dragon, painted in the blood of slain humans, would send a message.

Hestaby and her followers would take the blame for the night's slaughter, and for the escape of the prisoners he was about to set loose. The Romani boy hauled in by the locals would go free, and the Bitch-Wyrm's symbol on the wall would muddy the waters of responsibility.

He took stock; humans were dead and an elf had been freed from a cage. Hestaby and her minions would, at least briefly, bear the blame for it.

Talondel smiled. His orders had been carried out, and his Oaths fulfilled. His Prince's plans moved forward yet again. It had been an honor. He was content. He remained pure.

He was a Warrior, and none could stand before him.

THE UNTETHERED LIFE

(Attitude)

Here it is, friends. My very first published Shadowrun *work. I got this gig, I started this chapter of my story, by shooting line developer Jason Hardy a PM on an internet forum. He knew me from fan fictions I'd written prior, he wrote me back, and–as it turned out–he had a need for some intro fic.*

The rest, as they say, is history. Meet Saber, a shadowrunner who took his tactical Lone Star training, and extensive cyberlimb modifications, to the streets. You're gonna see a lot of him and his team in the next few stories, so here's your chance to meet him.

—RRZ

"Alarm off. Radio on."

Reid Sabelhaus sat up in his bed and glared at his clock. The harsh blaring stopped, and a talk radio show replaced it. The chattering voices of political spokesmen escorted him as he threw off the sheets and stood up. Motion sensors tracked his progress through the condo, lowering the volume of wall-inset speakers in one room and raising them in another, so that he never walked away from the shrieking metahuman rights activists despite yawning his way down the hall and into the bathroom. The volume automatically rose to compensate for the rushing hot water of his shower, then lowered again as it stopped, and the talking heads just kept talking. They cut to a commercial as he dried off.

"Radio off," he sighed.

Reid stood in front of his fog-covered mirror for a long moment, tossing his wet towel down for his Grimebuster to scoop up. He wanted to swipe a hand over the mirror to clear his reflection, but knew it would only remind him of how a cyberlimb—inhumanly perfect for so many tasks—could be perfectly inhuman for others. He hated the streaks it left, the squeak it made as his polymer and alloy hand scraped the glass, the way it sounded like setting a beer bottle on a glass coaster when his fingertips first touched the mirror. Reid didn't want to hear that again.

"Mirror," he said instead, clenching and unclenching both his carbon-fiber over gunblued fists. "Defog."

He stood there for a few more heartbeats, looking at himself as he did to start every day, taking inventory. Vents built into the wall and countertop banished the steam and brought clarity, and he stared long and hard at every puckered scar on his torso, relived every bullet and blade and tooth, and chided himself for letting them hit him. His gaze lingered where his arms and legs joined his torso, where meat suddenly gave way to metal, and he dwelled on every choice he'd made to get where he was.

Reid stared long and hard at the pink-smooth patch over his heart, the scar from the first work he'd paid the street doc, Aman Khayyam, for. He'd traded ten slap patches of opiates for a perfect circle of laser-marked skin where he'd had a tattoo removed as quickly and harshly as the street doc could manage it.

Reid Sabelhaus didn't work for Lone Star any more. He hadn't for years. They'd built him, then thrown him away when Knight Errant had invaded Seattle without firing a shot. He was glad he didn't have their company logo tattooed on his chest any more.

He made himself stare his reflection in the eyes and sent a mental command. The gunmetal-black framework built into and under his eyes flickered for an instant and his lenses snapped into place. Memory plastics formed a ballistic shield that protected his expensive ocular implants, but they served a psychological purpose, as well. They were a part of his new uniform. When the lenses blinked into place, he changed.

Reid Sabelhaus, Lone Star officer, was gone. Saber, the shadowrunner, stared him down in the mirror, all metal limbs and mirrorshade optics, scars and edge and attitude.

Reid had patrolled the Seattle streets with a partner; Saber worked with crews that came and went by the Juggler's whim and Mr. Johnson's budget. He used to requisition gear from a quartermaster or buy it from Weapons World with an employee discount; now he took knock-off guns from dead gangers and traded secrets to information brokers for ammunition. He used to believe in his job, working for the world's premier law enforcement corporation to make Seattle a safer place. Now he worked for a clever man who at least admitted he was just a weapon. He'd been surrounded by friends and coworkers; now he had contacts and business acquaintances. He used to be engaged and had been on the verge of buying a home. Now he rented crash-space by the hour. Reid had always arranged for Sundays off, but Saber was about to spend the day in Khayyam's back room, praying the junkie's hands wouldn't shake during a routine maintenance check on his artificial legs and an upgrade to his reflex/response hardware.

"I'm still alive," the street samurai said, glaring at every scar that hadn't managed to kill him. He was, it was true. But to stay that way, he still had to go to work. It was the only thing Saber had in common with Reid Sabelhaus.

Reid would've hated Saber. Saber, for damned sure, hated Reid.

IT JUST HAPPENED

(Conspiracy Theories)

You want to know a secret? I really wish I'd ended this story differently.

I had a pretty open-ended directive with this one, it just had to fit the theme of the host book, Conspiracy Theories. *I wanted something that just ended up nastier than it looked on the surface, something that sounded bad but ended up immeasurably worse. I wanted something wicked.*

I got all of that, and told a pretty fun shadowrunner-centric story, but in retrospect I wish more of these characters were still around for me to come back to later.

—RRZ

I didn't like it.

Match and Torque kept telling me I didn't *have* to like it, that shit like this came with the job. Their cynical reassurances didn't change the fact that the whole damned job felt bad from the start.

Not having Jangler set up our trip to DeeCee was one thing; okay, sure, he'd tried to pass off some Gila demon scraps as dragon hide and had gotten himself killed for it. Fine. Shit happens when your fixer's a crooked bastard hawking fake dragon parts, I get that. But him being a crooked bastard was what made him good at his job, damn it, and when I was trying to get myself shipped cross-country—especially with all the tension in the Federal District of Columbia, thanks to rifts and dragons and everything else—I *wanted* a crooked bastard to be handling the border security for me.

But no, our regular import/export mogul getting himself shot for pawning fake dragon bits wasn't the worst part. We'd found a way around that and gotten to DeeCee in one piece, without any hassles.

No, it wasn't the worst part by a long shot. The worst part was we were going into a job without any mojo on our side. No spellslinger. No summoner. No anything.

"I still say this sucks," I said for the millionth time.

"If it didn't suck, we wouldn't get paid to do it!" Match laughed.

"I'm telling you, quit worrying so much." Torque was calmer than either of us. "I know her rep. It's cool."

Torque had set up our meet with a DeeCee local, arranging it through his parts pipeline. Doc was vouching for the guy, too. Torque had his own little network of fixers and contacts from his old racing and smuggling days that still kept in touch. They made sure he had his fancy auto parts and semi-legit paperwork for all his cars.

Doc—well, Doc just knew everyone, everywhere, it seemed like. That's what we kept him around for.

"So he was just...dead?" Torque and Match both knew who I meant. "Not a mark on him? No shots fired? No blood? Nothing?"

"It just happens sometimes." Match tilted his head a bit and looked a little more smug than normal. Fucking elves. He was as mundane as a loaf of bread. Hell, he had so much chrome in him most mages would probably like the loaf of bread more. But he'd grown up in the Tír, so he knew more about magic than me or Torque, and he never let us forget it. "Mages go off into the astral and never come back. You know how touchy Twigs was about us moving his body, right? That's because he was scared he wouldn't be able to find it again."

"Yeah, but his body was right there in his room, man. No one moved it!"

"It just happens sometimes," Match said again, shrugging a little. Like repeating a lame answer made it make sense. "He went on a scouting run and just stayed in the astral, I guess."

Neither of them seemed particularly bothered that our mage had just left his body and never come back. Match had complained about the smell—he'd been the one to hit up Twiggy's apartment to check on him—more than he'd expressed any sense of loss. I think Twiggy owed Torque and

Doc money. Or he used to, at least. We'd found his corpse a few hours before we were set to leave Seattle.

"You really don't think it had to do with the Ares job?" I chewed on a fingernail, spat when I tasted blood. "I mean, what if they—"

"Stow it. Company's coming!" Torque's tusks flashed in what was probably supposed to be a smile as he saw Doc and our local contact sauntering up to the table. Doc looked rumpled like always. The local, though, had just the right curves for her jeans and a retro-style *Mercurial* tee.

"Hey, hey! Look who the cat dragged in!" Doc had met her first, Torque had spotted them, but Match was Match. He liked to act like he was our crew's leader, especially at negotiations. He reached for his "lucky negotiator glasses," the ones with the empathy software built in. I'd gutted a cute little emotitoy to make them for him a couple months ago, after losing a bet about a Screamers game.

"It's time for this gal—" The redheaded razorboy's custom shades were lifted up to cover his eyes.

"Don't say it," I groaned under my breath as she and Doc got closer.

"—to meet her Match!"

I screamed on the inside and groaned on the outside.

They weren't rank amateurs, Jenny decided quickly.

She'd worked with Doc back in '68, and he'd kept in contact ever since, like she knew he did with so many others. Jenny had also been a regular in the parts pipeline running to Torque and a few other West Coast racers for years, and she knew he was an experienced wheelman. Rumor was Torque drove cars as fast as she boosted them.

Jenny didn't need her astral sight to figure out the elf, either. She knew a street samurai when she saw one. Even ignoring his obvious combat-optimized cyberarm, there was an unnatural smoothness to his movements, a bulk to the artificial muscles of his meat arm, and a hint of chrome that betrayed custom cyberoptics (before he'd put those ridiculous glasses on, at least).

That left the skinny one with the chromed datajacks, and Jenny was bright enough to figure out what he did for a living.

Before she could get a better look at him, the burly elf stood up and flashed her a too-white smile.

"Hi there." He held out a hand with knuckles scarred and scarred again, and she could feel a fighter's calluses when they shook. He gave her that smile again. "I'm Match."

Doc had given her a good-natured warning when they'd met out front, letting her know Match had a tendency to try and mix business with pleasure, and ham-handed seduction attempts might be inbound. Jenny hadn't needed the warning; the elf was entirely not her type. Jenny didn't have a type. She never had.

"Jenny Q," she said, noting that they'd already set a small white noise generator on the table. She shook hands, gave him a curt nod. "Let's get straight to business."

The skinny one with the plugs in his head looked relieved. Doc grinned at an angry Torque like he'd just won a bet. Match, for his part, didn't seem to have noticed her brusque response. The meet was her idea, but she was no Johnson. She was an intrusion expert, and a damned good one.

They ordered beer and appetizers to keep the waitress off their back, then talked turkey; she was disappointed to hear their magical support wouldn't be along, especially since none of her regular local wiz-guys were returning calls lately.

Overall, though, she wasn't concerned. Nothing about their target made her think it would have serious magical support, and she told them so. The skinny one—Frostbyte-with-a-y, he'd introduced himself—looked relieved at that, and he listened intently as she shared what she knew of their security and how she'd bypass it.

I liked her, this Jenny Q. She showed us she was taking the job seriously, and she shared all the information she'd gathered so far in a quick download to my Hermes that I forwarded to everyone else. Doc and Torque pulled out their commlinks to scroll over it, Match used his Zeiss eyejobs to do the same thing. It looked good. Just another DeeCee brownstone on the outside, middle-of-the-road security on the inside; enough to show that they had something worth taking.

Nothing out of the ordinary for a group of their size and affluence, and nothing we couldn't handle. We all agreed to an even split, twenty percent apiece. Match triumphantly snatched his glasses off like he'd been some slick corporate shark the whole time, but Jenny didn't seem to be surprised or disappointed with cutting the profit five ways. She must have trusted her fixer to give a fair price, but that made sense; it was her home turf, after all. Torque, Doc, and I were fine with even shares, especially since Q had already done so much of the homework for us.

Much of it, but not all. We kept busy for the next four nights. Jenny and Torque's chop-shop buddies had hooked us up with the same big black SUV the Draco Foundation-types used, and with a few of the same mods. We'd have a comfortable ride as we handled our DeeCee business, and figured anyone in the know would recognize it as their style of wheels and leave us alone. Jenny said the streets were alive with DF whispers lately, and everyone was on eggshells around them, so we might as well take advantage of their rep while we were in town.

Torque spent most of his time in the storage facility Jenny had rented for us, tweaking the SUV. I didn't mind having a wheelman with his level of obsession—it meant he'd know the wheels inside and out when it came time to actually use them.

Doc and Match cleaned guns, mostly, but also took turns going with me or Jenny on recon trips or picking up gear from her local connections. Our cross-country trip had made it tough to bring in any major hardware, but Jenny's friends changed that. We cruised around in her Jackrabbit beneath the shadow of the Washington Monument and filled the trunk with all kinds of goodies over the next few days.

Match laughed at me when he caught me snapping photos, but I couldn't help gawking like a tourist. The brownstone was boring, but the rest of DeeCee was full of famous places I'd only ever seen on the trids. Boring was actually an understatement about this particular brownstone. We watched it day and night from behind the tinted windows of Jenny's Jackrabbit. It was some trendy cult hideout.

Everyone that came in looked normal enough, but I guess that was to be expected. There was a stream of everyday cars, along with people in business and casual clothes that you'd see on any street of any sprawl. No one strolled in and out of the place in blood-spattered robes or anything. We watched the place on and off for three days before Match got bored—that fucking suprathyroid of his—and just climbed out of the car all of a sudden. One second we were all chowing down on cheap takeout and Match was laughing at me as I fumbled with the chopsticks Jenny used so expertly, and the next he just said "I'm bored" and opened the door.

Jenny and I stammered at him from the car as he strolled across the street, putting on his lucky glasses, and just walked right in. His radio was quiet for almost an hour as the two of us called back to the storage facility and got Torque and Doc ready to roll in case we had to assault the place in broad fucking daylight. Just as those two radioed us back that they'd be here in five, Match came sauntering back out, smiling and shaking a bland, middle-aged corporate type's hand.

"All clear. I just told 'em I was thinking about joining," he said cheerfully, dropping back into the car and holding up his Hermes Ikon. "I didn't see any extra cameras or anything, and I even got some brochures with monthly dues discounts I can forward straight to you guys, if you want!"

I wanted to slug him, but I had two problems. From the back seat of a Chrysler-Nissan I didn't have any damned room to take a swing, for one, and Match could tear me apart without half-trying, for two. I settled for chewing him out instead.

Frostbyte was pretty good at his job, Jenny had decided. He knew just how much to yell at the cocky razorboy for pulling a stupid stunt without getting murdered, plus the kid was as good with hardware as she'd hoped. He'd helped Torque with a few extras for their big SUV, checked battery charges on all the hardware dripping off the team's new guns, and went over and over Jenny's own intrusion toys with her.

Most importantly, he worried. Jenny liked having a worrier around. It meant someone took the job seriously. That was important, these days more than ever. The margin for error in the DeeCee shadows had gone from slim to nil in recent weeks, but these four looked like they'd do. Doc and Torque knew their shit, and even Match's stupid walk across the street had panned out; he'd taken a head count while he was in there, confirmed that none of them seemed to be packing, learned a little more about their Cult of the Future Ascendant, and figured out they weren't—contrary to initial assumptions—tied to any of the dragon bullshit that had recently gone down.

It looked like it was just a plush, comfortable meditation house for overstressed DeeCee wageslaves and politicos, an escape from the self-help databases of some electronic bookstore, a trendy brownstone they could relax in to take a break from driving on the Beltway.

She preferred to work alone, but if she needed help, Jenny decided she could've done worse than this crew. When Johnny Swift had told her about the book and the job in the first place, he'd said bringing some muscle along as insurance would be a good idea. Swift and this team's dead mage buddy had worked together before, the crew had wanted some out-of-town work while laying low from ugly business with Ares last month, and all the pieces had fallen together. Jenny gave Swift a brief call just before go-time, and the fixer agreed; the book was as good as theirs.

I couldn't shake it. This Jenny gal seemed competent enough, and I agreed with her on all the specs. Even our pair of drive-bys to scout the place hadn't turned up anything that disagreed with her security assessment. No external cabling or increased thermal activity that would give away additional intrusion countermeasures. Their node was clean as a whistle, and no guards were out front. It looked like any other brownstone in a DeeCee suburb. So why didn't I feel more confident?

Twiggy had told us a cult used the place, had sold us on the job, had promised us DeeCee would be the last 'plex Knight Errant would look for us. Match had seemed eager to go, Torque had agreed, Doc went with the flow like he always did, and even I felt like it made sense to leave Seattle for a bit. Torque had heard about a smuggling job out of Chicago, but this job was as good an excuse as any, right? It should've all been fine. And everything matched what we'd been told before Jangler got geeked and Twiggy's body went empty. I just...I had a bad feeling.

I watched while we did our jobs. Torque's GridLink override worked like a charm, and I kept an eye on our registration as it changed every ninety seconds while we crossed town and parked. Doc went a few steps to the north and watched the street, Match did the same to the south. Both of them sported the hard, deadly bulges of short Colt rifles under their coats.

Jenny and I went straight to the door; I handled electronic overwatch on the approach. We both tricked the security at the same time; I convinced the cameras to replay the last three hours instead of showing the next three minutes, she silenced the alarms and opened the door. Match shouldered his gun and took point, Doc and Jenny just behind, then me, with Torque playing caboose.

We cleared the house, Jenny falling into the team like the pro she was; doorway by doorway, hall by hall, the occasional muttered "clear" the only sound, transmitted from Match's headware or the mics the rest of us wore slaved to earbuds. Jenny Q's astral sight confirmed what we all thought, and Match's augmentation suite agreed. We were alone, and the book wasn't above ground. That was part of the plan, though.

All the cameras were right where they were supposed to be, and there weren't any secondary floor panels or motion sensors. Jenny sliced through the old metal lock to the basement with the pick-gun she'd chosen earlier in the week. Everything went like a charm. I just couldn't shake my nerves. Jenny looked a little uneasy, too, but maybe that was just mid-job jitters.

We ghosted down the stairs, Match in front, the rest of us all stacked up. My Crusader felt good in my hands, reassuring, lethal, matching Jenny's HK, Torque's big Mossberg, and the paired carbines of Doc and Match.

We'd all done this before, I reminded myself. We all had plenty of trigger time, could shoot our way past anything we couldn't spoof or sneak. We were pros, we all knew the basement was an unknown variable, and we'd prepared. We were ready for anything.

Anything, God help us, but the *bugs*.

Bigger than me, bigger than *Torque*, all mandibles and huge eyes. Six of them, no eight. Ten. A dozen. Jesus. All rushing us, all at once. The stuff of nightmares.

Just some trendy cult house. Just some book. Twiggy's death "just happened." Just a few cameras. Just a few locks. Just another brownstone. Just, just, just.

Suddenly everything I saw, I saw in the strobe-brightness of muzzle flashes in the dark. Torque got shredded and went down, shouting and firing. My machine pistol chattered out a long angry burst at the bundle of eyes and claws that had tagged him, and Jenny shouldered her 227 and started in, too. I heard

Match firing short bursts behind us, further in the basement, and I watched as Doc got to work on Torque's wrecked belly, hands all swift and certain like he was back on a High Threat Response team again, responding to super-platinum contract holders. Jenny and I both emptied our magazines into the one that had gotten Torque—the one between us and the stairs out, *fuck the fucking job, we're leaving*—and I heard an explosion from behind us.

Match's gun barked again as I loaded a fresh magazine of explosive rounds and I saw him throw another grenade; close, so close the blast turned the tails of his longcoat into shredded streamers, but he weathered it just fine. I couldn't hear after the gunfire and the explosions, having lost my earbud somewhere between strolling down some stairs and finding myself in Hell. There was no sound but ringing, but I could feel Jenny's hand on my arm and see Match mouthing "GO" over and over again, half-turning to scream at us as he kept firing. Doc sent his full carbine skittering across the floor to clatter against the elf 's feet before helping Torque up.

The ork had three patches on his bloody skin, and whatever was in them was doing their job; his Mossberg's muzzle flash led the way back to the steps leading up and out. Doc gave the ork a shove toward life and freedom, then there was a spray of red and his head went tumbling from his body. Jenny mouthed words at me I couldn't hear and started moving.

I turned to fire over Jenny's head and past her as I stood on the third step, and I saw Match throw his Colt like a spear—pure adrenaline, pure frustration—a split-second before he kicked Doc's gun up into his hands to keep shooting. He had the carbine on full auto, just hosing left and right with it and blazing into a mass of twisted monsters that were too close to miss but too many to stop.

I told myself, later, that Jenny and Torque had made me leave. I told myself that they'd pulled me along, dragged me up the stairs and out.

I told myself that I hadn't liked the job in the first place, and that it wasn't my fault. I told myself Doc was dead before he'd hit the ground, and that there was nothing I could do to help Match. I told myself razorboys died all the time when jobs went sideways.

I told myself that, in this line of work...sometimes it just happened.

ROUND TABLE

(Way of the Samurai)

"Round Table" is a story I had a good chunk of fun writing, and one that I know not a ton of y'all have read. Way of the Samurai *has been a bit of a sleeper on the sales charts, probably my least-sold product to date. It was another chance to co-write (the sourcebook, not the fiction), and while I'm still fine with the end product, I'll admit it could have been better.*

The intro fic itself, though? This is a piece I like a fair amount. I got to show off an assortment of street samurai archetypes, I got to show who is and isn't a street samurai at all, and I got to introduce a couple of neat new characters I really gotta circle back to some day. Maybe some day soon.

—RRZ

They sat. In a half-lit corner of the Hollow Point bar, itself nestled in a half-civilized corner of the Puyallup Barrens, they sat. Coworkers and survivors, perhaps even friends, the small group washed down ideas with cheap beer, half-heartedly peppered their discussion with curses and threats, hammered out details and logistics, littered their table with empty bottles and a white noise generator, and tried to make a working plan. They weren't a crew in the strict sense, but they'd all worked together in the past, and they were considering working together again.

They were combat veterans, the warrior elite of the shadows, which made them a sort of aristocracy in the Hollow Point.

"I don't like it," Whitecap said around a reeking stogie. The dwarf had been Special Forces back east, but he was cagey about admitting which company, nation, or combination of those he'd served with. He'd been a lot of things in a lot of places. For this job, he was fire support and quartermaster all rolled into one, calling on a world's worth of contacts to get the guns this crew would need. Very few people could get ahold of firepower as readily as Whitecap could, and fewer still could make use of it as efficiently.

"You're too short to like anything." Red Stick laughed. He laughed a lot. He'd laughed his way right out of the Salish-Sidhe Rangers, to hear him tell it. He broke radio silence to crack about a superior officer's mother, then eventually hoofed it to Seattle. His eyes were as sharp as his tongue, though, and he was a hell of a shot, so his laughing hadn't gotten him killed yet. He was the long gun of the team, even if the only time he was patient and calm was when he was looking through a scope.

"I'm not happy about it either, 'cap." Saber made a point of ignoring the NAN sniper. "But it is what it is. Smiley gave us half up front, Smiley told the Johnson the job's as good as done, so we're in. We've got to find a way to make it work."

Saber didn't laugh much. It's part of why they listened to him. He wasn't some SpecOps hotshot, hadn't done time in the Desert Wars or globetrotted as a merc. He'd worked Lone Star Fast Response long enough to know how to handle himself, though, and he had a good head on his shoulders along with a solid street rep. He saw a lot from behind the black eyeshields he always wore.

People feared Whitecap and Shiv, they laughed alongside Red Stick, but they respected Saber.

"Shiv and I take the front, basic sweep and clear. Stick's got that new Barrett you arranged for, right? So he runs overwatch, taking shots through windows and laying down fire if back-up shows. You take the rear with your Ultimax. Let loose if they make a break for it." Saber talked matter-of-factly, laying out the closest thing they had to a plan. He knew Johnny Shiv was on board, even though the killer had ghosted into the Hollow Point's crowd for a fresh round of drinks. Shiv had agreed to the plan earlier, and Saber had never known the elf to change his mind on anything, least of all a plan that started with Whitecap scoring him a pair of new Cougar Fineblades.

"We're too short for this sort of thing," Whitecap butted in. Before the words even fully left his mouth, he was turning to glare at Red Stick, daring the Makah to drop a dwarf joke. "Short-staffed, I mean! The kill call went out to twenty gangers, Saber. Yeah, me and the kid can cover doorways and keep these punks bottled up, but even you and Shiv aren't good for ten guys each without problems. You sure you can't call anyone else on this one?"

"I know we could use a few more guns, but no luck. The new crew's got some prior engagements, so they're all no-gos," Saber said with a grimace. "Or we'd be in better sha—"

> *"–Ain't got no time for you cookin', vruken!*
> *Just check out my hez, I'm the bezzzzztt!–"*

As the MC Bacchus tune registered in the microcomputers built into his inner ears, Saber immediately located the source of the music, and his grimace deepened. He knew who it was before visuals confirmed it.

Woofer. *Damn.* This was a hassle he didn't need tonight.

> *"–I'm just here for your rohodo, ho!*
> *Rohodo, ho!*
> *Rohodo, yo!–"*

Woofer wasn't a former anything; not a cop or a soldier, not even a Mafia hitman like Shiv. He was just a chromed-up punk, and he seemed destined to die that way instead of growing out of it. The ork's faintly glowing cyberoptics caught almost as much attention as his brushed-chrome cyberarm, so the arm tried to make up for it by having an implanted speaker. That speaker perpetually blared orxploitation noise, giving the scowling gutter-muscle his own soundtrack.

"What up, breeder?" Woofer had to shout just to be heard over his own music, but he liked to shout. Saber knew Woofer would have been shouting even if the room was silent. The Hollow Point's thin crowd began to drift, inching out of the invisible path connecting Woofer and Saber's table. Their places were filled by a handful of burly orks flanking their cyberarmed leader, bristling with malice and packing guns tucked carelessly in their waistbands. Here and there exposed skin, stretched taut over enhanced muscles, was littered with slap patches. Black market drugs, Saber could tell when his optics zoomed in to identify a maker's mark. Nothing healthy.

"Why ain't choo payin' the fee, punk?"

"–Don't care what them ujnorts
say 'bout your warts!
I think you're hot,
so ready or not–"

"Fee?" Saber kept his tone neutral, gave Red Stick a silencing kick under the table to keep the rifleman from opening his mouth. He turned in his seat, facing Woofer with his glossy black cyberoptic lenses in place, inscrutable and unreadable, playing it cold as ice. "For what?"

"I tol' you what would happen next time I saw your fuckin' car, breeder." Woofer didn't blade his body like a pro, just glared at the whole table full of them, feet and shoulders squared, looking them full-on in the face. He trusted in his boys, rep, and 'ware to save him if shit went down. It was an inviting target, just the sort of profile people trained on. "You parkin' it in my neighborhood. You owe me a fee, or shit might happen to it. A part might break off."

It had been Saber's fault Woofer got that replacement arm, years ago. *That* part had "broken off" in a Fast Response Team raid back when Saber was still on the force. Woofer had pointed a gun at cops, but had been lucky enough not to lose his life for it. Saber felt he'd done the ork a favor. Woofer obviously felt differently, and he said so every chance he got.

"–I'm just here for your rohodo, ho!
Rohodo, ho!
Rohodo, yo!–"

<You want me to ...?>

The text rolled across Saber's field of vision, an open-ended offer from Johnny Shiv. Saber didn't bother scanning the crowd to find the elf; he just knew he was there somewhere, waiting and ready.

He thought about the offer. He thought about saying yes. He knew it would mean Woofer's death, and knowing Shiv it would be a blade high in the spinal column, maybe even a decapitation attempt. The elf would get his kill, but that would just let Woofer's crew off the leash.

High on who-knows-what, the gangers would open up. They'd go for Shiv first, and there were enough to kill him. Red Stick wasn't as good in close as he was at range, but he and Whitecap could take out at least a few. There'd be a lot of lead flying, though, especially given Stick's love of shotguns for indoors work.

It would cause a lot of civilian casualties and a lot of blood. Almost as bad, he'd be down a man, probably two. The job would be a scratch. No-go. Saber rewound in his head.

"–I'm just here for your rohodo, ho!
Rohodo, ho!
Rohodo, yo!–"

<You want me to ...?>

Saber played the scenario out again. He thought about saying no and going for his Ruger instead. The Thunderbolt had a nasty kick, but he knew his cyberarm could handle it. Woofer was chip-quick and plated up, so it might take two bursts to drop him though. A lot could happen between two bursts. Lord only knows what hardware Woofer had in that arm besides that stupid speaker, and the way the kid was standing, he was looking forward to drawing down on someone. Saber was fast, but he didn't know if he was fast enough. Once guns were drawn, there'd be no turning back.

Shiv would get a few or get away, Woofer would probably drop, but Whitecap might go for the frag grenade he always kept on him, and Stick's scattergun would tear up the crowd. If they even won, a lot of Hollow Point patrons would bleed. If a full-on firefight started, there'd be no way his crew would make it out bloodless. The job would be a scratch. No good. Rewind.

"–I'm just here for your rohodo, ho!
Rohodo, ho!
Rohodo, yo!–"

<You want me to ...?>

Play it out again. Saber considered accepting Shiv's murderous offer, but redirecting it. While Saber burst from his chair and popped his spurs, Shiv could probably take out two punks at once, stabbing low, going for the spots that hurt while they killed. The orks would be distracted enough that Red Stick could haul up that Defiance twelve-gauge he kept under his coat, Whitecap could go for his Predator, and the firefight would be quick.

In close, though? In close, Saber wasn't sure he could take Woofer without trouble. He knew how fast his arms, how powerful his legs, and how sharp his spurs were. He was practiced in a modified Kreysi style, adept at using his armored limbs to protect his head, lashing out with elbows and spurs. He knew he was good.

But was Woofer good, too? The ork was at least as strong as Saber was, probably stronger. He knew the kid's arm had started Evo-spec'ed, probably for bladework, and word from the gutters said the punk had some crazy new machete implant he was in love with. It would be brutal and close, either way... no. Bad odds. Still too many variables, too many orks too close to him and Shiv, too many blades from too many directions, too much risk, too many casualties. The job would be a scratch. No-go. Again.

> *"–I'm just here for your rohodo, ho!*
> *Rohodo, ho!*
> *Rohodo, yo!–"*

<You want me to ...?>

Saber considered going in close, fast and hard, but without the spurs. Not even answering Johnny Shiv, just bursting up from the table and launching himself, hydraulics doing their work, right at Woofer. Tangle him up, take him to the ground, wrestle and break the mad right out of him. Whitecap was professional enough he had to have some gel rounds or stick-and-shock on him, he could help take down a few orks before things got too bloody. Red Stick would pitch in, too, and with luck some Hollow Point staff would get in some licks. If everyone kept it clean and didn't kill any of the orks, maybe things wouldn't turn into a bloodbath.

But Shiv wouldn't be much help, his old bosses had only really used him for one thing. Shiv didn't go hands on, he went blades-in. Taking the time to go less-than-lethal would give the orks the edge, too, and there was no guarantee they would keep their kid gloves on, especially covered in slap-patches of Ghost-knows-what.

No. No, too many maybes were involved. Too much trouble, especially fighting with one hand behind their backs. The job would be a scratch. Again.

> *"–I'm just here for your rohodo, ho!*
> *Rohodo, ho!*
> *Rohodo, yo!–"*

<You want me to ...?>

The text rolled across Saber's field of vision, an open-ended offer from Johnny Shiv. Saber didn't bother scanning the crowd to find the elf, he just knew he was there somewhere. Waiting. Ready. Saber gave a small shake of his head.

Instead, he sent a mental command, and the black-gleaming ballistic lenses snapped away from his eyes, folding back into the metal framework on his face. Without them, his ocular implants looked almost normal. Almost human. Almost friendly.

Saber held his hands up, black chrome but unthreatening, fingers splayed to show he wasn't about to go for his blades.

"Fine. I'll pay your parking fee." It was the one response the ork didn't expect in the least. "But it counts as your up-front payment."

The rest followed his lead. Shiv didn't attack. Red Stick didn't laugh. Whitecap didn't do anything but puff on his reeking cigar.

Woofer looked terribly confused. "My up-front payment for what?"

"Have a seat, and I'll tell you," Saber said, turning halfway back around, nodding as Shiv emerged from the darkness to pull an empty chair up to their table. This was the only way to play without losing. To Saber, and the people that knew him, hired him, and trusted him, things like that still mattered. Someday, if he hung with the right crowd, that sort of thing might matter to Woofer, too.

"We're short a few guns for a kill-team tonight. If you and your boys can use the nuyen, do you have any time for a job?"

They sat. Honor can't be forced on someone, but it can be taught.

VOTER INTIMIDATION

(Dirty Tricks)

"Something about politics" was the theme I had to work with, and that was about the only direction I got. I took it and ran with it, slapping on a Seattle spin (the Ork Underground, our current hotspot), AND wanting to tie together a few of "my" storylines. I had Saber and his team on the one hand...and my latest character, an elf I cooked up for a novella, on the other.

Everybody ready to meet Jimmy Kincaid?

—RRZ

It was a panel van designed for hauling turn-of-the-century steam-cleaning supplies, not people. The back benches had been torn out decades ago, so the current passengers had to squat and lean against walls, using one hand to steady themselves while their others held their guns and clubs. It didn't help that the driver was obviously used to a smaller vehicle with better handling, or that they were bumping and skipping from pothole to pothole on ill-maintained Puyallup roads.

<I wish Torque was driving.> Frostbyte's headware commlink piped the whine to the muscle, the triggerman the streets called Saber. Truth be told, he wished the orkish wheelman were there for his brawn and his combat shotgun as much as his driving ability, but it seemed...impolitic...to say so to his team's new heavy. The scrawny hacker might have planned to mentally send something more, but a particularly sharp turn made him windmill one arm to stay upright.

Saber, for his part, held himself steady effortlessly. One cyberhand was braced against the bare metal interior of their ugly van, and magnetic panels did the rest of the work. A half-dozen other men—mostly white, like Saber and Frostbyte, and none of them metahuman—were jostled around in the van's cargo area, but Saber somehow stood steady and calm, with an aloof air. His slicked-back hair and matte-black cyberlimbs contrasted sharply with their shaved heads and white undershirts.

<Hell, I take it back. I just wish this van was new enough we could let it autopilot!> Frostbyte didn't fit in any better than Saber, but that had more to do with his skinny build than the dress code. The hacker was perfectly happy in faux-cotton, but out of sloppiness rather than conformity.

<If wishes worked, we wouldn't have a political rally to go to,> the street samurai sent back. <And you know as well as I do why Torque is out.>

Frostbyte almost dropped his baseball bat after they hit another pothole, and he started to open his mouth to complain. A stern glare from Saber kept him from doing so. Whether the pair were reasonably priced shadowrunner backup or not, sitting in the middle of a van full of Humanis Policlub thugs—the low-ranking and low-minded shocktroopers of the movement—wasn't a smart place to open your mouth and let something sarcastic out.

<which way u boys going 2 vote?>

In the passenger seat, Jenny Q, known as Jenny Quick in breaking-and-entering circles, typed furiously on her Hermes commlink. As an adept, she didn't have the implants the boys did, so her thumbs had to stay busy to keep in the conversation. As the van's sole female occupant, though, she also didn't have their comfort problem. She was securely seat-belted up front, her stubby little black HK submachine gun snug between her knees.

<Which time?> Frostbyte flashed a mischievous grin. Everyone knew the kid had a fake SIN for every day of the week, and probably more. He could probably cast a dozen votes if he wanted.

<I'm voting for it. Prop 23 will do good things to the Underground. If they want to be part of the system, the system should let them in.> Saber's implanted optic covers kept his features impassive, but it was easy enough to tell he meant it.

<A compelling argument!> Frostbyte gave Saber a thumbs-up, never mind the fact none of the Humanis thugs in the back of the van had any idea why. <Consider yourself having earned a vote.>

<ya rite,> Jenny's thumbs danced. <teh system sux. brackhaven makes it suck more. orks will be pissed w/ it soon enuf. they only want in b/c they dont know better.>

<Once they're in, they can work to change it.> Saber's reply was matter-of-fact, face blank as always. <They'll bring a lot of votes in. Votes Brackhaven won't have a handle on. The Underground's got a lot of people in it.>

<mostly w/o sin though. no id = no vote.> Jenny typed furiously.

Frostbyte swung his head back and forth, watching the argument unfold like a tennis match.

<If they can get enough votes to pass 23, they'll get enough votes to pass other bills. The system will work, if we let it.>

<even if ur rite, it sux tho. ork underground gets law & order, the shadows shrink a little more. 1 less place 4 people like us 2 hide out or do biz.> Jenny glared into the rearview to meet Saber's eyes, daring him to keep arguing.

The samurai turned his head just enough to make it clear he was looking at her reflected eyes, his optic shields still in place. For all his obvious inhumanity, though, one eyebrow quirked as he sent a headware response. <Is that what your contact said when he offered you this assignment?>

Jenny blinked first. She had to. Looking away, she pulled on some mirrored shades before glaring out the window and riding in silence. It had been her contacts who'd put them in touch with Humanis, though. Her business acquaintances had gotten the team the job, and her friends had offered them thousands of nuyen in exchange for dozens of bullets.

Frostbyte and his Fairlight commlink went to work, ignoring the sullen silence that had replaced the team-channel banter. Their whole Humanis crew had slaved their 'links to his, letting the Matrix specialist provide overwatch and security. A quick check with a pair of agents confirmed their timetable.

<The other van's on location already. The gun crews are in place,> he sent out to Saber and Jenny, thoughts transferred to text and displayed only to them. <Right where Saber told them to set up.>

They'd have a terrific field of fire from the rooftops the former Lone Star shooter had suggested. This Humanis chapter had a bold plan and a reasonable bankroll, but their tactics had been as outdated as their hardware. A drive-by shooting would have been ugly and not really effective. With the anti-Proposition 23 funds that had been funneled their way, they'd decided to invest in professional assistance. Jenny Q and her team of consultants had proven a wise investment.

Jenny's contacts had helped them get an assortment of black market weapons and vehicles that would never be traced to the policlub, upgrading their firepower and confidence with crates of European rifles and cutting-edge smartgoggles. Saber's tactical acumen was better than anything the Humanis chapter had, and he'd personally overseen weapons maintenance and basic firearm training in the weeks prior to the attack. Frostbyte's Matrix wizardry supplied agents to handle security cameras, surveillance drones, GridGuide, and inter-team coordination for the assault itself. What would have been a haphazard display of brutish violence had been refined into a four-pronged assault, with a pair of elevated positions laying down plunging fire in mutual support of each other. The icing was the two vans full of assault forces—including the trio of shadowrunners, who'd volunteered simply to see their plan carried out firsthand, free of charge—who would lay down a wicked crossfire and sweep up any survivors, fanning out into a gunline and then simply advancing into the kill zone.

The mostly metahuman crowd milling around at the Puyallup voting center wouldn't stand a chance. Heavily orkish and dwarven or not, the would-be voters weren't going to stand up to this kind of firepower.

As the team's Humanis Mr. Johnson had put it after Frostbyte had shared the plan over a flashy AR display, they would be mowed down like wheat before scythes.

It wasn't a bad plan, all things considered. They'd make up for their erstwhile companions' lack of training with sheer firepower, overcome the civilians' numbers through brutality coupled with coordination.

For a shadowrunning crew still without a mage, a team who'd recently lost two members, and a team leaving another regular on the outside for this job, it was pretty impressive work. For the shadowrunners, it would mean nuyen in the bank. For the Humanis Policlub, it would mean a righteous massacre, a glorious body count, the envy of other chapters, and every metahuman in Seattle thinking twice before going to any polling center or political rally for a long, long time. Everyone would win, except the poor metas pouring out of Carbonado to try and vote.

And who wanted them to win?

I never got my jollies on the rooftop jaunts, like so many of the freerunner kids and adrenaline junkie courier-types. Guys like Gentry, like my Alleycat Express neighbors. Maybe I'd smoked too much to enjoy a run like I used to. Maybe my shoes just weren't right for it. Maybe I worried about my fedora blowing off. Maybe it was this damned rain. My elven blood meant I wasn't getting old—physically slowing down, that is; mentally I felt like a dinosaur most days—so I knew it wasn't that, but the fact remains that I'm just not a fan of this sort of thing. Me, I liked keeping my feet on the ground, or failing that, on the pedals of a fast car. Clambering over low walls, sidestepping around air conditioning vents, ducking clotheslines and stepping on tar and pigeon crap? No thanks, pal. Jimmy Kincaid would rather be on the streets than high above 'em. Be that as it may, though, here I was. Doing anything for a paycheck, even monkeying around jumping between buildings like some sort of action-trid star.

Ariana loved it, the silly kid. Why shouldn't she? If I could fricking fly, I'd probably have a lot more fun up here, too. For someone who's clearly from the elemental plane of earth, so much so she shines like silver and copper and red rubies even in the muddy grey sunlight of Seattle, she sure does like being up high.

Ally spirits. There's just no accounting for taste. She didn't care a lick about nuyen and rent and bills, she just liked looking at the city from a new perspective. She enjoyed seeing the people of our neighborhood determined and upbeat and happy for once, all milling around and talking about exercising their rights as citizens.

Lon Campa himself, Puyallup's own and the Seattle Metroplex's only metahuman mayor, was footing my bill today. The ork had chucked my usual rates right out the proverbial window and offered me hourly pay in exchange for magically augmenting election-day security. Generous hourly pay. I was already on their books as a paranormal consultant, and I already had a solid rep with his office thanks to the work I did on their wards, but this was gonna be a big haul for me. It was gonna be a big day. It'd keep a roof over Ariana and me for months. That being the case, I could suck up having a roof *under* me for a little while, right?

I cupped my hands around a fresh Target and worked hard at an ignite spell to get it lit. Campa knew I got results. Campa knew I could handle mojo. Campa knew I'd been a cop (which made him trust me) but knew it had been a long time ago (which made his constituents trust me). Campa didn't know, though, that Ari did most of the magical heavy lifting nowadays, and he also didn't know how much I had to push to light a cigarette in the rain. Oh well. What Campa didn't know wouldn't hurt him. I'd get the job done. I always did.

Today's festivities promised to be something nasty. Word on the street said some Humanis punks with money to burn and a wish to be the next Alamos 20k were out looking for trouble. I'd heard mutterings from all over the place leading up to election day, natch, with every snitch and rat eager to pay for his next hit by telling you yesterday's news: this just in, metahuman agitation was high in the face of a Brackhaven re-election; news flash, Humanis doesn't like Proposition 23; we interrupt this broadcast to tell you that orks might get violent about Humanis harassment; and big screaming headline story, election fever makes people sweat nuyen. An idiot could see the trouble ahead; the tricky part was gonna be knowing when, where, and how it would come out.

No one knew exactly what was coming. No one but an old buddy from my Lone Star days, Sabelhaus. I'd been surprised when he came into my office, and even more surprised when he told me what he was up to. He'd never struck me as the plain old wetwork sort, but enough augmentation can change a man. I know what it's like to have a hole in you that just won't fill up, no matter what you throw in there. Mine had come from a vampire. His, maybe, had come from those gun-blued arms and legs of his, and the who-knows-what-else Lone Star had cut off and replaced with metal.

My former Fast Response Team buddy filled me in quick. Sabelhaus had heard exactly what was going down, and exactly where, and exactly when. He didn't even charge me for the dirt. He just wanted the authorities alerted and things nipped in the bud.

"Heh. 'The authorities,'" I muttered around my smoke, spitting my gum carelessly off the rooftop as I huddled against a wall in the rain. My mentor spirit would get a good chuckle out of *that.*

Ariana had us good and hidden, so I wasn't too worried about a little grumbling giving us away. She spun circles just over my head, dancing in the rain and sometimes peeking off the rooftop to watch the shining auras of the hopeful voters down below. I smoked and flipped up my collar against the rain and shivered and glared over at a half-dozen ignorant Humanis thugs as they set up a pair of RPK HMGs overlooking the crowd.

Lining the courtyard were street vendors, their cries and AR advertisements mingling along with the scents of the foods they offered. Ork Underground kids worked the crowd, selling gum and buttons and cheap t-shirts, AR badges and meat on a stick. The place was like a festival. A block party. Someone had linked up a half-dozen commlinks and their sound systems and had music playing. I heard the sharp, ugly, *chick-clack* of a skinhead machinegunner loading a belt of ammo.

"Yeah. The authorities. That's me." I flicked my cigarette away and reached for my Colt.

It was gonna be a big day, all right.

Frostbyte got a ping to his headware when the RPK machine guns, linked to his computer wirelessly, disengaged their safeties.

<Almost ti—> His update was interrupted by the pair of weapons opening up on the crowded square. The hacker couldn't help but jump; the reports were so loud as they echoed an hundred times off the brick and concrete of northern Puyallup. The screams started just a split-second later, drowning out the roaring autofire.

Frostbyte looked across the van at Saber, but the impassive street samurai just gave him a curt nod. <Everything's going according to the plan,> the shooter reassured him.

Their van screeched to a halt, and Frostbyte planted the butt of his baseball bat on the bare metal floor to shove off and half-vault, half-scramble out onto the sidewalk. The rear doors swung wide open and Humanis muscle came pouring out, fanning wide just the way Saber had drilled them. A dozen meters away, the first van opened and another eight thugs leaped out.

Saber moved at a herky-jerk quick trot, augmentations making him the quickest man there as he moved toward the first team. Jenny stayed in the passenger seat of the van, twisting, catlike, to level her HK out the passenger window and toward the square.

Their contract was officially over. The fire teams were in place, the machine guns were the cue for the ground teams to start. As consultants, they'd fulfilled their duties.

"Deadbolt is a go," Saber subvocalized to Frostbyte as he hefted his matte-black Ares Alpha. The samurai took in a deep breath. On either side of him, over a dozen Humanis punks shouldered their brand-new FN rifles and took up their shooting positions, matching smartgoggles in place, ugly smiles on their ugly faces.

"Fire!" Saber's bellow, in what Lone Star had used to call a "command voice," cut through the chattering autoguns and the screaming orks.

In the half-second between orders, Frostbyte worked his console-cowboy magic. Viruses, implanted weeks ago, were triggered and went to work. First, both vans' engines died. Then the hardware got hit. Every full magazine in the Humanis gun line dropped and clattered off the pavement, every bolt *snicked* back to send the remaining round glittering from an empty chamber, and every rifle shut down and rebooted for routine maintenance. Each set of smartgoggles whited out and dazzled their owners as their flare compensation protocols were reversed, then doubled and redoubled a dozen times over.

Several other things were also happening, mind you, all triggered by Saber's shout. Frostbyte tossed his baseball bat onto the sidewalk with a clatter and a grin. Jenny Q kicked straight backward, both long, athletic legs extending into their driver's ugly face. She held herself up by one hand braced on the passenger's side windowsill and her feet alone, smashing their Humanis escort's head away to spiderweb the impact-resistant glass of the driver's-side window. She twisted to line up her dancing laser sight and triggered a pair of short bursts into the backs of the first two Humanis shooters she saw. The stick 'n shock rounds sent them twitching and tumbling to the ground.

Frostbyte's bat rolled across the sidewalk until it stopped under the toe of a big, ugly, combat boot. 'Byte gave a cheery wave as a hulking figure bent over to pick the bat up; it was Torque, a wall of meat and tusks wrapped all in denim and leather who had materialized out of the scattering, screaming crowd of metahuman voters right on cue.

Torque gave the hacker a friendly nod and a toothy grin, giving the bat a practice swing as he advanced toward a half-dozen blinded Humanis punks. Strolling over discarded rifles and frantically removed goggles, the ork slipped into a practiced batter's stance and got ready to start bashing heads. Frostbyte scrambled backward into the van, sliding the door shut to protect himself from blood spatters.

Saber, meanwhile, carefully set his gun on the sidewalk. There were only nine of them, and they were blinded and disarmed; he wouldn't need to waste any ammo. The street samurai flexed his cybernetic hands, tensed his cybernetic legs. Hydraulics hissed as he launched himself headlong into the middle of their rabid little pack, lashing out with hands and feet as heavy and unyielding as crowbars.

Ariana's barrier spell did its job perfectly. Mine wouldn't have held up against a single large-bore round, but hers, shining silver-white, sent the dozens, then hundreds of RPK shots ricocheting harmlessly away from the crowd. That didn't stop the metas from screaming and scattering, and it sure as hell didn't stop the Humanis punks from just laying on their triggers and shooting longer and longer bursts, but it kept people in one piece. That's what counted.

At a little nod from me, Ari flitted over to the nearest gunner/loader pair. Her hair shone as she placed a bronze hand on each of their shoulders.

"You are *mean* people!" Her voice rang out with a child's certainty, indignation, and spite as she poured mana through their physical contact. Their auras were flooded with a raw power I couldn't come near to matching, and the pair of them slumped to the rooftop. That left me four, and every one of them was spinning to level their weapons—most of them big FN rifles, but another one with that other RPK HMG—right at my ally spirit.

"Hey!" My Colt barked and a pair of rounds slammed into the back of the leftmost shooter's skull.

"You no-good skells—" Another double tap, another dropped skinhead.

"—are under—" Another pair of shots.

"—citizen's arrest."

The last of them crumpled to the rooftop along with my empty magazine. They'd been dropped by gel rounds, and I was eager to get a mag of grown-up bullets locked and loaded. I slung one foot up onto the rooftop's low wall and leaned casually on my knee, watching the ruckus downstairs. I saw Ari's barrier flicker and vanish. Beyond it was a huge ork playing tee-ball with a handful of skinheads, and a leggy blond gal lit by the muzzle flash as she unloaded on another shooter from inside a van.

Meters away, my old buddy Sabelhaus—he went by Saber ever since Lone Star'd dropped him—tore through a pack of Humanis shock troopers like an unstoppable black wind.

The show was over awful fast. The team of shadowrunners all joined up in the rearmost van, with the big ork taking the wheel after pulling an unconscious lump of meat out. Sabelhaus climbed into the back and tugged the rear doors shut behind him, and the blond idly rolled her window up. Their van peeled away just as I saw Knight Errant's lights flashing a block away.

"Thank goodness," I snickered, "The police!"

I holstered my Colt and reached for my pack of Targets. Far below me, Humanis punks groaned and struggled to get to their hands and knees, only to be kicked back down into the gutter by Knight Errant jackboots, right on schedule.

I had a heck of a view of the festivities. Ah, maybe running around on rooftops wasn't all bad.

PART FOUR: KINCAID

BUST

(TWILIGHT HORIZON)

"Something in Las Vegas," was the main instruction on this one. I remembered it from a GenCon face-to-face freelancer meeting, all of us talking about Twilight Horizon *and pitching ideas for themed casino resorts. When I pitched for the intro fiction, I had all of Sin City laid out before me.*

And what's more fun than bringing Jimmy Kincaid up there, outside of Seattle and his comfort zone? Who better than a black-and-white noir PI to sling cards at a speakeasy? "Bust" was a fun way to remind people that Jimmy does jobs for city hall types (that's part of how he gets away with what he gets away with), to remind people that bounties on Technomancers are wrong and pretty evil, AND to remind people that all families are families.

PLUS there was another chance to show off what even a low-Force spell can do. Win/win!

—RRZ

"Hit me." I threw back my whiskey and gave the dealer a feral grin over a sixteen. I was on a lucky streak, a sensation that felt covered in dust and cobwebs. It had been a while. A long while. I hadn't gambled since before the vampire, before losing most of my Talent, before feeling everything positive and human and lucky about me getting torn away. But as it turns out, the luck was still there. Maybe I should've played more often. I was damned good at it. Who knew?

Jimmy Kincaid, Gambling Man had a pretty nice ring to it, compared to *Paranormal Investigator.*

I sat on my twenty and waved a leggy flapper over, and she cheerfully brought me another comped drink. Even if I hadn't been cleaning up at the table, the free booze alone meant the house was losing. This place, The Speakeasy, could afford to comp drinks but not a whole lot else. Two blocks off the strip, it was a second-rate themed joint, not one of the top end casinos that drew most of the tourists. My usual suit meant I didn't have to play dress-up the way everyone else did; mobsters and bootleggers were the veneer of the place, and I fit right in without any AR help.

"Another win, sir." Their pit boss, all plastic smile, three-piece suit, and slick hair, materialized at my shoulder almost as if by magic. He was lucky I was used to that sort of thing. Even so, I preferred my ally spirit doing it to this guy. He was a used car salesmen gene-crossed with a simple legbreaker. I hated him.

"Yup." I raked in my virtual chips, a negligent gesture that dragged the pile of them across faintly glowing lines. They shifted color as they left the dealer's bank, glowing slightly and neatly stacking themselves in with the rest of my imaginary hoard.

"Impressive." His faintly arched eyebrow spoke volumes. He hated me right back. I knew the cyberware scanners at the door had flagged me and the hardware crammed into my noggin, but I knew they wouldn't do anything about it while I was on the gaming floor, playing along.

"Yup." I drank down my next shot while their dealer flung imaginary cards around the table with flicks of his AR-gloved fingers. Our waitress in her flapper get-up caught me peeking at her and blushed as she poured me another drink, so I shot her a wink before I checked my card.

It wasn't just mine that mattered, though; it was everyone else's. We were in a tournament, after all, and if I was going to win it, I had to play against more than just the dealer. I glanced around the table, headware racing, people-reading knack in overdrive, emotive software integrating with both to help me out. The other players were a mixed bunch, but I read them like an assortment of open books.

A NAN businessman lounged next to me, sitting in a conservative suit with a small medicine pouch around his neck, his high cheekbones and pointed ears keeping me from being the only elf at the table. One pitch-black eyebrow always quirked when he was happy with his card, and the corners of his mouth tensed when he wasn't. I didn't even need my headware to spot that. A CAS vacationer sat on the other side of him, all blue jeans and Texas Rattlers bombat biker t-shirt stretched tight over an orkish bodybuilder's chest. He had on a zoot suit in the AR-overlay of this place, and it might've been the only suit he'd worn in his life. His cheeks flushed when he was happy, eyelids drooped when he was mad. Another easy read.

On my other flank was a salaryman with aspirations of being a high roller—perfect hair, flawless smile, biocosmetic work as expensive as his custom-tailored suit. His eyes gave him away, and there was a stiffness in his shoulders when he was disappointed in his initial card. He was used to boardroom deals, and it took my Talksmooth 3.7 'ware to initially pick up the faint adjustments in his body language.

I wasn't the only one soaking up comped liquor, but I could hold it better than any of the rest. I used the whiskey to strike a balance, to take the edge off while my mind raced. My Transys headware and the programs it was running gave me the leverage I needed, counting and calculating faster than I could alone. I waved the dealer off.

Another win.

Then another.

I lost the next hand, but raked in virtual chips in the one after that. The CAS ork grumbled about having to see a man about a horse, but we all knew he was really leaving because he'd been bleeding chips the last hour. Thirty minutes later, and twelve more winning hands for Mr. James Mitchell Kincaid, made the Sioux stalk off, too. It was down to me and the angry Japanese businessman. I knew his tell and I was on a roll. He never stood a chance.

They called in a new dealer when it was down to just the two of us. She was a perky little strawberry blond with a scattering of freckles across the bridge of her nose, so I didn't mind the change of scenery. Her cyberhands were long-fingered and slender, chromed and flashing, and she worked the AR table without need for gloves. She was their big gun. I saluted her with my next drink, then went on winning.

Pride kept my last opponent playing even after it was clear who had the upper hand, and the pit boss got called back over when he angrily tried to re-buy and get himself a fresh stack of chips. The tournament was over. The entertainment was finished.

No one was paying attention to me any more. While most of the nearby customers were distracted by the rising volume of Japanese cursing, I found myself flanked by a pair of shaved apes in ill-fitting suits.

Right on schedule.

"Please come with us, Mr. Kincaid," one of them said, wrapping a mitt like a steel vice around my upper arm.

My stack of chips made a *tickety-tack* noise as it vanished, virtually clicked-and-dragged into my credstick before I unslotted it from the table. I tossed down the last of my drink with my free hand, then politely slipped off with them while the argument behind me got even louder. I'd been expected them. I'd won too much, too fast. I knew what was coming next.

"Hit me," I said with a smirk as the elevator doors closed.

The beating started right on cue. I got in a few solid shots, but it felt like slamming my fist against a vault door. They pummeled me with jackhammers pretending to be fists, and I played along and went down, even though I would've been good for a few more swings. They didn't let up when I played possum, though, and after the second kick to the head I only had time for one more thought—*This was a stupid plan*—before the world went black.

"I've got a great plan for how to get in, that part won't be a problem," I waved away my client's concern with a smile. I felt Ariana, my ally spirit, tug at my conscience as I did so. Mr. Nelson only cared about my success, but she was genuinely concerned about my safety.

"And you're sure this will work?" Nelson was a bookish sort, with a faintly oversized head that made him seem even more so. He was one of the more reasonable men working in the Puyallup city building, though, and one of the few not in the Gianelli's or Kenran-kai*'s pocket. I liked him. I had to like him, or I wouldn't be taking this case that would drag me out of the city. He fretted as he followed me across my office to the door.*

"Positive, sir," I said as I reached for my hat and coat. I had a flight to catch. "I'll be back before you know it. I just need...ah...?"

"Yes. Yes, of course." He looked nervous as he handed me the credstick. I didn't blame him. I'd be nervous handing over my life savings to someone, too. If I had much to hand over, I mean. Working as a private eye meant "life savings" wasn't exactly a major concern of mine.

"This'll get me in there, Mr. Nelson. Don't you worry. I'll call you once I've got them." I looked longingly at my Colt, my wand, and my knife. The burner and the foci would've come in handy, and they were all legally licensed.

But no. Airport security, casino security, the plan itself, all relied on me not having them. Or Ariana.

I stuffed my hat onto my head and gave my client a reassuring nod.

"I'll get your family back, sir. As soon as I can."

"Nice to meet'cha, family," I said, sitting up and scanning my Corpsman bio-monitor's readout for serious injuries. I was perched on the edge of a bed, nodding to the father and son that stood, warily, across the room from me. I guess I couldn't blame 'em. I didn't feel much pain any more, but knew I had to look like a wreck.

"I'm Junior," the kid piped up, all big eyes and blond curls. He looked more like Roger than Jonathon, the Puyallup councilman who had hired me. His gambling, hustling, almost-kidnapping, husband-worrying dad stood behind him, showing himself to be the half of the Nelson marriage that had given their gene-crafted youngster that golden hair and winning smile.

"My name's Jimmy. Jimmy Kincaid." I held out one hand to return the young man's polite shake but glanced up at his old man when I said it. Recognition sparked in his eyes. Yeah. He'd lived in Puyallup long enough that my name rang a bell. The pair of them had been locked up in this room, this comfortable, well-insulated, soundproofed hotel room, since they'd gotten caught.

The furniture was well built in a traditional style, the mattress soft, the temperature comfortable. Hell, it even looked like some of this stuff was made with real wood. As cages went, they didn't come a whole lot more gilded.

"Mr. Nelson—the other Mr. Nelson—sent me to get you two out of here." The other Mr. Nelson. *Damn.* Maybe my biomonitor was lying and I really was concussed. "It's all gonna be okay, kiddo. Promise."

I looked back and forth from son to father, making sure they both believed me. Or at least believed me enough to go along with it. They did. The hope my presence gave them made me feel a little uncomfortable. I wasn't used to hope, any more than I was used to luck.

I dragged myself to my feet, checking my pockets and stretching to work out the kinks and check for twinges and tugs that might slow me down. Predictably, they'd swiped what little I'd had on me, including the fake SIN and the very real, very swollen, certified credstick. My Corpsman and I checked out, though. They'd roughed me up something fierce, but nothing that'd stick. They didn't want to permanently damage the meat before their business partners showed up, after all. Just tenderize it a little.

That's why I'd taken the job. Tamanous ties. One of the co-owners of The Speakeasy was a part-time organlegger, and rumors abounded concerning what happened to folks who cheated in this two-bit joint. Rumors about ghouls and other nasties. Vampires. I owed 'em.

"So here's what's gonna happen, fellas."

"It's all those fucking Screamers' fault," Jon Nelson had explained to me in my office. He paced, and I understood why. Sometimes moving was all you could do, and you had to feel like you were doing something. "Roger's not a bad man. He just...god, the fucking Screamers had such a bad year!"

I snorted at his understatement. Seattle's local brawl team had been scraping the bottom of the league all season. Even the usually-reliable Tacoma Wings weren't doing great. Only those chuckleheads from Cleveland were worse off.

"But he kept betting and betting. He said he had to. He was trying to make up for me, for my new position. You know how much we get paid." I knew it depended on how dirty they were. I knew I wasn't charging Nelson as much as I could for the office wards, because I knew he was one of the cleaner—which means poorer—ones.

"So what kind of people did he get in with?" I knew a lot of guys in local crews. I might be able to just call in a favor, and work out some sort of deal.

"Bad," was all he said. "The worst."

We didn't pretend to be sick, the way Junior thought we would. That only worked in tridshows, I told him.

Instead, I started shouting, ranting, raving at Nelson at the top of my lungs. He hollered back, shoulder-checked the wall, threw a lamp. In response, I hollered that I was gonna bash Junior's brains in.

The door opened and one of the thugs rushed in, his Ares Viper leading the way. I had a table leg in my hand, a head full of Lone Star Academy memories, and a spot just next to the door. His wrist broke from the first good overhand chop, and the toe of a wingtip sent the gun sliding across the carpeted floor. I slipped by his left cross, then let him have it. The wooden table leg was simple, straightforward, barely touched by metahuman hands or machinery. My spell to analyze it had confirmed my suspicions and gave me an uncanny feel for the weight of it, the life it had glowed with before being harvested, the feel and balance of it when I used it as a weapon.

It felt good. Easy. A natural extension of my arm. It whipped around like a live thing, smashing at him almost without me needing to do a thing.

The first mook dropped with a broken jaw and one temple caved in. His partner rushed in behind him. The stick spun and danced in my hand, and a quick backhand swing knocked his gun offline and sent his shot high and wide, flechettes tearing into the plaster roof instead of my vital organs. I gave him a good rap on the head, but this one had some bone lacing or maybe just a good mad-on, because it barely slowed him down. He caught my wrist to check my next swing, then drove his shoulder into me and me into a nearby dresser. The dresser felt like real wood, too. More's the pity. Should've hurt like a bitch, and would've if it wasn't for the Sideways dose I'd taken years ago.

I didn't feel pain, but that didn't mean I couldn't lose a fight. I'm no slouch, but he had thirty kilos of augmented muscle on me, and as we tangled up and wrestled I started to lose my early momentum. I knocked his gun away, he eventually twisted the club out of my hand, and it turned into a match of short, choppy punches, wicked knees, and attempts to twist the other guy to the ground. I smacked his nose across his face with a good head butt, but he clocked my hairline with a fist like a brick. I was seeing stars as his other mitt wrapped around my throat.

Then Mr. Nelson smashed him square on the side of the head with my club. The big hand at my neck went slack as the thug lurched around to face this new attacker, catching a second solid baseball swing as he clambered to his feet. I lunged and grabbed and got an arm looped around his neck as he advanced on my client's husband, and even as Nelson stepped into it to deliver another good shot, I twisted and pulled. The big body tumbled back to the carpet after a sharp, sick *crack*.

"See?" I panted, hands on my knees, forcing a grin. "Easy as pie. Just like I said it'd be."

Nelson looked at me like I was crazy while he clutched the bloody club. I could see white all around his irises. Then he blinked, heaved in his first gasp of air after surviving a fight like that, and let out a nervous little laugh. I knelt to toss the corpses, searching for anything worth taking, quick as only a Puyallup brat could be.

"It's...not exactly a missing-persons case, Mr. Kincaid," Nelson had said as I got up from my desk. "I know right where to find them."

"Yeah?" My enthusiasm for the case waned a bit. I hated to hear about a kid in trouble, but if it wasn't a missing-persons gig, I wasn't sure what he needed me for. I had a half-dozen divorce cases I should have been gathering evidence on.

"They're in Las Vegas."

"That's a bit outside my normal beat, Mr. Nelson."

"They told me what would happen if I didn't pay. They told me the ransom they want, told me how much it would cost me. They told me what they'd do to Roger if they didn't get it. It's...they know people in Tamanous."

Oh. Well, then.

"And what did Knight Errant say?"

"Jurisdiction issues. Problems because Junior isn't really...we weren't supposed to...he and Roger don't have SINs." Nelson looked ashamed when he said it, scared I'd rat him out to someone.

I sighed in frustration. Cops. Badges. Laws. They all had authority, but they only used it when they wanted to.

Nelson kept talking, "But Mr. Kincaid, there's another thing. I know why they set the ransom as high as they did. I know why they're not threatening to kill Junior. I know why he's worth so much to them."

I quirked an eyebrow. "It ain't just spare parts?"

"They're going to sell Junior, but not to organleggers." He swallowed, nervous. "He's special. There's a bounty."

"C'mon out of the bathroom, kid," I called out. I knew we didn't have a ton of time. I'd recovered the credstick and my lucky little flask—took a welcome pull of Jack before tucking it back into my pocket—along with their commlinks, two small rolls of assorted scrip, and both of the thugs' guns.

"You guys are doing great," I stood up, pistol in each hand.

"You were really brave back there." I said it to the son, but meant it for the father. "But we're not quite out of the woods yet."

I leveled one confiscated Viper at a corpse and pulled the trigger. It was just like I'd figured. The Slivergun refused to fire, its smartlink engaging the safety as the targeting reticule turned red in the corner of my eye. They had a touchlink system set up that activated fine, but smart-target software didn't let any of their weapons fire on guards.

Amidst their handful of other augmentations, they'd thoughtfully given their in-house wrecking crew ID implants. That meant security was on the way because they'd realize their men were dead soon—they probably had biomonitors like my Corpsman—but, most of all, it meant I wouldn't be able to shoot a damned one of them once they showed up.

"I need you to do a trick for me, Junior." A mental command ejected the magazines and racked the slides, and I twirled the empty guns by the triggerguards, holding their grips out toward his little hands. "It's okay, squirt. You ain't in trouble with me. I know you can do it, just like your dad knew you could help him with the slot machines.

"I need you to talk to these guns, kiddo. I can't do it. No one else can, only you. Your dad an' me, kid, we need you. Turn off parts that need to be turned off, make it let me shoot whoever I need to. If you do that for me, we're in the clear. I'll stop the bad guys. We'll be back home in no time. I promise."

It wasn't a lie. I'd flown here for speed, but after I arrived I dipped into the expense credstick to arrange for a rental car under my fake SIN. It was parked less than a block away. I had the building's layout in my headware, knew where the exits were, had a headcount of their security.

I'd runned and gunned with Lone Star's best in a Fast Response team. You put a burner in my hand, and I'll take care of what needs taking care of.

Junior looked to his dad, got a nod, then looked down at the guns. The boy closed his eyes and concentrated, tongue sticking out of the corner of his mouth. Viper in each hand, guns looking huge compared to his skinny arms and small hands, he worked in ways I couldn't. Even before I'd lost so much of my magic, I couldn't do what he was doing; almost nobody else could. He had a different kind of magic than I did. A different kind of amazing.

He was an illegal clone. He was a technomancer. But he was just a little boy. To me, the last one mattered more than the first two. But right that second, his knack with machines was pretty damned important.

He stuffed those guns back into my hands like he was afraid they'd bite him, and I quickly slapped their magazines home. One got tucked into my waistband, the other nestled in my palm like I'd been born with it.

"Good work, kid." I grinned and reached out to tousle his hair with my free hand, making him scrunch up his face in irritation. I laughed a little. "You hang onto your pop, and keep your eyes closed once we see any more of these palookas, all right?"

I knew what kind of hamburger it'd make once I started shooting tough guys in their unarmored faces. The kid didn't need to see that. I gave father and son a reassuring nod once he'd clambered up.

The muzzle of my gun led the way out into the hallway. It was time to get them out of here.

The house was losing this hand.

ADVERSARY

(ENHANCED FICTION)

When the latest set of SR rules, Sixth World Edition*, hit, I knew I wanted to get Adversary-the-mentor-spirit into my grubby paws pronto. He's been so central to Jimmy's stories for so long, I really wanted to be the one to stat him up for once, instead of nebulously basing him, in my head and in my writing, on the Fourth Edition version I'd started writing Jimmy with.*

My chance to write Adversary-the-mentor-spirit came by way of Adversary-the-enhanced-fiction, a short, punchy, little yarn that had some mechanics attached. This one's a pretty hard-hitting story compared to its word count, and I really wanted to use it as a chance to say a few things about some real-life issues; social commentary has always been a part of noir PI fiction AND Shadowrun*, and throughout my Jimmy stories, for sure…but this was probably the clearest and loudest I've ever been about it.*

—RRZ

They say everybody's got a little voice in their head. Mine's a little louder than most. He speaks to me—and yeah, I assume it's a "he," for the same reason I assume a serial killer making headlines is a he—in all sorts of different situations, at all kinds of different times. Sometimes it's in the ringing silences between gunshots, or in the breathless moment after a spell turns all the air in the room to fire and burns everything and everyone but me. Sometimes he speaks to me in the hissed intake of breath before throwing another punch. He can be the snarl of an engine, the growl of a dog, the sound of a bone breaking. I hear his voice when I'm first half-awake and not sure if life's still a dream or not, when I've stayed up too late and had enough to drink that reality goes fuzzy 'round the edges from exhaustion, when I take a good solid punch to the face and a concussion threatens. In those moments, I hear him clear as can be.

The whispers in the pointy ears of one James Mitchell Kincaid—Jimmy, to my friends—are real, you see. It's not my conscience warning me away, it's not memories of my mom or pop trying to steer me straight, it's not quite a god or devil, and it probably ain't even a chemical imbalance, quite. It's not even a vivid imagination and an imaginary friend-type of gig.

No, when I hear a bodiless voice commanding me to do bad things, I know just who it is. The cartoon devil on my shoulder watching the cartoon angel punch out at the end of the day and go home is actually a verifiable, quantifiable, metaphysically recognized entity; the pointy end of my moral compass, stabbing me until I bleed, is my mentor spirit. My totem. My life coach.

Adversary.

You ask an assortment of hermetic, shamanic, and everything-in-between-ic spellslingers to describe Adversary, and you'll get answers ranging from neo-anarchist manifestos about Robin Hood to Biblical warnings about the devil himself. And the thing is, none of them are wrong. That's his spectrum. That's him. Adversary is what you make of him, and what you let him make of you; he can urge you on to fight The Powers That Be, no matter how hopeless the struggle seems, or he can give you a wink and a nudge and the encouragement you need to kick a puppy, just because society says it's taboo.

That's between you and him, chummer.

I keep the bastard around because Adversary's more than bad life advice dribbling into my ear in moments of crisis; he's power. To a Black Mage like me, a mojo-man who lives his sorcerous life almost entirely by the adage of *do what works*, power is worth something. Worth everything. Worth all I've got.

I only have a few shredded tatters of magic left to me, you see. Ol' Jimmy Kincaid, well, I managed to end up on the wrong side of some vampiric fangs a while back, and then about a hundred klicks of bad road since then. I've had ugly luck, I've made ugly decisions, I've lived an ugly life, and it's taken cuts of my soul away from me. So I have to maximize what's left of my sorcerous potential. I have to do the best I can with what little's left to me, after all these years. I have to use leverage.

Adversary's my lever. He gives me that little extra *oomph* when I need it, especially when I'm acting in a way he approves of. He helps me take power from others and hold it with both hands. He's how I get the most out of my own little bit of power. He's how I scrape by. And just like any good lever—a crowbar, for instance—sometimes he works like a club.

This was all fresh on my mind because those whispers came back, with a vengeance, one particular night. A stray hold-out pistol shot from the back seat had busted the radio in my car, and I couldn't even lean on my skull full of Transys headware to get any tunes, because my favorite underground radio station, a 24/7/365 guerrilla jazz fest, was offline thanks to some Ancients shenanigans across town that had ended with a dump truck running headlong into their live studio set-up. There wasn't a distraction that would do the trick, so I found myself on a stakeout with nothing bouncing around in my head but dark thoughts and boredom, as dangerous and sickly-sweet a combination as Jack and Coke.

"You should just kill her," Adversary whispered to me.

I ignored him, glaring off into space as I scrolled through my case's files in my heads-up cyberoptics display. The files weren't really arguing against my mentor's dark urges, though.

Johnston, Mary Jo. Human. Female. Thirty-four years old. Husband, Marcus (divorced), two kids. The ex was the one who hired me, and those two kids had been why; Mary Jo had laid hands on them too many ways, too many times. Marcus had put up with her anger and her sickness for a long time, been poisoned by her deeply enough that he kept giving her new chances, internalized enough of the abuse that he thought he deserved it ... but when he walked in on Mary Jo leaving bruises and scars on their kids, internally and externally, Marcus found it in him to leave, and was lucky enough to have friends that could help him. Marcus was a clerk at Puyallup Hall, working for the city and handling the occasional paycheck or hot tip sent my way. Eventually, he reached out for my help.

MJ owed him alimony, and Knight Errant didn't have it in 'em to care. I was for hire, and didn't have it in me to let her off the hook, so here I was. Mary Jo wasn't at home or at work, so I was checking for her here.

The years since the divorce had done wonders for Marcus and the kids, but Mary Jo'd just turned her anger at other targets, taken out her vitriol elsewhere, spewed her bile on others. Johnston had gone full, bingo-card, pants-on-her-head extremist since then; hated elves, hated orks, hated trolls, hated dwarfs, hated changelings, hated magicians, hated Europeans, hated Aztlaners, hated NANners, hated, hated, hated. She'd racked up eight charges and sixteen months in a facility in the time since my buddy Marcus had left her, ranging from terroristic threats and destruction of property to battery and carrying an unlicensed weapon (to a political rally, no less, stirring up trouble at some of the Ork Underground debates). She had a head full of dumpster juice and a heart to match, and in the years since the divorce she'd just given up on being anything else.

"One to the back of the head, Jimmy. C'mon. You'd be doing her a favor," I heard. "*You know that much hatred comes from inside, not outside. Kill her. Break the cycle. You'll help her out, help out those kids, help out everyone else. Do the world a favor.*"

But I wasn't here to kill her. Honest. I was here to serve her papers, I was here to deliver a message, I was here to—maybe, if things went sour—put hands on her or any of her friends in self-defense only. Legal-like. Square. By the book. I was Jimmy Kincaid, Investigator For Hire, just serving some documents on behalf of an on-the-up-and-up legal employer. I was a good boy. That was the plan.

So there I sat, in the graveyard quiet of my Ford, trying to hum the tune of any song I could think of to take my mind off what a piece of shit this gal was, and to distract myself from the dark urgings of my vengeful mentor (who just hated to see me follow the laws). I was leaning hard on my cyberoptics from a block away, scanning faces as they came and went from the local Humanis chapter house, zooming in, trusting facial recognition protocols and pinpoint-accurate schematics of Mary Jo Johnston's facial features, and just waiting. She was a dumb, ugly creature without any friends anywhere else, so like a devil rat that only ran with the rest of her dumb, ugly herd, I knew I'd eventually find her here.

"Here" was where I found lots of dumb, ugly creatures without any friends anywhere else.

Puyallup's official Humanis Policlub chapterhouse had, once upon a time, been a humble office building. Small and simple, but productive. A part of the community. In decades past, someone had, I dunno, filled cubicles with workers, whiled away their work week, turned a profit or two, made a product, shipped goods, whatever.

These days, though? These days it was a tumor. A cancerous growth made up of hatred and fear in equal measure, with a dizzying assortment of flagpoles out front. Some were ancient symbols that everyone associated with bigotry and World- or Civil-War losses, some were newer logos imported from European haters or kit-bashed together by soulless marketing companies. Some were outright corporate logos, flaunting their favorite defense companies or hardline CAS and UCAS "buy native" jingoists.

Every flag was as ugly as the sumbitches I saw coming and going.

"Kill them, too."

I sighed.

"Burn those flags down. I'll give you the juice to do it, Jimmy. I'll help. Or I could lend you a spirit. A fire spirit! Slave it to your will, send it to destroy, and just sit here and watch the show."

"Nah." I spat my WhiteBrite gum out the window and popped in a fresh piece. "I'm good."

"'Good.'" Adversary snorted disdain at the very notion. "*You and I both know you don't really think that.*"

"I meant it like 'full.' Politely declining a—you know what, why am I even arguing with you?"

"You're right. Don't sit here talking to yourself, go update her file to 'deceased.' I'll give you the power you need, Jimmy. You can do it."

"We don't even know if she's in there, dummy." I chewed my minty, tooth-whitening, drug-laden gum. It kept me alert and awake, kept me sharp—and kept me agitated and energized enough to sit there and argue with my murderous, otherworldly patron. Out loud.

Plenty of Johnston's buddies had stumbled, half-sober at best, across the parking lot and to their parked trucks and SUVs to make their drives back to impotent mundanity, but no matter how late the night got, I hadn't spied *her* with my little eyes. Her car was there, though, and had been for hours. That might've meant she was in there, still drinking, serving drinks, playing cards and rambling incoherently with her friends, but that might've meant her car got left there earlier in the night, and she'd gone somewhere else when I ha—

"Hell-o, what have we here?" I sat up a little straighter behind tinted windows, squinted and refocused my cyberoptics to peer at an arriving panel van. It trundled past me and then backed awkwardly through the chapterhouse parking lot and tried to align its rear doors with the building's entrance.

A man and a woman climbed out of the front seats—both human, naturally—and I filled my Transys headware with their information to cross-check later for outstanding warrants, bounties, child support being in arrears, or any other reason I could get paid to fuck with them a little.

I eventually spotted my mark, MJ Johnston, climbing out the back of the van. Two things were different about her; her face had taken enough of a beating that my subroutines had trouble identifying her, and she was shoving an ork—an ork with her hands tied behind her and a face that looked like a fucking meatloaf—out of the van.

"It's her! Finally! Kill her!"

"Shut up." I focused on my headware and the heads-up displays on my optics, doing my stalwart best to ignore Adversary's blood-soaked urgings.

The ork came up a blank on my facial recognition scans, even when cross-checked with the district records and my licensed-investigator Knight Errant files. I didn't know if that meant she'd been beaten so badly she was unrecognizable to a headware commlink, or if she was SINless and wasn't in any particular records bank. I didn't know who she was, but that didn't matter compared to what I *did* know; I knew she was at a secondary location, and I knew she was an *ork* whose secondary location was a *Humanis chapterhouse.*

Nothing good was going to happen to a person like her inside that place.

I don't know what they had planned, I don't know which of them she'd made eye contact with or mouthed off to or fought back against to earn their ire, I don't know why they were feeling their oats. I wasn't gonna wait and find out. I wasn't just gonna serve some papers tonight, after all. Marcus would understand.

I sighed and swiped my thumb across the starter panel of my Frankenstein-monster Ford. The engine snarled to life.

"Summon Ariana," my mentor snarled along with it. *"Call down your ally spirit! Send her to wreak bloody vengeance! Defy their power! Destroy them!"*

"Nope." I tugged on my favorite driving gloves, wiggled my fingers into them for snugness and ritual. Then I reached up to fasten my safety belt and sent mental commands through my wireless network, checking on the ammunition load—very specifically—of the big, blocky, Colt handgun in its smart-holster on one hip.

"This is gonna hurt."

I reached down and pulled my wand from its own tactical holster and held it sidelong in my teeth, like a football player's mouthguard or the stick a Civil War soldier bit down on when a doctor grabbed a bone saw.

"Going in yourself?! Hah! Yes! Show the world you are strong enough with only me at your side! Get your own hands bloody! You don't need spirits for this! Do it yourself!"

"That's the plan."

My Ford was a beast. Me and an ex, herself a shadow legend and street driver named Turbo Bunny, had really done a number on it, back in the day. We'd had to chop up and reshape the whole frame just to make it work; the engine had literally belonged to a car twice the size, and it fed power meant for a sleek limousine into the body of an American-ugly semi-compact. It was lots of horsepower. Absurd horsepower. Too much horsepower.

As the door closed behind Johnston, her friends, and their prize, I floored it.

Adversary howled alongside the engine and my abused tires, and I fired my Ford like a bullet, up and over the curb, across their parking lot, a bullseye. I kept both hands on the wheel, white-knuckled under my gloves, and used a mental command to metaphorically lean on the horn. It blared, a warning, a war-cry, as the car hit home.

"Yes! Let them hear us coming. Let them know they can't stop us. Make them afraid!"

The ram bar smashed into the front doors like the fist of an angry god, and my car slewed to a stop halfway across their meeting hall amidst plaster, glass, fear, splintered tables, and confusion. I reeled against my seatbelt and trusted the harness do its job as I rolled with the impact and bounced around in the driver's seat.

The horn went quiet. The headlights went off. My cyberoptics went wide and white in the dark as I cycled through vision modes until I could see them clearly.

I spat my bloody wand into one waiting hand and bared my bloody teeth like a wild dog.

"Yes," Adversary purred, pleased with the damage.

My mentor spirit filled my head, heart, and stomach with rage, and my cyberoptics pierced the dark tint of my windows and the plaster dust and shadows in the air to find me targets. The Humanis goons were reeling, shocked, and terrified, but—only slowly—going for guns. Their orkish prisoner was prone somewhere, smart enough and scared enough to hug the ground, or maybe just knocked flat and stuck there due to her cuffs.

"Yes!" Adversary urged me on.

The raw, pure mana welled up inside me almost like it had in the good old days—the golden boy of Lone Star days, the trained combat hermetic days, the powerful days—and I held it in until I felt like I'd burst. Scanning for targets, scanning for targets, filling myself with power, pouring it into myself right to the brim, as I looked at the faces of the human-shaped monsters all around me.

"All of them," Adversary insisted.

All of them, I agreed.

"All of them," I breathed it out like a prayer. It wasn't my usual Enochian for Centering, but the *sentiment* was there, so the power flowed cleanly.

The belly full of mana blasted away from me in a hurricane of unadulterated power, swirling, eye-searing blue-white, a ripple in reality like lightning in a bottle. There was no attached elemental power, no piggybacking real-life energy involved. No plasma, no acid, no cold.

Just hurt. Just pain. Just force. Raw from the tap.

One good spell. One display of power. One overwhelming use of force. Adversary-style. Utter domination.

Every one of the bastards got blasted clean off their feet, more dead than alive.

Now, I won't lie, I wasn't the sort of mage that could sling that kind of mojo any more, not safely. It tore me up good, battered me as badly as slamming my car through a wall had, bruised me like going the distance against a boxer, wore me out like a wrung dishrag. I felt a rush of blood pouring from my nose, knew that if my eyes weren't cybered I'd've gone red and teary, and I reeled from it as my pulse roared in my temples.

Hell, Adversary pushed me to cast so hard, I hurt myself almost as bad as I hurt all of them.

Almost.

"Ma'am." My voice slurred as I hauled myself out of the car with my Colt in my hand. I shot the nearest whimpering Humanis punk as he tried to rise, blasted him back down to the floor.

Gel round.

"Wait, what?!"

"Ma'am, if you can hear me, you let me know." Another hint of movement, another shot. Another Humanis thug fell from his knees to lie face down.

Gel round.

"No!"

"Ma'am, it's okay, they won't hurt you, and neither will I. You're safe now. I promise."

"Kill them! Idiot!"

Another shot, another. Another. Another. Then I remembered bullets—especially gel rounds—cost money and my wingtips were already paid for, and I just started kicking them to sleep instead.

The ork finally clambered to her feet. She stood there, without my help, backlit by the city behind her, shoulders high despite the beating she'd taken.

The all-important kicking Mary Jo Johnston was a job I left to her. Serving those papers could wait. A little payback was more important than my errand.

"It's not too late! There's still time! Kill them all!" Adversary gnashed his teeth in my ear. I listened to the oncoming sirens, instead. We were in Puyallup, but not the Barrens part, and that meant they'd show up eventually. *"Your knife! Use your knife!"*

"Just take it easy," I said to her *and* to him, then I ignored him. I scanned the lot of Humanis wreckage on the astral, saw they were all, even if just barely, clinging to life. Their auras weren't dim yet, just their souls.

"I want to go home," the ork was able to mumble when she was done, which happened before Johnston was dead. I was impressed by her restraint. The orkish woman had taken a beating, but wasn't out. She had one eye swollen shut, was talking like she had a mouth full of glass instead of shattered teeth, but she lifted her chin. "Just get me out of here."

"Kill her, too! She can't tell you wha–"

"I can do that," I said, helping her to my car. We took down another section of wall on the way out.

I left Mary Jo Johnston and the rest of her hateful crew for Puyallup. Let the city decide.

Maybe the cops would show up and protect them all, get them medical attention, take down their story, fill out a report. Maybe their neighbors—staring at that hatred all day, every day—would get here before Knight Errant did, and none of that would happen. In the end, that wasn't for me to decide. It the cops got here first, fine. The bastards would keep. I knew where to find them.

Sometimes I listen to Adversary. Sometimes I follow the rules. Sometimes I do what I want.

Sometimes I do what's right.

OLD FASHIONED

For our final installment, something brand new! Something never-before-published! Something that didn't slip through the cracks in a sourcebook, no, something written specifically for this compilation. These are a few characters you might have seen before (and may see again) in our enhanced fiction line and an anthology or two, but they're another pair of not-quite-shadowrunners I'm really enjoying telling stories about.

Here's a little ditty about star-crossed lovers on the run from society's expectations! And, uh, also on the run from lots of other problems. Whew. Poor kids! They don't know exactly why, but they've got lots of trouble following them.

Which means lots of trouble they're dumping in Jimmy Kincaid's lap.

—RRZ

Dragons. I really hate their bullshit.

The name's Jimmy. I gotta pay my damned rent. I'm a private dick, I poke my nose in for money or favors, or not at all. Puyallup's my neighborhood, Puyallup's my home, Puyallup's my beat. I leave most of Seattle to Knight Errant, the pricks. The Knights patrol parts of my burg, too, but only parts of it. Most of Puyallup ain't worth their time, the way they see it, because if there's no System Identification Number, there's no complaint, if there's no complaint there's no contract, and if there's no contract, there's no coverage. Cops aren't worth shit, but Lone Star and Knight Errant, remember, they're not even cops, they're just corps.

So the everyday people—SINs or not, official or not, taxpayers or not—gotta pick up the slack. The people that live here police here. Like me.

Jimmy Kincaid, Paranormal Investigator, it says on my door (when the door ain't busted, and when there ain't a physical and augmented-reality eviction threat fluttering from the window). But the problem is sometimes investigating isn't enough, and the problems aren't just paranormal. Sometimes I'm juggling. Sometimes I've already dug up the dirt, or the dirt's been thrown right in my face, and sometimes instead of snooping, I'm talking. Or busting heads. Or shooting, on a bad day.

Sometimes it's not even about investigation, it's about follow-up. And there weren't many places I found myself following up in more than Sunny Salvo's.

A couple decades ago, when I was growing up here in the neighborhood, Sunny Salvo's was *the* birthday destination hotspot. Everybody knew you'd aced a report card if you hosted a shindig at Salvo's. Sunny Salvo's had it all; animatronic animals singing happy birthday your way, greasy pizza and plenty of cold soda to wash it down with, birthday cake that was at least half frosting, old-school skeeball and shoot-the-basket stuff *and* cutting-edge simsense arcade games (I was quite the hot hand with *Ultimate Bike Race Ninja Street Duel* back in the day, many a high score screen had a "*JMK*" on it, immortalizing my fame). Sunny Salvo's had been hot shit back in the day.

Problem was, Sunny Salvo's wasn't hot any more. It was just shit.

A few neighborhood kids came through, sure, but it was just enough business to make a lot of noise and keep up appearances. Brats these days, it's all virtual reality this, augmented reality that, wireless blah blah blah. Nobody wants to climb into a cockpit-pod and put on 'trodes any more, much less physically touch a rat-nasty skeeball that might still have traces of VITAS on it, y'know?

So it ain't much of a playhouse these days, no. What Sunny Salvo's *is* is a front and an office for a childhood not-quite-friend of mine, Enzo Gianelli. Of the Seattle Gianellis. Of the

Gianelli branch of the Finnigan family. Of the Three Families of the Seattle Mafia.

We grew up together, Enzo and me. My dad had helped run the correctional facility that held half of Enzo's family, so he and I, we'd lived just down the street from each other. Enzo's uncle Joseph, y'see, is the *Don* of the Gianellis. Enzo himself's a *capo*. Enzo's also a cokehead. Enzo's all right, for both of those things. I'd tussled with him before, but we mostly got along. I was halfway welcome at Sunny Salvo's, for better or worse. Mostly it was worse; I kinda hated the place, and I knew Enzo did, too.

I could already taste the heartburn as I sat across from him and gnawed on a slice of pizza. The idling arcade games made a racket around us, the lights were dim, and we would've had plenty of privacy even if the place wasn't empty. As it was, it was just us; Enzo Gianelli, street muscle dragged into respectability by nepotism, this kid Uranus, his mage-bodyguard-assassin from the Order of Merlyn, and little ol' me, Jimmy Kincaid, former Lone Star combat mage, current deadbeat makin' ends meet.

Just us. Nobody home but us killers.

Even my ally spirit, Ariana, wasn't hovering around. She was normally bungeed to me on the astral plane, ready to whip up trouble and protection alike on a moment's notice. She was across town, though, on loan to some buddies in the Hermetic Order of the Auric Aurora (try sayin' that three times fast). I was behind on my dues, just like I was behind on my rent. The wizard-nerds had reminded me I was once again in arrears on my contracted financial obligations to the group, and I'd offered 'em Ari's assistance with some ritual spells instead of cash on the barrel. They liked the sound of that, so she was off playing battery and spell-sustainer, and the fact she wasn't here was part of why Uranus felt like he could stand real close and eyeball me real hard.

Uranus and I had tussled before, too. I did a lot of tussling.

I was here on business. I'd gotten a call from one of the neighborhood's few Stuffer Shack franchisees, wanting to lodge a complaint. He'd promised me a slice big enough to cover my rent and some discounts on booze and Targets, my brand of smokes, in perpetuity, if I could help him out. That was worth the drive to Salvo's.

I finished a slice of cardboard-soy pizza as Enzo finished *his* version of how things went down.

"—So then I says to him, I says, 'Fuck you, you talk to me like that?!'" Enzo tugged his toothpick free every time he talked, then jabbed with it, stabbed with it, punctuated with it. The toothpick was new, the frenetic activity wasn't. Italian through and through, he loved talking with his hands. I wondered how much of it was genetic, how much was cultural, and how much was novacoke. He was agitated today. Excited. It was something more than riding the high of getting his knuckles split the day before and busting someone up.

"'Fuck you,' I say, and then I say 'And fuck your Stuffer Shack! You pay the power guy to keep the lights on, you pay the soykaf guy to deliver that coffee, you pay the *CHOCO-PUNCH* guy to bring you fuckin' candy bars. You pay everyone you need to pay to keep these shelves stocked, and out of every bill you got every month, you think it's *me* you can stiff? Huh?'"

It's riveting stuff, listening to a Mafia capo brag about how he handled a scrawny, teenage, cash register jockey.

"And all that woulda been fine, Enzo," I swallowed the last bite of pizza—it was greasy enough to go down smooth, although later would probably be a different story—and cut him off. "If you gotta tune him up a little, sure, you tune him up. But I'm tellin' you, shooting the place to bits like that, and the kid almost dying? That shit don't help. The neighborhood need—"

"What the neighborhood *needs* is to remember who's in charge, Jimmy. The neighborhood's gotta know I ain't some clown workin' out of a kiddie's pizza joint." Enzo's jabbed at me with the toothpick, eyes hard and cold. "The neighborhood *needs* to remember, or the neighborhood *needs* to be reminded. So yeah, I knocked a couple teeth out of his head to make room for the lesson to stick."

"Quite right, sir. Some cretins only understand violence." Uranus sniffed disdainfully at me from under his lame little hood like *he* wasn't the ganger-done-good and *I* wasn't the college-educated combat hermetic.

I did him the favor of ignoring him, *this* time, and instead I sighed at Enzo. "Yeah, yeah. So you gave the owner's punk-ass kid a beating, fine. You went a little hard on the kid, but sure. I know the rules, they know the rules." I went for my beer, washed the grease out of my mouth, and tilted the bottle his way, talking with the beer like he did with his toothpick. I'm good at acting like the people I'm around, when I try.

"But at least let me give the guy partial repayment for the damages. His kid's in the hospital, his windows are a wreck, his merchandise got trashed. C'mon, Enzo. Help him fix the place up, it looks good, yeah? Have him hold some stuff in the stockroom sometimes, maybe work something out longer term. But you gotta help him *make* the money for next month, so it don't gotta happen again, is all I'm saying." I took a thoughtful pull of my beer. "Show the neighborhood who's in charge, but who ain't being a dick about it. 'Specially to an elf."

Race relations were always tricky, especially in Puyallup. Me, I tried to get along with everybody, except folks who don't want to get along with everybody. Enzo's pretty chill on the metaracial front, too, following the Gianelli lead, hiring orks and the like when he could, including one of his doormen/valets. But a human *capo* beating an elf kid, it didn't look good. Not this close to Tarislar.

"Tearing the place up like that? Come *on*, Enzo. You know your uncle wouldn't have done that. Just like your uncle wouldn't work out of Sunny Salvo's here. It's just bad business. Think about the long term, and the rep! You know if you trash the joint, they *can't* pay you. Stores gotta have walls or they get looted, man, it's Puyallup. Stores gotta have merchandise on the shelf to make money, and they gotta make money to pay the bills."

"The bills," I called it, and "rent." What I *meant* was protection money. Part of my job was granting him legitimacy to stroke his greasy pizzeria ego.

Enzo twirled his toothpick, danced it across his knuckles instead of stabbing with it emphatically. He looked away. He fidgeted. My headware and my cyberoptics took it all in—in black and white, like I liked it, but I still didn't miss nothin'—and I gave him a knowing squint.

My information had been spotty, just the complaint from the dad, who'd gotten the complaint from the kid, and the kid *had* been tuned up pretty fierce. Most elves can't take a beating like I can. He said Enzo had demanded the money, hollered, cussed him out. He said Enzo came over the counter, beat him, and left him. And *then*, he said, then Enzo and his boys had sprayed the place on full-auto, while the kid was down and spitting teeth.

"Huh." I kept my eyes on Gianelli *hard*, reading him. He fidgeted. He glared around at the animatronic animals like they were gonna snitch on him.

We'd all *assumed* the shooting had been Enzo leaving a punctuation mark. But...

"The shootin' wasn't you, was it?" I cracked a grin and leaned forward in my chair.

"What Mr. Gianelli did or didn't do isn't any of your concern, Mr. Kincaid." Ugh, this kid. Uranus. Him and his spooky "magecoat" branded nonsense, his silly hood, his snooty tone. "I have been tasked with seeing to his security, and he will stay sec—"

"Shut up, kid. It's my concern if I say it's my concern." There wasn't real vinegar in my voice, though, I was having too much fun. My grin didn't waver, and my eyes didn't leave Enzo's face. "All that gunfire goin' on, what I heard from the kid it was you and your boys, Tweedledee and Tweedledumb, unloadin'. Full auto, it scared the shit out of him. I figured it musta been your Fort Lewis, illicit-black-market UCAS-Guard shit, big boomsticks sending him another message. But he was wrong, wasn't he? It wasn't you and your boys at all, was it?"

I almost crowed. Alright, alright, I did crow. "Hah! Enzo motherfuckin' Gianelli, the big, bad *caporegime*, did someone take a fuckin' *shot* at you yesterday?"

"I *said* Mr. Gianelli's security is *my* concern, not yo—" Uranus puffed himself up.

I cut him off, snickering. "In *broad daylight*, Enzo? Did someone take a shot at you in broad daylight?! Ha—"

"Fuck you, Jimmy, it ain't funny." Enzo flicked his toothpick at Uranus to shut him up, then fixed me with a glare that would—probably, and rightfully—make most Puyallup residents piss themselves. Me, I drank more, but pissed less than most.

"The fuckin' Dragons come at me, is what it was. Middle of the damned day, easy as you please. Rollin' up, guns out, and they let loose. Sloppy shit, Jimmy, not like men oughta do. Not like in the old days. Messy. Loud."

"Dragons" meant the Blue Dragons, the street muscle of Enzo's biggest rivals, the *Kenran-Kai* Yakuza. They were the gutter scum of the organization, the simple razorboys and razorgirls, a go-gang that was all about fast bikes, fast cars, and full auto. We'd tussled a few times. I'd tussled with *everybody* a few times, felt like.

He was right, though, this was how they did business. They'd done this drive-by bullshit my way before, a time or two. *Windows*, pal, were just not worth the trouble.

"Well that explains why you're in such a mood, and why your security boys are so big and bad today, all hawk-eyed out front."

That's why it was just the three of us in here, and why there'd been a few extra goons at the door. The ones that weren't guarding Sunny Salvo's were working the streets.

"So fine. Shootin' it up wasn't you. Even better! You show the neighborhood that *you* fix what the *Yaks* break! You give the store another month or two of grace. You toss 'em some nuyen to clean the place up and start turnin' a profit. You send the kid some, I dunno, some fuckin' flowers or chocolates or something, yeah?"

I finished my beer and slapped it on the table like a judge dropping a gavel. "In exchange, you get a piece of the Stuffer Shack's stockroom for whatever nefarious criminal enterprises you cook up, you look good and generous, *and* I don't tell half of Puyallup that someone took a swing at you in the middle of the afternoon, and that heads ain't rolled for it yet."

He glowered at that. "Oh, heads is gonna roll, Jimmy."

"Sure, sure." I waved his bluster away. It would wear off when the coke did. "But they ain't rolled yet. So, call it five K to the guy for repairs and restock? Plus ten percent for me?"

"Jimmy, you got some balls on you."

I grinned and reached for *his* beer. "It's why you love me, Enzo."

His bottle was stuck in place. Enzo's hands weren't anywhere near it.

"I don't love you, Jimmy," Enzo said, voice low, more serious than I'd heard it in a while. I tugged on the bottle again. It didn't budge. "I *like* you. I like you, and we got history, so I let you get away with a lot."

I glared at the bottle, then up at Uranus, Enzo's pet mage. The kid was squinting real hard, but not at me, at the bottle. Ah, that's the trick. Magic Fingers. He was using a minor telekinetic manipulation to keep me from snagging the bottle. Enzo was using the break in my momentum to take over the conversation.

Pricks.

"But I ain't payin' some keebler stiff five *thousand* nuyen as a prize for owin' me money, Jimmy. And I ain't payin' you no five hundred for doing the favor of eatin' my pizza, drinkin' my beer, and tryin' to shake me down in my *own fuckin' place*."

Sunny Salvo's. Half-closed, half-pathetic. Half-pizza. Half-hated by everyone, including Enzo. Some fucking place.

"So fine." I leaned back in my chair like I hadn't wanted the beer anyway. Uranus, the mob's leashed mage, sneered under his rune-chased hood. I paid attention to Enzo instead. "What'll it take, Enzo? If you won't pay me—and the shop—for working out the deal, what? You get storage in the Shack's backroom, plus...what? Let's work it out."

"Marie Hwang."

I squinted again. She was a gal from the neighborhood. Her big brother'd gone to school with us. Last I heard, she was working on cars or something. "Donnie's sister? What about her?"

"Old loan, I decided, has come due, since she did some work for the Dragons."

I sighed. My childhood buddy got a flat stare. "Enzo, you for real? So what, she makes money tuning up some Blue Dragon street racers or whatever, you gon—"

"Yeah, Jimmy, I'm gonna. I'm gonna call in her debt over it, no matter how little it is. She wants to be on my good side, she needs to *be on my good side*. The Blue Dragons gonna take a shot at me, I'm gonna remind people they gotta pick a fuckin' team."

He met my gaze, and we stared long and hard. I knew I'd win. I've got cyberoptics, he's got a novacoke habit. The day I blink first against Enzo is the day I hang up my hat and find honest work.

But then we got interrupted.

"You're the one standing here with your hat in hand, begging for charity, and you think you can tell Mr. Gianelli what debts to collect?!" Enzo's pet mage took a step toward me, shuffling, thinking he was taking his boss' side to help him win an argument.

I let Uranus run out of steam and peter off on his own. I held Enzo's gaze long enough to make it clear the staredown was *at best* a draw, got a resigned little nod from the capo, then I looked up at his magical advisor.

Me an' Uranus, we've got history that's a bigger deal to him than to me. We'd tussled, like I said, our very own mage duel once. During it, I'd chewed up his spells, spat them back at him, and then punched him in the face a bunch of times with my wand. He's had a chip on his shoulder ever since.

Knowing that Ariana—my ally spirit, my better half, the shining, bright, powerful side of my soul—wasn't here had Uranus feelin' his oats. Using Magic Fingers to keep me from picking up a beer bottle had him standing a little too tall.

I stood up, myself, and took a half-step toward him. I loomed, elf-tall, over him. I was broader in the shoulders, too. I had decades of experience on him. I may have lost most of my mojo to a vampire years ago, but I still had *finesse* over him, too, as a Lone-Star-trained-and-licensed combat hermetic, and a University of Washington honors grad in the Apotropaic Arts. He knew all of it.

So he took a full step back as I did so.

I pointed a finger at him as though it was the Colt 2061 or the wand on my hip, and he flinched.

"Obi-Wan Cannoli, I know you're on edge 'cause your boss is on edge. I know you're worried you're about to have to actually earn your fuckin' pay. I know you're about to fill those robes with piss 'cause you think the Blue Dragons might come through that door any minute. I know you're about half as good as you think you are, and I know workin' mojo is about confidence, so you gotta do your thing to *feel* like you can keep Enzo alive if the Dragons come through Salvo's and do you the favor of burning this shithole down."

Another half-step forward on my part, another half-step back on his.

"But if you interrupt me when I'm talkin' to *Mr. Gianelli* one more fuckin' time, my wand's goin' right down your throat, you hear me?"

My bark was pretty bad. Sometimes I had the bite to back it up. I let him wonder if I did, with Ari across town.

He looked nervously down at Enzo, but his boss was pointedly looking away, ignoring us; giving me permission to keep the newer generation in line and remind him there was a difference between standing near the table and *being at* the table.

Uranus gulped and nodded. I nodded back, matter-of-factly.

I reached down and grabbed my hat and coat, stuffing one on my head and slinging the other over my suit; even managed to get 'em right, despite the belly full of free beer and garbage pizza.

"Fine. Marie Hwang. I'll find her, you'll get your money out of her. Then you get me the money for the Stuffer Shack, I'll talk to the guy, tell him to set aside some stockroom for you."

Dressed and ready, collar flipped up, hands wedged into my pockets, I gave Enzo a raised eyebrow. We didn't have to shake, me and him, we had history enough a nod would do.

I got the nod. It was a deal.

I headed out.

Extra work. All 'cause of the Blue Dragons and their beef with Enzo.

Dragons. I really hate their bullshit.

I did what I do any time I had one of life's little questions to answer; I hit the streets. I didn't have to ask anybody about the Blue Dragons, they were the root of my problem, but not my problem itself. I already knew what I had to know about them. Their boss, their hang-outs, their hang-ups. I knew who they were and why they'd gone after Enzo. They'd *started* this shit, but they weren't the shit I was in now.

No, the Blue Dragons had just gotten the ball rolling. My problem *now* was Hwang. I spun up my Transys headware, a commlink/supercomputer that replaced a good chunk of my skull and was wired into a good chunk of my gray matter, and while I wracked my memories about her, I scrolled through her public records, too.

Hwang, Marie. Thirty-nine. Human. Female. Single. No kids. Parents dead. One brother, older, Hwang, Donald. She'd grown up in the neighborhood with us, gone to school where we went to school, had lived her life here in northern Puyallup where we did our best to act like we weren't a Barren.

I remembered flashes of her, and cross-referenced 'em with the records I found; gawky and coltish growing up, thick glasses and nerdy hobbies in school, Donnie's wild kegger to celebrate her scholarship to a vo-tech school, running into her half-sober and scrounging for parts at Black's Junkyard over the years, small-talking her drunk ass during Donnie's third wedding a couple years back, knowing she did electronics work on the white and gray markets when she needed beer money. She'd been a drinker as long as I had, I remembered that much.

The most recent gig I knew about her—from both my Matrix search and my memories—was keeping a local guerrilla station wired up. Matrix and radio rigged both, Re-Evolution had been an underground staple here in the Barrens for a while, with their lights on and tunes playing nonstop for years. They'd been a neighborhood fixture, and one of the few places to get jazz with any soul to it, for a decade or more.

Then came a fight between the Seven-7s and the Ancients a few months back, and a runaway truck—and a few grenades, the streets said—had done a number on their station. Re-Evolution was off the air for the first time in ages, searching for new place to hang their hat. Someplace with stable power wasn't always easy to find in Puyallup.

So Marie Hwang had gone back to freelancing, and had picked up some gigs working on the wires of street racers, including the Blue Dragons. Then *Kenran-Kai's* gangers were all about girls, guys, and guns, but also *gas*, like any go-ganger. They liked old-school engines that made noise and had torque, coupled with cutting-edge electronics that kept their rigs tuned and running razor-sharp. Marie had bounced around a few different tune-up shops and custom garages, then she'd picked up some less-than-legal work, wiring up the Blue Dragons' wheels for 'em.

But that had been a few weeks ago, last anybody'd heard.

Anybody *I* knew, at least. Anybody in Puyallup. Anybody working my favorite noodle joints and sandwich carts, anybody on the corners I knew best, anybody holding stashes, running gals, tuning bikes, hawking knock-offs. Anybody claiming turf, renting joy, selling chips. Anybody smuggling for talismongers, dopers, or street docs. Anybody who was anybody in the neighborhood, anyone who knew folks that knew folks, anybody with half a reason to know a local girl who was half-mechanic, half-electrical engineer, half-computer programmer, half-technician, half-drunk.

Eventually, I turned to Donnie himself. I knew him from my Golden Glove days, my varsity football days, my going-to-school-like-this-wasn't-Puyallup days. Before the magic, the college, the Lone Star, the vampire, the chips. I'd been a different Jimmy back then, but I kept in touch with the old crew. Puyallup was Puyallup. Nobody ever really left it behind. If you were born here, you died here.

I didn't lie to him. I told him why I was after her, and I told him who sent me. I stayed honest with my people whenever I could, or they wouldn't *be* my people. He appreciated the heads up. He said he'd rather I find her than some schmuck, and he knew Enzo an' me had history—he'd gone to school with the would-be *capo* too, after all—and hoped I could smooth things over.

Then he sighed, real deep. That sort of gusty exhalation that comes from the soul, not the chest. A sad sigh. Resigned.

"She needed some time away," he said. Like it was a vacation.

"She's at the Funhouse," he said. Like it was a graveyard. "Makin' ends meet."

I thanked him, promised to meet over lunch some time, wished him and the mister and the kids well, all the usual half-hollow crap, before I hung up. My Transys headware was already spinning, and the rest of my head with it. Head spinning, heart sinking, I climbed into my Americar and plugged in the autonav.

I sighed. The Funhouse. That meant *Redmond.*

Shit.

Now I've got some concerns about going up north and heading to Redmond, and they ain't all rooted in being a Puyallup boy, born and bred. It's true, there's a bit of a cross-town rivalry between Seattle's shittiest shitholes. Puyallup Barrens, Redmond Barrens, we're both the bottom of the Metroplex barrel, we've both got the least law, the most gangs, the least employment, the most SINless, the least money, the most fires, the least support. When it comes to Seattle, the two of us are tied for the race to the bottom, and being lumped in together like that makes us rivals. We're yoked together, so we hate each other, it's just a natural thing. Puyallup boys like me, we hate Redmond like Texans hate Oklahoma or Knight Errant hates Lone Star or megacorporations hate people breathing free air. So this is me admitting it, I'm bein' open about some bias here, okay?

But *man,* is Redmond a shithole.

Take everything that's bad about Puyallup, right? Scrape up the ash that adds us some mood and character, and replace it with motherfucking "Glow City," a literal nuclear-industrial wasteland. Take away Tarislar, the elven ghetto that's turned into an elven community and reminds the district that metahumanity exists in numbers that demand respect, and instead give the place a population that's three-quarters skewed to regular humans who look down on the rest of us. Double the friggin' population density, to make everything about metaracism, nuclear waste, abject poverty, and SINless life *worse*, right? It's awful. But, stay with me here, 'cause it gets worse.

Then you sprinkle some goddamned dragons on top.

First up, there's Kalanyr. Don't ask me why, don't ask me what good'll come of it, don't ask me what to do about it; but one dragon, this Kalanyr schmuck, has set up shop right there in Glow City. Word on the Matrix is he's got a bunch of money—like, y'know, a dragon—and owns property, stock, you name it, but for some reason this prick of a wyrm has decided to build himself a supervillain lair right in the middle of the glowing, nuclear heart of Redmond. The ol' Trojan-Satsop plant gave up the ghost a good, I dunno, fifty, sixty years back, contaminated the hell out of Beaver Lake, and it's there—in the middle of an irradiated Nothingsville—that one Redmond dragon has decided to hang his hat and start up a nice little cult-gang of followers and stuff.

So yeah, I'm real sure that's gonna work out fine in the long run, right?

But wait, there's more. You heard me, *one* Redmond dragon? Yeah. That's the reason I gotta drive up into this burg. A *second* damned dragon, right there in the same city, a dame named Urubia.

If Kalanyr's addicted to clicking Geiger counters, Urubia's addicted to partying with the little people. A good ten years or so back, she carved herself out a chunk of the Metroplex, along with her other completely transparent legal holdings, that she calls the Funhouse (so everyone else calls it that, too, she's a dragon, who's gonna argue?). A foursome of low-income apartments all squatting together, along with most of the *rest* of the surrounding blocks, got turned into her own weird little fiefdom. Three of 'em she rents out to folks to live and work in, but she bebops around and can be found perching dramatically atop each of 'em from time to time. It's the fourth tower that's the pain in my ass tonight, though.

The fourth one, you see, is her personal little party palace. She's filled up most of the building with every Awakened goofball in Redmond, every ganger in Redmond, and every full-time criminal piece of shit in Redmond, and rented out apartments to 'em for them to live in, play in, work in, do whatever.

The top half-dozen floors, though, are her playpen. Four stories of personal lair, is what I hear, but two stories are just...a party. A never-ending, nonstop, all hours, all days, sex, drugs, and rock-and-roll *party*; with a fucking dragon in the middle of it. She takes drugs, she dances to the music, she lets weirdos crawl on her, she bankrolls the whole thing. She's barely been seen away from her four towers of fun in years.

And, weirdest of all, it's *working*.

See, the Funhouse is a neutral zone to all of Redmond's gangs. Urubia don't want trouble, so there ain't no trouble. She wants a party, not a pit fight, so all the schmucks in the dragon's shadow, they do what the dragon wants. It's turned into no-go territory for most of Seattle's syndicates, gangs, and criminal outfits, that being the case; a safe haven for independents and folks on the run. When someone with gang colors rolls into Urubia's shadow, they do so quietly, and without malicious intent.

Nobody can out-malicious-intent a dragon.

So the Funhouse is a party and an apartment complex full of wannabes, small-timers, folks trying to slip through the cracks. Folks like Marie-fucking-Hwang. According to Donnie, she's laying low in the Funhouse, taking care of the light shows, speakers, amps, augmented reality stations, and whatever-else-the-fuck-anyway for Urubia's madcap little playpen. A permanent party takes a lot of juice from an unstable power grid like Redmond's got, and techies like Marie can make ends meet helping the party stay alive. That's the situation. That's the mess. That's what's up.

And then here's me. Jimmy Kincaid, asshole who just wants to pay his rent, having to roll up there. Waltz into a dragon's goddamned lair, in the *wrong* damned Barrens, to go fetch a neighborhood gal so my cokehead *capo* buddy can get his cash from her, so a Stuffer Shack owner can get his cash from him, so I can get my cash from them, and my landlord can get his cash from me.

Seattle, man.

So. That ain't me saying Redmond doesn't have gangs; it just has ones that behave close to Urubia's towers. It also, though, has ones that aren't terribly elf-friendly. My boys the Ancients aren't real popular in this neck of the woods, and for good reason. The Ancients like to claim all of Seattle as their playground, and they're more right than not, but realistically they're a lot more free to ride around in some places than others.

Puyallup, home, with Tarislar nearby? Elf-heavy streets they know by heart? That's the seat of their damned power, and every building might as well be painted acid-green.

Redmond? More metaracist, less elf-friendly, and full of enemy gangs that don't take kindly to their flashy bikes and green A's everywhere? Less so.

Redmond's home to charmers like the 162s. Where the Ancients are all-elf, these yahoos are all-Infected, each and every one has the Human/Metahuman Vampiric Virus. Most of 'em are ghouls—cannibals—but they've got a few full-on vamps hiding among 'em, I hear. They work for Tamanous, organleggers, and worse. Bad mojo. Bad people. Bad fellas.

Then you've got the Rusted Stilettos. They're not technically anti-elven, but they're fuckin' *weird*, 'cause they hang out in Glow City, soaking in the rads and spending their days and nights acutely aware of the death creeping up on 'em. They tend toward orks, trolls, and dwarves, the hardier metatypes that hang on a little longer, losing hair and teeth, but staying fighting mean and fighting strong. Not a lot of elves in an outfit like that.

Red Hot Nukes call the Redmond Barrens home too, this all-dwarf gig. They like explosions—bigger the better—and have *some* kinda history with every decent outfit in Seattle. Just like the pyro psychos in the Halloweeners, if you *like* blowing shit up or burning shit down, sooner or later you make a lot of enemies.

Crimson Crush? They're an all-ork bunch. Not the Ancients' biggest fans, these guys and gals. Whether we got pointy ears or not, it ain't like tuskers and keeblers get along, y'know? We live a long time, no matter how poorly. They live harder, faster, and uglier; society ain't their biggest fans, and everything capitalism likes about elves, it hates about orks. I don't blame 'em for having a damn big chip on their shoulder.

Last and not least on my headware's quick breakdown of major Redmond outfits, my memory gets jogged by the Death Heads. I did a gig for their leader, an ork gal named Fusion, a couple years back, but I don't know if that goodwill's gonna carry me through tonight's trip; her crew muscled in on an Ancients-traditional smuggling ring, so tempers flared. They and the Ancients scuffled, and hard, and the elves won. Acid-green chased black-and-chrome halfway across town, and the Heads are only chilling in Redmond 'cause the Ancients couldn't be bothered to follow 'em up here and finish 'em off.

Me? The streets know I get along with the Ancients okay; I'm not an affiliate or nothing, I ain't lookin' to slap a patch on my coat any time soon or whatever, but the streets remember. To get along in Puyallup, I get along with the Ancients.

And that ain't gonna do me no favors tonight. Not when the who's-who of Redmond is full of gangs they hate, and who hate 'em right back. I was rolling into the Funhouse counting on the Funhouse—counting on a drunken, drugged, dizzy dragon and her rules—to keep me safe.

Fuckin' great. I sighed. I drove. I thought about calling Trace and Skip for backup, or Pink, or whistling for Ariana, Order be damned. I didn't. Stubborn fuckin' fool, me.

Not far into Redmond, my Americar's autonav and the city's GridGuide gave out—spotty coverage where nobody in power cares about coverage—and I had to take the wheel and go manual. The place was easy to spot. Each tower was topped by spotlights slashing through the smog and the night sky to advertise the 24/7 party.

I just followed the lunacy, then parked as close as I could; if I was relying on draconic goodwill to keep myself safe, might as well rely on her draconic reputation to keep my wheels unmolested, too. My security system was up to snuff for the Puyallup Barrens, but that was *home*. All the wrong people knew my wheels, and half the chop-shops in my burg would get me word if someone rolled up with my modified Ford hot-wired. This was Redmond, remember. An altogether shittier Barrens.

I got the hairy eyeball from a couple of mooks out front of the project building, and I gave a hairy eyeball right back. My eyeballs're hairier than most. They and their nanotats and their scars and their slung AK-97s waved me on through. I tipped my hat, all polite-like, but never stopped glaring.

I felt their eyes on my back as I walked past and another pair of bouncer-ganger-psychos grabbed the door for me. The tension was as thick as the smell; gang-run housing projects are never nice places; cleanliness is next to godliness, and these palookas are pretty far from godly. The best answer is always to avoid the puddles and the stains, to not let my Sideways gene-treatment and its obsession with detail drag my gaze into the darkest recesses of the hallways, and to just focus—left foot, right foot, reassured by the gun and wand on my hip—on where I'm going.

I found *another* pair of street punks with big guns flanking the elevator. One of 'em had a commlink in his hand, with an unhackable direct line going straight from it up to his datajack, and he was staring at me real good. I saw they had a cardboard box in front of 'em, full of guns. I saw more boxes behind them. Lots more.

"Gel rounds only?" The other one grunted, as bored as if he was asking for my ticket to a concert.

I stopped and took stock for a second before I let myself accidentally lie, but once I was sure, I nodded, and they nodded back. None of their scanners beeped and got me killed, and we were all fine. Next thing I knew, I was in the elevator and the doors were sliding shut.

So, hey. Didn't have to ditch my Colt. Didn't have to fight anybody. Didn't have to take the stairs up a dozen or so levels, that's always good, right? Even better news, there was a trio of bullet holes where a speaker system oughta be, so there was no music on the way up. I figured I was on a genuine roll. Good night. Lucky streak. Feelin' good. Turnin' this whole damned day around, right?

Then the doors opened, and I got slapped in the face with darkness, light, and sound that had my headware and my cybersuites all a-tizzy, working to auto-compensate. My eyes hit up the anti-dazzle protocols and my ears muffled the loudest noises, but I still gave the party an angry squint as I stepped out—past yet another pair of overmuscled punks with big guns—and into the Funhouse proper. The bottom floor of it, at least.

It was, to put it mildly, a seething mass of sweaty metahumanity rolling and roiling in time with one another and the bone-rattling, bass-heavy, trog rock piping into the whole floor from somewhere unseen. Most of the non-load-bearing walls had been torn away—with various levels of professionalism versus enthusiasm—to make this whole floor of apartments into what felt like one huge, sprawling, dance floor, coupled here and there with the free-standing wreckage of what had been kitchens (and were now bars) and what had been bathrooms (which were still showers). Here and there a wall or two persisted, cutting off slices of the party for relative privacy, intimacy instead of showing off, the illusion of an enclosed space. They created a half-network of small nooks and crannies away from the laser-lights and the strobes for private deals, little corners set up for fog machines, stacks of amps and speakers, or just a stretch of wall for folks to lean against, looking cool.

It was a maze, filled with the funk of a desperate party, an undead thing, a nonstop celebration that existed before any one partygoer arrived and would persist long after any one partygoer left. The music would play on, the light show and augmented reality would dazzle whoever came along next, the darkness and sound would disorient, disguise, and distract someone *else* looking for the high of a dance, a drink, and a one-shot popper of some chemical cocktail.

It ain't quite my scene.

Maybe when I was a younger man. Maybe when me an' Turbo Bunny were still each others' long-running hook-ups, slotting Better-Than-Life chips, blurring them with hard liquor, and dancing on the line between reality and other-than. Maybe when the hole in me—the hole where most of my power had once been—was rawer, redder, more ragged around the edges. Maybe when I was hungrier to fill it. Maybe back then I could've fallen into, and fallen in love with, a place like this. Maybe Young Jimmy's out there on the dance floor right now, some other elf who tripped on hard times and rolled into this party, desperate for a release, a relief, and relapse. Maybe he's having a blast. Maybe Adversary left him here, instead of taunting him into standing up, dusting himself off, and grabbing for real magic again.

Maybe. But me? The real me? I was here on a job. I had a debtor to find and rent to pay. I had a case, or something like it. I grimaced around the last mouthful from my hip flask, tucked it back away, and went to work. It was time to be methodical. Professional. Precise.

I started by circling the leaping, grinding, half-dressed, last-lit and AR-shining masses. I tried to hug a wall, skirt along the edges of the party, and let my headware do its work. I ran facial recognition protocols while my cyberoptics scanned the roiling seas, and while my Transys commlink did what it did, I scanned for Marie myself.

My top-end optical suite cut through the light show and the spotty AR well enough, but by the time I made it to the opposite side of the building, and had scanned the perimeter of fully half the floor, I knew this would never work. Too many people. Too much movement. Too many people with unclear faces from dance-party masks, trendy hoods, or kissing someone too fiercely for facial recognition to split their heads apart. Too much going on, entirely too much, to even *really* get a good look just at the outer layer; and that was without even factoring in how to get to the chewy center of the seething, writhing, pounding mass.

"I need a drink." The party ate my voice entirely, even I didn't hear myself kvetch.

But hey, it was true. As my frustration mounted, the empty flask weighed more and more. Fuck methodical, professional, and precise, sometimes it's time to be a little bit drunker. Like the slogan says, "headware, don't care." My Sideways and little WhiteBrite betel gum could see to it I still accurately scanned the crowd no matter how buzzed I got, right? So I looked for a watering hole, or whatever passed for one. I figured something had to be in the smack-dab middle of the floor, and maybe it'd be someone who could pour me a drink and point me in the right direction.

I sighed at the wall of flesh. I adjusted my hat. I waded in.

I was immediately reminded that I was *too old* for this "wading in" bullshit.

The crowd was too rowdy for me to stroll through the beating heart of the mob. The trog rock blaring at us from speakers all over the place had 'em good and riled up. They'd spun up—here, in Redmond, a metaracially-charged shithole, with a strong human majority but plenty of hyperviolent metaracial minorities hanging out together, right?—*here*, in the Funhouse, they had spun up a cover song, a modern twist on a decades-atop-decades-old race-riot war-chant.

"So now I'm rollin' into Downtown with a shotgun,
These people ain't seen a pointed ear
Since their grandparents cropped 'em!"

It was a tune driven by pounding machines of bass and percussion, a song carrying rage and indignation in equal measure. The song was a giant middle finger to Humanis and the upper classes of humans—and elves, all too often—and a rallying cry for society's put-upon. Barrens-born metas, especially orks, loved this kinda stuff. *Loved* it. It got their blood up. Reminded 'em of the Night of Rage. Trolls, dwarves, you name it. Every broad-shouldered meta out there had a story about being spat on and looked down on for being in the wrong part of town.

And the counterculture smoothies? The humans and elves who hung in a joint like the Funhouse? They ate it up, too. Any song that gave voice to their frustration, their anger, their belly-deep rage, they liked. I couldn't blame 'em, not following Adversary. The way I see it, you sing along with whatever gets you through the night.

"So now I'm rollin' into Downtown with a shotgun,
These people ain't seen a pointed ear
Since their grandparents cropped 'em!"

The chorus hit the crowd again and again like waves hitting the beach. They moved in time to the music, but it wasn't dancing like I know it; swinging, leaping, shoving, roaring along. Headware helping me navigate or not, I had precious little idea just where I was in the maze of half-shattered walls and seething metahumanity when I finally wrestled my way clear of the crowd.

I found myself in a little oasis of relative silence and stillness, a watering hole amidst the manic, frantic motion of the rest of the party. The comparative quiet and openness was almost startling. It was an actual room, with actual walls on three and a half sides. Compared to the press of bodies all around us, there was only a handful of people scattered around a few tables, and one musician up on a makeshift stage.

And Marie-*goddamned*-Hwang.

Free of the overwhelming datafeeds of the crowd, I took in a snapshot of the scene in less than an eyeblink. I'd gotten lucky. I needed just a second to soak it in.

My razor-sharp cyberoptics, my running-hot Transys headware and wireless Matrix feed, my Sideways gene-treatment and the slow-motion it throws the world into, my WhiteBright and the betel it feeds me, they all worked together and sharpened the moment into perfect, detail-layered, focus. My headware threw brand names and model numbers at me for every piece of clothing and gear in my cone of vision. My facial recognition protocols threw names and, if they had 'em, System Identification Numbers at me, along with probabilities of accurate readings. Meanwhile, my mood-reading subroutines filled up my field of vision with tab after tab of helpful information about body language and pupil dilation. I got it all, suddenly, because instead of swarming hordes of people, there was only a relative handful of people.

I focused on Marie and the folks closest to her.

I recognized her with my own brain, but the Transys and uplink confirmed her identity with a 91% certainty rate based on the shape of her jawline, chin, and nose. More handsome than pretty after some rough years, but I still saw the childhood half-friend behind the harsher lines on her face, I still recognized her despite the long, pixie-cut hair and the clunky AR goggles that half-hid her face. My skull-computer spat data my way; *Hwang, Marie-Susan. Human. Parents deceased. Older brother, Donald, residing in Puyallup.*

She was wearing a holstered Nitama Sporter handgun, holster clipped onto an Ares Industrious "High-Tech Hard Worker" jumpsuit, topped off with jury-rigged smartgoggles my Transys couldn't find the brand name for. She had a compact toolkit and a mid-range electronics tech-deck on a rickety table between her and her friend, and lights flashed on her goggles as she ran a steady stream of diagnostics; she was keeping the nearby electronics up-and-running, was tracking and modulating power inputs and outputs as the unreliable Redmond grid gave them electricity in fits and starts. She had the look of someone sneaking in a quick break when everything was running smoothly. I knew the look. Hell, I took breaks every chance I got.

Next up was an elf gal I got an actual *REDACTED* response on and a string of gibberish character excuses for my lack of clearance. I knew from the exact error message it was a government, not a corporate, "error" at least, and that was a start. I also knew my buddy, Trace, had given me a novahot Skip 2.0 agent that would do yeoman's work getting me around that sort of classification, given enough time and cross-reference images.

The gal was a looker, though, with green hair that matched her large eyes and poured down to the small of her back. My biomedical diagnostic subroutines helpfully informed me it was likely a dye job. She had on Transys smartglasses—their "smartsport tactical" models known for quick and accurate smartlink integration—and precious few other electronics, just a cheap-as-hell MetaLink. The elf wore an Ares Light Fire 75 holstered on one hip, though, a top-end, integrally-suppressed model my headware spotted peeking out from beneath a Tír-surplus military jacket two sizes too big for her. Low-budget Stuffer Shack brand jeans, a Seattle Timber Wolves combat biker shirt and ball cap topped her off.

Huh.

So, to recap, she had a top-end, suppressed handgun spec-ops and wannabes loved, and also had good electronics to supplement the internal smartlink it carried. But she kept it slaved to a cheap, burner commlink, and she wore throw-away clothes meant to be as generic as possible in Seattle, basically a store-bought invisibility spell. Elven gal at a *party*, with a gun and glasses that run twenty times more expensive than her outfit?

I knew a shadowrunner, or a 'runner wannabe, on the run when I saw 'em. Lucky for her, I didn't care.

Last up, I focused on the ork on stage, 'cause my body-reading software told me Marie and the elf gal were both focused on him as much as on each other. That ork, it turned out, was the source of the roaring, pulsing half-riot going on all around us. He wasn't playing for a private audience, it was just that only the folks taking a break to hydrate and hook up were *watching* him play instead of listening. He had a bevy of wired connections and wireless fobs spiraling from his carbon-fiber-on-wood WireCaster smartguitar and datajack, linking him to a few old-fashioned amps arranged in a half-circle behind him, then off into the aether of the Funhouse, piping his singing, his six-string-sawing, and whatever his headware was doing to mimic the rest of a band, through the whole dance floor.

His jeans were tight and cheap, and his generic-ass shirt came from the Seattle Draco Foundation gift shop. The guitar was far and away the most expensive thing about him.

His silver-white-dyed hair blocked half his face as he rocked out—the kid was good-looking, for an ork—but eventually recognition protocols dug up something solid. I got empties on the first three databases, but in the Pueblo Corporate Council files I got a hit and a solid file. Name was Portland, Thomas. Tír-born. Criminal record. He was most recently wanted in connection to a Los Angeles shoot-'em-up with a tridshow-famous bounty hunter, and prior to that, his original charges had been kidnapping an elven gal from the Tír. An elven gal with a redacted name and a face I *swore* was just then peeking out under a Timberwolves ball cap mid-conversation with Marie.

Huh.

A heartbeat after my skull full of electronics fed it all to me, I sauntered over to their table. There were beers out and about, on theirs as well as a few of the other mismatches pieces of furniture, so I gave it a go.

"I'm not lookin' for trouble," I said, trying my best to sound friendly, "But I'm lookin' for an old friend and a drink."

I lifted my hands and opened my coat, showing the two ladies I was armed, but I wasn't going for anything. It was a peace offering. The elf with the dyed hair squinted at me, and I saw lights flickering across her smartlenses as she took me in.

Marie Hwang's face turned ghost-pale, and she almost dropped her beer.

"Easy. Easy, Marie." The elf gal across from her tensed up, I saw it in the oversized shoulders of her oversized jacket, but she didn't go for her piece. I didn't go for mine. Gun, wand, knife, all of it stayed put.

Instead, I wielded a smile. "C'mon. Even if Donnie didn't tell you I was coming, you had to know Enzo'd send *someone*, sooner or later."

Marie bit her lip beneath the bulky smartgoggles that hid the rest of her face. She looked like she was trying to figure out what to say, when suddenly a storm of red lights flashed and flickered in the AR hovering just off her face. She had a host of issues to worry about with the electronics piping Tommy Portland's angry cover song to the Funhouse floor.

Marie's body was tied in knots. She hesitated for long seconds, then ignored me and stayed wired in, working. She was on the clock. She was supposed to keep the strung-together sound system going, and she was doing it instead of trying to run from me. I respected that. Her fingers danced in the cyberspace just off her deck's surface, doing who-knows-what to regulate power flows, adjust wattage, and keep the Funhouse bottom floor's slapdash sound system working.

The elf stayed tense but tried to hide it, one hand on her bottle of water to look casual, the other tucked in close to her jacket, trying *really hard* to look casual as it crept closer to her gun. The devil on my shoulder, the monkey on my back, the mean whisper in my ear—whatever you want to call it, Adversary, my mentor spirit—told me to kill her if she actually touched the gun. I told Adversary to chill the fuck out. Marie, deep in her work, saved one or both of us.

"That's Mr. Kincaid. We grew up together," Marie said as her fingers danced in augmented reality, and her huge goggles made her subtle headshake to her elven friend not very subtle at all, actually. "Now he finds good people for bad people."

I swung a leg over a stool and took a seat. "Now, c'mon. I find all kinds of people for all kinds of people." I tried my best "aw, shucks" voice. It wasn't great. "It's just that bad people tend to pay more, and I got rent due."

The explanation was enough, for now, for the elf to relax. Her hand slipped away from the grip of her Ares piece. The darkest corners of my slipped away from brutal, proactive self-defense.

I smiled again, instead. "Nice to meet'cha. Call me Jimmy." I lifted an eyebrow toward her.

"Loriel," the elf responded after a long enough pause that I knew she'd thought about lying. Normally when someone in her general situation—on the run from freelancers and at least two different nations, living in clothes just a half-step up from vending machine one-shot outfits, and holding tight to a nice gun as a lifeline to freedom—paused just long enough to *think* about lying, and then *didn't* lie, it wasn't because they were going through fake SINs like nobody's business, and they had to try and remember which identity they were on.

It was because they were out of lies to tell. She was in that camp. She'd run out of fake SINs, run out of road, and resigned herself to just *be* herself, here, in the lawlessness of Seattle and the shadow of the dragon.

I gave her a long look—headware still scanning her face, trying to get a cleaner hit, databases slowly opening up—to show her I knew *something* was up, then my headware helpfully told me one of the nearby amps wasn't actually an old-fashioned tweed-faced noise-monster after all. It was a mini-fridge with a gimmick. Hah!

"I'm not lookin' for trouble," I said again, not quite lying. "But I just might shoot someone for a drink. I don't see a bartender, ladies, help a poor Puyallup boy out, in over his head in the big city?"

"It doesn't seem like your usual scene." Loriel nodded, and I saw more ripples of light on the lenses of her smartglasses. I wondered what she was looking up about me in return. She openly nodded to my outfit, though; rumpled longcoat, old suit, gun and wand on my hip. I *did* kinda stand out.

"I'm not a cop," I said, jerking my fedora off and tossing it onto the table. "Pinkie swear."

"Uh-huh." She gave me a skeptical nod.

"He isn't," Marie grudgingly agreed as a few red lights turned to yellow and she snuck in a few more words. "And he isn't a bounty hunter either."

That time *she* wasn't quite lying for me. It was handy, having an accidental accomplice.

"I'm not here after *your* legal woes." I nodded at the cooler again. "Right now I'm mostly just thirsty."

The elf held my gaze until I saw her eyes go a little out of focus, and realized she was up to a trick. An *astral* trick. An *aura-reading* trick.

I kept up my Masking. I had tricks, too. I knew my way around my own aura better'n most people do; I'd had years of practice at propping it up to make myself look more powerful than I was. I had to lie to my rivals, make myself come off as the potent Initiate I *had* been, not the burned-out Initiate I *was*.

"Grab a beer," she said finally, gesturing to the adorably stupid little fridge hiding as an amp.

When I straightened up with two and lifted an eyebrow her way, she shook me off. I took both anyway; either she'd change her mind or I'd get a second drink in me.

On my way back over, I returned the aura-reading favor.

I saw right off the bat she was a mage, too. Either a potent one—on par with me *prior* to my vampiric incident—or someone as good at Masking as I was who was projecting more power than she had. And, if it was the latter, the ability to *fake* the power was a skill in and of itself, and spoke of a certain level of training and experience.

Interesting. Dangerous either way, hermetically speaking, *and* she had that top-end piece holstered. Tír-trained, maybe? They made good mages, half of Tarislar said so, and the elven ghetto'd know.

I saw a bundle of power wrapped tight around her aura, too, a spell stringing out away from her, tethering her to the rockerboy, Portland. As I took a swig, I glanced his way, long and hard, and gave him an astral once-over, too.

He was an adept. Less refined than her, but more powerful than me. Blazing with potential, but even brighter with emotion as he sang, despite a few dark spots on his aura from cyber- and bio-implants. The spell she kept on him was one I recognized, and I fought a grin as I looked back to her.

I saw her green eyes on me, not a flicker of light on the lenses of her smartglasses any more, and a thoroughly elven smirk on her face. *I* knew *she* knew we *both* knew about the aura reading thing.

"Does he know?" I tilted my beer, a dull-as-can-be SoyBud, toward her beau.

"Know what?" She kept a playful smile on, but her eyes went brittle and hard. Afraid. Ready to kill me, depending on my answer.

Huh again. My mentor spirit, Adversary, prodded me to dig deeper, to dare her to try, to challenge her and kill her, but I decided to keep it light instead. I was used to his voice in my head.

"The spell you keep on him. Health spell, yeah? Increasing his force of personality, smoothing out his looks a little, that sort of thing. Does he know?"

"Oh. Yeah. He knows." She relaxed a hair, despite me calling her on it. Strange. I checked back in on my headware, toggled it to keep it reading her body language, trying to figure her out. What had she *thought* I was asking about? "He doesn't like it, says it makes him feel like a fraud? But he lets me do it. It makes gigs pay us better. He'll take the hit to his confidence to keep us fed."

"Good on 'im. And good on you." I toasted each of them, took another drink. The kid, Portland, was belting out another song, using the electronics in his guitar, his head, and Marie's rigged-up electronics deck to work magic. It sounded like a whole band was at work, while it was just him.

My headware pegged it as another cover song, though. "That why he only does other folks' music? Feeling like a fraud? Or other way around?"

"Little of both, I think," she replied, casting him a thoughtful look. Her gaze flicked down to the spare bottle I'd brought over with me. She wanted it, but didn't reach for it. "What else did you see?"

"He's an adept. I figure he knows that. Figure you woulda told him, if he hadn't figu—"

"He figured it out before he knew me," she said, sounding a little defensive. "He's smarter than people think."

"Easy, easy. I know orks ain't dumb. I ain't that kind of elf, okay? No offense was intended. I just meant, what with you havin' the evil eye and all," I said with a wink.

She relaxed another hair. Her green eyes kept darting, though. Up and down me, watching my hands, watching my face, watching over my shoulders, glancing at her boyfriend, glancing at Marie. She was a worrier, this one. A worrier and a *watcher*. She didn't like being on the run, but she was good at it.

I took another pull of my beer, then figured the best way to breach the subject was like I would a door, just go in hard. "Marie, you know when you're gonna be done here?"

Half the lights hovering near her goggles were still red. She either didn't hear me or pretended not to.

"Why do you have to take her?" Loriel gave me a serious look.

"Same reason she has to keep working her deck and keep your boyfriend rocking. A job's a job."

"Huh." Loriel squinted my way again. "A bounty hunter told us that outside Vegas."

"He in good shape?"

"She." The elf shook her head. "And no."

"That's too bad. If it's any help, Enzo ain't gonna hurt her. I promise. I won't let him."

"Enzo Gianelli. *Capo*." Loriel's voice was flat, faintly disbelieving of me. I figured out one of the things she'd been looking up with those smartglasses of hers. "And *you* won't *let* him hurt her?"

"I got weird friends," I said with a shrug. She didn't press. I gave her another look. "Some of those weird friends, y'know, could maybe teach you Mask. Heard of it?"

"I have."

"Dunno what this gig pays, but with it bein' a dragon and all, I bet you could afford lessons. I could make some calls. Maybe you get a few less bounty hunters up your ass that way, save money on hair dye and stuff."

"No." She shook her head, sounding certain, and just the littlest bit sad. "We've talked about it. We're not...doing that. Hiding like that. We're not even running, any more."

"Yeah? Word on the Matrix is he kidnapped you. You don't look very kidnapped to me."

"He didn't. That's just what they said to try and get me back."

"Who's 'they,' kid?"

"I'm not spilling *all* my guts your way, Mr. Kincaid. Not when you still owe me for the beer."

"Just like Marie still owes Enzo for whatever-it-was."

"How much?" Loriel looked my way, lip curling just a little. "To disrupt what she's got going here, what *we've* got going here, this work here at the Funhouse? How much does she owe him?"

I realized I didn't even know. I just knew I needed five hundred nuyen to make my rent, and for that to happen, Enzo needed Marie.

"Enough," I settled on for an answer. Blue Dragons and their bullshit. "She owes him *enough*."

"We don't make much. Marie and Tommy don't, I mean," Loriel said it in a way that *pointedly* excluded herself from the money-making side of things. Hwang ran tech and kept things working. Tommy Portland provided music. She felt like a taker, not an earner. Everyone felt like a loser sometimes. I knew that tone. I'd lost my share.

"You joked, earlier, about the dragon paying a lot?" Loriel shook her head. "She doesn't. Urubia's got a lot of music on tap. They do a couple hour sets a couple times a day. Techs do about the same, plus they loop stuff to fill in the gaps. I got us a good deal, a package gig, once we hooked up with Marie. But it's not...it's not what you'd think."

"Workin' the bottom floor of the perma-party doesn't pay the big bucks, huh?" I wondered what lunacy awaited on the higher floors. I wondered what it was like to try and drink, dance, drug yourself, distract yourself, with a dragon in the room. What kind of desperate edge did it add to a party, having a wyrm breathing down your neck?

"It's just cover songs down here, and techs keeping things barely strung together. Urubia wants creativity, people say. She doesn't want songs she's heard before."

"She's chasing new highs," I said with a nod, feeling almost-an-itch in my rows of 'jacks. I had plenty of plugs in my noggin, and I'd slotted plenty of chips in my time, most of 'em bad for me. I knew that feeling.

Loriel sighed and shifted in her seat, neither hand very close to her gun. For a few moments, her green eyes just settled on Tommy Portland, and she wasn't wary.

"He could do it. He could impress her," she said, certain.

"Sure," I said, less so.

"If he got a shot." She looked my way, eyes going wider, almost pleading. She just wanted a chance. I knew that feeling, too.

"Kid shoulda spun up some new tunes earlier tonight, then. Sorry, doll. Your boy's gotta play guitar, Marie's gotta keep the house's electronics stable, and I gotta find good people for bad people. We all got our jobs. If he's gonna impress her, he's gonna have to do it without Marie."

Then, royally fucking up my whole "a man has to live by a code" speech I was about to start on, I got two pretty important heads-up displays from the Transys commlink in my head.

One, her shifting and twisting and earnest leaning my way had revealed her t-shirt wasn't just tight across the top thanks to natural curves, no, it was tight across the belly, too. My diagnostic protocols, Corpsman-class, just like my own implanted biomonitor, told me she was pregnant, and plenty far along for an elf.

Two? I finally got a hit on her face and her name. She wasn't just Loriel, oh no. She was Loriel, formerly *Captain* Loriel of the Tír Tairngire Peace Force, a literal poster-child for their renewed combat mage recruitment drives. But worse! Because she wasn't just Captain Loriel, trained mage, though, no, she was Captain Loriel *Taylor*.

Her daddy was Connall Taylor, a Prince of the High Council of Tír Tairngire.

"You kiddin' me?!" I scowled at no one in particular.

Marie kept working. Tommy kept rocking. Loriel gave me a quizzical head tilt. "Jimm—?"

"Shut it, you." I reached an arm out for the extra beer—pregnant, no wonder she wasn't drinking it—and drew it back to me, flicker-quick. A wrenching twist sent the cap spinning, and I took a long drink.

"My dad?" she said, looking half-deflated, half-relieved.

I kept drinking, holding up a finger for her to wait. She knew, though. She knew what I was thinking. Had to. Fuck the Tír Princes of Magical ElfyLand for their nonsense snarling me up again. Fuck Tommy and Loriel for letting some ork with a record knock up *a literal Royal-Class* elf, fuck Marie Hwang for running here and making friends with 'em, fuck Enzo for sending me after her, and fuck the Blue Dragons for starting my whole stupid ball rolling into their business.

I nodded and sighed as I tossed the new empty SoyBud away to tumble off the table.

"Hell yes, your dad!" I looked, wide-eyed, at Marie, who had finally emerged from her cocoon of wires, both virtual and physical, and was watching my reaction. "And you! What do you think you're doing, hanging out with them?"

"You think I'm the only one hiding under Urubia's wings, Jimmy?" She leaned in toward me, hissing out an angry whisper like we weren't still under constant aural assault from Tommy and his amp-straining guitar. "Lots of people come here to get away from trouble."

"Not *her* trouble," I hissed back, feeling like schoolkids arguing in a library. A very loud library. A way, way too loud library. "Hell, no wonder you're up here, Princess."

"Captain!"

"*Princess*. Got the Ancients on your tail, huh? They always do the Council's dirty work, all along the coast. Bounty hunters are the least of your troubles! Hiding out in Redmond, where Ancients aren't so welcome, aren'tcha, Princess—"

She glowered. "Captain."

"Do you *know* who she is, Marie?"

"My friend," Hwang said, looking as stubborn as I remembered from twenty years ago. She tossed her head, snapping her bulky smartgoggles up to *snick* onto her forehead, and glared at me, eye to eye.

But the thing was, Marie wasn't running. She wasn't going for her popgun against me. She wasn't raising a fuss and getting any of Urubia's bullyboys to try and take me out. She wasn't even letting Loriel, her Captain Commando combat mage buddy, take a shot or three at me, much less calling over the burly boyfriend. She was sitting. She was sitting, and she was glaring at me over her friend.

"Fuck," I said to nobody in particular, settling back onto my stool.

"Alright." I fished for a pack of Targets, then squinted—*hard*—to let out a little of my anxiety and turn it into heat, glaring out a minor inflammatory spell to light my smoke. "I ain't gonna drag Marie anywhere. Okay? We'll wait until the next techie gets here to keep this mess of a party goin'. It won't fuck up your job. Then we'll walk out, civilized-like. But we got time until then."

I sighed out smoke and nodded at Loriel. "Let's hear it. How'd you end up here?"

Then she told me the whole story. Or at least what I thought was the whole story.

Old fashioned. A timeless yarn. Star-crossed lovers.

She and Tommy'd met when he was fresh out of the pen and she was fresh off the Peace Force. She was learning how to get grease under her nails and work with her own two hands, trying to get by without Mommy and Daddy's help by working at a tuner's shop. He was learning how to make a living *almost* on the right side of the law, making ends meet, barely, as a street racer, along with the occasional guitar gig instead of doing anything worse and bloodier.

Meet cute. Unlikely romance. Whirlwind relationship. Nervous reveal of family she was ducking. Cautious acceptance. Heavier romance. Pee test. Pregnancy. Trouble.

Running.

"My dad—" She sighed, looking longingly at a beer again, "—is trying. He's not happy about the baby, but he likes Tommy and he's *more* not-happy about the bounty and the fake kidnapping stuff."

"So if Pop didn't sign off on it, who did?"

"Another Prince. Or more than one? I don't know, exactly. But it would *have* to be, or Dad could just undo it."

"Wave a magic wand?"

"Wave an Ingram Smartgun."

I snorted. She kept going.

"We knew there'd be trouble, me and my folks had talked about it already, especially since he's—" she caught herself smoothly, but I noticed the almost slip as she shifted gears, made up a new way for the sentence to end, "—not married to me. The Tír is still the Tír, and some ork with a record, plus *me*, and just...it's bad enough."

She shrugged. I wondered what the "especially" really was. I wondered what she'd first thought I'd seen in his aura. It *was* bad enough. Her cover story, I mean, it *was* dangerous enough to maybe make them leave. So what was worse?

Huh.

"So we split. Got out, ugly, but out. Instead of causing trouble or drawing elven supremacists and stuff, we bailed. We went south, at first. Tried L.A."

"I read that file." I nodded. "Had a good gig going, then ran into that pretty-boy bounty hunter?"

"Chase." She grimaced. "Errant Knight. He's a dick."

"Kind of." I nodded. He'd done me a solid once, but he *had* been kind of a dick about it.

"So then we kept going into PCC territory. Then just...kept going, period. Trouble stayed on us. Lots of Ancients. We hit Vegas, Salt Lake, headed to Denver, but it got too hot."

Denver did that. I drank, she kept sighing and talking. Remembering close calls.

"Hopped a few borders, kept moving. He played or I fixed stuff to make ends meet, but we took jobs when we had to. Then just circled back, went west until we hit the Pacific, then rolled down the coast to Seattle. Figured maybe with everything going on, it might..."

"Be Seattle again? Feel free again? Its own little slice of chaos?" I nodded. We'd had a reputation, Seattle, once upon a time. We were getting it back. "Figured you'd duck into the Wild West, hide out close to home, but someplace they'd never look, in the shadow of a dragon, huh?"

Loriel almost winced at the d-word, and I don't mean duck.

She nodded. "Something like that."

She hid the tension—she *was* a real pro, I remembered—but there wasn't much I didn't see.

Someday I'll stop thinking dumb shit like "there wasn't much I didn't see."

Later, when Tommy Portland ran out of cover songs to waste his talent on, he joined us. He had water so Loriel wouldn't be alone in dodging the beers. Marie showed a moderation with the booze she hadn't had years earlier. Me? I drank my share, her share, and his share. We talked a few things over. The longer I thought about it, and the more I drank, the more certain I was that I had the solution to all our problems.

"I got an idea," I said, like *that* was ever a great way to start a sentence. I nodded at Marie. "If I take *you* back to Enzo and remind him what good work you do, you can work off whatever you owe him. Let him up his tech support a little, he's got that Highball kid doing some decking work, but nobody regular on the hardware payroll, yeah? You step in. Work for cheap. Can you rewire stupid fucking giant robot animals?"

"You mean, like, back at Sunny Salvo's?" She looked at me like I was a drunken idiot. I basically was. Then she grinned, and her face lit up like the teenager I remembered. I wondered what decades-old grudge she had against Salvo and the rest of his fuzzy crew. "I can gut those creepy animatronics and make something useful out of 'em? Yeah. *Yeah,* I can tear that drek down for Enzo."

"Radio station?" I lifted my eyebrows, glanced around to the tangled mess of speakers, amps, hardware boxes, wireless receivers, and sound all around us. The follow-up band that took over for Tommy was worse.

"You want me to...make a radio station? Like Re-Evolution?"

"Not like Re-Evolution. Re-Evolution. I want you palookas up and running again. If Enzo gives the station a home and takes a cut toward your debt, can you wire it up right?"

She looked at me like I was still a drunken idiot, thinking it over.

I still was, but I had an *idea.*

"And you." I nodded to Tommy, slurring a little. "You play there. And on the radio! The stage that used to have stupid robot dogs and stuff, you rock a little. Enzo gets more noise than he used to have, and some actual business some nights. Re-Evolution plays some of your stuff, you do live gigs, Enzo takes the money. You an' Loriel get more pizza than she and a growing baby want, maybe a roof over your heads, and you keep working with Marie. Yeah?"

"Yeah," Loriel answered for him. Tommy was still playing catch-up from missing most of the time we'd spent talking. It's okay, he was tired.

"So you do hardware work to get outta your debt while you two rock and roll and live in a mob boss's HQ to keep bounty hunters away. Enzo gets to store shit in a Stuffer Shack, makes enough money to be happy about it, and gets just the change in scenery his mid-life crisis fuckin' needs."

"Stuffer Shack?" Marie looked at me like, yeah, drunken idiot.

"Keep up, Hwang." I nodded matter-of-factly. "I can sell Enzo on this. I can make my rent."

"Rent?" Tommy looked from person to person, trying to make sense of me.

"We're gonna make all this shit fall right into place." I hauled myself up off my stool and hauled my hat up onto my head. We turned our back on the Archfiends, the all-guitars-and-one-bass elf band that had taken Tommy's spot.

"Don't sweat it, kid."

Someday I'll stop saying dumb shit like "don't sweat it, kid."

We got outside, the four of us, heading to our wheels. Marie had her silly damned Horizon-Doble Revolution waiting for her. Loriel and Tommy nodded to their Manticore pick-up, a Tír four-wheeler more at home the faster you drove it. I had my Frankenstein Ford, the best thing to come from me an' Turbo Bunny's dalliance.

None of us made it anywhere near our cars before I realized that the kid *should* have sweated it, and I *was* a drunken idiot, and I *had* dulled my headware, Sideways, and betel with enough booze that I'd missed something.

Lots of somethings.

A bunch of aggressive, armed somethings.

They fell on us from behind other parked cars, lunging into view, a few sliding across hoods, one launching himself at us straight up and over a Mercury Comet.

Ten. Ten was a lot. I didn't have Ari, I was drunk, Marie prob'ly wasn't much in a fight.

One went at Hwang with a taser and she folded, proving my theory.

Ten was a *lot.*

No muss, no fuss, Loriel just drew and started firing. I heard the muted *cough-cough-cough* of her Light Fire and one leather-and-denim-clad attacker stumbled and fell, dropping his bat. Tommy cursed, carefully set his precious guitar's hard case—Laina, he'd introduced me to her like she was a person—on the pavement, then straightened up into an uppercut that lifted his feet clean off the ground and sent an assailant flying, dropping an axe handle. At the moment of impact, there'd been a flash on my thermals; an adept trick, I'd seen them burn or shock people with their karate and shit before. The elf and ork stood back-to-back like they'd fought just exactly that way before but, well, ten was a lot.

One came at me in a tackle as I tried to whip up some combat mojo through a haze of beer and tiredness, and we fell together. My Sideways tried to keep up, my Puyallup gutter-kid instincts, my decades of scrapping, my elf-long reach. They were good, though, trained *and* mean, and just as lanky-strong as I was. We tumbled between a few parked cars, clattering some poor car's side mirror clean off, chains rattled as my attacker—some sort of ganger was all I could tell right away—tangled with me, rolled, spun, grappled.

I bucked, grunted, got in a bite, then a head butt. They recoiled from me, cursing and wide-eyed, then head butted me back. As we reeled apart, my Transys caught up to the action and cut through the booze. I knew them. I knew *her.*

"Squire?!"

Squire was a gutter-cat, an elf kid who'd grown up in the Ancients. She'd risen up the ranks in the shadow of Belial, who ran the whole Seattle outfit these days. Squire had taken care of his bike, carried his sword, and been like a kid sister or, well, a squire to him. These days she was twenty or close to it, lean, mean, and as lethal as any other Ancient.

"Jimmy?!"

I knew her, and she knew me. Ariana'd saved her life once, when the gutter-cat had just been a kitten. Like most kids, she'd been dazzled by my sweet Ari. I'd seen her grow up in the gang, just like everyone else had. I missed the kid she used to be, sometimes.

She wasn't wearing any Ancients gear. Not an "A" in sight. No flashes of acid-green. Tats were covered. No vests, cuts, or patches.

I heard glass shatter nearby, and recognized the sound of a skull hitting a car's side panels a split-second later. I wondered if Tommy'd put someone's head through a window then kept pounding them, or if the shoe'd been on the other foot. Oh, right. A fight was on.

Startled back into action, me an' Squire went at it again, and I reminded myself she *wasn't* that kid any more.

We tussled, spat, clawed, grappled. My ground game wasn't what it used to be, but it normally got the job done. Most of all, it was the chains that did her in. Like lots of gangers, she liked the flash and weight, she liked the look, the mass they added. One of her stealth-Ancients had brought a bat, another an axe handle, a third a taser. She'd planned on chains to knock someone silly with. Standard ganger-fare.

But every super-wiz loop of chains you're toting to look cool? It's a choke waiting to happen if you decide to wrestle someone.

I got my forearm wedged against her neck, through the loop of a rattling set of brushed-steel loops. She figured out the game as I started to twist and tighten, and—I gotta give the kid credit—she went for a blade out of sheer street-meanness. They'd started this fight as a non-lethal engagement, but when the chips were down, Squire went to stick me instead of blacking out.

I can respect that.

I ain't gonna just *let someone do it*, but I respected her swift pivot as I pinned her wrist, finished the fight, and hauled my tired carcass up to see who was next.

I dragged my Colt out of its holster as I dragged myself to my feet, and lifted it just in time to hear gunshots—unsilenced, not Loriel's Light Fire—and see another Ancient stumble, then sprawl, pummeled to the pavement by gel rounds.

"Marie Hwang." I grinned before shooting an Ancient in the back.

"Ares Industrious Jumpsuit." The Puyallup brat grinned right back at me, blasting away. "I got an electric-insulated model, given my line of work."

She was a lousy shot, and I was still drunk as hell, but between us we sent the Ancients packing.

"Let 'em go," I said, trying to sound like I was in charge. Loriel let me pretend I was.

If the Ancients stayed here and got caught, it'd mean dragon trouble chasing 'em back down into Puyallup. Hell if I wanted that. If we let 'em high-tail it outta here, slap-patching one another awake with stims and hurriedly dragging one another around by the leather-and-denim streetwear, nobody'd ever have to know it had been anything but a mugging attempt. Not a gang fight. Not organized business. Random crime, below Urubia's notice, nothing to start a Barrens-war over, I hoped.

Dragons. I really hate their bullshit.

Loriel reloaded and scanned the area as the Ancients took off. Marie gripped her little Sporter handgun real tight to keep her hands from shaking. Tommy cursed, raged, and threw dropped weapons after the retreating elves who'd threatened his unborn and his friends.

I smoked a cigarette.

I told everyone to stay mussed-up when we got to Sunny Salvo's. Tommy glowered real good and looked like a street-savvy brawler. Loriel looked serious and competent, then flashed her Tír-perfect smirk when Uranus peeked at her aura. Marie looked competent and well-equipped, and rattled off some power requirements when I asked her for razzle-dazzling tech jargon. I did most of the talking.

Enzo—high as hell, high enough to get excited about his hideout having a makeover—nodded along with us like it was a great idea.

Everything fell into place just like I wanted. Enzo gave me enough to cover rent, plus a smooth hundred nuyen that meant I'd also be able to eat a little something.

A couple weeks passed. The Stuffer Shack opened back up, with a new *Employees Only* sign on the storeroom that meant Enzo's people, not the owner and his kid. Marie got busy at Sunny Salvo's, taking the robots out, cannibalizing them and the virtual-pilot pods for the hardware Re-Evolution would need to open up and get back to filling my airwaves. Tommy Portland took to the stage that used to belong to animatronic stuffed animals, and—leaning into the street cred he and Loriel had from a live-cast gunfight with *Chase: Errant Knight* and a few grouchy Ancients who'd never speak of their fight outside of Puyallup—built himself a fandom and enough confidence for proper rockerboy swagger.

They invited me back to the Funhouse for his upstairs debut.

Tommy had his own material, honed razor-sharp in a mobster's playpen, and was ready to perform for the draconic host herself. Ready to rock. Ready to bring the street to the high-rise. Ready, with his guitar and his edge and *his own* voice, to make a real name for himself. Ready to dare the Ancients to come after him, dare a bounty hunter, dare the whole world to just try and take a swing. Ready to be immortal and untouchable under a spotlight, performing live for Urubia, Queen of Redmond.

This top floor beat the pants off the underbelly I'd seen. The power here was stable, taking priority from the other floors (which was why Marie and so many other geeks had to scramble to keep the sound going downstairs). It was clean. Clean*er*, at least. More booze. More of a party, less of a grungy pit. Good stuff. Bright lights. Big stage. Drones swirling, live-casting the action to the Matrix for smart-asses to enjoy without having to drive to Redmond. I wish I'd thought of that instead of letting Marie and Loriel drag me up here.

"This one's 'Call The Fire,'" Tommy growled into his mic, fingers sliding along the strings for a squawl of noise to draw every ear in the place. The song suited him.

He started in, calling forth lingering power chords that transitioned into shredding on his smartstring WireCaster. His hands, fingertips callused from steel strings and knuckles scarred from a life on the streets, danced flawlessly. His synthlink worked magic, guitar effects coming and going with just a flick of his mind. Hell, for all I knew, his *magic* worked magic, too, I had no idea what the adept could and couldn't do. His guitar, Laina, wailed like a banshee. He sang along with her, the crowd shouted along. The bass line became the heartbeat of the Funhouse, and everyone there moved in time with Tommy's mojo.

Even cynical, shit-hearted me. I found myself tapping a foot and bobbing my stupid head. Portland had heart, and he was pouring it out, angry and loud, with street-fast lyrics and a guitar sound that was half-chrome, half-tusks, all rock.

Ork or not, the kid was *born* for this.

As the song reached a crescendo, Urubia herself—red-scaled, cloaked in power and excitement, soaking in the energy of her hoarded party—lashed her tail, lifted her wings, and raised her strange mental voice. From time to time, Marie told me, she just liked to exclaim telepathically, *shouting* in that freaky, mind-invading way dragons had, adding her psychic voice to the noise of the crowd. Her wave of enthusiasm washed over the souls in the crowd. The crowd responded, doubling their enthusiasm.

But then her mind touched Tommy's, and something went all wrong and sideways.

His guitar screamed, and Tommy screamed with it.

Urubia's eyes went wide and glowed with power and confusion, then something like greed.

Tommy Portland writhed. Tommy Portland smoldered. Tommy Portland burst into flame, then just *burst*; warped, wriggled, swelled and twisted.

"Oh no," my cyberaudio suite clearly heard Loriel say, picking out her voice from all the background noise. Upset, but not surprised. "Not now..."

Tommy's scream turned into something else, trained rocker's volume giving way to something somehow even *more* powerful, more primal, more passionate.

The ork was gone. A looming dracoform stood in his place, broad-chested, broad-shouldered, a mighty Western dragon writ small. Wings flaring, head thrown back, roaring, the beast was bipedal, all bone-white scales, lashing tail, flames flickering from an open, fang-filled maw.

"Not yet." Loriel's hands rested on her belly as she felt a kick.

The party held its breath. Urubia flashed her fangs in something like a terrible smile.

Tommy Portland, drake, reached down and picked up his guitar. His claws danced on steel strings, and he played on, roaring.

Drones circled and broadcast, Urubia's tail lashed, and the crowd went stark, raving mad.

Dragons. I really, *really* hate their bullshit.

LOOKING FOR MORE SHADOWRUN FICTION, CHUMMER?

WE'LL HOOK YOU UP!

Catalyst Game Labs brings you the very best in *Shadowrun* fiction, available at most ebook retailers, including Amazon, Apple Books, Kobo, Barnes & Noble, and more!

NOVELS

1. *Never Deal with a Dragon* (Secrets of Power #1) by Robert N. Charrette
2. *Choose Your Enemies Carefully* (Secrets of Power #2) by Robert N. Charrette
3. *Find Your Own Truth* (Secrets of Power #3) by Robert N. Charrette
4. *2XS* by Nigel Findley
5. *Changeling* by Chris Kubasik
6. *Never Trust an Elf* by Robert N. Charrette
7. *Shadowplay* by Nigel Findley
8. *Night's Pawn* by Tom Dowd
9. *Striper Assassin* by Nyx Smith
10. *Lone Wolf* by Nigel Findley
11. *Fade to Black* by Nyx Smith
12. *Burning Bright* by Tom Dowd
13. *Who Hunts the Hunter* by Nyx Smith
14. *House of the Sun* by Nigel Findley
15. *Worlds Without End* by Caroline Spector
16. *Just Compensation* by Robert N. Charrette
17. *Preying for Keeps* by Mel Odom
18. *Dead Air* by Jak Koke
19. *The Lucifer Deck* by Lisa Smedman
20. *Steel Rain* by Nyx Smith
21. *Shadowboxer* by Nicholas Pollotta
22. *Stranger Souls* (Dragon Heart Saga #1) by Jak Koke
23. *Headhunters* by Mel Odom
24. *Clockwork Asylum* (Dragon Heart Saga #2) by Jak Koke
25. *Blood Sport* by Lisa Smedman
26. *Beyond the Pale* (Dragon Heart Saga #3) by Jak Koke

27. *Technobabel* by Stephen Kenson
28. *Wolf and Raven* by Michael A. Stackpole
29. *Psychotrope* by Lisa Smedman
30. *The Terminus Experiment* by Jonathan E. Bond and Jak Koke
31. *Run Hard, Die Fast* by Mel Odom
32. *Crossroads* by Stephen Kenson
33. *The Forever Drug* by Lisa Smedman
34. *Ragnarock* by Stephen Kenson
35. *Tails You Lose* by Lisa Smedman
36. *The Burning Time* by Stephen Kenson
37. *Born to Run* (Kellen Colt Trilogy #1) by Stephen Kenson
38. *Poison Agendas* (Kellen Colt Trilogy #2)
    by Stephen Kenson
39. *Fallen Angels* (Kellen Colt Trilogy #3) by Stephen Kenson
40. *Drops of Corruption* by Jason M. Hardy
41. *Aftershocks* by Jean Rabe & John Helfers
42. *A Fistful of Data* by Stephen Dedman
43. *Fire and Frost* by Kai O'Connal
44. *Hell on Water* by Jason M. Hardy
45. *Dark Resonance* by Phaedra Weldon
46. *Crimson* by Kevin Czarnecki
47. *Shaken: No Job Too Small* by Russell Zimmerman
48. *Borrowed Time* by R.L. King
49. *Deniable Assets* by Mel Odom
50. *Undershadows* by Jason M. Hardy
51. *Shadows Down Under* by Jean Rabe
52. *Makeda Red* by Jennifer Brozek
53. *The Johnson Run* by Kai O'connal
54. *Shadow Dance* by Aaron Rosenberg
55. *Identity: Crisis* by Phaedra Weldon
56. *Stirred* by Russell Zimmerman
57. *Veiled Extraction* by R.L. King
58. *Tourist Trapped* by Bryan CP Steele
59. *For a Few Nuyen More* by Stephen Dedman
60. *On the Rocks* by Russell Zimmerman
61. *Imposter* by Malik Toms
62. *CTRL Issues* by Bryan CP Steele

ANTHOLOGIES

1. *Spells & Chrome*, edited by John Helfers
2. *World of Shadows*, edited by John Helfers

3. *Drawing Destiny: A Sixth World Tarot Anthology*, edited by John Helfers
4. *Sprawl Stories, Vol. 1*, edited by John Helfers
5. *The Complete Frame Job*, edited by John Helfers

NOVELLAS

1. *Neat* by Russell Zimmerman
2. *The Vladivostok Gauntlet* by Olivier Gagnon
3. *Nothing Personal* by Olivier Gagnon
4. *Another Rainy Night* by Patrick Goodman
5. *Sail Away, Sweet Sister* by Patrick Goodman
6. *The Seattle Gambit* by Olivier Gagnon
7. *DocWagon 19* by Jennifer Brozek
8. *Wolf & Buffalo* by R.L. King
9. *Big Dreams* by R.L. King
10. *Blind Magic* by Dylan Birtolo
11. *The Frame Job, Part 1: Yu* by Dylan Birtolo
12. *The Frame Job, Part 2: Emu* by Brooke Chang
13. *The Frame Job, Part 3: Rude* by Bryan CP Steele
14. *The Frame Job, Part 4: Frostburn* by CZ Wright
15. *The Frame Job, Part 5: Zipfile* by Jason Schmetzer
16. *The Frame Job, Part 6: Retribution* by Jason M. Hardy
17. *Tower of the Scorpion* by Mel Odom
18. *Chaser* by Russell Zimmerman
19. *A Kiss to Die For* by Jennifer Brozek
20. *Crocodile Tears* by Chris A. Jackson
21. *See How She Runs* by Jennifer Brozek
22. *Under Pressure* by Scott Schletz
23. *Kill Penalty* by Clifton Lambert
24. *Kings of the Street* by O. C. Presley
25. *Clean Record* by Dylan Birtolo

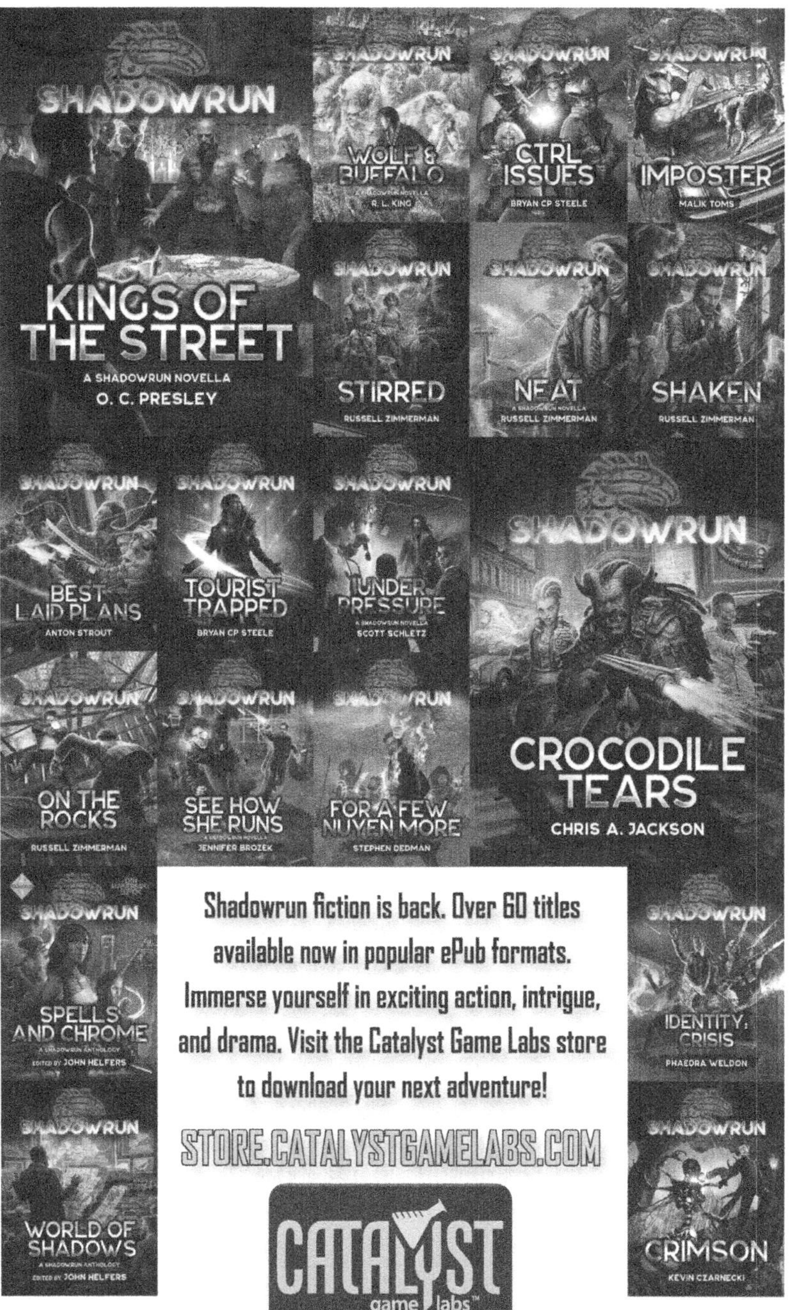
SHADOWRUN
KINGS OF THE STREET
A SHADOWRUN NOVELLA
O. C. PRESLEY
WOLF & BUFFALO
R. L. KING
CTRL ISSUES
BRYAN CP STEELE
IMPOSTER
MALIK TOMS
STIRRED
RUSSELL ZIMMERMAN
NEAT
RUSSELL ZIMMERMAN
SHAKEN
RUSSELL ZIMMERMAN
BEST LAID PLANS
ANTON STROUT
TOURIST TRAPPED
BRYAN CP STEELE
UNDER PRESSURE
SCOTT SCHLETZ
CROCODILE TEARS
CHRIS A. JACKSON
ON THE ROCKS
RUSSELL ZIMMERMAN
SEE HOW SHE RUNS
JENNIFER BROZEK
FOR A FEW NUYEN MORE
STEPHEN DEDMAN
SPELLS AND CHROME
A SHADOWRUN ANTHOLOGY
EDITED BY JOHN HELFERS
Shadowrun fiction is back. Over 60 titles available now in popular ePub formats. Immerse yourself in exciting action, intrigue, and drama. Visit the Catalyst Game Labs store to download your next adventure!
STORE.CATALYSTGAMELABS.COM
IDENTITY CRISIS
PHAEDRA WELDON
WORLD OF SHADOWS
A SHADOWRUN ANTHOLOGY
EDITED BY JOHN HELFERS
CATALYST game labs™
CRIMSON
KEVIN CZARNECKI

Made in United States
North Haven, CT
26 August 2024

56580451R00153